The Altmann Circle

The Altmann Circle
A Novel

by

David P. Spencer

Dedication

To Jos Kuerten a true friend and colleague, whose love of the city of Berlin, great knowledge of German history and the German language, enthusiasm and unwavering support through thick and thin enabled me to write this book. And not to forget our various adventures on the east side of the Berlin wall during the dark days of the divided city. Thanks a million!

And a debt of gratitude to my musical partner Denise Tandy, whose countless hours of work spent correcting my numerous mistakes editing and proofreading this manuscript are greatly appreciated. Thank you.

Foreword

I first started work on this novel in 2002. I'd been forced to retire early because of ill health and fished around for something to occupy my now plentiful spare time. I've been a student on the subject of Nazism for many years now and thought it would be a good idea to write about a subject about which I had some knowledge. The main characters in the book are all young people whose lives have been deeply affected, for good or evil by the Nazi regime.

Young people in Germany quickly became the focus of the Nazis from before 1933 as they knew that the young could be moulded into their perverted idea of the *ideal* from a very young age, and that they would become the standard-bearers of the Third Reich. They insinuated themselves into every aspect of a child's early years from the classroom, to the sports field and later to the universities. The Hitler youth movement, which became compulsory for all German youth from 1936, had grown to a total membership of eight million young people by 1938 ninety percent of children from the age of ten to eighteen. The indoctrination of youth encompassed every aspect of their lives.

Hitler said of the Hitler youth movement that once young people had joined then, '*They will never be free for the rest of their lives.*'

The main characters in the book are all young people. Dieter who has been so seduced by the regime that he is prepared to betray his father to the Gestapo to achieve his aims. Rudi, whose own father dies inside a concentration camp after being betrayed by Dieter, setting Rudi on a course of resistance. Bruno, his communist father murdered by the Nazis. Ruth, the young Jewish girl whose love for Rudi is forbidden and dangerous. And Paul and Alex, who come close to having their homosexuality discovered, putting them in grave danger and on course to being sent to a concentration camp.

Although these young people are fictional, the situations that they encounter in the book are all based on fact. From the persecution of the German Jews to the loss of basic human freedoms, with the ever present threat of the concentration camp for anyone who dared to speak out against the Nazi regime; which would eventually lead down the path to a place called Auschwitz, and the deaths countless millions of innocent people.

David Spencer
Broadway, 2016

By Way of Introduction

Berlin. No city has impressed and inspired us, David Spencer, the author of the book you're about to read, and myself, more. Berlin, the city that has been the focal point of world history for the bigger part of the Twentieth Century. Berlin, that has seen the staggering metamorphosis from a divided and partly embattled and encircled city to the attractive, open and vibrant metropolis and capital of a reunited Germany that it is today. But Berlin has also been the capital of another Germany, a Germany that had denied and abolished most of the values with which it was identified by the civilised world during the previous centuries. Berlin, the capital of Nazi Germany, of the Third Reich. It is this sinister, dark and menacing city that serves as the backdrop for the story that unfolds in this magnificent historical novel.

Although this novel is entirely David's work and he takes the full credits for its creation, I've had the privilege to witness and even to be part of much of the fascinating process of its coming into being. David and I share a vivid interest in contemporary European history and we frequently engaged in lively talks and discussions on this subject. What made a huge impact on both of us was a visit, in 2005, to the former concentration camp of Auschwitz-Birkenau, now a memorial and a museum in the Polish town of Oświęcim. The impressions gathered there most certainly found their way into the novel. On a couple of occasions in the mid-eighties of the previous century we also visited Berlin together. This happened well before the fall of the Wall on 9 November 1989 and the subsequent collapse of the German Democratic Republic (GDR). The border between West- and East-Berlin was still firmly in place and crossing was for us only possible through two border posts, Friedrichstraße railway station and Checkpoint Charlie. Once across, we were suddenly surrounded by an alien and bewildering environment of a society based on political and economic premises diametrically opposed to those prevalent in the West. Everything was different: the traffic, the shops, the restaurants, but most obvious was the apparent obsession with security. East-Berlin, the capital of the GDR and tantalisingly close to the island of affluence and freedom that was West-Berlin, teemed with members of security forces of any kind and description. Both East-German and Soviet, as at that time Moscow still was the true and undisputed master of the GDR.

Historically, of course, the division of Germany was the direct consequence of the Second World War, which, in its turn, would never have taken place without the rise and the eventual complete political dominance of the Nazis. David's novel, albeit a work of fiction, meticulously describes the factual background of the German society of these days and is therefore, in this respect, historically entirely correct and authentic. The author actually went to great lengths to check every historical detail depicted in this novel.

The story is written for a universal audience. Especially young readers, however, are likely to take a peculiar interest in this book. As time goes by, less and less direct witnesses of the period during which the story takes place survive. The power of this novel is that, through its historical accuracy and eye for detail, it very cleverly and imaginatively evokes the atmosphere of Nazi-ruled Germany. Ever since I have started reading the various drafts of the manuscript, I can no longer walk the streets of Berlin without recalling in my mind the scenes of this novel. I still remember very clearly the utter surprise and fascination that almost physically grabbed me as I read the short story that later turned out to become the nucleus of this wonderful and well-researched novel, for which David is to be congratulated and that I most emphatically recommend to your attention.

Berlin, November 2015
Jos Kuerten

'First they came for the communists
but I was not a communist so I did not speak out.
Then they came for the Socialists and Trades Unionists
but I was not one of them, so I did not speak out.
Then they came for the Jews
but I was not Jewish so I did not speak out.
And when they came for me,
there was no one left to speak out for me.'

Pastor Martin Niemoeller
1892-1984

1

The train gave a slight shudder and started to pull slowly out of Nuremberg station, wisps of black smoke drifting past the carriage window as the train gained speed. Dieter Hoffmann, the eldest by a few months looked over at his two companions. They were all seventeen years old. The three boys wore the summer uniform of the Hitler Youth movement, with khaki shirts, black shorts and knee length socks. Around their necks each wore a neckerchief fixed with a toggle rather like that worn by boy scouts. On their left arms they were wearing a swastika armband and had a ceremonial dagger attached to the left-hand side of their belts.

'God, I'm tired,' said Rudi, to his companions, 'I'm going to get my head down.'

Paul nodded his agreement. It had been an incredible week: one that they would never forget. They were exhausted. All that is, except Dieter.

Staring into space, he felt a sense of the most incredible exhilaration and would, until the day he died, remember the events of the past few days. Closing his eyes, he could see the SA, the SS, the Hitler Youth, row upon row of them. The swastika flags and banners … he could hear the military marches played by the SA and SS bands, the music going over and over in his mind. Most importantly of all, he could hear the voice of the Führer, Adolf Hitler. When he spoke, he held the crowds in the palm of his hand and there was total silence, as if the crowd were holding their collective breath. Every time he paused, there erupted a huge roar as thousands of the faithful shouted, 'Sieg Heil, Sieg Heil, Sieg Heil'. They adored him. He was the new Messiah speaking to his disciples. This genius was going to solve all of Germany's problems and his new Reich would last for a thousand years. The Nuremberg rally was over for this year. Next year, Dieter promised himself, he would be wearing the uniform of the SS.

The train taking them back to Berlin was speeding along and rocking from side to side. Dieter's two companions were sleeping, their faces looking childlike in repose. In the next compartment some Brownshirts were singing the 'Horst Wessel' song with maudlin drunkenness. An SS officer walked passed Dieter's compartment, looked in, smiled and nodded. Next year I'll be wearing that uniform, Dieter promised himself. However there was a nagging problem that wouldn't go away no matter how much he wished it — his father.

Professor Klaus Hoffmann was professor of mathematics at the University of Berlin and was very highly thought of by friends and colleagues. He was a big, powerfully built man and Dieter was more than a little afraid of him. Being a very promising student Dieter was one of those boys who seemed to sail through life with ease. He had a natural ability, no matter what he did, to do well.

When he'd broached the subject of the SS with his father, the Professor had looked over the top of his half-moon glasses and said, 'Dieter the first thing that you will do is complete high school and then go on to university. After that you will have plenty of time to think about your future.' He had made very clear by his tone of voice that there was to be no argument.

His mother, Greta, had said in a conciliatory voice, 'Your father's right Dieter, there's no need to rush into anything; you've plenty of time to decide what to do in the future.'

Dieter realised how futile it was to argue. Inside he'd been seething with anger and resentment but had said nothing. He'd asked permission to leave, got up and walked out. Dieter's parents had looked at each other. Neither said anything, but there passed between them a look of fear, which showed their dismay at the events overtaking their country with such incredible speed.

When the Nazis had finally come to power in 1933, Dieter, for all his young years, had taken with both hands all that the New Order had to offer. He was the first in his class to join the Hitler Youth and seemed to be mesmerised by Hitler and the Nazis. The professor and his wife were worried but said nothing. They hoped that this phase that Dieter was going through would pass quickly, but it didn't. Klaus Hoffmann, his wife, and many of their friends had watched the rise of the Nazis with horror. The whole of Germany seemed to have gone mad, and they were powerless to do anything about it. They were afraid. You no longer knew who you could trust, fear stalked the streets and the secret police seemed to be everywhere. You had the feeling that the state was looking over your shoulder. It was.

The two boys started to stir. Rudi opened his eyes, stretched and gave an enormous yawn. Opening his eyes, Paul untangled his long, lithe body. One leg had somehow managed to get entwined with Rudi's during their sleep. They were like young puppies, Dieter reflected. Although they were all more or less the same age, Dieter felt so much older than them and certainly much more superior. They were like children. Rudi, for example, was his oldest and best friend. They'd started at kindergarten together and their parents were old friends. The two boys had naturally formed a deep friendship, but over the past few months their relationship had cooled. Rudi treated the Hitler Youth as if it were all a big game. Dieter had told him about his dream of joining the SS.

Rudi had looked at him strangely and said, 'But Dieter, I thought that we were going to the university together?'

Dieter had answered very seriously, 'You go to university if you wish. I have more important things to do.' Dismissing it, as if it were of no importance.

For years the two friends had laughed and joked about what fun they would have at the university, but that had all changed almost overnight. Rudi was hurt, but said nothing. For him their friendship would never be the same again. Anyway, he intended to be an engineer like his Father and to do that he would have to complete his education.

Paul Lindmann was a tall, slim, good-looking boy with brown hair who was a highly gifted young violinist. It was said that he would go to the very top in the music world. The Brownshirts in the next compartment were still singing old party songs. It seemed the more schnapps they consumed the louder they became.

With a look of distaste on his face Paul said, 'For Christ's sake, I wish those bastards would shut up, they're driving me crazy.'

Rudi froze, his eyes instinctively turning towards Dieter.

Dieter, who didn't like Paul, looked at him coldly and said, with ice in his voice, 'If it were not for those BASTARDS, Lindmann, Germany would still be a cesspool fit only for people like you to live in. I'd be very careful what you say in future or you could find yourself in a lot of trouble.' The threat in his tone was implicit.

Paul's face had gone the colour of chalk and he started to stutter an apology.

Rudi cut him off, saying, 'Oh, do lighten up, Dieter, he didn't mean anything by it; anyway it's getting on my nerves too.'

He was challenging Dieter but Dieter said nothing. He just looked at them as if memorising this incident for the future.

Rudi tried to break the icy atmosphere that had suddenly descended on the compartment by saying, 'Who's for a game of cards? Come on, Paul, let's have a game.'

Giving Rudi a look of gratitude, Paul nodded and Rudi, taking a pack of cards out of his knapsack, began to deal.

Rudi looked at Dieter out of the corner of his eye and said to himself, 'Now I know why I don't like you anymore, Hoffmann, you bastard.'

2

The train finally pulled into the Berlin Zoo station in the late afternoon. The three boys lifted their knapsacks onto their shoulders and prepared to leave the compartment. Doors were flung open along the length of the train and the SS, Brownshirts and Hitler Youth groups started to move along the platform. The jackboots of the SS and SA men made a metal staccato as they marched along. Paul muttered something and hurried away, as if glad to be out of Dieter's presence. He was to have a few sleepless nights after the incident with Dieter in the compartment. Rudi was still very angry over it and was determined to confront Dieter. Not so long ago the two boys, laughing and joking, would have headed to the tram together, as their homes were very near to each other. Those days seemed far away now to Rudi. Dieter turned away. Putting his hand onto Dieter's arm, Rudi squeezed hard and forcefully pulled him around to face him. The two boys were evenly matched in size and build and Dieter's hand instinctively dropped to the dagger at his side.

Rudi looked Dieter directly in the eye and said in a very quiet voice, 'Don't even think about it, Dieter. Just give me the excuse to give you a good hiding.'

Both Dieter and Rudi were big boys and no one in their lives would ever accuse them of being cowards. Dieter sensed that this was not the time or the place to take things further. He just stood there and looked at Rudi with a sneer at the corner of his mouth. However, he wouldn't forget the incident.

'If there's something that you want to say get on with it. If not let go of my arm,' said Dieter coldly.

Rudi looked at Dieter and dropped his hand. The two boys stood facing each other. In the background they could hear the announcer saying that the 17.30 train to Frankfurt was about to leave. They sensed rather than saw the people milling around them. It was if they were on their own private little island.

'Why did you attack Paul on the train like that? Who do you think you are? The Gestapo? You're turning into a stranger, Dieter. Before long you'll have no friends left.'

Rudi for the first time hated the uniform that he wore and the crooked cross on his left arm. He didn't wait for Dieter to reply but just turned and walked away.

'Shit!' Dieter murmured to himself, a pulse of anger beating in his forehead, as he left the station and headed towards the Tiergarten, the large area of parkland situated in the heart of the city, beloved of Berliners. He was in no mood to face his father and mother. During the journey he'd decided that no matter what his father said he would apply to go into the SS on his eighteenth birthday in two month's time. Dieter was beginning to suspect that maybe there were other reasons that his parents were against his enlisting in the SS. Now that he thought about it, they'd never shown any enthusiasm for the new government although, to be honest, he'd never heard them say anything against it either. At least not in front of him. Dieter was intelligent enough to realise that maybe there was a good reason for that.

The Tiergarten was full at this time of the evening, and young couples were strolling around arm in arm. There was a small group of Wehrmacht soldiers playing football, shouting and laughing, and having a wonderful time. How he envied them. Realising how hungry he was, he headed towards a wurst stand and ordered a bockwurst and beer. Sitting on a grassy knoll, he looked over in the direction of the Brandenberg gate. To the left he could see the gutted Reichstag building, set on fire by the Dutch communist Van der Lubbe in February of last year. He'd followed the case with great interest in the newspapers. Van Der Lubbe had been found guilty and been beheaded in January. The Führer had shown what a strong leader he was then, Dieter thought admiringly.

3

Professor Hoffmann arrived home from the university at about 17.30 that evening. Entering through the front door, his face was grim and Greta could sense the anger that was not far from the surface. She knew better than to ask him what was troubling him, and knew that he would tell her in his own good time.

It was because of the Professor's anger that the evening's events would take the turn that they did. In his anger, and his wife's preoccupation with looking to her husband's needs, they both forgot that Dieter was due to return that evening. If they had remembered, things would have perhaps been different. The Professor would have been far more circumspect. If only …

Klaus Hoffman looked at his wife and, taking her hands in his, said seriously, 'This evening, after dinner, Robert Wagner is coming over for a drink. Perhaps it would be a good idea if you were to go over and visit Astrid?'

He then went on to explain what exactly had happened at the university that afternoon, concerning his colleague Professor Lindblom.

Professor Joseph Lindblom was in his late sixties and was professor of modern physics at the university. He was highly respected and liked by both his colleagues and students. He was also a Jew. That afternoon he'd been summoned to the rector's office in the administration building. The rector was new and his Nazi credentials were there for all to see: he wore the party swastika badge in the lapel of his jacket. Knocking, Lindblom had waited politely to be told to enter. In the old days, he reflected, when his old friend had been in charge, he would have just knocked and gone in. Now he waited. Having been called in, he stood in front of the Rector's desk. The Rector was writing and made no attempt to acknowledge the professor's presence. After a few minutes he put down his pen and looked up.

'Ah, Lindblom,' he said, 'thank you for coming to see me.'

He didn't offer the professor a seat and let him stand there like a student who'd misbehaved himself. Lindblom, who was a rather meek and quiet man felt himself starting to get angry; to be treated in this way by a man half his age was inexcusable.

'I've called you here to see me to give you some news. I've been instructed by a higher authority to tell you that your services will no longer be required.'

Lindblom started to go cold. He couldn't believe what he'd just heard.

'I don't understand, Herr Rector,' he stammered.

The rector lifted up his hand and silenced the Professor in mid-sentence.

'Look, Lindblom, you're getting old. It's time to make way for new blood.'

'Someone wearing a badge like yours', Lindblom thought bitterly.

'We ... I,' he quickly corrected himself, 'would like your resignation by the end of the week.'

A sense of total and utter defeat overcame the old man. He knew that to argue was futile. He was a Jew and that was enough to end a long and distinguished career. He looked calmly at the rector and said, 'If the future of our young folk is to be in the hands of people like you then may God help Germany.'

'Get out, old man,' snarled the rector.

Lindblom turned and walked slowly towards the door, his shoulders slumped. There was no fight left in him.

Entering the faculty staff-room quietly the professor had tears streaming down his face. His whole world had been destroyed in just two minutes. Seeing him enter, Klaus knew immediately that something was wrong and crossed the room in two strides, taking hold of the old man's arms.

'What is it, Joseph?' he asked.

The old man looked at him with infinite sadness and said, 'They've sacked me Klaus. After twenty years, they've sacked me.'

'I don't understand, what do you mean?'

'I mean that there's no room for an old Jew like me anymore,' he said bitterly. 'Klaus, I'm a German. I fought for the Fatherland at Verdun. I was awarded the Iron Cross First Class.' The old man faltered, tears streaming down his cheeks.

'I'm so sorry, old friend.'

Klaus Hoffmann felt a hopeless rage engulf him. What could he do? What could he say? The other members of the staff who were present averted their eyes.

'What can I do now? I'm glad my Clara never lived to see this day.'

The old man brushed the tears from his eyes, straightened his back, and walked out of the door. There was a hush in the room; even the men present wearing the party badge said nothing.

Climbing to the top of the stairs Professor Joseph Lindblom opened the door which led out onto the roof of the university building. Looking around, his mind went back to the time that he'd first come here as a young proud student. Giving a sigh, he walked to the edge of the roof and without any hesitation threw himself over the top, his body landing with a thud in the quadrangle below.

A silent crowd of students and teachers stood in a circle looking down at the professor, a pool of blood seeping from beneath his broken body. Someone had called the police and a policeman and a Brownshirt had arrived, pushing their way through the crowd and looking down at the corpse. The rector walked over to them and spoke quietly.

The Brownshirt looked at the policeman, smiled and said in a loud voice, 'Well that's one less for us to worry about.'

The Policeman standing next to him gave a nervous grin. No one present said a word.

4

Walking quietly up the drive to the front of his house, Dieter noticed Robert Wagner's car parked at the front. Some instinct, which he couldn't explain, made him cautious. There were lights on in the drawing room and he noticed that the curtains were drawn, as he put his key quietly into the lock and opened the door. He immediately heard his father's voice, not raised, but full of rage. He stopped, took off his rucksack, and quietly walked towards the partially open drawing room door. He sensed that something important was happening and heard his father's voice again. Although he couldn't see whom he was talking to he knew that it must be Robert Wagner.

'I can't believe what happened today. What has Germany come to? The State murdered that old man, just as surely as if it had put a gun to his head and shot him. Why? Because he was a Jew. That barbarian, Hitler and his filthy crew have dragged this country back to the Dark Ages.' There was a pause and then the professor carried on, 'And my son has become one of them. Every time I see him in that filthy uniform I want to vomit.'

'Try to calm yourself, Klaus,' said Robert Wagner quietly, 'This madness can't go on forever, surely the people will see sense? They'll get rid of Hitler and his gang as soon as they see what's going on.' There was a hint of pleading in Wagner's voice.

At first, Dieter couldn't believe what he was hearing. An ice-cold anger swept over him. How dare they criticise the Führer and the party like that. Who do they think they are? Almost shouting aloud, Dieter had to fight an urge not to burst into the room and confront the two traitors. He'd heard enough. His Father and Wagner had damned themselves with their own mouths and would have to take the consequences. He turned, walked to the front door and let himself quietly out.

Five minutes after he'd left, Greta Hoffman entered through the front door, and immediately saw Dieter's rucksack lying on the hall floor. Walking into the drawing room, she smiled at the two men and said, 'Where's Dieter. Have you seen him?'

Klaus looked at Greta and replied, 'Dieter's not here, I haven't seen him.'

'That's strange, his rucksack's in the hall.'

Klaus shrugged and said, 'He must have left it in the hall and gone back out again.'

'I wonder where he is. It's starting to get late and I wonder why he didn't tell you that he was back?' she murmured, feeling a moment of apprehension.

The taxi pulled up outside 8, Prinz-Albrecht-Straße, and the driver looked strangely at the boy wearing the Hitler Youth uniform sitting next to him. It was the first time that he'd had a fare to Gestapo headquarters. The address was already beginning to strike fear into the hearts of ordinary Germans. Dieter paid the driver off and walked up the stairs to the main entrance. He pushed open the large doors and entered. To his right, seated at a desk, was a sergeant wearing the black uniform of the SS. He looked up as Dieter entered. Dieter lifted his right arm in the Hitler salute. The sergeant returned the salute casually and said, 'And what can we do for the Hitler Youth this evening?'

It only took Dieter a few minutes to explain why he was there. The sergeant looked at him seriously and said almost to himself, 'That's worth a trip to Dachau at least.' He looked up at Dieter as if about to say something more and then thought better of it. Pointing, he said, 'Take a seat over there.'

Lifting the receiver of the telephone he dialled a number and spoke in a low voice, too low for Dieter to hear what he was saying. Looking around him, Dieter was surprised how quiet it was. There were a few people walking around, some in uniform, some in civilian clothes. He had imagined that the place would be a hive of activity and in a way he was disappointed.

A door opened just along the corridor from where he was sitting. A man stood there in civilian clothes, and he beckoned Dieter over. He walked towards the man, not sure whether to give the Hitler salute or not. He didn't.

'Come on in, young Hoffmann,' the man said affably. Dieter wondered how the man knew his name. Of course, he'd told the sergeant at the desk. He looked at him and thought, '*he looks like a schoolteacher, not like a Gestapo agent.*' Standing to one side the man let Dieter enter the office, a little smile at the corner of his mouth. The officer motioned for him to take a seat and said. 'Now Dieter, you don't mind if I call you Dieter do you?'

'No, not at all,' he answered.

The man took a cigarette from a packet on the desk and offered him one. The boy shook his head in refusal.

'My name is Langers,' he said quietly, 'Now why don't you tell me all about it, from the very beginning,' he said, blowing smoke towards the ceiling.

He listened intently to everything that the boy had to say, occasionally writing notes on a pad. When Dieter had finished Langers looked at him and said, 'I'm proud of you, the Führer would also be proud of you.' He was impressed with this young man. 'You've done the right thing by coming here tonight. Tell me, was your Mother present when this conversation was going on?'

'No, Sir, she wasn't,' replied Dieter.

Langers looked a little disappointed, but said nothing. He lifted the telephone and dialled. While he was waiting for a reply he looked at Dieter and said, 'Do you know the address of this man Wagner?'

Dieter replied that he did. Someone answered the phone at the other end and Langers spoke for a long time. After he had finished speaking he put down the receiver and asked Dieter what his ambitions were. Dieter told him about the SS. Langers looked at him and said, 'I think that after tonight you should be enrolled at one of the Adolf Hitler schools as a boarder; you're just the type of student they need. I'll arrange it,' he said with finality. 'You do realise that after tonight you won't be able to stay at home. How would you like to stay with my wife and I, at least until we can make other arrangements?'

'Thank you, Sir, that would be very kind.'

'When will you be eighteen?' Langers asked.

'In two month's time.'

'What are your grades like at school?'

'Very good. I'm always at the top of my class,' Dieter replied, with pride in his voice.

Langers grunted, 'Perhaps we can find a place for you at the SS officer training school at Bad Tolz. Would you like that?'

Before he could reply there was a knock on the door and two men entered dressed in civilian clothes. Langers nodded at them.

'Take the boy with you and go and arrest Professor Hoffmann. I'll arrange for another car to fetch this other man Wagner.'

The two men nodded, looked at Dieter, and waited.

'Go with them Dieter. I'll see you when you get back. Heil Hitler.'

Dieter gave the Hitler salute and followed the two men outside.

5

Klaus Hoffmann and Greta sat side by side on the couch. Greta was worried but couldn't really say why. Robert had left just after they'd discovered Dieter's rucksack in the hall. Where was the boy? They both heard the car draw up outside at the same time and looked at each other. 'Who's that?' they both wondered, glancing up at the wall clock. It said 10.30pm. They heard the car doors slam, the crunch of feet on the gravel and then the bell ringing. Klaus went to the door and opened it. There were two men standing at the entrance, with Dieter just behind them. One of the men said, 'Are you Professor Klaus Hoffmann?'

'Yes, I am,' answered Klaus.

The Gestapo agent who'd asked the question lifted an oval metal badge and showed it to Klaus.

He said, 'You're under arrest for treason against the State. I'm taking you into protective custody.'

Greta's hand flew to her mouth. Klaus was surprisingly calm and, like Professor Lindblom, he knew that for him the time had come. He also knew that sooner or later his arrest would have been inevitable. He couldn't have stood by and done nothing. Although he was now very frightened, he had no regrets for his actions that evening. A feeling of deep sadness overcame him. To be betrayed by his own son was too much for him to grasp. How could it have happened? The boy must have heard every word and gone to the Gestapo. Turning to Greta, he hugged her and gave her a kiss, and said with deep regret, 'Don't worry my dear, I'll try to be home soon.'

Dieter stood there looking at them, feeling no emotion whatsoever. Klaus turned to his son and said very gently, with great calm, 'How could you do it? Your own father?' he shook his head and continued, 'I'm sure that now, Dieter, you'll be able to join the SS.'

Dieter looked at his father, a little smile playing at the corner of his mouth, as he said nothing.

The two Gestapo agents took hold of Klaus's arms, led him to the car, and opened the back door. He took one last look at his wife over his shoulder and climbed in. Dieter sat in the front with the two Gestapo men. Greta stood in the open doorway in a state of paralysed shock as the car pulled away. That was the last sight that father and son were to have of her for a very long time.

The closed Gestapo van pulled slowly up to the entrance of the camp. Written in the scrollwork of the camp gates were the words 'ARBEIT MACHT FREI' — 'Labour Liberates'. The prisoners were manacled together and their faces were badly swollen. Their whole bodies ached from the beating that they'd received at the hands of the Gestapo. Now they were about to be handed over to a new set of torturers. The back doors of the van were opened and they climbed painfully out straight into the arms of the SS guards.

Dieter stayed with SS Colonel Langers of the SD and his wife until his eighteenth birthday, the pair becoming surrogate parents. At the age of eighteen he was enrolled as an officer cadet in the SS and was sent to the officer training school at Bad Tolz.

Six months later, Astrid Wagner received a letter from the camp authorities informing her of the death of Robert from pneumonia. Mother and son sat down together and cried. Rudi, his heart full of hate, swore an oath that one day there would be a reckoning between him and Dieter and that he would do everything possible to resist the regime.

6

Swinging the pick in a huge arc over his head, Bruno Meyer gave a grunt of satisfaction as it bit into the hard earth with a sharp crack. Stripped to the waist, the muscles of his upper torso rippled with each swing of the pick, as he hummed under his breath, 'Deutschland, Deutschland, über Alles.' Looking over at Paul, Rudi smiled, winked, and nodded towards Bruno, as if to say, he's at it again. Paul smiled and lifted his eyebrows. All around them the area was a frenzy of activity as the young men of the 'German labour front' worked on the farmland. The supervisors were wearing the brown uniform, swastika armband and green hunting hats of the service. They kept a close eye on their charges, shouting an instruction from time to time. Paul, Rudi and Bruno were digging a drainage ditch and were all in high good humour, especially Paul, who'd been counting the days from the beginning. They had just three more days before the end of their service and would then be free to return to their studies at the University of Berlin.

The young men of the German labour service came from many levels of society. Students worked alongside working-class boys, doctor's sons with the sons of steelworkers. For many, it was the first time that they'd had work of any kind. The pay was bad but it was at least work. Many of them were grateful to Hitler for that.

Bruno came from a working class-family. His father, a communist, had been shot and killed in 1929 by the SA, although it was never proven. Himself a communist, Bruno was far too intelligent to advertise the fact, although sometimes his bravado and devil-may-care attitude brought him close to danger. Loathing the Nazis, he'd do anything to help destroy them and was in fact being groomed by a group that even he knew little about. He was aware that he would be wanted for something in the future, but was not sure what. Living alone, his rent, university fees, and general living expenses were paid by a mysterious benefactor whom he'd never met or had any contact with. He suspected, but couldn't be sure, that the communists were behind it all. The only contact he had was with a man whom he called the 'Controller.' They met regularly, at least once a month. Bruno would be handed an envelope containing enough money to last him until the next month. Neither Rudi nor Paul was aware of any of this, not because he didn't trust them, but for their own safety. Like Rudi, he was a student of engineering, and on graduation he planned to leave Germany. He wouldn't do anything to help the Nazis and was determined not to serve in the armed forces, something that he'd have to do when he left university.

The three friends made an unlikely combination. Rudi and Paul were from wealthy and privileged backgrounds. When his father had died in the camp, Rudi had inherited a considerable fortune. His uncle, a banker in Basel, administered his inheritance. His mother had inherited money of her own on the death of her father.

Paul, along with Alexander Kraus, a brilliant young eighteen-year-old concert pianist, was already the talk of Berlin musical society. His mother, a rich divorcee, knew everybody of any importance in Berlin society. She was on first name terms with most of the prominent Nazis. Paul could easily have escaped the rigours of the labour service but when his mother had raised the subject, he'd refused even to consider it. That was his nature. Bruno, of course, knew all about his friend's backgrounds, but their friendship was far more important to him than their money. Rudi's and his own father's death at the hands of the Nazis cemented the bond between them. Rudi and Bruno sensed Paul's vulnerability. Neither of them understood it, but both were protective of him. The three friends all had something in common: Rudi and Bruno hated the Nazis — Paul feared them, with good reason.

The three young men were working side by side, Paul and Rudi using long-handled shovels to dig the area that Bruno had loosened with his pick. They were sweating even though there was a cold north wind blowing through the valley. Bruno seemed oblivious to the cold. Wearing a pair of heavy-duty gloves to protect his hands as much as possible, Paul had been the butt of many good-natured jokes from the others at first, until he'd been asked to play his violin to them one evening, when they quickly realised that they were in the presence of a very fine musician. After that, no one said anything, not even the supervisors, whose idea of good music was the 'Horst Wessel' song. On many evenings, Paul was asked to play by the other men in the hut, and was happy to oblige, no matter how tired he was. After supper, he would go to the hut where all the equipment was kept and practice for two hours. It came to be known as Paul's 'music room.'

Paul looked at Bruno who was still swinging his pick as if it were a child's toy. He'd changed from humming the German national anthem to the 'International'.

Paul said, 'I can't wait until Friday. The first thing I'm going to do is soak in a red- hot bath.'

Rudi nodded and replied, 'Yes, me too, and I've promised to take mother to dinner at Kempinski's.'

Bruno stopped his wild swinging, looked in turn at the two boys and said, in mock seriousness, 'You two are a disgrace to the Fatherland. Our great and beloved leader, Adolf, has given you the opportunity of a six-month holiday in the country. There's lots of fresh air, but you're so ungrateful you want to get back to the smog of Berlin. Shame on you.'

The two laughed and Paul said ironically, 'To quote Charles Dickens, "What larks!" eh Rudi, "what larks!" Bruno frowned, realising that he'd missed something.

Rudi smiled and looked at his watch, 'That's enough labour for the Reich for one day. Come on, I wonder what's for supper?'

'Indigestible stew, of course' grumbled Bruno.

The three boys shouldered their tools and started to walk in companionable silence in the direction of the camp. All around them the others were doing the same.

As they entered the barrack block, they immediately noticed a group of young men standing listening to the radio at the far end of the barracks. They walked over.

The announcer was saying in strident tones. 'Today, the German army at the invitation of the President of Austria crossed over the frontier to complete 'Anschluß.' Austria is now part of the greater German Reich. Joyous crowds have greeted the triumphal German army. The Führer is planning to visit the city within the next few days. Heil Hitler.'

Loud martial music came from the radio at the end of the announcement.

Bruno said in a loud, serious voice, 'Gentlemen, our great and beloved Führer has shown his genius again. At a stroke, he's just expanded Germany by another few million people. It won't be long before our 'Kultur und Volk' embrace the whole world. I for one think that we should all join together in a chorus of the 'Horst Wessel' song.'

He started to sing loudly, his voice sounding like an off-key bullfrog. Rudi, with a smile, took his cue from Bruno and started singing, closely followed by the other young men in the room. Bruno stood in the centre, waving his arms, giving his impression of a conductor. No one was ever sure whether Bruno was serious or not, which was just as he wanted it. The young Nazis in the room, and there were many, had no choice but to give him the benefit of the doubt and join in. Anyway, there was not one person there who was prepared to challenge him. No one would forget in a hurry the incident of the previous January.

One bitterly cold evening, the three friends had decided to walk into the small town of Northeim a couple of kilometres away. A full moon lit up the frozen countryside as they made their way to a local bar, used regularly by the young men of the labour front. The group leaders used a bar in another part of town. Walking down the stairs, they entered. The bar was full of young men drinking beer and smoking. The room was hot after the dry cold of outside; a large room in rustic style, with a tiled heater in the corner which glowed and was red hot to the touch. Cigarette smoke filled the room, hanging in the air like a cloud. Rudi bought three beers and handed them around. Bruno took a long drink, a look of pleasure lighting up his whole face. There was a hum of conversation. Two pretty young barmaids were kept busy and were good-naturedly fending off the attentions of a succession of randy young men. The three had stood at the bar, talking amongst themselves. They were aching from the physically hard labour that they were now expected to do. For Paul it was particularly difficult, but he made no complaint. They were all in the same boat.

There had been a group of four young men from the labour front sitting over at a table in the far corner of the bar. One of them, a blond and ruggedly built young man, had noticed the three friends enter. His face was flushed with the beer and schnapps that he'd consumed that evening and his name was Heinrich Heinz. At twenty-five, he was older than most of the others, a cunning, as well as intelligent, young man with ambitions to go into the Gestapo. His father was a high ranking SA leader. Like his father, Heinrich was a bully. He'd seen the three friends together often in the past month and he'd heard that the skinny one played the violin; that alone was enough to earn Heinrich's hate. He disliked the three of them for their obvious friendship and this evening was in the mood for a fight. Heinrich stood up and walked over towards the three friends at the bar, and, as he approached, he purposely bumped into Paul, spilling his beer over him.

'Look out you fucking little queer,' Heinrich said aggressively.

Paul was trying to brush the beer off himself. Gently pushing Paul to one side Bruno had looked at Heinrich and said, 'What did you say?'

'I wasn't talking to you,' Heinrich said, 'Keep out of it.'

Bruno looked him up and down and said very quietly,' You're talking to me now.'

Rudi and Paul started to try to calm things down, but Bruno cut them off with a sharp gesture with his hand. Things were now beyond their control. Bruno had met people like Heinrich many times and could imagine him wearing the uniform that he detested with so much hate. Bruno could smell people like this little Nazi in front of him.

Heinrich had sneered at Bruno and said, 'What's this? Is he your fucking bum boy or something?'

If Heinrich had taken the trouble to look closely at Bruno's eyes at that moment, he would have seen how much danger he was in. Bruno's anger at this remark was ice-cold and calculated. The conversation in the room started to die down as people realised that something was going on. It went very quiet. Bruno looked at Heinrich, and with a little smile playing at the corner of his mouth, had said very quietly, 'I'm going to give you one chance to apologise to me, and more importantly to my friend here. Now, what's it to be?'

No one in the bar said a word as Heinrich at last realised the danger he was in, but it was much too late for that. He'd backed himself into a corner.

'I'm not going to ask you again,' Bruno had said very quietly.

Heinrich suddenly felt very afraid. All the drink that he'd had that night began to have an effect, and his bravado started to evaporate. Starting to sweat, he had sneered and taken a swing at Bruno, his right fist aimed at Bruno's head. The fight had been over almost before it had started. Bruno stepped easily to one side, blocking Heinrich's arm, and he then brought his right knee up with tremendous force into Heinrich's testicles. Giving a squeal of agony, Heinrich jack-knifed forward. Bruno was waiting. This time he'd used his left knee, making brutal contact with Heinrich's face as it was coming down. Everyone in the room heard the bone in Heinrich's nose break. Blood spurted from his face and at the same time he vomited and rolled in agony on the floor, covering himself in his own blood and vomit. Bruno looked down at the broken figure for a second, squatted, and said very quietly so that no one else in the room could hear him.

'If you ever cross my path again, you piece of Nazi shit, I'll fucking kill you.'

He had then got up, beckoned to Paul and Rudi and without a word had walked up the stairs and out of the bar. A hum of conversation followed their departure.

One of the young men had said to his companion, 'The last time I saw a fight like that, it was between a 'Brownshirt' and a communist in 1930. The 'Brownshirt' also got the worst of it.'

Heinrich had been taken to the hospital, where they operated and removed a testicle. They could do nothing for his smashed nose. He carried that particular scar with him for the rest of his life. Heinrich's belongings were removed from the camp the next day and nothing official was ever said about the incident. It had been just another bar room fight between two young men who'd had too much to drink. Everyone present had sworn that it was Heinrich's fault and that he'd provoked the whole incident. He'd got what was coming to him. The matter was quietly dropped.

Both Rudi and Paul had been shaken to the core. The cold, calculated viciousness of Bruno's attack had opened their eyes to a side of Bruno that they'd never seen before.

The next day Bruno had been back to being his normal self, as if nothing had ever happened.

Three days after the German Army had walked into Austria, Rudi, Paul and Bruno stood in the corridor of the train as it pulled slowly into Berlin Zoo station. The day that they'd all being waiting for had at last arrived. Paul's heart was singing with happiness, just a few more hours he thought to himself.

Bruno said, 'Well boys, we've done our duty to Führer and Fatherland, perhaps they'll leave us alone for a bit.'

Rudi replied gloomily, 'Yeh, it's the army next.'

'Over my dead body,' said Bruno, ominously.

'Oh come on you two,' said Paul, 'cheer up and think of the weekend.'

'You're right, said Bruno,' his face lighting up, 'Tonight I'm going down to Mutti's bar and fill myself with Bockwurst and beer and if I'm really lucky the beautiful Sophie might be there. I hope she's in the mood to do her duty for a young warrior of the Reich. I'm feeling very randy; six months without a woman's too long for a red blooded young German like myself.'

The others laughed. Bruno looked at Paul, gave a smile, and said, 'And what of our young, musical genius? Do you think that we haven't noticed all those letters that you've received over the past six months? She must be really sweet on you.'

Paul laughed and replied, 'What you don't know won't hurt you, Bruno.'

'Don't give me any thought will you? Nobody loves me,' said Rudi.

The train slowly shuddered to a halt and the three boys jumped down. They walked to the station entrance, laughing and chattering good-naturedly. Rudi and Paul said goodbye to Bruno and agreed to meet him on Monday morning at the university.

'Come on,' said Paul,' we'll get a cab, my treat.'

'Thank you kind sir,' said Rudi, giving a mock bow.

They hailed a cab, jumped in and sped away.

7

Paul jumped out of the taxi, took his suitcase and violin, and paid off the driver. He walked up the stairs to the entrance of the luxury apartment block, pushed open the glass doors and entered the marble foyer. Sitting in a reception area to the left was the concierge, a middle aged man wearing a smart dark suit. Paul disliked him intensely. A few months earlier, he'd replaced the previous concierge. He'd been a nice old man. Paul had no illusions about his replacement. This one was a Blockwarden, wearing a clean suit. Paul nodded to the man, walked into the lift and pushed the button for the third floor. He pushed his key into the door and went in. The door opened onto a spacious hallway. As he entered, Trudi, the general help, came through the lounge door. She was a small, podgy woman with greying hair and rosy cheeks and had been with the family for years. Paul adored her. When she caught sight of Paul her face lit up, she gave a little cry and said, 'Master Paul, you're home at last.'

She waddled over and wrapped her arms around Paul and gave him a big, wet kiss on his cheek.

'You're very thin,' she scolded, 'Have you been eating enough?'

'Trudy, my love,' said Paul, 'How is the most beautiful girl in the world?'

He held Trudy at arm's length. She gave a little giggle.

'To answer your question, yes I have been eating enough.'

'Humph,' she scoffed, 'I don't believe that for one minute.' She gave a little scowl and then her face brightened, 'Not to worry, I'll soon get some meat on your bones.' She scurried off and headed towards the kitchen saying over her shoulder, 'I'll make you a sandwich; you must be starving.'

She'd gone before Paul could reply. He gave a little smile to himself and walked over to the telephone on the hall table. He was excited and lifted the receiver, quickly dialling the number that he knew by heart. The phone at the other end was answered on the second ring, as if the person was waiting for the call.

Paul said, 'Hello, little one'. There was a cry at the other end of the phone that nearly burst Paul's eardrum. He moved the receiver away from his ear slightly while the person at the other end chattered on excitedly.

'Stop, stop!' he said. 'Listen, I'll be with you in about two hours … no, be patient,' he laughed, 'I need a soak in a hot bath; you don't want me coming over all smelly, do you? Be patient, I'll be with you soon, yes, I promise.' Paul smiled and put the phone down.

He walked over to the lounge door and entered. It was a large beautifully decorated room, full of antiques and dominated by an exquisite chandelier hanging from the ceiling. There was a fine oil painting of his mother as a young woman, hanging over the fireplace. His mother was sitting on a long, luxurious couch reading a magazine. She looked up as Paul entered and gave a lovely smile, her whole face lighting up as she stood. Paul walked over, embraced her, and kissed her on both cheeks.

'Paul, darling,' she exclaimed, 'how are you? How was that dreadful camp?'

'I'm fine mother, the camp could have been worse, not much, but...'

'Oh, Paul if only you'd have let me talk to somebody.'

Paul cut her off and said, 'Mother we've been over this a thousand times before, I don't want any special favours from your friends.'

She gave a little sigh, 'You're so stubborn,' she said, 'just like your father.'

Paul laughed, and said, 'You look absolutely ravishing tonight, dear Mother.'

It was true, Rosa was a beautiful women. She had long, blond hair, strikingly blue eyes, and a peaches and cream complexion. She looked much younger than her forty-five years. The beautiful white evening gown and lovely diamond necklace with matching earrings showed her off to perfection.

'Where are you going tonight?' asked Paul.

'Oh, some boring reception at the Italian embassy,' she replied. 'We'll probably go out to a club afterwards, which should be fun.'

Paul was just about to say something when the door opened and Trudy entered carrying a tray with a huge plate of sandwiches and a glass of milk. To her, Paul was still a little boy.

Paul laughed when he saw it and said, 'Trudy, you're an angel, but I think that I'd prefer a scotch and soda.'

'What a good idea, darling, could you fix me one too?' said Rosa, taking a cigarette from a silver cigarette box.

'What are you doing this evening?' Rosa asked Paul.

'I'm going to soak in a hot bath, and then I'm going out to have a wonderful time.'

Rosa looked at Paul and said, 'All right, darling, but be careful what you're doing.'

Paul smiled and replied, 'I will, mother, I promise. Now I'm going to soak that camp away.' He took his scotch and the plate of sandwiches and started to leave the room.

'Oh, Paul, I took your car to the garage, it's full of petrol and the tyres have been checked.'

'Thanks Mother. Oh, by the way, say hello to Doctor Goebbels for me,' said Paul, ironically.

'Yes, darling, I will.' The irony was totally lost on Rosa.

Later, Paul took the lift down to the basement garage, got into his Mercedes and drove out. He got onto the Kurfürstendamm, heading in the direction of the Olympic stadium towards Spandau. His speed built up to sixty kilometres an hour as he gave the powerfully-built car its head. He was so happy. *'If only I could share my happiness with Bruno and Rudi … but sadly that can't be,'* he thought. Driving off the main road and into a quiet street in the suburb of Spandau, he pulled up in front of an old apartment block that had seen better days. To Paul it looked like heaven as he entered the building and raced up the stairs.

Pausing outside apartment number three he could hear the strains of Beethoven's 'Emperor' piano concerto. He put his key into the lock and pushed the door open and entered quietly, closing the door behind him. The young man sitting in the armchair didn't see Paul at first, giving Paul an opportunity to study him. The boy was totally lost in the music and Paul could see his face in profile. There were still signs of childhood in his features, which belied his eighteen years. He had beautiful black curly hair, dark, almost black eyes, and a smooth olive complexion that was almost Mediterranean. He was incredibly handsome, shorter and stockier than Paul by a few centimetres.

'Hello Alex,' said Paul.

Alex looked up, a look of joy spreading across his face as he came back to earth and recognised Paul. Jumping out of the chair, he flung himself into Paul's arms. They clung together in a tight embrace, never wanting to let go. Alex's head was pressed into Paul's chest as he gently stroked the boy's hair, at the same time planting small kisses at the base of his neck.

'Oh, God, I've missed you so, Paul,' said Alex, his voice muffled. 'Promise me that you won't ever leave me alone again, I think I'd die.'

'I promise Alex,' said Paul. He meant it. There were tears of happiness in his eyes. He cupped Alex's chin and gently, with great tenderness, lifted his face so that their eyes met. Lowering his head, he kissed Alex gently on the lips. Alex returned his kiss his tongue probing. Paul opened his mouth and their tongues met.

The two boys stood exploring each other's bodies for what seemed like an eternity.

They parted. Looking into Paul's eyes, Alex said, very quietly, 'Please make love to me, Paul.'

Paul nodded. He looked at Alex and with his voice filled with emotion said, 'Have you any idea how much I love you, Alexander Kraus?'

'Yes I think I do,' replied Alex.

Paul put his arm around Alex as they walked into the bedroom and closed the door.

8

S tanding in front of the full-length mirror, Dieter Hoffmann looked at his reflection, a smile of satisfaction playing at the corner of his mouth. Wearing the working uniform of a lieutenant in the SS, he buttoned the top button of his jacket. The earth-grey uniform was an immaculate fit. On the left hand side of the collar were the three pips and double bar, silver on a black background, which denoted his rank of first lieutenant. On the right hand side were the two SS flashes, and on the lower part of his left arm, picked out in silver on a black-diamond shaped background, were the letters SD. At his waist he wore a black leather belt with a closed holster containing a Luger automatic pistol. Newly promoted, he'd arrived the previous evening at the SS barracks in Lichterfelde, a district of Berlin. Today was to be his first working with his mentor SS-Colonel Langers at Prinz-Albrecht-Straße. Walking over to a table in his spacious quarters, he sat and poured a cup of coffee from a silver pot that had been delivered a few moments ago by an orderly. He reflected on the events of the past four years.

All that time ago, the bus taking him and twenty-four other new cadets had pulled slowly into the forecourt of the officer training school at Bad Tolz. The driver turned off the engine, stood and opened the door. A breeze of cold mountain air filled the bus. In the distance you could see the snow-covered, towering peaks of the Bavarian Alps. The cadets stayed where they were, waiting for something to happen, all of them more than a little apprehensive. A picket gate set into a set of massive double doors opened and a man dressed in the uniform of a captain in the SS stepped out.

Climbing up the stairs into the bus, he looked around at his new charges. Taking a list out of his pocket, he said quietly, 'Good morning, Gentlemen.' Without waiting for a reply, he continued, 'Answer your names.' The twenty-five cadets meekly obeyed, each trying to make his voice sound authoritative and impress his fellow cadets. The formalities over, the Captain, whose name was Muller, said, 'Right, get off the bus and fall in. I want you in two ranks. Don't talk, move.'

The young men had fallen over themselves in their haste to obey. The morning had passed quickly, everything being done at the double, the senior N.C.O's giving them no time to ponder their circumstances. By lunchtime they'd been given a mountain of uniforms and equipment.

A ferocious sergeant-major, by the name of Klein, gathered them into their barrack room, their home for the next few months. 'Stand to attention and stand by your beds,' he growled. 'Listen to me carefully. After lunch, at 14.00 sharp, you are to parade in the gymnasium. The Commandant will talk to you and I suggest, Gentlemen, that you listen very carefully to what he has to say.' At that moment, Captain Muller entered the room. Sergeant-Major Klein came to attention and raised his right arm in the Hitler salute.

Muller returned the salute, his gleaming black jack-boots reflecting the overhead lights. Tucked under his arm, he carried a riding crop, his whole bearing that of an officer of the Prussian school. 'I will be your company commander during your stay here and I warn you all now, that the discipline here at the academy is of the highest order. You will obey the orders of your superiors without question. Our job is to make SS officers of you and anyone who fails to live up to our standards will find themselves out of here very quickly. Is that understood?' There was a murmur of agreement from the assembled cadets. 'I can't hear you, shout.'

They all raised their voices, 'Yes, Sir.'

'That's better.' Turning to Klein, Muller continued, 'Take them to lunch Mr Klein. I'll see you all at 14.00 hrs.' He turned and left the barrack room.

The new recruits stood in line in the mess. Delicious odours wafted from the hotplates, making them realise how hungry they were. The mess hall was almost medieval, the rows of tables filled with older, more experienced cadets. The new arrivals attracted a lot of attention, with many knowing smirks from the older cadets, as if to say, we hope you know what you've let yourselves in for. Dieter felt a sense of euphoria. I've arrived at last, he said to himself.

At 14.00 sharp the new intake lined up in three ranks, standing rigidly to attention. Muller and Klein were talking quietly to each other both keeping an eye on the entrance to the gymnasium. There was a movement at the door. It opened and a tall slim man entered wearing the black uniform of a colonel in the SS. Muller and Klein came as rigidly to attention as their young charges. Their right arms came up in unison in the Hitler salute.

The salute was casually returned by the commanding officer. Looking towards Klein, he said, 'Stand them at ease.' The order was given and the young men relaxed slightly. 'Welcome to Bad Tolz, gentlemen.' The colonel passed his eye over the young men in front of him, and continued, 'Today is your first day, the first day of what I hope will be a new career for you all. That is, all of you that make the grade. Make no mistake, my standards are high and I expect one hundred percent effort from you all. You will be expected to give unswerving loyalty, both to me and to your instructors. When you eventually pass out from this place you will be commissioned officers in the SS. While you are here you will learn that when you are given an order, you will obey that order without question. Your loyalty to the Führer must be absolute. If there's any man in this room who feels that they are unable to comply with this rule, you should say so now.' There was a silence in the room. No one moved a muscle. 'Good. We, Gentlemen, are a relatively new organisation and we have our enemies. There are those who would like to see us fail; they don't like the idea of an elite body of men whose unswerving obedience to the National-Socialist cause is absolute. The regular German army is suspicious of us as they see us as a threat. We are not a threat, except to those who would like to see our cause destroyed. Our aim is to serve the Führer and Reich alongside our army colleagues; we should complement each other. My job is to turn you into officers and gentlemen, the equal of our brothers wearing field grey and that, along with my staff, is what I intend to do.' He turned towards Muller and Klein, nodded and said, 'Dismiss them. Heil Hitler.' He turned and with his boots beating a tattoo as he walked, went out.

At 05.30 the next morning, the barrack room door burst open and the room was flooded with light. 'Out! Out! Come on you lazy swine,' shouted the two SS corporals who were both dressed in tracksuits. 'Come on, I won't say it again, get your feet on the floor,' continued an instructor upending one of the beds with the unfortunate occupant still in it. The new recruits jumped out of bed as quickly as they could, shivering in the cold early morning air. 'Right, listen in. You have five minutes to get your PT kit on and parade on the road downstairs. We're all going for a run around the Alps before breakfast, now move it!'

The young men scrambled to obey. Their long, hard regime had begun.

Dieter had loved every minute of it and had excelled at everything he did. He became popular with his instructors who recognised his potential and his fellow recruits whom he did everything to help.

'Hoffmann! Hoffmann!' Dieter had been on the rifle range, his rifle tucked into his right shoulder and his finger curled around the trigger. Distracted, he eased the pressure and looked towards the sound of the person calling his name. All around him was the crack of rifles being fired as he laid down his weapon and ran towards the instructor who'd called his name. His boots sank into the slight coating of mud on the range as he ran, causing him to stagger slightly, his black, coal-scuttle helmet feeling like a ton weight on his head. Skidding to a halt in front of the instructor, he came to attention. 'Go and get cleaned up and report to the commandant's office in one hour. Go on, Hoffmann, don't be late.' Dieter, saying nothing, did an about turn and ran towards the barrack block. 'Shit!' he said to himself, 'I wonder what he wants?'

Less than one hour later, Dieter stood in the corridor outside the commandant's office and waited.

A door opened and the adjutant came out with a file tucked underneath his arm. Looking Dieter up and down as he approached, he said, 'Ah, Hoffmann, the Colonel will see you now; you can go straight in.'

'Thank you, Sir.' Walking towards the office, Dieter knocked and waited.

'Enter,' said the voice from within the office.

Dieter marched in and came rigidly to attention, his right arm coming up into the Hitler salute. 'Cadet Hoffmann reporting as ordered, Sir.'

'At ease, Hoffmann, sit down.' The Colonel gave a little smile. 'I've been looking at your file. You're doing extremely well. Your instructors are saying very nice things about you.'

'Thank you, Sir. I feel very much at home here.'

'Good. I received a letter from Berlin this morning. They are also interested in you.' He raised an eyebrow slightly and continued, 'How would you feel about joining the SD when you pass out?'

'SS Intelligence?'

'Yes, they're very interested in you. In fact I've been instructed that when you do leave here you're to be sent to Hamburg to continue your training as an intelligence officer. Believe me, it's a very good move for you career-wise.'

Dieter felt his heart soar, 'Sir, that would be wonderful. I'd love it.'

'Hoffmann, we still have many enemies both inside and outside of the Reich. You could make a valuable contribution to hunting them down. Captain Muller tells me that you'd make a superb field officer, but for the moment at least, it looks as if your talents are wanted elsewhere.' He looked directly at Dieter, put his hand to his mouth and stroked his upper lip with his forefinger. 'I know about your father. That was a brave thing that you did.'

'Sir, I did no more than my duty. I would have done the same no matter who it was. Traitors to the Reich deserve no sympathy. My father and Wagner were traitors. They got what they deserved, nothing less.'

The commandant nodded. 'Well said, Hoffmann. You will make a very thorough intelligence officer.' He smiled and continued, 'I wouldn't want to be an enemy if you were on my trail. That's settled then; it looks as if your future career's being mapped out for you.'

'Thank you, Sir, I'm delighted.'

'By the way, how's Colonel Langers?'

'Oh, very well, Sir. I spend my leaves there. He and his wife are like parents to me and treat me like family.'

'Good, we all need family, Hoffmann. Will they be coming to see you pass out?'

'Certainly, Sir. Just two more months now.'

'Very well. Perhaps the two of you will work together in the future.'

'I'd enjoy that very much, sir.'

Nodding, the Colonel said, 'Alright, Hoffmann, you can go now. Take the rest of the day off. Go into town and have a few beers, you deserve it.'

Dieter's eyes lit up, 'Yes sir, thank you very much.'

'Tell the adjutant that I said you should have a pass for the day. Off you go.'

His heart singing with happiness, Dieter had stood, saluted and left the office.

It had been a beautiful morning on the day of the passing out parade a few months later. The morning sun had hit the ice and snow on the top of the Alps, causing it to gleam and sparkle. It was a perfect backdrop to the scene being played out on the parade ground below. A warm breeze gently blew down from the mountains and the flags and banners stirred slightly. Of the twenty-five young men who'd arrived at Bad Tolz all those months ago, twenty remained. The whole of the school was on parade, standing stiffly to attention in three straight ranks. The SS band stood to one side, the brass instruments catching the sun. Sitting on a platform at the far end of the Parade Square sat the family and friends of the cadets passing out that day, including Colonel Langers and his wife. The twenty cadets stood in their immaculate black SS uniforms, the red armbands with the white circle and black crooked swastika standing out against the coal-black of the uniforms. The twenty cadets were split into four groups of five, three facing forwards and one facing inward on either side. Standing in front of each group, stood an SS officer holding the swastika flag straight out in front of them, parallel to the ground, the long flagstaff supported underneath their right arm. The most important part of the ceremony was about to begin. Each cadet touched the flag with their left hand and, raising their right hands, they swore in loud voices the oath of allegiance to Adolf Hitler, the Reich and *Obedience unto Death.'*

Each of the twenty cadets was presented with a ceremonial SS dagger. Dieter was also presented with an SS sword, as he was deemed by his superiors to be the most outstanding cadet of his cohort.

The strains of a Johann Strauss waltz played by the band could be heard as the newly-appointed SS Second lieutenants and their guests drank champagne. They were standing in small groups, laughing and joking, the young men proud.

'Well, Dieter, it's finally happened, all of your dreams have come true, eh?' said Colonel Langers with a smile playing at the corner of his mouth.

'Oh, yes Sir, you can't imagine. Although I always believed that this day would arrive; my whole destiny is with the SS. I can feel it.'

'Two weeks leave now, Dieter,' said Ilse Langers. 'Are you coming to stay with us?'

'Well, Ma'am, if you don't mind, I intend to spend a few days in London. I've always wanted to go there and now seems like a good opportunity.'

Colonel Langers chuckled, 'A very good idea my boy; go and enjoy yourself.' He paused and looked at Dieter quizzically, 'You have a good camera, don't you?'

A look of surprise crossed Dieter's face, 'You know that I have, Sir; you bought me one for my last birthday. Why do you ask?'

'Well, the thought just occurred to me that as you'll be in London it might be a good idea if you were to put your time to good use.' Dieter looked puzzled as Langers continued, 'Why don't you take a few discreet photos? Places that would be of interest to us. You know the sort of thing: railway stations, bridges … the East End docks are, I believe, very interesting.' He raised his eyebrows.

Grinning, Dieter said, 'What a marvellous idea. Yes, I'll do just that.'

'Oh, you SD men, always the spy,' said Ilse.

The Colonel looked at Dieter and winked. Changing the subject, sure that Dieter had understood, he continued, 'Your first posting will be useful to you. You should learn a lot. Who knows, we may work together in the future. Oh, by the way, in a few month's time I'm going to order that your father be released from the camp. He can stew for a while longer. I don't believe that any useful purpose will be served by leaving him there forever. He's no threat to us. Unfortunately, it's too late for the other fellow, what was his name? Oh, yes, Wagner. He died last week; pneumonia, I believe.'

Dieter gave a slight shrug of his shoulders, 'As you like, sir.' He hadn't thought of his family for months; it was almost as if they'd never existed. He found that he was shocked to hear about Rudi's father.

'Any more champagne, anyone?' Langers had said jovially.

Coming back to the present with a start, Dieter glanced at his watch. Smiling to himself he reflected that it wouldn't be a good idea to be late on his first day at Prinz-Albrecht-Straße. Standing, he put on his peaked cap with its death's head badge, adjusted it to a jaunty angle and left the room.

9

Walking up the stone steps to the entrance, Dieter pushed open the main doors and went in. The reception area was to his right, just as he remembered it. There was much more activity today he thought, and he felt an immense sense of pride at the achievements that had brought him here. As he approached the desk, the young SS private who was on duty stood and came to attention, lifting his right arm in the Hitler salute.

Dieter returned the salute and said, 'Lieutenant Hoffmann, I'm to report to Colonel Langers.'

'Yes, Sir, just one moment,' replied the private. He lifted the telephone and dialled. After a short pause he said, 'Lieutenant Hoffmann for you, sir.' He replaced the receiver, looked at Dieter and said, 'If you just go down the corridor, it's the third door on the right, Sir.'

Dieter looked at the private, said, 'Thank you, I know the way,' and walked towards the office that he remembered so well.

Straightening his back almost instinctively as he approached the door, Dieter knocked and waited to be told to enter.

'Come on in, Dieter.'

Recognising the voice of Langers, he pushed open the door and entered. Coming to attention he clicked his heels together and gave a straight arm Hitler salute. Langers casually returned the salute, jumped up from his chair and approached Dieter. He was wearing the uniform of a colonel in the SS and his face was creased in a smile. He put a hand on each of Dieter's shoulders and said, 'Dieter, my boy, how nice to see you. Did you have a good leave? We've had good reports of you from Hamburg, how long has it been since you passed out?'

'Just about three years now. How are you? I'm sorry that I haven't seen you much recently, but I'm sure that you understand how it is.'

Langers chuckled and said, 'Of course we understand. Ilse missed mothering you, but you have your own life to lead. Come, sit down.'

He ushered Dieter over to two armchairs by his desk and offered him a seat.

'It's a little early in the morning, but I think a celebratory drink's in order.'

He took a bottle of whiskey and poured two drinks. The colonel came over, gave Dieter his drink and sat down. He continued speaking, 'By the way, you're to be working on my staff — Division 111, counter-espionage. Our job is to make sure that our enemies within the Reich are hunted down and taken care of. I know that you're more than up to the job.'

Dieter said very seriously, 'I can guarantee that Colonel. It's much the same as I've been doing in Hamburg. '

'I've been reading your file this morning and it's very impressive. You've excelled yourself as I suspected you would. Oh, by the way, thanks for the photos that you took in London; they were very useful and we have them filed away. Now to other business. Firstly, we've an important visit to make this morning. You should be very flattered, Dieter, the chief's taken a personal interest in you.'

'The chief?' inquired Dieter.

'Yes. Heydrich. He wants to see us both this morning. Oh, and Dieter, a word of advice — don't ever be stupid enough to underestimate him. He's one of the most powerful men in the land. If he has his way he'll become even more powerful; be very careful,' said Langers quietly.

'Oh don't worry, Sir, I know all about him. In fact it will be nice to meet him. I'm a great admirer of the man. However, I'd never be that stupid and I value my head too much.'

'Come on, Dieter,' said Langers. 'Let's go up there now.' Langers rose and Dieter followed. They left the room and walked up the main staircase. The two men entered a large ante-room. Sitting at a desk was a young SS lieutenant, working on what, to Dieter, looked like lists.

He looked up and said, 'Good morning, Colonel. The Obergruppenführer is expecting you. Please wait one moment.' The lieutenant got up, smiled at Dieter, and walked over to a pair of enormous doors, knocked and entered. He was gone for a matter of seconds and when he returned he nodded and said, 'He'll see you now.'

Langers and Dieter marched in side by side and in step with each other. They halted and raised their arms in unison in the Hitler salute. The man sitting at the huge desk in front of them looked up and returned the salute. Seeing the man for the first time in the flesh, Dieter was amazed to see how young he was, in his thirties. Even sitting behind the desk, Dieter could tell that he was a tall man. He had a high forehead, small eyes which seemed to look everywhere at once, a long nose, and his mouth was wide-lipped. When he spoke, the first thing that Dieter noticed was how high-pitched his voice was and how his speech was nervous and staccato.

'Good morning, Gentlemen. Welcome to my team, Hoffmann.'

'Thank you, Sir,' said Dieter.

'I've read your file with interest. I believe that you've become very proficient at hunting down our enemies since you graduated. Congratulations!'

'Thank you, Sir.' Dieter looked down at Heydrich's long, lily-white hands and thought, '*He does have the hands of a strangler.*' Something he'd heard whispered before.

It was nice to meet you, Hoffmann. Keep him up to scratch, won't you, Colonel?'

He looked at Langers for the first time.

'I certainly will, Sir,' said Langers. Heydrich nodded as if to say 'Dismissed.' The two men were about to start to about-turn when Heydrich interrupted them.

'By the way, Hoffmann, there's one very important thing that you must never ever forget in our job.'

'And what's that, Sir?' said Dieter.

'You can never know enough about people.'

'Yes, Sir. I won't forget.' Heidrich nodded. The two men about-turned and marched out of the office.

Once in the corridor Dieter and Langers allowed themselves to relax a little. Lighting up a cigarette, Langers said, 'Well, Dieter, what did you think about your new boss?'

Dieter looked across at Langers and said, 'A bit frightening to be honest. I wouldn't want to be an enemy of his that's for sure.'

Langers roared with laughter. 'Oh, yes, my boy, make damned sure that you never cross him because if you do you'll live to regret it.'

The two men returned to Langers' office. At the entrance, Langers turned and looked over at a pretty, young secretary who was busy working on a typewriter.

'Heidi,' he said, 'be an angel and bring us some coffee, will you?'

'Certainly, sir,' she replied, rising from her desk and walking away.

Dieter and Langers entered the office.

'Your office, by the way, is next door,' said Langers, nodding in the direction of a door set in the opposite wall. 'Don't hesitate to come and see me if you need anything or have any problems will you?'

'No, Sir, I won't,' replied Dieter.

'Alright,' said Langers, 'I'm working on a very interesting case at the moment and I want you to take it on for me — it's important.' He continued, 'We know that there's a communist cell working out of Wedding.'

'But I thought we'd cleared Wedding of communists?' said Dieter.

Langers laughed. 'The only way to clear Wedding of communists would be to shoot all of the inhabitants and raze the place to the ground. Even the rats there are red. Yes, I admit we picked up all of the well-known faces in '33, but these communists breed like rats. We know for a fact that they're being helped by our Russian friends in all kinds of ways.'

Dieter nodded, knowing that the working class district of Wedding was a hive of communist activity. He was just about to say something, when there was a knock on the door and Heidi entered carrying a tray with a pot of coffee. Dieter eyed her appreciatively. She was of medium build with brown hair and was wearing a tight, white blouse which showed her breasts off to perfection. A short, black skirt showed her long, shapely legs which were encased in black nylon stockings. *Very nice indeed*. Dieter thought to himself. Smiling he looked her straight in the eye, a look that she returned. She licked her ruby lips, showing her beautiful, white teeth. A *frisson* of sexual excitement passed between them.

'Heidi, my dear,' beamed Langers like a benevolent uncle, 'Thank you. This is Lieutenant Hoffmann who's joining our little team. I've no doubt that he'll be giving you some work to do from time to time, won't you, Dieter?'

Heidi held out her hand and Dieter took it, holding it a little longer than strictly necessary. She looked him straight in the eye and said, 'Welcome Lieutenant. It'll be my pleasure to do any work that you may have for me.'

Langers chuckled. He had a knowing look in his eye.

'Thank you, my dear. Now run along, we've work to do.'

She gave them both a little smile and left the room.

'Charming girl,' muttered Langers to himself.

Langers poured them both coffee and continued as if there'd been no interruption.

'I suspect that this cell is small. I think that the people involved are young and that there are no more than four or five of them. They're distributing leaflets and we've even found some slogans daubed onto walls.'

'Very brave or very stupid,' said Dieter.

'We picked up a suspected communist yesterday. He's downstairs at the moment helping us with our enquiries,' said Langers sardonically. 'After coffee we'll go down and see how things are going, although I'm not over-optimistic.'

Dieter nodded. He'd often wanted to see the cellars of the Prinz-Albrecht-Straße. Now was his chance. The two men sipped their coffee and talked of inconsequential things.

Langers and Dieter walked down the stairs to the cellars beneath the building. At the bottom there was a long corridor stretching ahead of them with overhead lights at intervals. The corridor had rows of cells on each side. From some of these cells you could hear the occasional groan of someone in intense pain. Langers walked over to a door, turned the handle, and walked in. Dieter found himself inside a windowless chamber. There was a smell of burnt flesh in the air. He wondered for a moment where it was coming from. Incongruously, he noticed a large cast-iron bath complete with taps in the far corner. A single overhead bulb lit the room, as if someone wanted to save electricity. In the centre of the room, strapped to a chair, was a middle-aged man, naked from the waist up, his head lolling forward onto his chest. There were two men in the room, both with their sleeves rolled up as if they had a busy day ahead of them. Dieter was surprised at how humid it was down here. He'd expected it to be cold and damp. Langers walked over to the man in the chair who was making a wheezing sound through his open mouth. Taking hold of his hair, he jerked his head back. His face was hardly recognisable. The flesh around his eyes was black. The man's nose was completely out of joint and his mouth was swollen and bleeding. Dieter noticed that a number of his teeth were missing, leaving gaping, bloody holes, and there were a number of cigarette burns on his chest.

'Well?' said Langers, raising an eyebrow.

'Nah, Chief, this one knows nothing. He's even giving us names of people that we picked up in '33. Do you want us to work on him some more?'

The other Gestapo man, who'd remained silent, was smoking a cigarette. He finished it and casually stubbed it out on the man's chest.

The prisoner gave a squeal, his whole body convulsing. *He sounds like a wounded rabbit*, Dieter thought to himself.

Langers looked at the prisoner thoughtfully and said, 'Let him stew for a few hours in the cells, then work on him again for a while. If he doesn't tell you anything of interest, get rid of him.'

'What would you like us to do with him, Chief?' said the second Gestapo agent.

Langers looked at the man and said testily, 'It's a matter of complete indifference to me what you do with him. Use your initiative man and report to me if you come up with something useful.'

'Yeh, Chief,' replied the man.

Dieter looked at the Gestapo man and said, 'You could always put a bullet in his head. That's what you'd do with a useless horse.' He gave a cold smile.

Langers nodded at Dieter, smiled and indicated that they should leave. Both men headed for the door and walked out. They walked up the stairs and headed for Langers' office. Once inside Langers said, 'Well, I didn't hold out much hope, but it was worth a try.'

Langers looked down at his hands. He gave a look of distaste as he realised that there was blood on them. He walked over to a small sink in the corner of the office and washed his hands fastidiously. He looked back over his shoulder and said to Dieter, 'You and I are not here to get our hands dirty, Dieter. Leave that to the people downstairs. Believe me when I say that the Gestapo has no shortage of people like those two down there. There are plenty only too willing to do the dirty work.'

He paused, and then continued like a professor giving a lecture.

'No, Dieter, our job is to make sure that the machinery is well-oiled and runs smoothly. All we have to do is to tell the Gestapo who we want and they see to it. It's interesting, isn't it, that the SD has the ultimate power. The Gestapo don't like it one little bit at times.'

'Yes I know. In Hamburg we very often didn't leave our desks; just picked up the phone, told them whom we wanted and they'd do the rest. We're the ultimate power behind the throne, eh? Now, what about this cell?' asked Dieter.

'Don't worry, we have agents and informers all over Berlin. Sooner or later they'll make a mistake and then we'll have them.'

Sitting in his office after a large and enjoyable lunch spent with the beautiful Heidi, Dieter felt happy that he had taken the opportunity to invite her to dinner that evening. As he was reflecting on the pleasures that he hoped were to come, the buzzer went on his desk. Pressing the lever he said, 'Yes?'

'There's a Frau Von Klein asking to see you. Shall I send her in?'

'Yes please, Heidi,' replied Dieter.

A well-dressed woman in her mid-forties entered the office. She was obviously from a middle-class background. She was a strikingly attractive woman, with just the right amount of make-up, and she was wearing a small hat set at a jaunty angle on the right side of her head. She looked at Dieter and said, 'Thank you so much for seeing me, Lieutenant. There's something that you should know, I think.' Deiter noticed that she had a very cultured voice. She paused and then carried on, 'I discussed it with my husband at breakfast this morning. He's a lawyer you know.'

Dieter nodded, wondering what was to come next.

'Anyway, we had a dinner party last night, just a few friends.'

She paused and then continued. 'We were having a discussion after dinner. I tell you, Lieutenant, I was shocked.'

Dieter wished that the woman would get to the point.

'Our neighbours, the Klebers, had the audacity to say that the Führer would, in the end, bring this country to ruin. That there would be a war between us and the English and that it would end in defeat for Germany just like the last time.'

She stopped. There was a look of genuine shock on her face and then she continued, 'The Klebers have been our best friends for twenty years, but my husband and I felt that we just had to report it to the authorities.'

She took a deep breath and said, 'After all that the Führer has done for this country. I mean, there's hardly any unemployment now. I agree with him not trusting the Jews either. They certainly can't be trusted.'

Dieter lifted his hand as she was about to continue, and said, 'Thank you very much, Frau Von Klein, for this information. I'll ask you to make a written statement of what you've just told me. If you'd then sign it, I'll make sure that it's passed on to the relevant authorities.'

She said, 'Thank you so much. It's a weight off my mind, I can tell you.'

Dieter looked at the woman and asked, 'Tell me, are you and your husband members of the party?'

'No, Lieutenant,' she replied. 'We're not at all political. We know that we're in good hands with the Führer. We have complete faith in him.'

Dieter nodded and pressed the buzzer on his desk. He asked Heidi to take the lady's statement.

'Thank you for coming in to report this matter to us, Frau Von Klein. You've proved yourself to be a good loyal German. Just leave it with us now.'

The woman smiled and nodded, got up, and left the room.

Dieter looked at the door for a few minutes after the woman had left. 'There's no doubt our system's working very well indeed. People are doing our job for us,' he said, half aloud to himself with a little chuckle.

Later that evening the Klebers were arrested.

10

The rehearsal room was filled with the beautiful sounds of the Beethoven sonata, the overhead light reflecting off the mirror-like surface of the Bechstein grand piano. Paul and Alex were totally absorbed in the music. The two young musicians played together almost as a whole, the one complimenting the other, as sparks seemed to be flying between the two of them. The piece was reaching its climax. The music dropped to a pianissimo and started to crescendo, the tempo gathered pace, moving from allegro to presto to vivace, all the while getting louder. Paul's whole body was moving to the tempo of the music and his fingers raced over the strings of the violin. Alex was sitting at the piano and the fingers of his large, strong hands were flying over the keyboard at incredible speed. The piece ended with three fortissimo chords played by both instruments. The two boys visibly relaxed, taking a few seconds to come off the musical plateau that they'd been on for the past twenty minutes.

Paul looked down at Alex, smiled, and said playfully, 'Not bad for a beginner, Alex. I could tell that you'd been practising.'

Alex snorted, smiled and said, 'Bloody cheek! A few more years and you just might be up to my standard.' The two were always duelling in this way knowing that the one was the equal of the other. Paul smiled, quickly looked around, bent down and gave Alex a kiss on the lips.

'You played like an angel as usual, Alex,' said Paul, giving the younger boy a playful clip around the ear.

Alex ducked and said, 'I fancy a trip down to the Black Cat for a beer — how about it?'

'Yes, let's go and see Gustav.' Paul put the violin into its case and the two boys left the room, turning the lights out behind them.

The Black Cat was in a side street near to the zoological gardens. During the time of the Weimer Republic it had been a favourite haunt of homosexuals. On any night of the week the bar would be filled with good-looking male prostitutes and their clients. The weekends would be party time, with transvestite shows and cabaret and everyone having a wonderful time. The place still had a regular clientele. Anyone who was outside the Nazi ideal seemed to congregate there. People were more discreet out of necessity except, that is, Paul and Alex.

Parking the car a short way from the bar, Paul and Alex climbed out and walked towards the entrance. They went down the long flight of stairs below street level into the *Jungendstil* room. In the centre was an oval-shaped bar, while on two sides, running the whole length of it were dark brown, leather-covered benches. Fixed onto the wall on both sides were mirrors with the shape of a cat etched on them. Lamps at intervals gave out a mottled, amber glow. From the ceiling above the bar hung a circular five-branched lamp. Facing the benches were round marble-topped tables with wooden chairs, the place having the ambience of a private club that had seen better days. As they entered, Alex said to Paul, 'My God! This place is dingy — look at the carpets — but you know I love it here, Paul. Do you remember the first time that you brought me here?'

'Of course I do, silly, how could I forget?'

Alex giggled and said, 'If my father could see me now he'd go mad.'

'I promise not to tell him,' said Paul with a smile.

The bar was dimly lit and there were only a few customers this evening. Standing at the bar were a couple of young prostitutes, who were still quite pretty and who both knew Paul and Alex very well. Further along the bar two Jewish men were having an animated conversation. Sitting at a table in the corner were two lesbians who seemed to be having a row. There were a few other people scattered around the bar, drinking and talking quietly. Everyone minded their own business in the Black Cat. Gustav, the barman, gave the two boys a smile and a nod, lifted two fingers up and raised his eyebrow, as if to say, 'the usual.' Paul nodded agreement. As they approached the bar, one of the prostitutes looked up, smiled and said, 'And how are the two boy geniuses this evening? Still taking the Berlin musical scene by storm?'

'We try, Lisle, we try. How's business?' asked Paul.

'I've given up for tonight. All the clients are at home with their wives,' Lisle replied.

Her companion, peroxide blond, wearing a low-cut, red dress laughed and said, 'She wants to take you home tonight, Paul, and give you some lessons.'

Paul smiled and replied, 'No thanks Rita, I prefer the real thing.'

Alex said in a camp voice, 'If she tries that, I'll scratch her eyes out.' As the four of them laughed, Gustav came over and put two beers down on the bar.

Alex said, 'Thanks Gustav.' The barman nodded and walked over to serve another customer. He wasn't the type to make idle conversation, unusual in a barman.

Paul said, 'I think we'll sit down and have our beer, girls. It'll soon be time to take the little one home and put him to bed.' Alex scowled and punched Paul on the arm.

'I'll bet,' said Rita with a smile.

Paul and Alex picked up their beers, walked over to a long, padded bench set against one wall of the bar and sat down side by side. Alex rested his head on Paul's shoulder and Paul put his arm round Alex, gently stroking his hair. Lisle and Rita stayed at the bar talking. Smoking and taking the occasional sip from their drinks they took no notice of the two lover-boys sitting behind them. Lisle was standing facing the stairs leading down to the bar. Rita had her back to them and Lisle was only half listening to her companion's conversation. Rita was complaining about a client that she'd picked up the previous evening. Lisle happened to glance up towards the top of the stairs and, by chance, she immediately noticed two pairs of gleaming jackboots slowly descending the stairs, their owners not yet in sight. She hissed at Rita, 'The Police. The boys, quick!' Paul and Alex were totally oblivious to the danger. Lisle grabbed hold of Rita's arm and pulled her towards where the two boys were sitting. Rita caught on immediately and the girls rushed over to the boys Lisle roughly forcing her way between Paul and Alex. Paul started to protest but Lisle shut him up with a look, and he quickly realised that something was wrong. Lisle put her arms around Paul and kissed him on the lips.

'Police,' she whispered in his ear, 'Kiss me again.' Rita was doing the same thing with young Alex, who'd also realised that something was wrong. By now the two policemen were standing at the foot of the stairs. They looked around, staring at the clients. Paul and Alex had their arms around the girls like four lovers on a night out.

Gustav said to the two policemen, 'Evening gents, would you like a beer?'

'No, we're on duty,' growled the older of the two policemen. Gustav shrugged his shoulders, as if to say, 'suit yourselves.' The policemen saw the two Jews sitting at the bar; they had stopped talking and were looking fearfully at the officers. The policemen walked over and looked the Jews up and down. The more senior officer said, holding out his hand, 'Papers.'

The Jews started to fumble in their inside pockets for the documents, both looking terrified. They managed to get them out and handed them over. The senior policeman opened the papers and scrutinised them carefully, as his younger colleague looked on, his face cold. The older policeman finished looking at the papers but instead of handing them back, he threw them on the bar. He bent forward and said menacingly, 'I suggest that you two Yids get the fuck out.' The two Jews picked up their papers and, without a word, left the bar. The two policemen turned around, looked over at Paul, Alex and the two girls and walked over. Paul's heart was in his mouth. As the policemen approached Lisle said brightly, 'Hello, officers.'

The older of the two replied, 'Hello Lisle, I see you're set up for the night.' He raised an eyebrow.

Lisle smiled and replied, 'No, officer, they're just friends.'

The officer grunted and said warningly, 'You girls had better be careful; it's much more than a fine nowadays for being on the game.'

Lisle gave a little smile and replied. 'No, it's not like that officer. I've got a job now, haven't I Rita?' Rita nodded.

The policeman looked over at her and said, looking at Alex, 'He's a bit young for you isn't he, Rita?' Rita just smiled and said nothing. The two policemen turned around. On the way out, they stopped and looked at Gustav.

The younger one said, speaking for the first time, 'You'd better be careful who you're serving in this shit-hole, or we'll have to arrange a visit from the SA.' The policemen walked slowly back up the stairs and out of the club.

Gustav watched them go and said quietly, 'Bastards! I suppose they want me to put up a sign saying "Jews not allowed" like most of the other bars in town.'

Paul and Alex both breathed a sigh of relief when the two policemen had left. Paul gave Lisle a peck on the cheek and said, 'Thank you, both of you; Alex and I are in your debt.'

'Yes,' said Alex, 'thank you.'

Lisle laughed and said, 'Who'd have thought it! I'm now in the business of babysitting a couple of homos. Come on, the least you can do is buy us a drink.' Becoming more serious, she said, 'Be careful you two. We won't always be around to save your arses. It's no picnic in one of those camps from what I hear.' Paul and Alex both nodded soberly. Unfortunately, they were not yet frightened enough to listen.

11

Jack-knifing upright, his heart beating rapidly, his whole torso covered in a film of ice cold sweat, Klaus Hoffmann opened his eyes. His pyjama jacket was soaking wet. The same dream, always the same dream and the camp — always the camp. That place of evil, the hell on earth that he'd been consigned to by his son. He shuddered and looked over at the clock sitting on the bedside cabinet; it was 3 am. Stirring, Greta opened her eyes and looked up at her husband, knowing that the poor man had been dreaming again, her heart going out to him. She came awake quickly, sat up and said, 'A bad dream again, Klaus?' Nodding, Klaus felt his heartbeat starting to slow down, a shudder shaking his whole body. Leaning over, Greta turned on the bedside lamp, placed her hand gently on Klaus's shoulder, and said, 'You're soaking wet, put on some fresh pyjamas. I'll go down and make some tea.' She climbed out of bed, put on her dressing gown and left the bedroom. Moving slowly, Klaus felt like an old man as he went over to the chest of drawers and took out a fresh pair of pyjamas. The dream was beginning to fade as he changed, put on his dressing gown and slowly walked down the stairs. Entering the kitchen, he saw that Greta was busy getting the tea things ready, her back turned towards him. Klaus walked over to the kitchen table, sat down, and lit a cigarette — a habit that he'd never had before the camp. He'd started on his release. They helped somehow. Greta walked over to the table, sat down and took her husband's hands in hers. 'Better now?' she asked.

Klaus nodded and said, 'Will this never end Greta? I don't know how much longer I can go on.' He was close to tears.

When he and Robert Wagner had arrived at the camp they'd been immediately escorted to the guardroom. There were three SS men present, the guard commander, an SS lieutenant, a sergeant and a corporal. The brutality had started straight away. 'Stand over by that wall and keep still,' snarled the sergeant.

The two men had stood to attention, the corporal walking casually over to them, saying, 'If you two dog turds think that you're here for a fucking holiday you can think again.' He lifted his right arm and hit Robert on the cheek with full force, using the open palm of his hand. Robert staggered, his cheek on fire.

The corporal, carrying a riding crop, looked at Klaus and said, 'You'll learn fast who's in charge here, if you have any sense. Who the fuck are you to criticise the Führer? You piece of shit.' He lifted the crop and brought it down with full force onto Klaus's shoulder. Giving a shriek of agony he had almost fainted with the pain. They'd been made to stand rigidly to attention for what seemed like hours, as the guards shouted abuse at them. Robert thought that his bladder would burst and he was in agony, but had been too frightened to say anything. The SS had filled in the appropriate forms for their 'protective custody'.

The sergeant had said, 'I suppose that you pair of bastards are wondering how long you're going to be our guests?' He sneered and continued coldly. 'Well, I'll tell you. We decide how long you'll be here. It might be a month, a year, or forever — you'll never know.' He looked across at the lieutenant who'd been doing the paper work and said, 'Have you finished with this garbage now, Sir?' The senior man had nodded. The guard had shouted, 'Get out! Move, move!' Robert and Klaus had fallen over themselves in their haste to get out of the guardroom as the process of their dehumanisation had begun.

They'd had their heads shaved, been given the prisoner's striped uniform and a number. They were now in the system. A wall, with a ditch and a live, barbed-wire fence surrounded the camp, with watchtowers placed at intervals. There were two rows of seventeen wooden huts facing each other with a road in between. At the far end of the camp there was a large concrete building which housed the kitchen, laundry and showers. Behind that there was a prison block. Just outside the wall of the camp was a crematorium.

Separated immediately, the two men had been assigned a barrack room. The huts had wooden bunks down each side, a washroom and latrine at the end. The daily routine in the camp started at 4am and finished at 9pm, 'lights out' in the summer. In the winter, reveille was at 5.am. Working time was from dawn to dusk. The labour was wretchedly hard and the food inadequate. The brutality of the SS was unimaginable. This place was indeed 'hell on earth.' At 4am the doors would be flung open by the guards, the barracks would be filled with the shouts of the

SS. 'Out! — Raus, raus! — Schnell, schnell! Move you pieces of shit!' The prisoners would jump out of the bunks, falling over themselves in their haste. It was a case of every man for himself and God help anyone who delayed for a second. Roll call at 5.15am was the first ordeal of the day, as the prisoners stood row upon row, rigidly to attention no matter what the weather. Many times Klaus and the others had stood in torrential rain and freezing snow, their masters walking up and down the lines counting over and over again, until they were satisfied. The commandant would often be present, pacing up and down impatiently, slapping his riding crop against his leg: a very dangerous man to be avoided at all costs. The number of prisoners in the camp while Klaus and Robert were there was two thousand three hundred.

Each day after roll call, the prisoners were given their labour for the day, which was always hard and backbreaking. The SS, of course, oversaw them and would beat anyone mercilessly whom they thought wasn't pulling their weight The punishments in the camp were numerous and varied, including being made to stand to attention on the parade ground for hours at a time. Punishment drill, harder work, beating with a stick or whip; the list was endless. The method only depended on the whim of their SS masters. The homosexual prisoners came in for some of the most brutal treatment. These poor men, who could be recognised by the 'pink triangle' that they wore on their camp uniform, were often singled out for special treatment. The SS called them *'Arschlecker,'* and would often give them the most arduous tasks. One day, one of these prisoners, an old priest, could take no more and threw himself onto the electrified fence. Each day became a nightmare of fear and pain.

One morning a prisoner had been hanged by the SS. As they set up a gallows on the parade ground, all the prisoners were lined up on three sides. They were forced to watch as the guards tied a rope around his neck, stood him on a stool and, when they were good and ready, they kicked away the stool. The prisoners were forced to watch as the life was choked out of him.

Robert's health had started to deteriorate and he was in almost continual pain from the many beatings that he'd received. One day, a group of prisoners were put to work moving a large pile of sand. Robert's group was shovelling the sand into large barrows, as other prisoners were pushing the full ones away. Robert had hardly had the strength to lift the shovel, his face creased in pain. Giving a cry as a jagged white pain shot across his chest, he had dropped the shovel and fallen to the ground. A guard, seeing this, walked over and, lifting his foot, kicked Robert in the ribs.

'Get up you idle piece of shit!' shouted the guard, giving him another kick with his heavy jackboot. Robert had tried to rise, but it was impossible. Even if the guard had started to beat him to death, he couldn't have lifted himself. One of the guard's kicks had pushed the broken rib into his lung and he started to expel a pink froth from the corner of his mouth. The SS man saw this and called two prisoners over. 'Take him over to the barracks,' he ordered.

Later that evening, after roll call, a *Kapo* had sidled over to Klaus and said quietly, 'Your friend Wagner's asking for you. He's in a bad way. I can get you in to see him.' The man's lips hardly seemed to move.

Klaus, without looking at him, said, 'Thank you, I'd be grateful.'

'Follow me,' said the *Kapo*. They had walked over to Robert's barrack and entered. The man said, 'He's over there, don't take all night.'

As Klaus walked over to Robert's bunk, the other prisoners moved away to give the two men some privacy. Looking down at his old friend, he sat on the edge of the bunk thinking '*What can I do to help you old friend? This is all my fault. May God help me.*'

Robert's brow was covered in sweat, his face white. His breathing came in short gasps. There was still a pink froth coming from the corner of his mouth. As Robert opened his eyes and looked at Klaus, he had tried to smile, and say, 'Hello Klaus,'

Klaus had to bend down to hear him as Robert coughed, his face wracked with pain. More bloody froth came from his mouth, 'I'm afraid it's all up for me. If you ever get out of here alive, promise me that you'll tell Astrid and Rudi that I love them, please.'

Klaus had taken his friends hand, squeezed it and said, 'Of course I will, but you'll be able to tell them yourself.'

'No. We both know that's not true,' Robert interrupted. 'It's not only my lung, it's my heart. I couldn't have taken much more of this place anyway.' Tears were streaming down Klaus's face and he blamed himself for Robert's plight; if only he hadn't asked him over that night, none of this would have happened.

The *Kapo* had come over then, tapped Klaus on the shoulder and said, 'You'll have to go now.' Klaus nodded.

Robert had looked at him and whispered, 'Goodbye old friend, may God bless you.' Klaus looked at his friend and, through a mist of tears, said, 'Goodbye, Robert.' He stood up and shuffled out of the barrack block like a very old man. At 1am Robert Wagner died. For him the suffering was over. He wasn't the only one to die in the camp that night; there were many. The bodies of the dead were loaded into a cart, taken to the crematorium and burned, like so much rubbish. Many times after that, Klaus had looked over at the electrified fence and contemplated ending it all. The only thing that stopped him was his promise to Robert.

The months had dragged by, the routine never ending. One bitterly cold morning in early December of 1936, Klaus was on a working party, when a guard shouted his name. Klaus had frozen, his heart beating rapidly. Straightening up and running over, he took off his cap and had stood to attention, trembling, waiting for what was to come next. The guard stood with his hands behind his back, his feet apart. He looked Klaus up and down and said, 'Report to the guardroom, now. Go on move!'.

Klaus replied, 'Yes Sir.' He moved around the SS man and started to run, his heart beating with fear. As he passed, the guard raised his riding crop and hit him across the buttocks. Klaus hardly felt the pain. Running towards the guardroom, his breath coming in heaving gasps, Klaus had knocked, entered, and waited to see what was coming, his heart beating a tattoo in his chest. The SS man sitting behind the desk looked up and had some papers held in his hand. Klaus stood in front of him, breathing heavily. The SS man looked at Klaus and said, 'Well Hoffmann, I have a New Year's present for you. 'Klaus said, 'Yes, Sir'

The SS man nodded and replied, 'Someone on high has decreed that you should leave our establishment. I'm sure that you'll be sorry to go.'

Stammering, not daring to believe what he was hearing Klaus said, 'I don't understand, sir.'

'You're being released, you fucking idiot. The Gestapo, or should I say the SD, in their wisdom, have decided that you're no longer a danger to the Reich.' Klaus closed his eyes and gave silent thanks to God.

'If you ever come back Hoffmann, I promise you that you'll never leave here alive. I advise you to keep your nose very clean from now on and keep your mouth shut. Now read and sign this.' The man handed over a document, which Klaus read.

He was warned never to talk of what he'd seen and heard in the camp on pain of being returned. If he was returned it would be for a much longer period, under much stricter conditions and maybe forever. He was reminded what much stricter conditions meant and was instructed to find work, any work. Warned not to be a burden on the state he was instructed to reintegrate himself into the German Reich. Also he was forbidden to have any contact with former prisoners and was told to report to his local Police station twice a week. He was forbidden to leave his home city without written permission.

Klaus had read the document and signed it. Handing in his uniform, he had received back the clothes that he'd been wearing the day that he'd entered the camp. When he had put them on, they hung loosely on his body. He'd been a prisoner for seventeen months. SS-Colonel Langers of the SD had signed his release order. It was early February 1936.

Coming back to the present with a start, Klaus took a sip of the tea that he'd left standing on the table. It was almost cold. Looking over at her husband, Greta had a mixture of anxiety and worry on her face, feeling useless and angry. Klaus never talked about his experiences in the camp. If he had then perhaps she would have been able to help. Taking Klaus's hand in hers, she said, 'Better now? Perhaps it would be a good idea if you spoke to Dr Kleber?'

Giving a tired smile, he said, 'I'm afraid that Kleber can do nothing for me, my dear, and I'll probably have these nightmares for the rest of my life. At least I'm still here to have them, but poor Robert.....' His voice trailed off.

Greta interrupted him and said, 'Klaus my love, you must stop blaming yourself for Robert's death. It wasn't your fault, but the fault of those Nazi barbarians.' She hesitated and carried on quietly, 'And our son.'

Klaus looked at her and said, 'Yes, our son. Where did we go wrong, Greta? What did we do to turn him into such a monster?'

'It wasn't us that turned him into a monster, it was them,' answered Greta. 'Do you ever wonder what's happened to him?'

Klaus gave a bitter laugh, 'Oh, I'm sure that Deiter's serving his masters well. After four years, he'll now have been turned into the image of his beloved Führer. He was only seventeen when it happened, so young,' mused Klaus.

Greta gave a sigh and said, 'Yet you hear about it all the time now.' She continued, 'What a world we're living in, Klaus.' She glanced over at the clock on the wall. It was 5am. 'It's too late to go back to bed now; why don't you go and soak in a nice, hot bath while I make some breakfast?'

'A good idea. At least it's Saturday, we can relax a little.' Klaus got up from the table, left the kitchen, and headed up the stairs to the bathroom. Watching her husband go, Greta remembered the day that he'd come home from the camp.

She'd been upstairs making the bed when she'd heard the bell ring. Going down quickly, she'd opened the door. At first, she hadn't recognised the figure that stood in front of her.

Klaus had said very quietly, 'I came home as soon as I could, Greta.' He had then burst into tears. As Greta had thrown her arms around him, she could feel his malnourished body under her hands and she too had started to cry, huge sobs wracking her body.

'My love,' she'd repeated over and over again, 'what have they done to you?' She had tried to control her emotions as she'd led him through the front door and into the living room. She'd made coffee and they'd talked for hours, the suffering etched onto his face. Over the months, she'd been able to put some flesh onto his bones, but had been able to do nothing to heal the scars of his mind. Word soon got around of his release and old friends from the university had called to see him.

One of the first to come had been Astrid and Rudi Wagner, a meeting that he'd been dreading. He'd embraced Astrid and then Rudi, and said through his tears, 'I'm sure that you want to hear all about Robert?' Astrid and Rudi had nodded in unison. Klaus had put his arms around them both and said very quietly, 'Let's go into the library and I'll do my best to tell you everything.' Holding nothing back, he told them the whole story. Greta left the three of them alone.

One day a few days after he'd come home, he'd received a visitor, one of his old students, Franz Krux. Franz had said to him, 'My father and I heard about your problems, Herr Professor, and we wondered if you would be prepared to come and work with us in the office? We can't offer you much in the way of salary,' he'd said apologetically, 'but we would both be honoured if you would consider coming to join our little firm.'

Klaus could have wept with joy. He'd said, 'It would be a great honour for me to work for you and your father, I would be delighted.' He'd hesitated, and then continued, 'I'm very grateful to you both, thank you.' After that things had been easier.

Coming out of her reverie with a start, Greta looked at her husband as he entered the kitchen. Looking over at her he said, with a trace of his old self, 'I thought you were making the breakfast my love. Come on, stop daydreaming, I'm starving.'

She laughed and said, 'All right, you old bear, I'll do it now.' She paused, and then continued, 'Oh by the way, Astrid and Rudi are coming over later.'

Klaus beamed and said, 'Good, I'd like to have a talk with Rudi, if he has time for an old man like me.' Klaus and Rudi had become close. Rudi had lost a father and Klaus had lost a son. Klaus was feeling better than he had for a very long time.

12

Sitting in the study after breakfast reading through the newspaper, Klaus heard a car pull into the drive. Putting down the paper he walked to the front door and opened it, a huge smile creasing his face as he saw Astrid and Rudi getting out of the powerful Mercedes. He gave them a little wave. Astrid was a striking woman of medium build with auburn hair done up in a bun at the back. She was wearing a well-cut suit, looking every inch the well-off lady that she was. Added to the inheritance of a very large sum of money on the death of her father, was the considerable fortune that Robert had made. Fortunately, Robert's money was safely deposited in his brother's bank in Basel, safely out of the hands of the Nazis. Rudi had been well provided for in his father's will, making him a wealthy young man.

Klaus said, as they approached the front door, 'Astrid, Rudi, welcome. Come in, it's nice to see you both.' Astrid and Rudi smiled.

'Klaus, how nice to see you you're looking better than you have for a long time,' said Astrid.

'Thank you, my dear. I must admit that I'm feeling a lot better today. However I did have a bit of a bad night. And how are you, Rudi? Keeping well I hope?'

'Oh, I can't complain, Professor,' replied Rudi.

'Where's Greta?' said Astrid. 'In the kitchen, I suppose, preparing lunch. You men!' she chided, 'All you can thing about are your stomachs. I'll go on through and leave you two to have a chat.' She smiled and headed in the direction of the kitchen.

Klaus put his arm around Rudi and said, 'That's a good idea. My boy, let's go into the study for a quiet drink. We can keep out of the women's way.'

'A very good idea, Professor.' The two men entered the spacious study. Walking over to the sideboard, Klaus poured two generous measures of whiskey and handed one to Rudi, sitting next to him in a comfortable, leather armchair.

Rudi nodded his thanks and said, 'How are you really feeling, Professor? I must say, Mother's right, you are looking a little better.'

'I'm still having these dreadful nightmares,' said Klaus. He hesitated and then carried on, 'The camp, you know … but, I don't know why, my morale seems to be improving. Do you know, Greta and I mentioned Dieter this morning for the first time in a very long time.'

Rudi looked at Klaus, took a sip of his whiskey and said, 'Do you hate him for what he did to you and papa?'

Klaus sighed and replied, 'Sadly, Dieter is a product of our times. If there had been no Nazis …' he trailed off, 'But to answer your question, I honestly don't know. If he walked through that door now I can't say what my reaction would be. You, however, must hate him for what happened to Robert?'

'What I hate is what he represents. Do you know, it's a pleasure to come here and be able to say what one really thinks.' Rudi stopped, paused, and then continued, 'You know better than I what happens to someone who says the wrong thing. No one dares say what he or she thinks and you have to continually look over your shoulder; you can trust nobody anymore.'

'And that is exactly how they want it. People don't seem to realise or don't care that this country is now a vast concentration camp. We Germans are all prisoners. The Austrians too, now. Every aspect of our lives is controlled,' continued the professor. He glanced down at the newspaper that he'd been reading earlier and said, 'Take the press. Before they came to power, we had a press that was the envy of the world. Now the few papers that we have all say the same things. We're allowed to know only what they want us to know. Between ourselves, and I mean between ourselves, Rudi,' Rudi nodded. 'often, when Greta's gone to bed, I tune into the BBC. That's enough to put me back into the camp. Rudi, I warn you, what happened to me and your father in that evil place could easily happen to you. Be very careful what you get involved in.'

Rudi said, 'I hear you Professor, but it's so frustrating. I hate those bastards but what can I do? After graduation, I'll be conscripted into the army. I don't mind serving my country. I'm loyal to my country and would defend her if she were threatened,' he stopped and then continued, 'just as you and father did during the last war, but to serve these Nazis … do you know that we have to swear an oath, not to our country, but to Hitler.'

'My boy, that oath is going to cause a lot of good Germans many problems in the future. We are a race that takes oaths very seriously, and when you start swearing an oath to an individual, especially one like Hitler…..'

Rudi nodded and said, 'I think I see what you mean, but what can we do?'

'What can we do? Very little, I fear. The Nazis have total control of every aspect of our lives. I, as an ex-concentration camp prisoner, have to report to the police twice a week. I'm sure that I'm under surveillance and, believe me, I'm very careful what I say on the telephone.'

'You mean …?'

'Oh yes, I wouldn't be surprised. If the phone was in this room I'd be very careful what I said. In fact, I would go and have my conversations, especially ones like this, somewhere else.' Klaus paused, looked Rudi in the eye and continued, 'Rudi I know from my own experience what these barbarians are capable of. I also know, as surely as there is a god, that these people will eventually be destroyed. My big fear is that Germany will be destroyed with them.'

Rudi nodded and said, 'I think that you're right.'

Greta put her head around the door, looked at them and said, 'I suppose you two have been putting the world to rights? Come on, lunch is ready.'

'We're on our way, my love. I don't know about you Rudi, but I'm starving.' They got up and left the room.

On the way out Klaus looked at Rudi and said, 'Remember Rudi, for the love of God, be careful.'

'Don't worry, Professor, I will; but I'm going to do something. I don't know what yet, but …'

Lunch was a festive one, as if Christmas had come early. Looking over at Klaus as he entertained everyone, smiling, joking and making them laugh, Greta couldn't believe that this was the same man who a few hours earlier had been so low in spirit. She prayed that maybe things would now get better for him.

There was one serious moment when Klaus had raised his wineglass and said, 'To absent friends.'

'To absent friends,' replied the others.

After lunch, Klaus said to Rudi, 'Come with me, there's something that I want you to see.' He led Rudi up the stairs to the very top of the house. 'This house, Rudi, was a wedding gift to Greta and me from her parents. I certainly couldn't have afforded to buy it on my salary as a teacher.' He looked at Rudi and continued, 'Do you see that cupboard against the wall over there?' He pointed while Rudi nodded, mystified. The cupboard was flush with the wall and was quite small, about four feet square. Klaus walked over to it and opened the door, squatting down and indicating to Rudi that he should do the same. 'Watch this,' he said. Putting his hand into the top right-hand corner, he pushed with some force. The back of the cupboard swung quietly open onto a small room. You could smell the stale odour of the years. The door hadn't been opened for a very long time. Klaus looked at Rudi and smiled. 'Greta's father showed me this room on the day that we moved in. Do you know, I've never said anything to anyone about it, not even Greta.' Rudi was even more mystified. He said nothing, waiting for the professor to get to the point. Klaus continued, 'If you crawl through, there's a small room under the roof and you can close the door from the inside.'

'Very interesting, Professor, but what's your point?' said Rudi.

'Oh, I suppose it goes back to what we were discussing before lunch. Don't you think that that room would be very useful for anyone looking for somewhere to hide?' Klaus continued, 'I admit that if someone wanted to do a very thorough search it would eventually be discovered, but it would have to be thorough. You see that wall's solid brick, so anyone tapping it would think that the whole wall was. I'm going to reinforce the back of that cupboard so that it doesn't sound hollow if it's tapped'. Klaus looked at Rudi and smiled, 'Just remember that it's there, Rudi. Only you and I know about it.'

Rudi was beginning to understand. 'What about Dieter?' he asked.

'Only you and I,' repeated Klaus. The two men walked back down the stairs. 'There's just one more thing,' said Klaus, leading Rudi into the study. He opened the desk drawer; inside was a large automatic pistol that was well oiled. There was a magazine of ammunition in the butt of the weapon and next to it there were two full clips. 'Do you know how to use one of these?' asked Klaus.

'Certainly, that was one of the things that we learned to do in the Hitler Youth. In fact, Dieter and I became very proficient.'

'I've had it since the World War. If you ever need ...' Klaus trailed off, looked at Rudi, and said, 'These are indeed strange times that we live in, Rudi. You never know. Oh, yes, take this too.' Klaus put his hand into the drawer, fished around for a moment and came out with a key. He handed it to Rudi and said, 'This is the key to the front door; keep it and use it at any time.'

'Thank you, Professor.' Rudi wasn't sure what exactly had passed between him and the professor at that moment. But he knew that it was something very important.

Klaus looked at Rudi, put his arm around his shoulder and said, 'Rudi, don't worry too much, your conscience will tell what's the right thing to do.' The two men left the room.

Astrid and Greta were just coming out of the living room. Greta said, 'So that's where you two are. You're both acting very mysteriously?' Klaus looked at Rudi, smiled and winked.

Looking at Rudi, Astrid said, 'It's time that we went Rudi. Thank you both for a lovely time. You must come to us soon.'

'It's been our pleasure,' said Klaus.

Greta nodded and said, 'Yes it's been wonderful.'

Putting his arm around Greta's shoulder, the two of them led Astrid and Rudi to the front door. They stood and watched as Rudi helped his mother into the car, got into the driving seat, sounded his horn, and drove off with a wave.

Klaus looked at his wife and said seriously, 'You know my dear, with young men like that around, perhaps all is not lost for this country.'

Greta replied, 'I hope that you're right, Klaus. You know, there's been a big change in you today,' she said.

'Perhaps that young man gave me my courage back,' replied Klaus. Looking closely at her husband Greta was puzzled but relieved.

13

S itting at his desk in Gestapo headquarters, Dieter Hoffmann glanced up at the clock on the wall. It read 1am. The lamp on the desk threw shadows onto the walls as he lifted another file from the pile at his left elbow. He gave a sigh, stretched, yawned and took a swig of lukewarm coffee. Sitting in shirtsleeves, his uniform jacket was draped over the back of the chair. He glanced down at the new file in front of him and reflected that Heidrich was right, you could never know enough about people. The file that he was looking at now was a good case in point; the subject was a mid-ranking Nazi official. This man, whose name was Krutz, was married with two children. He had a young mistress, which was not a crime in itself, but the young lady in question was known to have connections with the communist party. Suspected of being a spy working for Russian intelligence, she was under twenty-four-hour surveillance and it was hoped that she would eventually lead the SD to her communist cell. It was suspected that her controller was a high-ranking attaché working in the Russian Embassy situated on Unter den Linden. The Nazi, Krutz, had no idea of his mistress's background and would have been surprised to know that he wasn't the only man in her life. She was spending time with a captain serving with the German navy, who was based in Kiel and who commanded a warship. The girl was known as Christine and the file on her was growing thicker every day.

The shrill ringing of the telephone at his elbow shattered the stillness and quickly bought him out of his reverie. Lifting the receiver he said, 'Hoffmann.'

The SS operator answered, 'I have a man on the line asking for the duty officer, Sir. Sorry, but he refuses to give a name.' Unsurprised, Dieter was used to this; people very often preferred to remain anonymous.

'Put him through. See if you can trace the call while I'm speaking to him,' said Dieter.

'Very good, Sir,' said the operator. There was a short pause as the call was transferred.

The person at the other end came through and Dieter pressed the record button on the tape recorder on his desk.

Dieter said, 'Gestapo.'

A man's voice answered very quietly, 'I believe that you're looking for a group who are distributing anti-Nazi pamphlets?' Before Dieter could reply, the voice carried on, 'You don't need to say anything, just listen. If you go to this address, tomorrow night, you'll be able to pick them all up. Now write this down,' he ordered, giving Dieter the address. He then continued. 'I would suggest that you and your men get there at about midnight. You should catch them all red-handed.' The voice paused for a second, said 'Heil Hitler', and then the line went dead.

Dieter said to the operator, 'Well?'

'Nothing, Sir, the call was too short.'

'Thanks,' said Dieter, as he replaced the receiver and looked thoughtfully into the air. Standing, he walked around the desk and looked at the large map of greater Berlin fixed to the wall, a look of puzzlement etched on his face as he looked at the map. The address that he'd been given by the anonymous caller had come as something of a surprise. 'Charlottenburg,' he murmured to himself as he walked back to the desk, lifted the telephone and dialled a number. It was answered immediately. 'Hoffmann here,' said Dieter. 'I want to know who lives at this address; name and anything else that you can tell me, as soon as possible.' He gave the address. Thoughtfully he glanced upward. Charlottenburg was the last place that he would have expected. The phone rang and he lifted the receiver, said 'Well,' and listened. He made a note on the pad in front of him and said, 'See if we have a file on this man; if so, bring it into me. Thank you. Pastor Neuffe, well, well, well,' Dieter murmured to himself. The file, when it arrived, proved to be interesting. The good Pastor had over the past two years preached a number of sermons which were not exactly friendly towards the regime. The man was obviously no fool, as these Sunday sermons were couched in language that was not too obviously anti-Nazi. Without mentioning the party by name he'd made a number of remarks which could be interpreted as being detrimental to the State. Wondering why the man hadn't been picked up before, he supposed it was because the party did not want to be seen to be too obviously against the church. Shrugging his shoulders, Dieter thought, 'Well it looks as if we might have him now.' Standing up, he walked over to the door, went into Langers' office and placed his report onto his chief's desk.

14

Knocking on Colonel Langers' door, Dieter walked in and gave the customary Hitler salute. 'Morning Chief,' he said, 'I had an interesting night.'

'Morning, Dieter. Yes, I saw the report. We seem to have quite a lot on this man.'

'Yes, he's the pastor of a large church in Charlottenburg.'

Langers grunted and said, 'What about our anonymous caller?'

'Nothing, but he had a cultured voice, that's all that I can tell you really. I have it all on tape of course.'

Langers smiled and said, 'Now we know why our communist friend downstairs could tell us nothing.' Langers' manner changed and he said coldly, 'I want these people, Dieter, and I don't care who they are. For Christ's sake, Charlottenburg's right next door to here. I don't like anybody making fools of us, especially under our noses.'

Dieter nodded. Since he'd known Langers, he'd noticed how the man could change instantly from being jovial and full of bonhomie, to being ice cold.

'Tonight, I want you to go and raid the place. If our caller's correct, have the Gestapo arrest them. The charge will of course be treason. Have them taken to Plötzensee prison. If we need to talk to them downstairs, we can have them sent over.'

'Alright, Chief. I suppose they'll be handed over to the "People's Court" for trial?'

'Oh, yes, in this instance I think that that would be the best course of action. We can make sure that the case receives a lot of publicity. Sends a loud message,' said Langers.

At 11.30 that night, three black cars drove out of Prinz-Albrecht-Straße, turning right and then taking a left into Wilhelmstraße, driving past the air ministry and Reich Chancellery. Turning left into Pariser Platz, they sped under the Brandenburg Gate and headed towards Charlottenburg. Sitting in the front of the lead car, the only man wearing uniform, Dieter idly glanced out of the window. In each car sat two men. The three cars glided silently to a stop outside Pastor Neuffer's house.

Dieter and the five Gestapo men got out. Walking over to a car parked a little further up the street, Dieter bent and tapped on the window. Sitting inside were two men. The driver looked out and said, 'Evening Lieutenant, the good Pastor's at home. A man and a woman went in about two hours ago and they're still there.'

Dieter nodded, 'Alright, come with us.'

The house was in darkness, except for a light in the hallway. Directing two of the Gestapo men around to the back of the house, Dieter and the others walked up the short drive to the front door. Drawing his pistol, Dieter nodded to one of the men. A large well-built man, he carried a sledgehammer in his left hand. Lifting the hammer over his shoulder, he brought it around in an arc and sent it crashing into the door. There was a sharp crack as it made contact with the door, shattering the lock. Taking the lead, Dieter and the five Gestapo men walked quickly into the dark hallway. Looking to his right, Dieter could see a light shining from an open doorway. This obviously led down into a cellar. Dieter quickly led the men down and pushed open the door, lifting his pistol as he entered. There were four people in the room, two men and two women.

'SD,' said Dieter, looking around. To his left there was a small printing press. Standing on a table was a large stack of leaflets. Dieter walked over and picked one up and glanced at it; one look was enough to tell him all that he needed to know. The four people present said nothing. With no trace of fear in their faces, they looked calmly at Dieter and the others. Dieter put his pistol back into the holster, sure that he wouldn't need it.

'Which one of you people is Pastor Neuffer?' said Dieter.

'I'm the Pastor,' replied a tall, thin man wearing a pair of spectacles.

A small woman with grey hair standing next to the Pastor said, 'I'm the Pastor's wife.'

'And you two?' demanded Dieter looking at the other couple.

'My name's Muller and this is my wife,' replied the other man.

Dieter's men were walking around the room looking at the press and leaflets. One of the Gestapo men was reading through one of the leaflets. Giving a whistle he said, 'You people are in really big trouble.'

The Pastor looked over at the man and said, 'Young man, our consciences would not allow us to stand by and do nothing.' Lifting his hand, the Gestapo man hit the Pastor with full force across the face. A stream of blood poured from his nose as the Pastor reeled and fell to the floor, his wife trying in vain to save him.

Frau Neuffer looked at the Gestapo man and said with contempt, 'How brave you are hitting an old man. It doesn't matter to you that he's a man of God.'

The man sneered, looked at Frau Neuffer and said, 'You'll need more than your God to save you, you shrivelled old cow.'

Herr Muller turned towards Dieter and said, 'I take it that you're the officer in charge? Are you going to stand by and let your men abuse the Pastor and his wife like that?'

His face filling with fury, Dieter looked at the man, walked over and punched him full in the face. Muller's head shot back and hit the wall, dazing him as he too started to drip blood.

Dieter shouted, his voice filled with a cold anger, 'Now, is there anyone else here who would like to say anything?' He paused, looked at the senior Gestapo officer and said, 'Arrest these people.' Addressing the four prisoners he continued, 'You can talk to the judge. Perhaps he'll be interested to hear what you have to say. Take them away, the men to Plotzensee, and these two to the women's prison.' The Gestapo men handcuffed the four prisoners and led them from the room.

On the way out Frau Muller, who up to this moment had said nothing, looked Dieter straight in the eye and said, 'God is watching what you do.'

'Get them out!' snarled Dieter.

The Gestapo took away the press and leaflets that night.

15

The People's Court sat in a chamber in the Berlin law courts, decorated with three large swastika banners and busts of Frederick the Great and Hitler. Situated at one end there was a long table. Sitting at the table were two Nazi judges who wore long red robes with a German eagle and swastika on the left hand side of their chests. At the table with them were the five other people that made up the tribunal. These men were all loyal Nazis from the ranks of the party or the SS. Arriving just before the court sat at 10am, Dieter, dressed in uniform, sat at the front of the full courtroom. The seven men of the court entered at exactly 10 o'clock. Everyone in the room stood as the judges took their places and sat down, the senior judge telling a policeman to bring in the accused. With their hands manacled behind their backs, the Neuffers and Mullers were escorted into the court, all four having an air of tranquillity about them and showing no sign of fear. They'd all been mistreated, their faces swollen and bruised. Dieter, who'd been present at the interrogation, knew that the four had suffered at the hands of Langers. The colonel had been determined to find out if anyone else had been involved with the group, angry that they'd operated right underneath his nose. Standing facing their accusers the four old people looked directly ahead, while their faces showed defiance.

The senior judge, a little man with pinched features, looked over at the four and said, 'You're standing before this court charged with high treason. The evidence against you is overwhelming.' He lifted one of the pamphlets into the air, holding it between his thumb and forefinger as if it were contagious. 'You were caught red-handed by the Gestapo printing this filth.' He paused and then continued, 'How dare you write and distribute these lies against the Führer and the people? What gives you the right to undermine the work that's been carried out in the name of the German Reich?' The judge looked around the court and he gave a sneer as his eyes came to rest on the prisoners.

'Do you have anything to say for yourselves?' he barked.

Pastor Neuffer, his back straight, looked across at the judges and said with great dignity, '*You* say that we've printed filth and lies. Every word in those pamphlets is the truth. This regime, that you represent, is evil. This is not a court of law. Where is our defence? You are our judge and jury. Our fate has already been decided and I say to you before my God …'

'Silence!' snarled the judge, his voice dripping with venom, 'How dare you challenge the rights of this court?' His face was screwed up with rage. 'We sit here as a legally constituted body of the Third Reich and I will not have filth like you challenging my court, or me.' The judge looked to the other members of the tribunal and lifted his eyebrow, as if to say, 'Well?' The other members nodded. 'As I've said, the case against you four is overwhelming and you can expect no mercy from us. You've proved by your actions here today that you have no sense of remorse. This court will send a message to anyone who thinks that they can flout our laws with impunity that they are wrong.

Frau Neuffer interrupted the judge and said in a loud voice full of contempt for the whole court to hear, 'There is no justice in your Third Reich but, as God is my witness, one day this whole Godless edifice will come crashing down around your ears.'

The judge slammed the palm of his hand onto the table. The crack resounded around the courtroom. He continued very quietly, his voice filled with menace. 'We find you guilty as charged. The sentence of this court is death. Take them away.'

The seven men of the tribunal stood and left the courtroom. Dieter sat and watched as the prisoners were taken to the cells. They look like everyone's favourite aunt and uncle he mused.

Sitting in the court that morning was Pastor Hardt, a good friend of the Neuffer's. He had a little smile on his face. He was well pleased with this morning's result. One of his parishioners had mentioned, in confidence of course, that the Neuffer's were producing pamphlets. Neuffers parish was far wealthier than his own, and now he could apply for it. The call to Gestapo headquarters had been easy. After all, producing anti-government leaflets was illegal, wasn't it?

16

The days later, Dieter drove up to the entrance of Plotzensee prison. It was about half an hour before dawn as he got out of his car, walked over and rang the bell at the gate. As he waited he looked up at the sky. 'It's going to be hot again,' he mused half aloud. 'A nice day to die.' The gate opened. He showed his pass and entered. The four prisoners had been informed of their execution the night before by a public prosecutor as was required by law. They'd then been transferred to block three, known as the death house.

Standing in the execution shed with the other officials, Dieter looked over at the guillotine, its blade gleaming in the overhead light. Situated in the centre of the room, the executioner stood next to it, waiting.

They brought Frau Neuffer first. Her hands were tied behind her. As she walked in she held her head high and her back straight. Looking around, she spotted Dieter standing at the very front almost next to the guillotine. As she approached she stopped. One of the warders tried to hurry her on but Dieter lifted up his hand. The warder and prisoner came to a halt. Looking Dieter straight in the eye she said, very quietly and with great calm, 'In a few minutes, I'll be standing before my God. You, and that uniform that you wear, are an abomination in the eyes of God. One day, you too will stand before your Maker, you and your vile regime. What will you say to justify yourselves? Do you know, I almost pity you.

Dieter's face turned white. A wave of anger swept over him. He looked coldly at the woman standing before him and said, 'You're standing here today because you're a criminal. You and your fellow conspirators have broken the laws of the Reich. Your crime is treason and the penalty for that crime is death. You madam are now going to receive that penalty. Give my best wishes to your God,' he sneered. 'Take her away.'

The execution was handled both quickly and professionally. The victim was placed face down, her neck on the block. Falling with great speed, the blade neatly severed her head, and great gouts of blood shot from her body as her severed head fell into the container below. Frau

Neuffer went to her death, as did the others, with dignity and serenity. The words that the brave women uttered to Dieter, just before her death, had no effect on him whatsoever.

17

The hot August sun beat down on the city, a cool breeze taking off the worst of the heat and making the temperature bearable. Rudi felt marvellous, the sun shining down on the back of his neck as he strolled up the Kurfürstendamm. That Saturday morning he'd taken a stroll around the Tiergarten, had some lunch, and then browsed around the shops, finishing off at Kranzler's for coffee and cake. It was now late afternoon and he decided to head back to his car, which he'd parked in Fasanenstraße, a side street just off the Kurfürstendamm. Ahead of him, in the distance, he could see three Brownshirts walking under the S-Bahn Bridge, laughing and joking. As he was walking past the entrance to an apartment block he thought he heard a groan. Stopping, he listened carefully, but couldn't be sure. Yes, there it was again. Looking around, he walked over to the dimly-lit entrance of an apartment block. Lying in the shadows just inside the doorway, he saw the figure of a man lying on the ground. Quickly walking in, he crouched down over the prone figure and placing a hand on the man's shoulder he turned him over. His face was covered in blood and was already beginning to swell. As Rudi touched him he gave another groan.

'Here, let me help you,' muttered Rudi, pulling the man into a sitting position.

The man's head fell forward onto his chest. With an effort, he lifted his head and looked at Rudi. He said, 'Thank you, sir,' through swollen lips. Helping the man to his feet, Rudi steadied him as he swayed from side to side. Taking out his handkerchief, Rudi gently wiped the blood away from the man's face. The man said again, 'Thank you, sir, I'll be alright now.'

Rudi looked at him, 'You won't be all right and stop calling me 'sir.' What's your name? Where do you live?'

'My name's Goldmann, Otto Goldmann,' replied the man.

Rudi was beginning to understand. 'It was those three Brownshirts wasn't it?' he said. Goldmann said nothing. 'Bastards,' muttered Rudi. 'Come on, let's get you home.' Goldmann tried to pull away.

Understanding his fear, Rudi continued, 'Don't be afraid, we're not all like those swine, you know. Come on, my car's just up the street.' It was obvious that the Jew needed help.

Reluctantly he allowed Rudi to help him, saying, 'Thank you, sir, it's not far … if you could just take me to my front door.'

Rudi smiled, in spite of the circumstances, and said, 'Please, Herr Goldmann, stop calling me 'sir,' my name's Rudi. Arriving at the car, Rudi glanced to his right and, as he was helping Goldmann inside, noticed the synagogue opposite. He turned. 'Now where do you live again?' Rudi asked.

'Savignyplatz. I have a small jeweller's shop,' explained Goldmann.

'Oh, just around the corner. I'll soon have you there.'

'Thank you,' said Goldmann again. Hesitating, he said quietly, 'Rudi.'

Smiling, Rudi pulled away from the curb, turned first left and headed towards Savighny Plaz a short drive away. They travelled in silence, Goldmann occasionally rubbing his bloody nose with Rudi's handkerchief. Rudi turned the car left into the street as directed by Goldmann. They pulled up in front of a row of five shops, all Jewish-owned judging by the names on the front of the windows. Goldmann's shop was the first in the row. As the grill was pulled down, Rudi supposed because of the Jewish Sabbath, the shop was closed. In the row there was a furrier, a delicatessen, a gentlemen's outfitters and an antique shop.

Rudi took all of these in, as he slowed to a stop outside Goldmann's. 'Here we are, Herr Goldmann, let me help.' Rudi jumped out of the car, walked quickly around and opened the door, helping Goldmann out. 'You're still a bit unsteady, put your arm around my shoulder. That's better. Which door?'

Goldmann pointed in the general direction. He fumbled in his pocket, searching for his key. 'I'm very grateful to you, Rudi. I hope that you'll come in for a few moments?'

'I'd be delighted, Herr Goldmann.'

'Now you must stop calling me 'Herr Goldmann.' Smiling, he winced, his swollen lip causing him pain. 'My name's Otto.'

Putting the key into the lock, he turned it and the door opened into the shop. There was a bell over the door that gave a little tinkle as they entered. Looking around, Rudi could see a glass-covered counter that also served as a display case. It was full of gold rings, bracelets and all kinds of other jewellery. To the right, there was a large display cabinet full of silver and behind the counter, running the length of the back wall, was another display case. To the left of that was a door.

Rudi gave a little whistle and said, 'You did say a small jewellery shop, didn't you, Otto?'

Otto chuckled, forgetting for a moment the pain in his lip. 'Compared to some it's small, Rudi.' He was about to say more when the door opened behind the counter. Standing in the doorway was the most beautiful girl that Rudi had ever seen. Looking first at Rudi and then at her father she gave a gasp, her hand flying to her mouth.

'Papa!' she screamed, a look of horror on her face, 'What's happened? You're hurt.' She rushed forward.

'Rachel, Rachel, calm down. It's not as bad as it looks. Just help me upstairs.'

Rudi looked at Rachel and said, 'My name's Rudi Wagner. I found your father ...' his voice trailing off, feeling like a schoolboy.

Rachel said, 'Help me with him, up the stairs, over there.' They led Otto up to a large living room on the first floor. 'Sit at the table, Papa, I'll get some hot water and antiseptic.' She left the room and after a short while she returned with a bowl and a small brown bottle. 'What happened?' she asked. Otto explained.

'Filthy pigs!' she said, her face screwed up in anger. She started to bathe Otto's face. 'It's not as bad as it looks fortunately, but your face will be sore for a few days, Papa.' Rudi had been watching her all the time that she'd been working on her father's face and he was totally captivated. She had the most beautiful brown eyes, a small button nose and lovely red lips. *Just made for kissing*, thought Rudi. Her brown hair cascaded down to the small of her back. Her breasts were small and she had slim hips with long tapering legs. She was about eighteen, he guessed.

Looking at Rudi she said, 'Thank you for helping my father. You can't be one of them or you wouldn't have helped him.'

Rudi came back to earth with a jolt. 'No, I'm certainly not one of them. Anyway, I should be going. I'll leave you both alone.' He hesitated; the last thing that he wanted was to leave.

Otto came to his rescue and said with a little gleam in his eye, 'You'll do no such thing, young man. The least we can do is to offer you a drink. Come, sit down.'

Rudi looked at Otto thankfully and said, 'Well, I could certainly do with a drink, thank you.' Rudi sat down on the couch.

Really noticing Rudi for the first time Rachel thought, '*He's so handsome.*' She started to blush. '*What am I thinking? I don't know this young man, although I'd like to know him better,*' she thought to herself. 'Oh, please excuse me, I was so wrapped up in Papa.' She hesitated slightly, gave Rudi a dazzling smile and continued, 'What would you like?'

'Have you a scotch?' asked Rudi.

'An excellent idea. Have something yourself, my dear.'

'I'd love a glass of sherry,' she said.

A look of alarm suddenly crossed Otto's face. 'Where's Sam?' he asked.

'Don't worry, Papa, he's staying over at the Goldberg's this evening.'

Otto gave a sigh of relief. 'You can't be too careful now. Sam's my son, he's fourteen,' he said in explanation. 'Now, Rudi, tell us a little about yourself.'

Telling them his history, Rudi explained about his father and his hate for the Nazis. Facing him, her hand cupped under her chin, Rachel listened to his story, a cloud of sadness passing over her face as he told of his father's death. Rudi kept glancing at her as she nodded and smiled at him from time to time. Totally captivated by this young girl, he couldn't think of a more pleasant way of spending an evening and hoped that it would never end.

Otto nodded occasionally, his eyes never leaving the young man.

'Rudi,' he said, 'I'm so sorry about your father, these are very bad times that we're living in. Now, how would you like to stay for supper?'

'Oh, yes, please do,' said Rachel excitedly. 'I'll start straight away.'

Rudi beamed and said 'Thank you. I'd be honoured, if it's not too much trouble?'

'You're very welcome. It's no trouble at all.'

'I hope you don't mind my asking Otto…' he hesitated, and then continued, 'Your wife?' he stopped.

'Sadly, she died giving birth to Samuel.'

Rudi stammered, 'I'm so sorry.'

Otto lifted his hand, 'I admit it's been difficult bringing two children up alone. You know, Rudi, one thing about us Jews, we do look after our own. Our enemies say that about us, as if it's something to be ashamed of.' He paused for a moment then continued, 'My children had many mothers as they were growing up.'

'You know Otto, until you mentioned it, I'd forgotten that you were Jews.'

'Oh, Rudi, you're a nice boy. Sadly, there are many of our fellow countrymen out there who don't feel the same way. Like the Brownshirts this afternoon, for instance. I just can't understand why these Nazis hate us so much. We're no longer regarded as German citizens and we have no rights.' He paused, 'I have great fear for our future, not so much for myself, you understand, but for Rachel and Sam.' Rudi nodded.

'So, you have no reason to like them either,' continued Otto.

'Like them, I detest them,' he said, his voice filled with venom.

Otto looked at Rudi and said, 'You poor boy, to lose your father in those circumstances and betrayed by your best friend. What is the world coming to? 'One day,' continued Otto, 'there were two Brownshirts standing outside the shop. They had a placard on which they had written: GERMAN CITIZENS DO NOT BUY FROM JEWS. One of my oldest customers, Frau Schmitt,' Otto paused, smiled and continued, 'she must be eighty … saw these two men standing there with the placard. She walked over and said to them, "How dare you tell me where to shop!" She lifted her umbrella and poked one of them in the chest.' Otto and Rudi were beginning to laugh. 'She then said, "You should both go out and get proper jobs, instead of harassing honest citizens." You should have seen their faces, these Brownshirts, they didn't know what to do.' Otto, Rudi and Rachel were rocking with laughter. 'Stop!' pleaded Otto, 'My face is sore.'

After a while, he became serious again and said, 'I can't even go for a drink in my local bar anymore, after thirty years. They have a sign up saying: NO JEWS ALLOWED,' he sighed. 'But what can we do? Not everyone hates us, people like Frau Schmitt for example.'

'The problem is,' said Rudi, 'there are too many people in this country who are prepared to do nothing.'

They were interrupted by the sound of the shop bell downstairs. Rachel said, 'Ah, there's Sam.'

There was the sound of someone running up the stairs, the door burst open and Sam came in. He stopped abruptly when he saw Rudi. Looking at his father, he frowned and scowled when he saw the marks on his Father's face. 'Have you been attacked again, Papa?' Without waiting for an answer, he continued, 'Who's this?' looking at Rudi.

'To answer your questions young man, yes, I've been attacked and this is the man who helped me.'

'Are you Jewish?' asked the boy.

'Sam!' said Rachel.

Rudi smiled and said, 'No, Sam, but I hope that you won't hold that against me?'

Sam, a tall skinny fourteen-year-old, had brown hair and eyes, like his sister. His features were just beginning to make the change from childhood to manhood. Stepping forward, he gave a little grin and said, offering his hand to Rudi, 'Thanks for helping Papa. I'm Sam.'

'I'm pleased to meet you, Sam,' said Rudi gravely.

'Sam, five minutes to supper, go and have a wash,' said Rachel. Sam lifted his eyes towards the ceiling, as if to say, 'sisters.' Everyone laughed.

The rest of the evening passed too quickly for Rudi and from time to time his eyes would meet Rachel's. A small smile would pass between them. Rudi had fallen totally in love.

After coffee, Rudi looked around at everyone and said, 'Thank you all for a wonderful evening. I haven't enjoyed myself so much for a long time.'

'Are you coming again soon?' said Sam.

Rudi replied, 'Certainly, if you'll have me.'

Otto looked at Rudi and said, very seriously, 'Rudi you will always be welcome in this house and at this table.'

'Thank you,' murmured Rudi. He stood up, shook hands with Otto and Sam, looked at Rachel, and said, 'It's such lovely summer weather, would you like to come to the zoo with me tomorrow?' He held his breath and looked imploringly into Rachel's eyes.

She gave a little smile and said, 'Thank you. I'd like that very much.'

Otto beamed. Sam just raised his eyes to the ceiling.

'I'll pick you up at about 10am. if that's all right?' said Rudi.

'That's fine. Come on, I'll see you out.'

As he walked to the door, Otto held his sleeve, and Rudi paused. He said very quietly, 'Look after her Rudi, won't you?'

'You have my solemn promise.' Otto smiled and nodded.

Following Rachel down into the darkness of the shop, Rudi took Rachel's hands in his and they looked deep into each other's eyes. 'Until tomorrow,' murmured Rudi, as he bent his head forward and gave her a kiss. At first she didn't respond, his tongue gently probing. Soon, forgetting her inhibitions, she opened her mouth slightly in response. Their tongues met, duelling with each other, both of them quickly starting to become aroused, forgetting where they were for an instant. Pulling away, Rachel said, a little breathlessly, 'I think that you should leave now, before we do something that we might both regret.'

Laughing lightly, he replied, 'You're right. I hope that we will have plenty of time together. Goodnight, Rachel. I'll see you tomorrow.'

He quickly left the shop. In the car on the way home his heart was singing, but he knew that he and Rachel were in an impossible situation. He didn't care and made a silent vow to himself, 'I will not let those animals spoil this for me.'

Watching the car disappear around the corner, Rachel was filled with both longing and fear. Turning, she slowly walked back up the stairs.

18

Rudi arrived promptly at 10am. The sun was shining, with a slight cooling breeze, making it very pleasant. Coming out of the shop doorway, Rachel had a spring in her step and a smile on her face as she approached the car. For once she was allowing herself to feel happy, even though she had a doubt lurking in the back of her mind. She knew only too well of the dreaded Nuremberg laws of 1935, which forbade marriage or sexual contact between Jew and Aryan and stripped the German Jews of rights of citizenship. She sharply pushed the thought aside.

Leaning over, Rudi opened the passenger door, gave a smile, and said, 'Good morning, Rachel, I hope that you slept well?'

'No. I didn't sleep a wink, thanks to you.'

Rudi grinned, and said, 'Neither did I. To the zoo?'

Rachel hesitated, and said, 'Rudi, do you think that's wise? There are so many people.' She stopped.

Putting his hand over hers he said, 'There's no law in this country, as far as I know, which says two people can't take a walk around the zoo.'

'Not yet,' she said bitterly. 'Perhaps this wasn't such a good idea.' The fear was almost ingrained in her mind.

'Please, Rachel, don't let's spoil such a beautiful day.'

She was immediately contrite, 'I'm sorry Rudi, it's just that …'

'I know,' said Rudi.

Rachel looked at Rudi and said, 'Rudi Wagner I think that you're a very good man.' She smiled and said, 'The zoo it is.'

'That's better,' said Rudi, 'Come on let's go and enjoy ourselves, and we can worry about them later.' He drove off and headed in the direction of the zoo.

They had a wonderful first day together. At first Rachel was tense, but soon relaxed as she quickly fell under Rudi's spell and was soon laughing at his silly little jokes, as he did everything that he could to make the day special for her. They walked around, looking at the different animals. Rudi loved the gorillas and mimicked them, pulling his face into impossible shapes as she roared with laughter at his childish antics. She loved the gentle gazelles; a noise disturbed them and they sped away with grace and agility, making her smile. The zoo was full of Berliners out enjoying themselves in the August sunshine. Rudi and Rachel shared an ice cream and before long they were holding hands. She became nervous when a group of SS and SA men walked past. Rudi gently whispered into her ear, reassuring her. They ate sausage and potato salad, washing it all down with ice cold beer, feeling completely at ease in each other's company. On the bandstand there was an army band giving a concert, playing a Strauss waltz, the clarinet players' fingers running up and down their instruments at lightning speed. They both giggled as the fat Bandmaster's ample bottom seemed to sway with the tempo of the music. In the afternoon Rudi drove them out to the lake on the Havel and they sat on the manmade beach watching the sailing boats, the sun gleaming off their sails. Later, they took a walk through the wooded area of the Grunewald and Rudi put his arm around her waist. She couldn't remember how long it had been since she'd felt so happy. They sat down in the shade of a huge, old oak tree and Rachel, her head resting lightly on Rudi's shoulder, gave a sigh of contentment.

'Happy?' asked Rudi gently.

'I was just thinking how happy I am. Thank you for today, Rudi.'

'Today will be the first day of many, if that's what you want?' replied Rudi.

'Do you really think so?' she asked hopefully. 'There's so much against us. What about the Nuremberg laws? We can't just ignore them, you know.'

'I've thought about nothing else since I first set eyes on you. I'm in love with you. You know that, don't you?'

'I'm in love with you too, Rudi. Was it only yesterday that we met?'

Rudi smiled and said, 'For once, the Brownshirts did us a favour, Rachel?'

'Yes,' she answered.

Rudi hesitated, 'Would you like to go to my house?' Shyly, he continued, 'I have the place to myself. My mother's staying with my uncle in Switzerland.' He looked over at the lake, frightened at what her answer would be.

'Rudi, look at me.' Turning his head towards her he looked into her eyes, 'I would love to come, but please don't hurt me.'

Taking her hand in his, a look of longing etched on his face, he replied, 'I promise never to do anything to hurt you.'

At first they made love with a sense of great urgency, both of them eager for each other. Later, they slowly explored each other's naked bodies, taking their time, discovering each other. She gave a soft moan as he entered her for the second time, moving slowly in the beginning, playing a delightful sexual game. The two of them became one, as a sense of exquisite pleasure overwhelmed them. His tempo became faster as they both neared their climax. Giving a cry, they both reached their peak simultaneously, their orgasm seemingly endless. Afterwards, their bodies entwined, they looked into each other's eyes and knew real love for the first time.

Walking into the room carrying a tray of coffee, Rachel placed it on the table, sat next to Rudi and took his hand in hers. Using his free hand, Rudi stroked her hair, and said, 'No regrets, darling, I hope?'

'No, none.' She gave a little smile, and continued, 'You do realise that we're both now criminals?'

Giving a snort, Rudi said, 'Criminals! Only in the sight of those perverted barbarians.'

Giving a sigh, she said, 'But what are we going to do, Rudi? We have to be realistic.'

'No. What we have to do, at least for the moment, is be discreet. Tell me, would you consider leaving Germany?'

She laughed, 'And go where?'

'If you had the chance,' he persisted, 'would you?'

'If it meant that we could have a proper life together, I suppose I would. But what about Papa and Sam? I can't just walk away and leave them.'

'Do you know, I was lying in bed last night dreaming about us.'

She slapped him playfully and said, 'I bet you were.'

Grinning, he said, 'No, seriously, I was, and I had the beginning of an idea. Listen, darling, I want you to trust me. I can't say too much at the moment but I think that I can find a solution that will suit us all. Don't say anything to Otto or Sam at the moment. Please try to be patient, and in the meantime we'll just have to be discreet, just trust me.'

'Alright, Rudi, I'll be patient and wait.'

'What time did you say that you'd be home this evening?'

She shrugged, 'No special time, why?'

Looking her straight in the eye he grinned and with a motion of his head indicated the bedroom upstairs.

Smiling, she said, 'Oh, yes please.'

The two of them walked hand in hand up the stairs and into the bedroom.

19

Crack! There was a clap of thunder. A streak of lightning lit up the afternoon sky and the heavens opened. The rain started to hit the pavement and bounce, making small explosions. 'Just in time,' muttered Bruno to himself. The day had been humid, the storm threatening to break since early afternoon. Humming the Horst Wessel song to himself, Bruno walked down the stairs, looked around, saw the person that he was there to meet, and walked over. Walking past the bar, he smiled at Gustav and ordered two beers, receiving a nod of acknowledgement. Joseph was sitting at a corner table with a good view of the entrance and he smiled at the brawny young man as he pulled out a chair and sat down. Idly picking up one of the cards that were lying on the table, Bruno looked casually at the picture of a black cat, with the address and telephone number of the bar written in the bottom right-hand corner. Playing with it for a few seconds, he slipped it into an inside pocket. The light was reflected off Joseph's glasses as he toyed with an almost empty glass, saying nothing. Walking over, Gustav put two glasses of beer onto the table. He leaned forward, speaking quietly with respect in his voice, and said, 'There are no strangers in tonight.'

Joseph nodded and replied, 'Good. Keep your eyes open.' There was a command in his voice. Gustav nodded and walked away, leaving the two men alone.

'Excuse me a moment. I need a pee,' said Joseph, standing and walking over to the end of the bar and through the door marked 'WC.' Bruno looked off into space, thinking back to that night in 1929.

Glancing up at the clock sitting on the mantlepiece above the fire, the young Bruno had looked at the time. *He's late tonight,* he thought, shrugging his shoulders. He reflected that it wasn't so unusual for his father to be this late. He had just about finished his homework and had been thinking about going to bed, when the bell rang. He walked over and answered the door.

At the door stood Joseph, a friend of Bruno's father. 'Good evening, Joseph,' the boy said. 'Papa's not here at the moment.'

There was a look on Joseph's face that made Bruno uneasy. 'Can I come in Bruno? I'm afraid that I've some bad news. Reluctantly stepping back, Bruno let Joseph enter the small room.

'What is it?' the muscular fourteen year old asked.

'Sit down. There's no easy way to tell you this, Bruno. I'm very sorry but your father's dead.' Staring at the man sitting opposite him, he hadn't been able to believe what had been said to him.

His eyes filled with tears as he stammered, 'I don't understand, Joseph, was it an accident?'

'No, I'm afraid not. His body was found in an alley about two hours ago. He'd been shot in the head. You know that your father was a member of the communist party?'

The young boy nodded.

'He'd been to a meeting tonight and we believe that he was killed on the way home.'

'By who?' Bruno had asked.

'We don't know for sure, but think that it must have been the Nazis. Conrad had a lot of enemies, being so high up in the party.'

Tears streamed down Bruno's face. He'd adored his father and couldn't believe that he'd never see him again. 'I'm so sorry, Bruno, go and pack a few things. You can come and spend a few days with me.'

Getting to his feet, the young boy walked over to his bedroom door and entered. Taking a small bag from his battered wardrobe, he had thrown a few clothes into it and snapped it shut. The older man and the boy left the dingy tenement block together.

Standing at the side of the grave three days later, Bruno had looked at his father's coffin as it was lowered into the ground. His face was set, showing a mixture of both grief and anger. 'I promise you Father, that one day I'll have my revenge for this, I swear it,' he had said to himself. There were a large number of mourners there that cold winter morning. Conrad had been a popular man. Looking across the graveyard, Bruno had noticed a small, muscular, swarthy man standing a little further away than the other mourners. He didn't recognise him and assumed that he must be a friend of his father's, but when he looked a few moments later, the man was gone. The mourners solemnly filed past Bruno, each shaking his hand, many of the men promising that his father wouldn't be forgotten and would, given time, be avenged. *Don't worry,* the boy had thought to himself, *I'll avenge my father.* A cold hatred of the Nazis was born in his heart that day.

Sitting in Joseph's luxurious apartment after the funeral, the older man had looked at the boy and said, 'Now we must talk. Your father is gone and we have to look to your future. You're a big strong lad and more than able to take care of yourself. It's been decided that you should continue to live at your old apartment. There's nothing to be gained by moving you, and Frau Hoffer has agreed to look after your needs— food, washing and ironing, things like that. Also, the members of the party have agreed to keep their eye on you. You need never think that you're alone. You know where I live and I promise to come and see you at least once a week.'

'But who's going to pay? My father had no money.'

Joseph smiled, 'Bruno you have more friends than you think so don't worry about that. You'll be well taken care of and I promise that in time I'll tell you everything that you need to know. In return,' he continued, 'you must make me a promise. You show great talent at school. You'll go a long way in this life. I want you to promise me that you'll continue to work hard as that's what your father would have wanted. Will you do that?'

'Yes, Joseph, I promise.'

For two years, Bruno had done as he'd promised and had indeed been well looked after, even receiving a small weekly allowance. Just after his sixteenth birthday, Joseph had called round one evening, accompanied by another man.

Joseph stood in the doorway and next to him was a tall, slim man with blond hair and incredibly blue eyes, who stood erect with his shoulders held back like a soldier. The first thing that struck Bruno was the man's sinuous strength, like a coiled spring. In his late twenties or early thirties, Bruno guessed.

'Hello Bruno,' said Joseph, 'May I introduce Werner?'

Smiling, Werner held out his hand, 'Hello Bruno, I'm pleased to meet you.' The handshake was strong and firm.

Liking him instantly, Bruno said, 'Hello Werner, please come in.'

The two men entered and Werner said, 'It's the start of the summer holidays next week I believe; how would you like to take a little trip with me to the Alps?'

'I certainly would,' Bruno replied, 'I've never been there.'

'That's settled then. We'll go for about two weeks. This place is very isolated. There are a few things that I want you to learn. How about it?'

'Sounds great!' Bruno said, his voice full of enthusiasm. He'd taken an instant liking to this man.

'You're certainly a strapping lad, Bruno. I think I'm going to call you "Tiny".'

Bruno had laughed, '"Tiny"— yes, I like that.' From that time on Werner was to call Bruno by that nickname.

The place that Werner had taken Bruno to was certainly isolated, standing high in the Bavarian Alps. It was a three-bed roomed ski lodge with a large cavernous barn attached. Standing in the large living room, humming the Horst Wessel song to himself, Bruno waited for Werner, wondering what exactly they'd be doing that day.

Putting his head round the door, Werner said, 'Tell me, Tiny, do you like that tune?'

'Like it! I loathe it. But every time I sing it, it reminds me of them. You know, the Nazis, and I don't ever want to forget them.'

Werner chuckled, 'Good for you! Let's keep it that way. Now, what do you know about firearms?'

'Not a lot,' Bruno admitted.

Giving a grin, Werner said, 'Well, we'll soon put that right.'

Later, in the barn, Werner had set up a target in the shape of a man, the type used by the army. Standing just behind Bruno to his right, he said quietly into his ear, 'Lift the pistol until it's pointing towards the target. That's right. Now, take a breath and hold it. Gently squeeze the trigger. Squeeze it, don't jerk or pull it.' Crack! The pistol fired, pulling Bruno's arm up slightly, the bullet just grazing the target. Bruno turned his head and looked at Werner, who was smiling. 'Alright, now do it again and this time squeeze the trigger, don't pull it. Imagine it's a fucking Nazi. Doing as he was told, Bruno lifted his arm in a fluid movement and fired, the bullet passing straight through the target's heart. 'Good! Now do it again— and again.' Bruno had kept on firing until the magazine was empty. Clapping his hand on Bruno's shoulder, Werner said, 'My boy, you're a natural.' By the end of the two weeks, Bruno was as good as any marksman in the German Army. He had also been taught a number of very dirty tricks, which if used properly would severely maim or kill an opponent.

Coming back to earth with a jolt, Bruno saw Joseph sitting opposite him, a little smile playing at the corner of his mouth. Taking a swig of his beer, Joseph said, 'Well, how was the labour service?'

'Fucking awful. It's a good job that Rudi and Paul were there, otherwise I'd have gone mad.'

'That fight that you had was, shall we say, unwise.'

Bruno looked at him, and said, 'Isn't there anything that you don't know about? Anyway the bastard had it coming.'

'I'm glad that you mentioned Rudi. What do you think of him?'

'I'd trust him with my life.' He looked at Joseph, 'But you know him.'

'Yes, but not as well as you. What does he think of our Nazi friends?'

'He hates them, after what they did to his father,' Bruno's voice trailed off. Rudi's problem is that he's frustrated; he hates the bastards, but doesn't know what to do. Why, do you have something in mind?'

Joseph nodded, 'Do you think that he'd join us?'

'If he can do anything to hurt the Nazis, I'm sure that he'd jump at the chance.'

'That what I think too, let's set up a meeting with Rudi. Don't mention me, of course.'

Bruno nodded, 'How about if I suggest the two of us meet for a drink at his house, say, tomorrow evening? I'll talk to him, sound him out.'

'Good idea. If he seems interested, call me. I'll drive over and we can have a long chat.'

Bruno smacked his forehead, 'There's something that I'd forgotten. It's important — our Rudi's in love. Her name's Rachel, she's Jewish.'

Joseph raised his eyes. 'Well, well,' he muttered, 'Give me a ring.' He finished his drink, got up, and walked out, nodding to Gustav on the way.

20

Finishing classes for the morning, Rudi had seen Bruno and he'd suggested that the two of them have a drink at Rudi's house that evening. Rudi readily agreed as Rachel was looking after some young Jewish children that evening, so they couldn't meet. Walking along the corridor, he almost collided with Joseph Altmann, the head librarian of the university. 'Oh, excuse me, Joseph, good morning,' said Rudi.

Joseph smiled. 'Be careful Rudi, I'm too old to be trying to dodge you young students. Do you have time for a coffee?' he asked.

'That's a good idea, Joseph.'

'Let's go into my office in the library, it's quiet at the moment.' The two walked down the corridor and through the swing doors. The library was huge, with row upon row of books. A few students were sitting at long, polished tables, studying quietly, some whispering to each other occasionally. Joseph had a staff of four men working for him and he nodded to one of them indicating that he would be in his office. The man smiled and lifted his hand in acknowledgement.

'Come on in, Rudi,' said Joseph. There was a coffee pot simmering quietly on a small stove in the corner of the office. Walking over, Joseph poured two cups and offered one to Rudi. Beckoning to him to sit down, he asked 'How's life treating you, Rudi?'

'Oh, not too bad. We have to make the most of it don't we?' Rudi replied.

'Yes… difficult times,' mused the older man. 'I was sad to hear of your father's death, Rudi. How long has it been now? Four years?' Rudi nodded. 'Do you know the saying by Heinrich Heine, "This was but a prelude; where books are burnt human - beings will be burnt in the end"?' Joseph said quietly. 'I'll never forget the night that they burned my books.' There was a note of bitterness in his voice. He continued, 'You know, it was the students themselves who burnt the books, not the Nazis. They were rubbing their hands with glee. The students did their dirty work for them.'

Rudi looked at Joseph and said, carefully, 'Yes I'm sure Goebbels was delighted.'

Joseph smiled, 'Oh, I'm sure that he was. Can we be candid with each other?' He gave a little chuckle. 'I'm sure that you won't be going down to Prinz-Albrecht-Straße to repeat this conversation?'

'Joseph, believe you me, there's no chance of that. After what they did to my father,' he faltered.

Joseph nodded, 'Things will get a lot worse before they get better, but what can we do?' he asked, raising his thin shoulders.

Rudi answered, 'Yes, that's the question. I wish that there was more that we could do, but what?' The two men made desultory conversation for a few minutes. Rudi thanked Joseph for the coffee, got up, and left the office. Joseph's eyes followed him. Lifting the telephone, he dialled the operator and asked for a number in Switzerland. After a pause someone answered at the other end. 'Hello, Max,' said Joseph, 'Is Stefan there?' Listening for a second, he said, 'Put him on would you?' He waited again for a few seconds.

Stefan Wagner came on the line. 'Hello, Joseph. 'Do you have some news?'

'I think so, Stefan. I'm meeting him this evening, but I think he'll be amenable. I'll call you later on tonight.'

'Very good.' The line went dead. Joseph replaced the receiver and looked reflectively into space.

21

Later that evening, walking up the long well-kept drive that led to the Wagner's imposing house, Bruno, who as usual was humming the Horst Wessel song under his breath, looked around him and gave a whistle. 'Very impressive,' he murmured to himself as he rang the bell and waited. He heard someone approach the front door which opened and there stood Rudi, his face lighting up with pleasure. 'Bruno, welcome,' he said, offering his hand.

'Evening, Rudi. If I'd known this place was so grand I'd have put my best suit on.'

Laughing, Rudi punched him on the shoulder and said, 'You're lucky I'm not charging an entrance fee. Come on in.' The two young men entered the imposing hallway. 'Mother's gone over to the Hoffmann's for the evening. We've got the place to ourselves. Let's go into the lounge,' said Rudi leading Bruno into a large, well-furnished room.

As they entered, Bruno glanced over at a glass-fronted cabinet. Walking over, he looked at the numerous Meissen figurines displayed inside and said, 'Wow, Rudi, these are beautiful.'

Nodding, Rudi replied, 'They're mother's, she's been collecting for years. Father used to buy her a piece for her birthday and Christmas every year.'

Turning, Bruno looked around the room, 'Is there a telephone in here?' he inquired.

'No,' said Rudi, 'Why?' His brow creased.

Bruno shrugged, and said, 'Oh, no special reason, I just wondered. Mine's a scotch and soda. Normally, I'd ask for beer, but in such prestigious surroundings, I'll have the best.' He paused, and then continued, 'If the comrades could see me now.'

Rudi laughed, 'Yes, they'd probably sack the place and shoot me.' Rudi poured two drinks then they both sat down in leather armchairs. Rudi continued, more seriously, 'Fortunately, the Nazis couldn't touch this place. It belongs to mother, a wedding gift from father. Also most of father's money's in Switzerland where those swine can't get their hands on it.'

Bruno suddenly became serious and said, 'How long have we been friends, Rudi?'

Looking at Bruno, Rudi frowned. He was puzzled by his friend's question. 'About three years, since the start of university. Why do you ask?'

'What do you know about me? I mean *really* know,' Bruno asked.

'Well, now that you come to mention it, not very much.'

'For example, have you never thought where the money's come from to pay my university fees?' asked Bruno.

'Well, no I haven't.' Rudi had to admit it was true. 'I think you're here for more than a social visit tonight, aren't you?'

'Yes, I am. You know, Rudi, I'd trust you with my life.' He paused for a second, took a sip of his drink, and then continued, 'Ever since my father was killed, I've been groomed, if you like, to resist the bastards that run this country. 'I've been very well trained, Rudi. All of my training will soon be used to try and destroy these thugs. I've no illusions and it will take a long time, but I'm determined to see it through to the end, come what may.'

'Can I ask who you're working for?'

'Before I answer that question, let me ask you one. How much do you really hate them? Do you hate them enough to put your life on the line? Would you be prepared to die, possibly horribly? Think very carefully before you answer.' Bruno looked at Rudi, his face set and serious.

After a moment, Rudi answered, 'Listen to me Bruno. I've seen my father murdered by them and they've turned this country into a sewer. I'm not allowed to marry the girl I love because of their obscene racial laws, and they control every aspect of our lives. Everyone walks in fear, so yes, I would do anything to be free of them, even if it cost me my life.'

Bruno smiled, he said, 'I was hoping that you'd say that. To answer your question, at the moment I'm not sure who I'm working for. I'm hoping to find that out tonight. Do you want to work with me?'

'Yes,' answered Rudi, 'I do.'

Bruno looked at Rudi and a big smile crossed his face. Standing, he crossed over to Rudi, picked him up in a huge bear hug and, as if he weighed nothing, whirled him around the room.

'Stop, Bruno,' shouted Rudi, 'That's enough! Put me down.' Laughing, as if a big weight had been taken off his mind, Bruno put him down and they both became serious. 'Where do we go from here,' he asked.

'Can I use your phone? There's someone that I'd like you to meet; he's my chief.'

'Of course, it's in the hall.'

Bruno left the room and Rudi heard him dialling, followed by a short pause, Bruno speaking for no more than a few seconds. Returning, Bruno looked over and smiled, 'He'll be with us in about half an hour.'

'Bruno, I should have guessed that there was more to you than meets the eye. I'll never forget the night of the fight, a side of you that I'd never seen. You made a real mess of Heinrich.'

'If there hadn't been so many witnesses, I'd have killed him.' Rudi could tell by his tone that he wasn't joking.

The two young men sat around talking and waiting for their visitor, feeling tense, Rudi wondered who this mysterious person would be.

The bell rang, making Rudi start. Looking over at Bruno, he said, 'You'd better go and let our visitor in.' Bruno got up and left the room. There was the murmur of conversation in the hallway. The lounge door opened, Rudi looked up. Standing in the doorway was Joseph Altmann. 'Good evening, Rudi. I'm so glad that you've agreed to join our little circle.' His spectacles reflected the light from the overhead chandelier.

'Joseph,' he said unable to believe his eyes.

Joseph looked at him and smiled, 'I'm the last person that you expected to see, eh, Rudi? Believe me, that can have its advantages. After all, who would suspect the mild-mannered librarian? Be a good chap and fix me a drink, would you?'

Rudi nodded, walked over to the sideboard and poured three drinks. He looked over at Joseph and said, 'You were testing me this morning, weren't you?'

Joseph smiled, and replied, 'Our group has had its eyes on you for a very long time as a potential recruit. I for one have never doubted your commitment and, believe me, if I didn't think that you could be trusted, I wouldn't have come anywhere near you tonight. Now, let's sit down and have a chat. By the way, this is your last chance to back out because once I tell you about the organisation, you're in. So if you have any doubts …'

'Joseph, I'll say to you what I said to Bruno, for years I've been frustrated wanting to do something but not knowing what, now I have my chance to do something.'

'Alright, you're both going to learn some surprising news tonight. Firstly, the man that we're all working for is your Uncle Stefan, Rudi.' Both Rudi and Bruno gasped. Joseph raised his hand to stifle any questions. He continued, 'Stefan Wagner's a very rich and influential man who knows many people. He has friends in high places: Nazi, Swiss and British intelligence.' He paused, then carried on, 'Take the Nazis. Many of them have been feathering their own nests for years, using your Uncle's bank. Stefan hates the Nazis. He has enough on a lot of them to send them to the guillotine. This leaves them wide open to blackmail.' Joseph looked at the two young men and smiled, took off his glasses and polished them vigorously with an immaculate, white handkerchief. Bruno and Rudi waited patiently. Joseph put his glasses back on.

'My father and your uncle go back to the 1914 war. My father, Frederick, commanded a regiment at Verdun. Your uncle was his adjutant and they became very close friends. Today, Frederick Altmann is a general serving on the General Staff here in Berlin. My father's an officer of the old school. He loathes Hitler, calls him 'the little corporal'. He believes that the Nazis will destroy this country and he's not alone. There are others of the same opinion. Father and your uncle have always kept in touch and used to meet regularly in Basel. However, they both agree that that's too dangerous now as the Nazis have their eyes and ears everywhere. My father has access to a great deal of valuable information with contacts in the criminal police and the Abwehr.' He stopped, looked at Rudi and said, 'Pour me another drink will you, Rudi? There's a good chap.' Rudi got up and refilled Joseph's glass. Joseph continued, 'My father, after a lot of soul searching — believe me, it wasn't an easy decision for him to make — approached your uncle; he asked him to use his contacts to pass on vital information, to, shall we say, interested parties. That's why we're sitting here tonight.' Joseph paused, took a sip of his whiskey, smiled and said, 'I'm sure that you both have a number of questions?'

Rudi looked at Joseph and said, 'I certainly have. Firstly, why didn't my uncle ask me himself?'

'Oh, that's easy. He wanted you to make the decision for yourself. You see, he thought that if he approached you, you might agree out of loyalty and he wanted you to make the decision alone.'

'Does my mother know about this?' asked Rudi.

'Yes,' replied Joseph. 'She hates them as much as any of us.'

Bruno looked a little puzzled, and said, 'So who's been paying for my education and living expenses for all these years?'

Joseph chuckled, and replied, 'I'm sorry to disappoint you Bruno, but it wasn't the communists. No, Stefan's been paying for everything for years. Again, this goes back to the 1914 war. Your father served in the trenches under Stefan's command and so they knew each other. Your father was a good man and wanted you to have the best education possible. When he was killed, I spoke to Stefan and he agreed to help. We could both see your potential. He hoped that one day you'd agree to work for him. You see, we decided to let you carry on thinking that it was the Communists. In fact, it's true to say that they have been keeping their eyes on you for years, but only to make sure that you were safe, not in a material sense. Don't forget that your father was one of them.'

Bruno nodded. He looked a little disappointed, and then he smiled ruefully and said, 'Well, I don't suppose it makes any difference. I owe a great debt to your uncle, Rudi.'

'I'm sorry, Bruno, but the Russians have no particular interest in the German communists; those Germans that left Germany and went to Russia when the Nazis came to power have been bitterly disappointed.' Joseph paused for a moment, and then continued, 'From time to time, there'll be certain documents on microfilm to be taken to Switzerland. That's where you both come in. The film will be passed on through a prearranged system; we can work out the details later. I'll be contacted and pass on the time and place of the drop and then tell you where to go, etc. The idea is that you work as a team, watching each other's backs. We can't afford to be a bunch of amateurs about this.' Joseph became very serious. He pushed his frail body forward in the chair, and said, 'We're all playing a very dangerous game and if we're caught we can expect no mercy. I, for one, will never allow myself to be captured. Don't worry I have no illusions about how I'd stand up to Gestapo torture. Also, remember that we're all responsible for each other's security. It's a huge responsibility; we're not playing games here.'

Bruno nodded and said, 'If they ever get anywhere near me, I'll take some of the bastards with me before I go. To be honest, it makes no difference who I'm working for just as long as I can help destroy them. Tell me, do you know who was responsible for killing my father? Because if you do, I want to know.'

'Sorry, Bruno, only that it was the Nazis and that's not one hundred percent certain. To be honest if we did know, he'd be dead by now.' Turning to Rudi, Joseph said, 'I'm going to call your uncle tonight, Rudi, and I'll tell him you're in.'

Rudi nodded and said, 'It's funny, I was going to talk to Uncle Stefan anyway, I was going to ask his help.'

Joseph said, 'Your girlfriend?'

'Yes, and her family.'

Joseph smiled, 'Don't worry, if anybody can help, he will. In fact I'm sure that one way or another he'll be able to get them out. If I were you I wouldn't worry too much.'

'What does a man have to do to get a drink around here?' said Bruno, 'Come on Rudi, let's drink a toast. I'm going to enjoy working with you.'

Rudi laughed, and said, 'Yes, a toast, a good idea.' He stood, collected the glasses and poured fresh drinks. 'To the downfall of our country's enemies.' The three men lifted their glasses.

'Can you get away for a few days?' asked Joseph.

'Yes of course,' replied Rudi, 'I need a holiday. I can think of more pleasant company to spend it with than that bear,' he shrugged. 'But, as it's in the line of duty ...' He smiled at Bruno as he punched him playfully on the arm.

'OK, Bruno, I want you to take him out to the chalet, our friend Werner will be there, he'll brief you.'

Bruno laughed, looked at Rudi and said, 'I hope that you're fit, Rudi, our Werner is a tough customer. By the time he's finished with you you'll certainly know how to look after yourself.'

Joseph looked at Rudi and said quietly, 'If I were you Rudi ... if it ever comes to it ... well, don't let them take you alive.'

22

Taking the long drive to the farm at a leisurely pace on a glorious sunny early September day, the two young men were having a wonderful time. Laughing and joking, a bond grew quickly between them, closer now than ever, both aware that their lives might at some time depend on each other. They arrived at the farmhouse in the early evening but there was no sign of Werner. After supper, as the boys were enjoying a quiet beer together, they heard a car pull up. The door was slammed shut and there was the sound of footsteps approaching the front door. The chalet had been chosen because of its isolation. The door opened and Bruno and Rudi looked up.

Werner stood in the doorway. The tall, wiry man looked at Bruno and said, 'Hello, Tiny, it's been a long time.' Bruno and Rudi stood up and Bruno walked around the table. Werner smiled and said, 'Come on, Tiny, go for me.' Bruno didn't hesitate. As quick as lightning, he went towards Werner, his right arm swinging at great speed. If it had connected it would have floored the older man. Side-stepping, Werner grabbed hold of Bruno's arm using Bruno's speed against him; twisting his body and using Bruno's arm as a fulcrum he threw the younger man over his shoulder. Bruno flew through the air and landed with a huge thud on his back. Walking over, Werner looked down at the winded Bruno and said with a grin, 'Not bad, Tiny, you'd have probably got away with it with anyone else. What's this I hear about you giving young Nazis a good hiding? Laughing, he bent over and took Bruno's arm to help him up. Bruno grabbed hold of the proffered hand, twisting his body at the same time. Werner was unbalanced and fell. With incredible agility, Bruno turned Werner onto his stomach, climbed onto his back and twisted his arm up towards his neck. Werner gave a cry of pain and said between gritted teeth, 'Alright Bruno, you've got me; you don't need to break my arm.'

Bruno gave a laugh, stood up and this time offered his hand to Werner. Werner took it and the two men looked at each other and embraced. 'See, I didn't forget everything that you taught me. Rudi stood watching the two men, his mouth open.

Werner looked at him, smiling. 'You must be Rudi,' he said. 'I'm very pleased to meet you, and I'm glad that you've decided to join our little club.' He paused and continued. 'Our friend over there and myself are going to teach you a few tricks.'

The next two weeks passed quickly. Like Bruno before him, Rudi learned how to look after himself. Werner was impressed with his shooting skills and taught him how to disable or even kill an enemy in several different ways. He taught the two to work together as a team, the one covering the other's back. They drove into Munich and spent hours learning how to follow someone without being seen, and how to spot a tail, as well as how to lose someone who was following them. Werner was an expert in the game of espionage. They learned nothing about him; all that they knew was his name.

After supper one evening, the three were sitting around the table. Opening three bottles of beer, Werner passed one to each of the boys. 'Prost,' he said. The two lifted their bottles in salute. Looking at them he smiled and said, 'It's time that you learned a little more about me, especially as we're going to be working together a lot in the future.' Rudi and Bruno looked at each other in surprise. 'My name,' he continued, 'is Werner Koenig. I'm a major in the German Army and I'm the aide to General Altmann. It'll be me who you liaise and work with.' Werner looked at the two young men opposite him. 'My life and the lives of brave men like the General will often depend on you. I've been impressed with the both of you. However, never become complacent,' he said with force, 'because if you do, you could be signing all our death warrants. One thing I can promise you, it'll be a very unpleasant death.' He looked from one to the other, 'We're involved in treason, at least the Nazi scum will call it treason. Not only them, but many of the members of the General Staff would also call the General a traitor. Let me tell you, General Altmann is one of the most honourable men I've ever known. He had to fight with his conscience long and hard before he came to the decision to give secrets to a foreign power. He wants to see Germany free of these Nazis. He knows that Hitler wants war. In fact, war is inevitable sooner or later. Unfortunately, Germany will have to be defeated before we can be rid of these people.'

'Werner, you don't know how much of a relief it is to me that at last I'm doing something positive,' said Rudi.

Werner smiled and said, 'I know you're very brave young men. A wise man should also know the meaning of fear, because fear of what might happen to you just might keep you alive.' He stopped and took a swig of beer.' Now, when you get back to Berlin, Joseph and I will take you to a safe house and we'll meet you there from time to time. I'll give you the film or documents-it could be either-for you to take with you. It's then up to you to get them out and into Stefan's hands. He'll then pass them on. If you get into trouble, go to the safe house and we'll arrange to get you out of Germany, if we can. I'm sorry but there are no promises. Now, work together as a team and look after each other's backs.' Werner smiled, looking from one to the other, he said, 'Well, gentlemen, the time for talk's over. Here's to a long and successful partnership. Remember, look after each other.'

Rudi and Bruno raised their bottles in a toast. Bruno grumbled, 'Does this mean that I have to call you "Major", or even worse, "Sir"!' Werner laughed and clipped him around the ear.

23

Leaving the isolated chalet before dawn the next day, Rudi and Bruno drove along each wrapped up in his own thoughts. They were both silent for the first part of the journey as Rudi reflected on the incredible past two weeks — part of him was exhilarated, the other part was apprehensive. No fool, he was well aware of the danger that lay ahead and yet this was something that he'd been searching for. Perhaps now he could help to make a difference; all of the impotence of the past few years had been taken away. Likewise, Bruno was not by any means stupid and for all his bravado was aware of their huge responsibility. That the two of them would make a fine team was not in doubt.

Turning to Rudi, Bruno, said, 'Well partner, how does it feel to be involved at last?'

Rudi glanced over, smiled, and replied, 'To be honest a little scary, but at the same time I feel exhilarated. How about you?'

'The same, although Werner's right, we've a lot of responsibility.'

Rudi nodded, 'Yes, we're going to have to start thinking like a couple of twins.'

Bruno asked seriously, 'When it comes to it, will you be able to kill in cold blood?'

'A good question and to be honest I don't know the answer. Do any of us?

Bruno nodded, 'Do you know, Rudi, I think that our partnership is going to be a long one. I can feel it.'

'You could be right there. I suggest that we get our heads together and work out exactly how we're going to operate. As far as I'm concerned my education is on hold until this is all over. I'll spend the minimum of time at the university, without attracting any suspicion of course.'

'I agree. Have you given any thought to our military service?' asked Bruno, 'I mean, sooner or later we're going to be called up.'

'Bruno, I have a feeling that Uncle Stefan's already thought of that, and we're no good to anybody in the infantry or whatever. As soon as I get back to Berlin, I'll talk to him. The sooner we see him the better. After all, you're as much a part of this as I am.'

Bruno's face lit up, 'A trip to Switzerland, great! It's time that I broadened my horizons.'

Rudi smiled, 'I suppose that you want to go mountain climbing while you're there?'

'That's not a bad idea. Do you think that I could learn to blow one of those big horns?'

Rudi laughed, 'An Alpenhorn, you idiot.' He became serious and gave a sigh, 'I've got to find a solution to the problem of Rachel and her family, Bruno. I've got to persuade them to get out, before it's too late.'

Bruno nodded, 'Don't worry, your uncle will be able to help, I'm sure.'

'I hope to God that you're right.' They drove along in companionable silence. After a while, Rudi pulled in to a petrol station. There was a radio playing loudly on the forecourt. An announcement boomed from the Propaganda Ministry:

IN THE EARLY HOURS OF THIS MORNING, GERMANY, GREAT BRITAIN, FRANCE AND ITALY SIGNED AN AGREEMENT RESTORING THE CZECH SUDETENLAND TO THE REICH. OUR GLORIOUS ARMY WILL BE ENTERING CZECHOSLOVAKIA TO LIBERATE OUR SUDETEN BROTHERS TOMORROW. HEIL, HITLER.

The radio announcer finished speaking as music from Wagner's *Rienzi* came through the speakers.

Rudi looked at Bruno, 'What's today's date?' he asked. Bruno thought for a moment.

'September 30th,' he replied. Rudi said nothing and walked over to the fat owner to pay.

'Good news, eh, comrade?' said the fat man. Grunting, Rudi threw some Reichmarks onto the counter, walked out, jumped into the car and roared away.

Rudi drove fast, beating a tattoo with his fist in anger and frustration on the steering wheel. 'The bastards! They've done it again. What the fuck are the British and French doing?' Bruno was surprised. It was rare for Rudi to curse like that. 'This is the second time in less than a year they've just walked into a sovereign state and taken over. Not a shot fired. My God! Will this never end? Where next?' He looked over at Bruno, 'That madman thinks that he can walk roughshod over whoever he likes. From now on Bruno, I don't know about you, but I'm at war with these bastards.'

Giving a cold smile Bruno said, 'Suits me.'

Arriving home in the late evening, Rudi parked the car and walked into the house. 'Mother, I'm home,' he called.

'I'm in the lounge, darling,' shouted Astrid.

Walking in, Rudi embraced his mother and gave her a kiss on the cheek.

'You look fit, Rudi, country air must suit you. Have you heard the news?'

'Czechoslovakia? Yes, I've heard it. Would you like a drink? I could murder a scotch. We need to sit down and have a long talk, mother.'

'Yes, we have a lot to talk about Rudi. I spoke to Stefan while you were away and he wants you and Bruno to go to Switzerland in about two weeks' time. There should be something for you to deliver by then. I've also made a big decision while you've been away. I'm leaving Germany for good. I've decided to go to Switzerland. I've nothing to keep me here.'

'Thank God for that. Now that I'm involved in this business it'll be one less thing for me to worry about. We must talk about Rachel, too. You know that I'm head over heels in love with her? Mother, I have to get them out.

'I know that you are, darling. You're right, there's no future here for them.'

'Look, I've an idea. Let's invite them over for dinner, and then we can have a council of war. It's not going to be easy to persuade them, especially Otto and I don't think Rachel will leave without him.'

Astrid nodded, 'We'll get Stefan to pull a few strings with some of his Nazi friends. Don't worry darling, it'll work itself out.'

'I hope so, mother. I've great fear for the Jews in this country. I'm going to phone Rachel now. How about early next week for dinner?'

'Yes, a good idea. What am I thinking of? You must be starving. You go and phone Rachel, I'll make us some supper.'

Rudi put his arms around Astrid and kissed her on the cheek. 'Mother you're an angel. You've made a good decision about getting out.'

Astrid smiled, 'I'm proud of you, Rudi. Your father would have been too. I'm glad that you decided to join the group, but please, for the love of God, be careful.'

'Don't worry, mother, I will.'

24

Pulling into the drive of the lovely old villa, Paul turned off the engine and turned to Alex, who was humming the slow movement to a Beethoven concerto. Coming from the interior of the house the two young musicians could hear a haunting melody being played on a violin, 'Listen, Paul, it's beautiful.'

'Yes, I can't place it. What a lovely sound he produces.' The two boys sat and listened for a moment, the violin seeming to hold them as if by magic. 'It's a shame to disturb him.'

Alex nodded, 'You could listen all day, couldn't you?'

'How lucky I've been to have such a wonderful teacher.' Paul stirred, 'Come on, let's go and say hello to Papa. They got out of the car and, taking his violin case, Paul headed towards the front door with Alex. Paul rang the bell. The violin stopped playing and after a short pause, they heard a shuffling coming from the interior.

'I'm coming, I'm coming,' a voice muttered. The door opened. Standing there was a stooped old man of about seventy-five years, with a shock of white hair and a small moustache. He was wearing a pair of baggy trousers, old carpet slippers and a grey cardigan that had seen better days. His face lit up when he saw the two boys. 'Paul, Alex, my two *wunderkinder*, how good to see you.'

Paul opened his arms and embraced the old man affectionately, kissing him on the cheek, 'Hello, Papa, how are you?'

'Oh, not so bad for an old man,' Papa Stern said as he turned to embrace Alex. He pinched Alex's cheek. 'How is my young pianist today? Still practising the Brahms, I hope?'

'Oh, yes, Papa,' Alex gave a boyish grin. 'Those first few bars are impossible. I have to get them right for the big concert.'

Papa chuckled. 'Difficult my boy, not impossible.' The old man lifted a finger and wagged it under Alex's nose. 'Come, don't keep an old man standing on the doorstep.' He gave a mock shudder. 'It's too cold for me,' he said, leading the two boys into the house.

The young Paul had been coming here since the age of six when Papa had recognised instantly the boy's incredible talent; more than a talent in fact, a gift from God. The old man was awed. He'd never seen such musicianship in one so young. Papa himself had been a child musician and as a young man had played with some of the finest orchestras in the world. He'd played under the baton of the great Jewish composer Gustav Mahler with the Vienna State Opera. The two men had become firm friends. Often, during the performances of Wagner at the opera house in the early 1900's, there stood in the audience, as he couldn't afford a seat, a young man. Listening with rapt attention, he was transported to another mystical world. His name was Adolf Hitler. Papa had finished his career as first violinist with the Berlin Philharmonic, the members of the orchestra had stood with tears streaming down their faces and shame in their hearts as Papa and the other Jewish musicians had been forced to leave. Now Papa made a living as best he could by giving lessons, often to mediocre talent.

'The others should be here soon. They're so excited to be able to play Schubert's *Trout* with the young Alex.' Alex grinned and pulled his tongue out at Paul. 'Don't let it go to your head, young man,' Papa admonished, with a smile. In the corner of the room was a beautiful Bechstein grand piano. Alex walked over and looked at it lovingly as he sat and started to play the opening bars of Beethoven's *Moonlight* sonata. 'Ah! Such music,' said Papa. 'It brings joy to an old man's heart.' They were interrupted by the sound of the doorbell. Alex stopped playing as the bell sounded again.

'I'm coming, I'm coming,' said Papa, as he shuffled towards the front door. Paul looked over at Alex and blew him a kiss and Alex smiled, nodded his head and winked. There was a commotion as one elderly man tried to get himself and a huge double bass through the door at the same time. The other musician came bouncing in with a cello tucked under his arm. The two were chattering away to each other in Yiddish. 'Gentlemen, you all know Paul,' said Papa,' and this is Alex.' The two men came forward and solemnly shook hands with both Alex and Paul.

'It's a great pleasure to be able to play some wonderful music with you,' said the old bass player, the bass almost bigger than he was.

Alex looked at him and smiled, 'How did you manage to get the bass here?'

'Oh, that was easy,' replied the man, whose name was Isaac, 'I borrowed the kosher butcher's van.' They all laughed.

'It's true, Alex,' said the second musician whose name was Samuel, 'I had to sit in the back with it and my cello.'

Samuel, the cellist, said, 'If you can smell anything funny, it's him.' They were all laughing and chattering away. Looking at the three musicians, Paul felt a little sad, *these wonderful old men,* he thought to himself. *Such brilliant musicians; all that talent wasted.* Not thinking, lost in the moment, Paul tucked his violin under his chin, placed the bow onto the strings and started to play the slow movement to Mendelssohn's violin concerto. The sound of the beautiful melody filled the room. The four men stopped talking as Papa's face turned white as he became agitated.

'Paul, Paul, please stop!' he begged, 'the Brownshirts will come.'

Paul stopped playing and was immediately contrite. 'Papa, gentlemen, forgive me, that was thoughtless of me.' At that moment, Paul felt ashamed to be a German. 'The Brownshirts wouldn't know such beautiful music,' he said.

Papa looked sad and patted Paul on the shoulder. 'I don't suppose that you'll ever be allowed to play that concerto in Germany, not in my life time.' For a moment the atmosphere in the room was solemn.

Alex, trying to lighten things, started to play the opening bars to Wagner's *Tanhauser* overture. He stopped, looked at each musician in turn, and said, 'Gentlemen, I'm very glad that Wagner didn't write a piano concerto.' The three old men tittered, their heads nodding up and down in unison. The music stands and chairs had been set in a semi-circle facing the piano. Sitting at the violin stand Paul waited for Papa and the others to join him. For this piece Papa would be playing the viola.

Looking at Papa sitting next to him, Paul smiled. He had a lump in his throat and his love for this old man was overwhelming. Leaning over, Isaac muttered something into Papa's ear. Papa nodded and looked at Paul and Alex. 'We have something to ask you both.' He stopped, hesitating. The two boys looked at the three musicians quizzically. 'We would like to give a concert,' Papa said, 'for needy Jews. There are many now who can't find work.' We spoke to the Rabbi who said we could use the hall next to the synagogue.' Papa hesitated again. 'We wondered if you would like to play with us? If you don't want to, we quite understand.'

Alex gave a cry of delight. Paul beamed. 'What a fantastic idea,' cried Alex, 'What shall we play?'

The three old men's faces lit up with joy. 'The *Trout* of course,' said Isaac.

'Yes, of course, but what else?' said Alex.

Paul interrupted, 'I know, first, Alex, you play...' he stopped and thought for a moment, 'a Beethoven sonata?'

Samuel said excitedly, 'The *Moonlight*?'

'The *Appassionata*?' said Isaac.

Alex laughed, 'I'll play the two' he decided.

Paul thought for a moment. 'I could play the Schubert *Rondo*, with you accompanying me, Alex.' Paul was getting caught up in the excitement.

Alex nodded, 'We need an encore after the *Trout*'

'How about the Brahms quintet in F minor?' asked Papa.

'Yes, said Paul.' The five musicians were smiling at each other.

Papa said excitedly, 'When people know that you two are playing, it'll be standing room only.'

'What shall we wear?' asked Alex.

Paul was about to say something like, 'Clothes, you idiot.'

Isaac said very quietly, 'For us it would be very nice to wear our evening suits. We don't have the opportunity to wear them very much anymore.'

Paul said, 'Yes, white tie and tails, a super idea. We'll make this a night to remember.' They all started chattering excitedly.

Papa tapped his bow on the top of his stand and with a smile said, 'Perhaps we should practice a little?'

'Yes,' said Alex, 'but when will the concert be?'

Papa thought for a moment and said, 'How about the middle of October, the fifteenth?' The four other players nodded in unison.

Paul, as leader, said, 'Are we ready?' He looked around. There was a silence; now they were thinking only of the notes on the paper in front of them. The four string players lifted their instruments into the playing position and looked towards Paul. He lifted and bought down his upper torso in the exact tempo. The *fortissimo* chord opened the piece by the strings, answered by the piano. Alex played with a maturity which belied his years. All five musicians played this beautiful piece with love, the music coming to an end as it had started with three *fortissimo* chords. For a few seconds there was silence as the five came back to earth, all nodding their contentment.

Papa smiled and looked from one to the other. 'That was well played,' he said with satisfaction. They had coffee and cakes together and afterwards they played until late into the evening, none of them wanting to stop.

25

On a cold evening in early October, Rudi and Bruno walked down the stairs and into The Black Cat. The bar was crowded this evening, the air full with the smoke of numerous cigarettes and the babble of voices.

As they entered, Gustav saw them and motioned to them to come over to the bar. As they approached, looking around he said, above the noise, 'They're waiting in the back room. Go through the door over there.' He indicated to the door at the far end of the room, marked 'toilets'. 'It's the first door on the left.'

Nodding their thanks the two young men headed in the direction indicated and walked through the door. Facing them was a long, dimly-lit corridor, stacked crates full of empty bottles stretching down one side. Directly in front of them, at the end of the passage was a door which led into an alley at the back of the club. Just on the right was a staircase which led up to a disused bar. Going further up into the darkness the stairs led to Gustav's living quarters. The bar's toilets were just down on the left-hand side. Opening the first door on the left, Bruno and Rudi entered. Sitting at a table were Werner and Joseph, an overhead light casting shadows over their faces. 'Evening, Tiny, Rudi,' said Werner.

Joseph nodded and smiled at the two young men. 'Come in, take a seat.' Bruno and Rudi sat as Joseph filled two glasses, shoving one to each of them. We're going to show you our little den in a few moments. I expect that you'll use it a lot in the future.'

'Where is it?' asked Bruno.

'Right here, in this building,' replied Werner. 'It's perfect. Gustav's one of the team. No one's going to take much notice of anyone entering or leaving a bar. If for any reason you need a safe place to go, you can come here.' Bruno and Rudi nodded, 'You can trust Gustav, he's a good man.'

Joseph said, 'Anything that we have from my father we'll hand over here, away from prying eyes.' Joseph looked from one to the other, 'Let's go on up.' The four men got up from the table, their drinks left untouched. As they left the room a man was coming out of the gent's toilets. They waited for him to pass before heading towards the stairs, Joseph leading the way. Climbing the first flight, they arrived at a large landing. Directly in front of them was a door. Joseph opened it and turned on a light. Inside, were a number of tables and chairs, and a large bar in the corner with a huge mirror behind it. There was no window in the room. 'We're now on street level. This bar's no longer used,' said Joseph, turning out the light. Carrying on up, the four men reached a second landing, smaller than the first. They faced another door. 'This is Gustav's living quarters,' Joseph explained. 'He has a flat … very luxurious too.' Walking up the final set of stairs to the second floor they came to a door. Reaching into his pocket Joseph produced a set of keys. He inserted one in the lock and turned it, the door opening easily into a hallway. Directly in front of them were two doors, one leading into a sitting room, the other to a bedroom. To the right there was a small kitchen, while at the end of a corridor there was a bathroom. Joseph entered the living room which was dimly illuminated by the light coming from the streetlights outside. Walking over to the windows he closed a pair of heavy curtains. 'You can turn on the lights now.' Rudi obliged and the room was lit by soft lighting.

Bruno gave a whistle, 'Wow! This place is nice! Can I move in permanently? It beats my place in Wedding, and it has a bar downstairs!'

Werner smiled, 'No you can't! Business use only. Come with me.' He led Bruno and Rudi over to a large chest of drawers and pulled open the top drawer. Inside there were four Walther automatic pistols, their black surfaces dull and menacing. A large number of magazines and ammunition were beside them. Rudi whistled. 'That's not all.' Werner opened the second drawer; inside were half a dozen British hand grenades.

'That's a nice little arsenal. I'm impressed,' said Rudi.

Walking over to a small cupboard, Joseph opened the door and took out a briefcase, opened it, and showed the contents to Bruno and Rudi. Inside there was a small fortune in Reichsmarks and Swiss Francs. 'Emergency funds. If you ever need to get out in a hurry, you'll need cash.'

'I've never seen so much money in my life! Can I have a sub?' said Bruno with a grin. The others smiled.

'There's one other thing … it's important, come with me.' Joseph led them to the bathroom. 'Look up there,' he said, pointing to the ceiling. Looking up they saw a hole about half a metre square. 'If you push the wooden trap door, it opens up and you can crawl along to the next building. There's another trap door, which opens above another bathroom. You can drop down an escape hatch.'

'Who lives there?' said Rudi.

'No one. It's an office building.' said Werner.

Rudi puffed out his cheeks, 'Someone's thought of everything. This is impressive.'

'Come on, let's sit down,' said Joseph. The four men returned to the living room and sat in the armchairs. 'Your uncle, Rudi, owns this building and the office next door. The business next door is legitimate, by the way. This has all been set up over the past three years. Your uncle saw the need for a bolthole like this when my father approached him. As far as Stefan's concerned this is money well spent, and hopefully we could be using this place for years to come.'

Werner nodded and said, 'Now, I have something for you both, When are you going to Basel?'

'Next week,' replied Rudi.

'Alright, here's the microfilm.' He produced a small film cartridge, 'This was shot using a Riga Minox miniature camera, a beautiful little thing. There are fifty photographs on there; you don't need to know what's on them. In the future if there's something here to be collected either Joseph or I will contact you. Whatever it is, film or documents, they'll be left in the small cupboard where the briefcase is. Hand me the film Rudi.' Rudi handed the film to Werner. 'Leave it here until you go to Basel.' Werner put the film inside the cupboard and closed the door.

'That's it then, gentlemen. Here are your keys. Oh, by the way, the kitchen's well stocked … you shouldn't starve, if you need to hole up here,' said Joseph.

'What about the telephone?' said Rudi, indicating the phone on the cupboard.

'Only use that in an emergency.'

'And if it rings?' said Bruno.

'Then answer it. If it does ring it'll be important,' said Joseph. The four men got up, turned off the lights and left, locking the door behind them.

Descending the three flights of stairs, they arrived at the corridor leading to the bar. It was empty. Saying their farewells, Joseph and Werner left by the back door.

Deciding to stay for a beer, Rudi and Bruno walked towards the door leading to the bar and opened it. The bar was still full and something made Rudi look around the room before he entered. His eyes came to rest on a table on the far side of the bar. He froze, putting his hand behind him to stop Bruno from entering. 'What's the matter?' Bruno asked.

'Look over there, in the corner. Isn't that Paul and Alex?'

Bruno looked over Rudi's shoulder, 'Yes it is. Let's go over and have a drink together.'

'Bruno, look closely,' said Rudi, a note of exasperation in his voice. The two young lovers were sitting with their arms around each other's shoulders. As Rudi and Bruno were watching, Paul lent over and kissed Alex on the cheek.

'I see what you mean, they certainly look more than just good friends.' Bruno sounded shocked.

Rudi managed to catch Gustav's eye and he gestured urgently for him to come over. Saying something to one of the waiters, Gustav walked over and approached Rudi and Bruno who were standing in the shadow of the open doorway.

'What's up?' enquired Gustav.

'The two young men sitting over in the corner ...,' said Rudi.

'Paul and Alex, the two homos?'

'You know them?' asked Rudi. Bruno was standing with his mouth open.

''Course, they're always in here.'

'Are you sure that they're homosexual?'

'Rudi, I've seen enough homos in my life to know. Anyway, you saw them, all lovey-dovey. They're always in here and they don't make any attempt to hide what they like to get up to in the bedroom. They were nearly caught by the police recently. Fortunately, two young whores saved them that time.'

The last sentence made Rudi's mind up for him. Both he and Bruno loved Paul like a brother. Normally he'd say nothing, but if Paul was carrying on like that for the entire world to see ...

'Listen, Gustav, can you ask them to come in here,' said Rudi, indicating the room where they'd met Werner and Joseph earlier on.

Gustav nodded, 'Sure. I suppose I should have warned them myself. I forget that this isn't Weimer anymore.' Gustav shrugged and walked back through the door heading towards Paul and Alex's table.

Rudi led Bruno into the small room. The light was still on. 'Jesus, this is going to be delicate.'

Bruno seemed to be in a state of shock. 'I would never have guessed,' he said.

The two young men didn't have time to speculate anymore as the door opened and Paul and Alex were standing there: Paul, looking tall, slim and extremely handsome, while the shorter stockier Alex, equally as attractive, stood by his side.

Paul's eyes opened in surprise as he saw his two friends. 'Hello, Rudi, Bruno,' he said anxiously. You know Alex, don't you?'

'Who doesn't? You two are the talk of Berlin. Look, Paul,' he hesitated, 'You'll be the talk of Berlin for other reasons if you're not more careful.'

Straightening up Paul, put his arm around Alex and looking Rudi in the eye, said defiantly,' Rudi, I'm not ashamed of what I am. In fact, I'm relieved that you now know.'

Rudi lifted his hand. 'I'm sorry, Paul, I put that badly. For Christ's sake, we could've been the Gestapo,' he said it angrily. 'Paul, you know that both Bruno and I would do anything for you, especially after all that we shared together in the labour camp.' Bruno nodded. 'It's not our affair, what you … you know, like to do in bed …' Rudi looked a little sheepish.

'He's right, Paul,' said Bruno quietly. 'If you're caught … you'll both end up in prison.'

'Or worse.' Rudi walked over to Paul, embraced him and kissed him on the cheek. He smiled and tried to lighten the atmosphere. 'If I was that way inclined, I'd probably … well, you know …'

Paul smiled.

Bruno, not to be outdone, said, 'I wouldn't, you're far too skinny for me.' He paused, looked at Alex and said, 'Now you, Alex, you've got some meat on you.' All four laughed.

Rudi became serious again, 'Listen you two. Please be more discreet. It would break our hearts if anything were to happen to you.'

Paul nodded and looked at Alex; the love that they had for each other was obvious. Rudi couldn't pretend that he understood.

'It seems so unfair somehow,' said Paul, his voice tinged with sadness.

'Life's usually unfair, especially here. You have so much talent, both of you. We're all green with envy you know. Please be careful.'

Alex, who'd been silent all this time, said, 'He's right, we've been stupid. Perhaps we should be more careful.' Paul nodded.

'Come on,' said Alex brightening up, 'let's go for a drink.'

'Now, that's the best idea I've heard all evening,' said Bruno. Putting his arm around Alex, he led the way into the bar. Rudi and Paul followed.

The four headed towards the door, entered the bar, and Bruno called over for four beers. They found a table, Paul sitting next to Rudi. Alex and Bruno were soon in conversation, laughing and joking with each other.

Paul turned to Rudi and smiled, 'I've given you a shock tonight, haven't I?'

'Yes, I suppose you have. I'm curious, Paul, how did you know? I mean…'

'Oh, I've known for years. I suppose you think that we're all effeminate with limp wrists?' He smiled, flicked his hair from the front of his eye and continued, 'The first time, strangely enough was at a Hitler Youth camp. I was sharing a tent with another boy, you know, I can't even remember his name. Ironic really, not being able to remember your first lover's name. Well, as I said, we shared a tent. We were wrestling together, you know how you do?'

Rudi nodded. Bruno had Alex in stitches over something. Paul looked at the two of them, then at Rudi and smiled. He continued, 'We both found that we were getting excited. I'm sure that you know what I mean? Well, one thing led to another and we had sex. It was the most incredible experience of my life.

'How did you and Alex …?'

'Well, when he first came here to Berlin from Frankfurt, I tell you, I was attracted to him from the start, as we're both pretty good musicians.'

'"Pretty good"— that's the biggest understatement that I've ever heard in my life.'

Paul shrugged, 'Well, I suppose it was only natural that we should play together.' He smiled. 'Music, I mean.' Rudi grinned. Paul continued, 'I tell you Rudi, I was totally in love with him. One evening, when he was only seventeen, we'd been playing a Beethoven sonata together. You know, Rudi, he's a brilliant pianist and one day he'll be great, when he's matured a little. Well, we decided to go for a walk together in the Tiergarten and I could tell that he was unhappy and thought that he was homesick. We sat down together on the grass and I was aching to put my arms around him. I'm not embarrassing you am I, Rudi?'

'No, I'm fascinated.'

'He started to cry. Then I did put my arms around him. It all came out: how he was homosexual, how much he loved me, how much I'd hate him and not be his friend. Rudi, I tell you, I cried with joy. We both went back to his flat that night and made love for hours. I never wanted it to end. Listen, Rudi, I want you to try and understand something, difficult as it may be. This is not just about sex, although God knows that's wonderful, but there's much more to it than that. We love each other. I'm not stupid; I know that even without the Nazis, society would be against us. "Queers," "bum boys", "perverts" that sort of thing' he said bitterly, 'but I truly love him and if necessary would give my life for him. That's why we like coming here. You know what this place used to be in the old days? No one looks down on us here. The trouble is that when we're together we sometimes forget to be careful.'

Looking sympathetically at Paul, Rudi nodded and said, 'So, all those letters that you were getting when we were at the labour camp …?'

'Yes, from Alex. Let me tell you Rudi, I've never been so happy in my life.'

'Paul, I believe that you really are. I can't pretend to understand. I'm not homosexual, but …'

Paul smiled, 'Yes I suppose it must be difficult for any heterosexual man to understand.' He looked directly into Rudi's eyes, 'But believe me when I say that I'd die for him.'

'I do believe you, Paul, but promise me that from now on you'll both be more discreet.'

'I promise.'

The four boys had a wonderful evening together.

26

Sitting in the library, Rudi could smell the delicious aroma of roast duck. His mother was helping the cook/housekeeper, Sarah, in the kitchen. He was excited. If his plans for this evening came to something, hopefully Rachel would soon be out of Germany. This was going to be more than a convivial social evening. Hearing the doorbell ring, he jumped up and rushed to answer it. Opening the door, he saw Rachel standing there, looking absolutely ravishing. God, I love her so much, he thought to himself. Giving him a radiant smile, she entered. Closing the door, he took her in his arms and they embraced, their lips touching in a passionate kiss. Pulling away, he held her at arm's length and studied her. She moved a little from him and took off her coat. She was wearing a tight, white blouse that showed off her breasts to perfection, and a figure hugging black skirt, which came to just above her knees. Her long brown hair cascaded down to the small of her back.

Their lips met again in a passionate kiss, and then once more they parted and looked into each other's eyes. 'Good evening, sweetheart,' murmured Rudi.

'Hello, my love.' She gave a little shiver. 'Winter's coming. It's nice and warm in here though.

'I know. It would be even warmer in bed. I wish we were alone tonight.'

She smiled, 'You men, you have only one thing on your minds. It would be nice though. Anyway, Rudi Wagner, I came early. Papa and Sam will be over in a little while. They're just shutting up the shop. I came to see if there was anything I could do for your mother?'

'You mean you didn't come early to see me?' he said, a smile playing at the corner of his mouth. Come on, let's go and have a sherry.'

'What about your mother?'

'Oh, she's fine, Sarah's with her.' He put his arm around her waist and led her into the library. Pouring two glasses of sherry, he sat on the settee next to her, handed her one, and said, 'Cheers, here's to a splendid evening.' They sat holding hands, saying nothing.

Looking back on the past few weeks since they'd first met, Rachel couldn't believe that she was this happy or that she could be so passionate. They'd made love at every opportunity, using all their ingenuity to find private places, which was not always easy. Yet underneath the surface, she had a nagging fear that wouldn't go away. Rachel hadn't forgotten their day together at the zoo and what Rudi had said. Perhaps this evening he'd tell them more of his idea?

She gave a sigh and rested her head on his shoulder, 'It's so nice here … peaceful … I wish ….'

'You wish what? Tell me.'

'I wish that life wasn't so complicated.' She sighed once more. 'What are we going to do, Rudi?'

'Don't worry, sweetheart, be patient. I do have an idea. After dinner tonight, we'll all have a long talk.'

They were interrupted by the sound of the doorbell. 'That'll be Papa and Sam.'

Rudi stood, offering Rachel his hand, 'Come on, let's go and meet them.'

They walked out of the library. Astrid was already there, having beaten them to it. Pausing in front of the hall mirror, she checked to see that her hair was in place and went to open the door. Standing there were Otto and Sam, both of them dressed in their best suits, Otto holding an enormous bunch of roses in his arms. The man and the boy bowed slightly in unison. Rudi smiled. It looked as if the pair of them had been rehearsing that little bow on the way over. This was the first time that Astrid had met either Otto or Sam.

Otto offered his hand. 'Good evening, Frau Wagner. It's so nice to meet you. This is my son, Samuel.'

Astrid gave her most charming smile. 'It's so nice to meet you at last, Herr Goldmann. Please come in.' She stood to one side as Otto and Sam entered.

'Hello, Otto, Sam,' said Rudi. 'Let me take your coats.' Rudi shook hands with them both. 'You're looking smart tonight, Sam.'

'So are you,' replied Sam, running his finger around his collar, as if it were too tight. He looked around him and said, 'You have a beautiful home, Frau Wagner.'

'Thank you Sam. Come, let's go into the library. Pour some sherries Rudi, darling. A small one for Sam?' She looked at Otto enquiringly. He nodded. 'Why not?

'Come, Madam, I would very much like to get to know you.' He gave his most charming smile, and offered his arm. He led Astrid over to a large settee and waited for her to sit. 'It's so nice to meet you at last. I owe your son a debt.'

'Herr Goldmann, you owe my son nothing. He only did what any decent young man would do. Those barbarians are a disgrace to this country.'

Otto nodded. 'Yes, they're difficult times for us. But what can we do?' he shrugged his shoulders. 'I hope that this country will soon come to its senses.'

Astrid said, 'So do I, but I fear things may get a lot worse. Now Hitler has the Czech Sudetenland, what next?' She looked over at Rachel, Rudi and Sam. She continued. 'It's the young people that I fear for. You know, Herr Goldmann, my Rudi adores Rachel.'

'Yes, but what future can they have here? To be honest, Frau Wagner, it worries me. You know, the Nuremberg Laws ...'

'Herr Goldmann, I'm a woman and I can see that Rachel's as much in love with Rudi as he is with her. Are we to allow these barbarians to stand in their way? Tell me, do you have any objections to them on religious grounds?'

Otto smiled. 'No, why should I? Like you, I believe that they do love each other. If you could see the way she moons around the house. But what can we do to help them?'

'After dinner, Herr Goldmann, I suggest that we all get together and talk about just that.'

Dinner was a convivial affair with lots of banter, fun and laughter. Sam had a great time, passing jokes between himself and Rudi. Astrid looked at the two of them. It was obvious that Sam adored Rudi. She thought they were like brothers, and what a wonderful daughter-in-law Rachel would make. She knew the solution and hoped that Otto would agree. After dessert she suggested that they have coffee in the library.

Standing in the centre of the room, coffee cup in one hand, Astrid looked around, very much the mistress in her own home.

'It's been a wonderful evening so far. Dinner, however, wasn't the only reason that we invited you here this evening.' Otto, Rachel and Sam looked at each other, wondering what was coming next. 'Firstly, I've decided that I'm leaving Germany. Since my husband was murdered, I have no reason to stay. With these barbarians in control, things can only get worse. I fear that they'll be ruling Germany for a long time to come.'

She paused, took a sip of coffee and continued. 'I've decided to go and live in Basel. My brother in law, Stefan, lives there. I hope that you don't mind my saying so,' she looked at Otto, 'but I fear that things can only get worse for your people. Otto nodded. 'I have a suggestion to make and hope that you'll give it serious consideration.' She paused and looked across at the portrait of Robert hanging on the wall. She continued. 'Stefan is both rich and influential. He's a banker and has many friends, a lot of them Nazis. At least, they think he's their friend. In fact nothing could be further from the truth. He hates them as much as we do. Rudi's going to Basel in the next few days.' Rachel looked at Rudi as if to say, *you didn't tell me that*. Rudi looked a bit sheepish as Astrid continued. 'I think it would be a good idea if Rudi were to carry on.' She went and sat down next to Otto.

'Mother's right about the Nazis. It'll take a war to get rid of them. Hitler wants war. He also wants the Jews out of Germany. I believe that things will get a lot worse, especially for the Jews.' The Goldmanns were listening with rapt attention. Rudi continued, 'Mother's already spoken to my uncle. He's more than happy to use his influence to get you all out of Germany.'

There was a long silence as Otto looked from Astrid to Rudi then he said, 'Do you mean that we should just leave everything and go? That's impossible. I mean, my business. Switzerland is already full of jewellery shops. Things can only get better here.'

'Herr Goldmann, please be realistic, It's my opinion that things can only get worse,' said Astrid. Otto looked perplexed. This was all too much.

Rudi said, 'Thousands of Jews have already left Germany and made new lives for themselves. Why not you? Look, Uncle can arrange for you to transfer your capital to his bank. You sell the business here and start again. In fact, he's told me that he's prepared to buy the shop including all the stock and the contents of the apartment. He'll give you a very fair price.'

Otto said with some anger, 'You're missing the point. I'm a German. Why should I be driven out?'

'Otto, tell me, how many times have you had your shop windows broken? How many times have you been beaten up?' said Rudi, 'What about Rachel and Sam? Sam has no life. He can't get a decent education and the other boys treat him worse than an animal. Why? For one reason only…. because he's a Jew. Sam, we're talking about your future so how do you feel?' asked Rudi

Sam looked at the four of them and said, 'Things are bad. Us young Jews are always being beaten up.' He straightened his shoulders and continued, 'But should we run away?'

Rudi answered, 'Sam, we admire your bravery but alone you can do nothing. Every day in our schools young children are taught to hate Jews; what kind of society is that? One day Sam, you'll have the chance to fight them on an equal footing, that I promise you.' He paused and looked longingly at Rachel. 'And what of us?' he asked, quietly, 'We both know that there's no future whatsoever for us in this country.'

'Rachel looked at him. She knew without any doubt that she loved him and would gladly marry him if he asked. 'But if I'm in Switzerland and you're here what good does that do us?'

'Look,' said Rudi, 'I've already made up my mind. Within one year I'll have finished my degree and after that I'll be called up to do my military service. That is something that I'm not prepared to do. Please remember that they murdered my father. I'll not serve them and so will have no choice but to get out, and then we can be together.'

Otto gave a sigh, almost of defeat. 'Perhaps you're right. Maybe it's time to take our heads out of the sand. Tell me, would we all have to leave at the same time?'

'What do you have in mind?' asked Astrid.

'Well, if Rachel and Sam could leave ....'

'I'm not leaving without you, Papa,' said Rachel.

Otto raised his hand. 'I was going to say, it would give me time to sell the business. Put my affairs in order.' He paused. 'You know, I think that you're right. I lost my wife. I couldn't bear to lose my son and daughter. If you could arrange it we'd be grateful.' Sam and Rachel smiled as they looked at each other.

Looking at Otto, Astrid put her hand on his shoulder and squeezed. 'You've made the right decision Herr Goldmann. God willing, these people won't last forever. Now, to be practical, I intend to leave Germany on the first of November. That doesn't give us much time, especially as we have to wait for your exit visas to come through. On that subject I beg you not to worry. I know my brother in law and if he says that he can get you your visas then he can.' She smiled, and continued, 'Perhaps it's better not to ask too many questions. So I suggest that you, Rachel, and you, Sam, come with me. I'm flying from Tempelhof and think that we should, under the circumstances, travel together.' She looked around and waited.

'Alright,' said Otto, his mind made up, 'You two go with Frau Wagner, I'll try to join you by Christmas.'

Astrid smiled, 'Well that seems to be that. It's settled. Now I suggest a drink would be rather nice, brandy everyone?'

Looking at Rachel, Rudi smiled, took her hand and said to everybody, 'Would you excuse us for a moment?' Without waiting for a reply, they left the room. Leading Rachel into the library he turned and faced her, stroking her long hair lovingly. Their lips met and they embraced passionately. 'I love you so much Rachel. I'd die if anything were to happen to you and I admit I was so worried that your father might refuse.'

'It was a difficult decision for him to make but I think that it's the right one. We'll be separated though.'

'Yes, but only for a short time. I have something that I must tell you. I can't say too much, but recently I've become involved with an anti-Nazi group; this group is very efficient and deadly serious. So am I, and I intend to fight this regime. It'll be dangerous, and you of all people have a right to know.'

She gave a gasp. A look of fear passed over her face as she said, 'Thank you for telling me, trusting me. I admire your courage and you must do the right thing. But will you promise me something?'

'Yes, anything.'

'For my sake,' she hesitated for a fleeting moment, and continued, 'and the sake of our child, please, please be careful.'

Cupping her face in his hands he looked deep into her eyes, 'Are you sure?'

'Yes and I have no regrets. I've loved you since I first set eyes on you and know in my heart that you love me.'

A surge of joy passed through him.

'A child, our child! Oh, I do love you so much.' Making his mind up in an instant, he said, 'I'm flying with you to Basel; we can be married straightaway — a civil ceremony. I'll get uncle to arrange it. That is if you'll have me?'

'Of course, I'll have you. Now, not a word to anyone, not just yet.'

'You have my word.' His heart was singing.

Bringing his lips down to meet hers, they kissed. It seemed to go on for an eternity.

27

Rudi opened the door that led from the large kitchen into the garage and pressed down the switch, flooding the room with bright white light. He walked over to the gleaming Mercedes and squatted down by the front left-hand wheel, wrenched off the hubcap, and took it over to a workbench that ran the length of one whole wall. He picked up the microfilm which fitted snugly into the palm of his hand and wrapped it in waterproof canvas. Taping the film securely, he put it inside the hubcap and clipped the cap back onto the wheel. As he left the garage, he turned out the light. He and Bruno were leaving Berlin early the next morning and they planned to go via Leipzig, Frankfurt and Freiburg, taking four days in all. Rudi was on the one hand excited, as it seemed that at last his life had some real purpose but, on the other hand, was apprehensive. He knew the penalty if they were caught, but the first thought was by far the stronger of the two. Rudi looked back to the day four years ago when he and Dieter had almost fought on the train, the day his father had been betrayed to the Gestapo. Since then, he'd been looking for some way to fight the regime and now at last he'd found it. No longer did he feel the sense of frustration that had dogged him for so many years, and on top of all that he'd fallen head over heels in love with Rachel. He'd now do everything in his power to get her and her family out of Germany. Rudi had the feeling he was embarking on an adventure that would stretch far into the future and he couldn't possibly know the outcome. He took some comfort from the thought that, although he wasn't particularly religious, his fate and the fate of the others were in the hands of some entity. Wishing his mother goodnight, he set his alarm for 6am and slept like a baby.

Rudi pulled up outside Bruno's apartment at 7.00 a.m. and pipped his horn. Bruno came running out of the apartment block carrying his battered suitcase. He opened the boot, threw his case on top of Rudi's, and slammed it shut, making Rudi wince. Opening the passenger door, he jumped in.

'Morning, Rudi. What a nice, fresh morning for a sightseeing trip,' he said, with a grin. 'Did you bring something for breakfast? I'm starving.'

'Morning, Bruno, and yes to all of your questions.' Rudi smiled at his friend's boisterousness as he pulled away from the curb.

'Do you realise, Rudi, that this is my first trip outside of Germany,' he said, munching on a sandwich that he'd found on the back seat near a flask of coffee. 'Mind you, I never saw the sea until I was twelve. It's funny though, going out of the country in these circumstances.'

'Yes, you're right. I think that we're both going to learn a lot over the next few days. I can't wait to meet Uncle Stefan. It's been some years since I saw him last. Eh! Save some of those sandwiches for me. We haven't even left Berlin yet and you're half way through them.'

'Well, I'm a growing boy.'

They finally drove through the outskirts of Berlin and on to the autobahn heading towards Leipzig. The two young men were in holiday mood over the next three days, the bond between them growing stronger day by day. They became more subdued, however, as they approached Freiburg, the last stop before the German-Swiss frontier.

They spent the night in a small hotel in the town, got up early, had breakfast and were heading towards the frontier by 8am It was a cold, sunny day and there'd been a slight frost during the night.

'We've about 70 kilometres to go before we get to the border crossing,' said Rudi. 'Nervous?'

'Yes, I am. I feel naked,' replied Bruno.

'I don't think that we need to worry too much, unless they're on to us, of course.'

Bruno nodded.

'If they are on to us, it'll be over before it starts.'

They drove in silence, each occupied with his own thoughts, as they passed through the small village of Schliengen and on to the last part of the journey to the border. They rounded a bend in the road and saw the border crossing point about two hundred metres in front of them.

'Here we go,' said Rudi, his heart thumping loudly in his chest. Directly in front of them, there was a red and white striped pole stretching across the road, while to the right there was a long, single-storey building. By the entrance, hanging limply from its pole was the swastika flag. There was already a car parked outside the customs building which had Frankfurt licence plates. As they slowed down, a policeman of the *Grenzpolizei* walked over towards them, indicating that they should pull in behind the other car. Rudi and Bruno were very aware that these border police came under the control of the Gestapo. The green-uniformed man had a pistol in a holster at his waist and a 9mm MP38 sub machine gun slung over his shoulder. Rudi wound down his window and the guard bent down and looked into the car.

'Heil Hitler,' he murmured. 'Please get out.' The two young men obeyed. 'Take your passports and papers into the office,' he said, indicating the door behind him. 'Give me your keys.' He held out his hand. Rudi handed them over, and he and Bruno headed towards the interior of the building. To their left were a number of benches that were obviously used for the inspection of luggage.

Over on their right, sitting at a high desk rather like those that schoolteachers use, was an officer of the border police in conversation with a fat, well-dressed businessman. He glanced over as the two young men entered. Standing behind him was a man in civilian clothes. 'Gestapo', thought Rudi. The police officer smiled, said something to the well-dressed man, and stamped his passport. The man gave the Hitler salute, said 'Good morning' and left. Finding himself standing in front of the officer Rudi felt remarkably calm. Sensing Bruno behind him, he could hear him softly humming the Horst Wessel song.

'Your papers, please,' said the customs officer holding out his hand. Rudi could feel the eyes of the Gestapo man watching him, looking for signs of nervousness. Handing over his papers, the officer opened his passport, looked at the photo and then at Rudi. 'Going for a holiday are you?' he asked.

'Yes, we're going to spend a few days with my uncle in Basel.'

'Your first visit to Switzerland?' he asked, raising an eyebrow.

'Yes, at least since I was a child.'

The officer nodded.

'Have a good holiday,' he said, stamping Rudi's passport and handing it back. Rudi turned and made way for Bruno. As he waited, he looked through the large picture window. Outside, the guard had the boot and car doors open, busily looking into the interior of the car. Rudi could hear Bruno behind him, chatting to the officer as if they were old friends.

He sensed, rather than saw, the Gestapo man standing slightly behind him.

'Nice car you have there,' he said quietly. 'Must have cost a few Reichsmarks, that?'

'Yes, it's a nice car, a bit expensive, but … '

The Gestapo man grunted.

Rudi heard Bruno say, 'Yes, Officer, thanks a lot, Heil Hitler. See you on the way back, perhaps?'

He turned as Bruno approached, glad to distance himself from the Gestapo man. Bruno looked at his friend, then smiled and nodded towards the Gestapo officer.

'Nice day,' he said, giving his most charming smile. The man looked at Bruno, said nothing, and walked away.

'Arrogant bastard,' said Bruno, under his breath.

The two young men walked towards the door, Rudi reaching the entrance first. He almost stopped in full stride, but checked himself. The border guard was squatting down looking at the front left-hand tyre. Rudi's heart was in his mouth as the guard looked up when they approached

'I'd have that tyre checked if I were you. It looks like you may have a slow puncture.'

Rudi smiled, his heartbeat returning to something like normal. 'Yes, thanks, I'll see to it when I get over to the other side.'

'You can go now.'

The boys closed the boot and back doors. They climbed into the car, turned on the ignition, and waited for the barrier to be raised. They drove through to the Swiss side of the border.

'Jesus! That was a bit nerve racking,' said Bruno.

Rudi looked over at him, smiled and said, 'You were talking to that officer as if you were old friends.'

'Yeh, the piece of shit,' muttered Bruno.

They were driving slowly towards the Swiss frontier and could feel that they were under observation. The control on this side of the frontier was almost identical to the German side. They stopped the car, climbed out, nodded to the Swiss border guard and entered the customs building.

'Gentlemen, welcome to Switzerland,' said the Swiss customs officer. A door opened behind him and there standing in the doorway was a man with a military moustache. He was wearing the uniform of a major in the Swiss border police. The two boys handed their passports over once again for inspection. The major held his hand out and the other man passed them over to him. He glanced at the passports and handed them back, smiling at the two young men.

'And how are our German colleagues over the other side this morning? Not too thorough I hope?' he laughed. 'No, if that had been the case you wouldn't be talking to me now. I'm sorry, let me introduce myself. I'm Major Weiss. I'll always be glad to be of service. Please, Herr Wagner, give my best wishes to your uncle. Have a nice stay in our country.' He turned and walked back into his office, closing the door behind him.

On their way out Rudi turned to Bruno, 'I think that we've just been given an important message.'

'Yes, it looks like it. Now, where are the mountains? I can't see any.'

Rudi laughed, punched him on the shoulder and said, 'Idiot!'

28

Driving up the hill into Münsterplatz they came into the beautiful, cobbled square, which was enclosed on three sides by exquisite 18th-century houses. On the open side stood Basel Cathedral, its twin spires soaring into the sky, trees and lamps at intervals around it.

Rudi pulled up outside No 14 which faced the Cathedral. They looked around them.

'This place is beautiful, isn't it?' said Rudi.

'It certainly is. Makes my place in Wedding look like a hovel. Your uncle must be really wealthy to live here.'

'He is. Come on, let's announce ourselves.' The two young men got out of the car and rang the bell.

The door was opened almost immediately. Standing there was a short, stocky, muscular man. He had black, curly hair cut close to his skull, a swarthy complexion and a nose that looked as if it had been broken at least twice during the owner's lifetime. He was immaculately dressed, wearing a black jacket, a white shirt with a silver-grey tie, and pin-striped trousers with highly-polished, black shoes.

'Good morning, Gentlemen,' he said, in a gravelly voice. 'Welcome to Basel. I'm Max, Herr Wagner's manservant.' He looked at the two boys. 'Which of you is Rudi?'

'That's me. This is Bruno Meyer.'

Bruno looked closely at the man, knowing instantly that he'd seen him before, but where?

Max bowed slightly. 'Please come in. I'll take your luggage from the car shortly. If you'll give me the keys, I'll put the car in the garage. May I ask... er ... the film ...?'

Rudi was surprised. '*Who is this?*' He wondered to himself. '*More than a servant,*' I think. He told Max where it was.

'I'll get it. Someone will be coming to pick it up shortly. Now, let me take your coats'. They were standing in a hall with thick blood-red carpet on the floor, and walls panelled in dark mahogany. At intervals were large oil paintings in gold frames, the furniture was all Louis XIV, and Rudi thought he recognised at least one Rembrandt. Max led them through into the well-furnished library, its walls lined with leather-bound first editions. Above the fireplace was a portrait of Rudi's mother and father, painted when they were a young couple. A fire was blazing away in the comfortably warm room.

Max smiled for the first time, showing even, white teeth. 'Your uncle apologises that he's not here to meet you, but he has important business in Bern. He'll be back early this evening. In the meantime, please make yourselves at home. Would you like a drink?'

'Thank you, Max, a whiskey would be nice,' said Rudi. Max nodded and poured two drinks from a crystal decanter. Bruno was looking around the room with awe. He'd never seen such opulence.

'Please sit down. I'm going to make you some lunch. I hope that cold meats will be alright? When you've had your drinks, I'll show to your rooms. I'll unpack for you later. Herr Wagner's taken the liberty of making an appointment with his tailor for you, Herr Meyer. This afternoon at 4 p.m. It's very easy to find. In fact, I suggest that after lunch you might like to do a little sightseeing?'

Bruno looked uncomfortable. 'Oh, thank you,' he said and thought to himself, *Where do I know you from Max?*' The time and place eluded him.

'Now, let me show you to your rooms. I must move the car and retrieve that film.' Max looked at Rudi and Bruno.

'Perhaps I should explain? I know exactly what's happening. In fact, the three of us will probably be working together a lot in the months to come. Now if you'll come this way.'

He led them out and into the vestibule. They climbed the stairs to the first floor where their bedrooms were adjoining, with ensuite bathrooms. The furnishings here were equally as sumptuous as downstairs and each bedroom had a huge four-poster bed. The walls were adorned with valuable paintings. Max left them together saying that lunch would be in about half an hour. Bruno looked at Rudi. He was in a daze. He'd never seen anything like this in his life.

'Rudi, I know him. I've seen him before but can't place him.'

Frowning, Rudi said, 'Are you sure? I don't see how that can be possible.'

'I tell you I've seen him before. Perhaps I'm mistaken. No I'm sure.' He shrugged. 'Don't worry, it'll come to me.' Changing the subject, he continued, 'What am I going to the tailors for? My wardrobe's not much I know but I did bring my best suit … ,' his voice trailed away.

Rudi smiled.

'Don't worry, Bruno. Uncle just doesn't want you to feel out of place. In fact, I know that you're in for a bit of a surprise tonight. Uncle will explain everything over dinner this evening'.

'Oh, come on, tell me.'

'No, be patient. Let's go and have some lunch, I'm starving.'

Bruno shrugged. He had no choice but to be carried along with it all.

On the way downstairs, Bruno whispered to Rudi, 'Did you see the muscles on Max? I wouldn't care to tangle with him.'

'Me neither,' said Rudi.

After a leisurely lunch, the two young friends walked into the town and spent the afternoon looking at the shops, stopping from time to time for a beer. Bruno gave a gasp of astonishment every time they passed one of the numerous jewellery shops, looking at the Swiss watches with envy. They found the tailors and went in. Bruno was more than a little apprehensive as he entered but he needn't have worried as the proprietor was charming. He soon had everything that he could possibly need, which would be delivered as soon as possible. He was given an evening suit and a day suit to take with him for immediate use. They left the shop, the proprietor telling Bruno that everything would be charged to his account. *What account?* Bruno wondered. Rudi just smiled and said nothing. They arrived back at the house at 5pm.

Max answered the door and let them in, taking their coats,

'Herr Wagner's back. He's bathing at the moment but suggests that you all meet in the library at 7.30 p.m. Do you have evening dress now, Herr Meyer?'

Bruno nodded.

'Very well. In that case Herr Wagner suggests that you dress for dinner. You're going to the Restaurant Spillmann, I believe'.

Rudi and Bruno thanked Max and went up to their rooms. It was a little later, after a long soak in the bath and as he was getting dressed, that Bruno began to think how puzzled he felt about many things — Max and the tailors, for instance. Rudi wasn't being very helpful and Bruno was sure that he knew more than he was letting on. His thoughts were interrupted by a knock on the door.

The door opened and Max entered, smiled and said, 'Is everything all right, Herr Meyer? I suppose it's all a bit strange for you at the moment?'

In that instant it came back to him. Max had been the stranger at his father's funeral. 'I've seen you before, haven't I?'

'You have a very good memory. It's almost ten years since your father's death.'

'It was at the funeral, wasn't it?'

'Yes it was. You know, you're the spitting image of your father when he was your age.'

Bruno's mouth opened. 'You knew my father?'

'Oh, yes, we were old comrades, and served together all through the last war. He was a very brave man. I was so sorry to hear of his death and came to the funeral to say goodbye to an old friend. I promise you that if I ever find the person or persons responsible for his death, I'll tell you. If it's any consolation to you, he died fighting those bastards. He loathed them you know. Herr Wagner was our company commander.'

'Is that how you became his servant?'

'Oh, I'm more than his servant. By the end of this evening you'll know everything. Anyway, it's nearly time to go down.' Max headed towards the door.

'Max,' said Bruno. Max turned. 'Would you tell me something about my father, sometime?'

'Bruno, I'd be delighted.' Max smiled and left the room.

There was a tap on Bruno's door. Rudi was standing there.

'Wow! Look at you! Very smart I'm sure.'

'Fuck off!' growled Bruno, 'I feel like a stuffed turkey. You look smart.'

'Thanks. You do too. It suits you, you know. Are you ready? Come on let's go down and meet Uncle.'

The two young men walked side by side down the stairs and into the library.

Standing with his back to the fire, Stefan Wagner was sipping a glass of whiskey and soda, the library lit by the pleasant glow from three table lamps. Stefan was a dapper little man, standing no more than five feet two inches, and with the bearing of a person who'd seen a number of years of military service. The top of his head was completely bald, while the neatly trimmed hair at the sides was dark brown, flecked with grey. He wore his moustache in a clipped, military style. The two young men entered the room. Beaming, Stefan looked first at Rudi and then at Bruno, opened his arms and embraced Rudi, stepped back and put his hands on each side of his shoulders.

He looked into Rudi's eyes and said, 'Rudi, my boy, it's good to see you. It's been too long. You're the spitting image of your father when he was your age.'

He turned towards Bruno and embraced him.

'You're also like your father, Bruno. Max tells me that you know now that we both knew him? We all served in the trenches together. Anyway — a drink. Would you pour, Rudi?'

Rudi smiled.

'Of course, Uncle.' Rudi handed a drink to Bruno. The three men lifted their glasses in a silent toast.

'You got through the frontier alright this morning, I take it?'

'Yes, Uncle, no problem. Although it was a bit nerve-racking, I must say. Oh, by the way, a Major Weiser sends his best wishes.'

'Ah yes, Weiser, a good man. He, shall we say, sympathises with us. A very useful man to have on your side. We have many things to talk about tonight.'

He turned to Bruno who up until now had remained silent.

'I'm sure that you must have a thousand questions that you want answering?' He said smiling. 'I promise you that I'll tell you everything over dinner. Oh, by the way, the film was collected this afternoon.'

'I must say, sir,' said Bruno, 'there are a number of things that puzzle me. For instance, until half an hour ago, I had no idea that you knew my father personally.'

'Bruno, your father and Max were sergeants in my regiment. We all served together throughout the 1914 war. General Altmann was our commanding officer. My God, you should have seen your father and Max in action. They were a formidable team. Max, by the way, is far more than my servant and has saved my life at least twice. He's as involved as any of us in all of this and I'd trust him with my life. You should do the same. It's dinnertime so let's continue this conversation over a good meal, shall we?'

'That's a good idea,' said Bruno, 'I'm starving.' The other two men laughed. They all headed out into the hall, Max was waiting there, and he helped them all on with their coats.

Stefan turned to Max and said, 'Don't forget our visitor this evening Max. He should be here at about 11 p.m.'

'I won't forget, sir,' answered Max, nodding.

'Good,' said Stefan chuckling. 'We'll have a council of war and see if we can't do these Nazis some real damage.' Stefan opened the front door and led Rudi and Bruno out into the cold, autumn night.

The three men linked arms and walked across the dimly-lit, cobbled square. They walked down the hill. In the distance, at the bottom, a tram went clanking past, the passengers illuminated by the yellow, interior lights. At the bottom they turned right. Spillmann's Restaurant stood a few yards in front of them on the right-hand side just before the bridge that crossed the fast-flowing Rhine.

As they entered, the headwaiter saw them immediately and rushed over. 'Good evening, Herr Wagner. Welcome. Your usual table's ready, if you'll follow me.'

Stefan said, 'Thank you, Felix.' The waiter led them to a secluded table, set in an alcove. There was a large window with a view looking across the river, and you could see the lights of the buildings twinkling on the other side. The three men sat and ordered apéritifs, the waiter handing them the menus and leaving. All around them was the buzz of conversation and the tinkling of glasses and cutlery from the other guests. They were sitting far enough away for it not to intrude.

Looking at Bruno, Stefan began, 'I promised you an explanation, Bruno. Well, here goes. After the war, your father returned to Berlin, his native city. Max and I came here. You see our father had set up a banking business in the 1890s. The bank had prospered and I went into the business with him. Your father, Rudi, preferred to follow his career as an engineer. He served in an engineer battalion during the war. When our father died, it was 1920 and I took over the bank. I heard nothing of your father, Bruno, for many years. Joseph Altmann of course, knew him well. He was a committed communist and became one of the leaders in Berlin. Right from the beginning, he was virulently anti-Nazi. As you are both aware, it was all-out war between the two groups. There were some very vicious street battles. Konrad was a big man, as you know Bruno, and was totally fearless. This I know from our experiences in the trenches together. Anyway, when he was killed, Joseph told his father, who in turn told me. I knew about you and decided to do all in my power to help. Joseph had told me how bright you were.'

Stefan was interrupted by the arrival of the headwaiter.

They ordered and he continued, 'I invested a certain amount of money in your name. Over the years that investment's done very well indeed in fact, and your whole education has been paid for out of that investment. You are now a rich young man and the investment's getting bigger every year. The original money was repaid a long time ago so now it's all yours. However, that doesn't mean that you can buy a luxury apartment and a Mercedes.'

Stefan smiled.

'Our friends over there would get very suspicious if an impoverished young student were to start flaunting lots of money.'

Bruno's mouth was wide open — the shock and surprise were written all over his face.

'I can't believe this. I owe you so much. How can I ever repay you?'

'Bruno, you owe me nothing. It's been a pleasure to help the son of an old comrade.'

The first course arrived and the three men started to eat with relish.

After a while, Stefan turned to Rudi and said, 'Now, to your little problem, Rudi. I was in Berne this afternoon talking with some contacts in the Swiss Government.'

Rudi and Bruno were again alert, hanging onto Stefan's every word.

'It won't be a problem to get entry visas for the Goldmanns. I've guaranteed employment for Otto and Rachel and also Sam's education costs. I'm owed a few favours. You know the sort of thing: free investment advice. All they have to do is go to the Swiss Embassy and ask for Herr Reichling. By tomorrow he'll be expecting them. They have no need to worry. This afternoon I also made a phone call to Nazi-party headquarters on the Wilhelmstraße.'

He laughed and then continued. 'I had a conversation with a particularly odious man by the name of Rudolph Nieper. He's a deputy gauleiter, very high up in the party. He's been siphoning off party funds for years and made a very nice little nest egg for himself. I've told him to expect a visit from Max. All that I said was that he would be carrying an important letter from me. It would be in his best interests to help. What I plan to do is to use the carrot-and-stick method. If he helps ... don't worry, he will.... I'll offer to make his bank account healthier. If, on the other hand he refuses, then someone will send documentary evidence to our friends in Prinz-Albrecht-Straße. That should put the fear of God into him. I'll also tell him that if anything were to befall Max, he'll be dead within a week.' This was said in a very matter of fact way, but it was clear that Stefan was deadly serious. 'I'll suggest, very politely of course, that it would be in his interests to make a few calls to the various departments that the Goldmann's will need to visit. That should do the trick.'

'God, I hope that you're right, uncle. We have to get them out.'

'Don't worry, my boy. It will happen. He's not the only one, you know. I have a list, a very long list, and everyone on that list will do as I tell them or they'll suffer the consequences.' Stefan's voice was ice cold as he said it. 'I've enough on these people to send them all to the guillotine and it would give me great satisfaction to do it.' He looked at the two boys, smiled and said, 'The next thing is Otto's business. The way things are in Germany today it'll be almost impossible for him to sell to another Jew. They have enough problems of their own without taking on any more. If he sells to a German, he'll only get a fraction of its value. There are many Germans ready to take advantage of the Jew's plight. Today, I spoke to my lawyers in Berlin and told them to draw up some legal documents. I'm going to make an offer for the business. My name won't appear anywhere. The buyers will be one of my companies. I'm offering to buy everything, shop and stock, even the furniture. That way we'll be able to have the furniture shipped here without any problem. I want you to phone him tomorrow and tell him to go to their offices and sign the papers. The money will then be transferred to his account very quickly.'

'I must say, that's very generous of you, Uncle.'

'Not at all, it's a very good business. Now, the next and most important point. Since the fifth of this month, that is October, the Jews in Germany have been forced to have the capital 'J' stamped on both their passports and identity cards. That is along with the added insult of having to have the name Sara or Israel on their documents. This capital 'J' business is due in great part to the Swiss government. They've put pressure on the Germans mainly because they fear a mass exodus of Jews over their frontier. Scandalous I know, but there it is. Without the 'J', the Goldmann's will never be allowed into Switzerland and so it's crucial that that's been done. When you phone Otto tomorrow, Rudi, please tell him to make sure that their papers have all of the correct stamps. If they turn up at the Swiss Embassy without that 'J', they'll be turned away.'

'Alright, Uncle, I'll see to it.'

'Good, I hope that all your questions have been answered satisfactorily? Now, what's for dessert, I wonder?'

29

The three men left the restaurant at 10.30pm. There was slight drizzle in the air as they walked up the hill to Münsterplatz. Bruno was in a complete daze. 'What other surprises would tonight bring?' he wondered They entered No 14 and Max took their coats. Rudi excused himself for one moment.

Entering the library, Bruno turned to his benefactor and said, 'Sir, I'm truly lost for words; 'thank you' doesn't seem enough, but believe me when I say that I'm grateful.'

Stefan put his arm around Bruno's shoulder and said, 'Listen, young man, I've never married. I'm an old bachelor. With your permission, I would like to think of you as the son that I never had. To be able to do something for you has been a pleasure. I've followed your progress ever since you were a teenager with great interest. Joseph has kept me fully informed and I'm very proud of your achievements.'

Bruno, looking at the older man, said, 'Since my father died, having no family to speak of, Rudi and I are like brothers. I'd give my life for him and know that he'd do the same for me. Now, I have a new father. You don't need my permission, sir. I would be very honoured.'

Smiling, Stefan said, 'Good,'

At that moment, Rudi walked in followed by Max.

'Let's have some brandy. Would you pour, Max? Have one yourself.'

The doorbell rang. Max excused himself and went to answer it.

'That'll be our visitor,' said Stefan.

The door opened and a tall, slim man came striding in. Like Stefan, he had the bearing of a military man. He was about sixty years old, with short grey hair and he wore an immaculate pin-striped suit, a waistcoat with a gold chain for a pocket watch, and the regimental tie of the Grenadier Guards.

He looked at everyone in the room, gave a little bow and said in faultless German, 'Good evening, gentlemen.'

Stefan stepped forward, held out his hand, and said, 'Hello Claude, let me introduce everyone. Max, you already know. This is my nephew, Rudi, and this is Bruno.'

Claude Brown shook hands with everyone. Rudi was surprised when he realised that Mr Brown was English. They all sat down. Max poured the brandy, including one for himself. He joined the group.

Stefan said, 'Claude works at the British Embassy. He's, shall we say, fully aware of our little group and our activities. In fact, all of the information that we've collected over the years has been passed on to his organisation.'

Nodding, Claude began, 'Yes, thank you for the latest. The film that you brought over today went into the diplomatic bag to London this evening. I've been given a message for you. Someone who's very important and I suspect will become even more important in the future has asked me to say thank you for all of your efforts. He's very aware of the grave danger that you face.' He paused, looked at Rudi and Bruno, and continued. 'In the British Parliament this gentleman said, about the Munich agreement, of which he's ashamed, "This is only the beginning. The first foretaste of a bitter cup, unless by a supreme recovery of moral health and martial vigour, we arise again and make our stand for freedom." Mr Churchill, gentlemen, spoke those words. He's not fooled by Hitler and his promises of no further territorial claims in Europe. He's been warning the British people for years about Hitler. The trouble is no one wants to listen.'

He stopped talking. Everyone could tell that he was angry.

'Mr Churchill is being kept informed of all that you and the General are doing, unofficially, I might add. The General confirms what we already suspected, that is, that Hitler will take over the rest of Czechoslovakia within six months. There's nothing that we can do about it.'

Rudi looked at Mr Brown and said, 'What, in your opinion, will happen next?'

'There'll be war. It's not a case of if but when. My opinion, and that of Mr Churchill, is that we have about a year. Mr Chamberlain came back from Munich waving his useless piece of paper and talking about "Peace in our time." The only good thing to come out of this damned agreement is that we've been given a respite, some time to prepare. Make no mistake, that madman wants war. That's why every piece of information that your group can pass on to us could be vital.'

Stefan looked around and said, 'Well, it's nice to know that our efforts are appreciated. We'll of course carry on. If we can help to destroy Herr Hitler and his crew, then we will.'

Looking at Rudi, Claude Brown asked, 'Do you speak English?'

'Yes, I do. Why do you ask?'

'What about you, Bruno?' said Brown.

Bruno hesitated, shook his head and replied in German, 'No, I don't.'

'No matter, you can always learn.'

'Why do you ask?' persisted Rudi.

'We'll come back to that in a moment,' said Brown, 'I've the germ of an idea. However, I'll have to sell it to my superiors. The problem is that, at the moment, Mr Churchill holds no government post. That, I promise you, will change once we're at war. Britain will need a strong leader and I think that Churchill will be the man. I must say that we're very impressed with the way your organisation's being run — very professional. You can rest assured that there are very few who know about you. We're keeping it on a need-to-know basis and I promise you that it'll stay that way.'

'There's something that you two young men should know,' said Stefan. 'Max, here, is a frequent visitor to Germany. He goes across the frontier from time to time, don't you Max?'

Max nodded.

'Sometimes not quite legally. If you're ever in trouble, he'll do his best to get you out. Try to call this number if at all possible. All you need to say is ... let's think of a code word.'

'I know,' said Rudi, who'd been an avid reader of Dickens as a boy, 'How about, "Pickwick"?'

Brown roared with laughter, 'A very good choice, my boy.'

Bruno frowned.

'Pickwick,' he repeated, in a strong German accent.

'Let's take a break for a while. Some coffee would be nice, I think. Would you do the honours, Max?' Max nodded and left the room.

Stefan watched him go and said, 'Boys, remember, you can trust Max with your life. He's got me out of some very dangerous situations in the past. Don't think for one moment that you're alone out there, because you're not. We've spent a number of years building up this group, as Claude here says. We're very well organised and will do everything in our power to help keep you out of trouble.'

Max came back into the room carrying a tray of coffee and some sandwiches. 'Ah! Wonderful,' said Stefan.

Bruno lifted his hand as if he were at school and said, 'What Rudi and I want to know is, what's going to happen when we graduate? It's only a few months away now and then it'll be the military for us. I tell you now I'll not serve them. If I did, it would make a mockery of all that we're trying to achieve now.'

Nodding his agreement, Rudi said, 'Bruno's right. We have to have an answer to this question this evening. I for one want a definite solution.'

Stefan said, 'You're both quite right. Here's my answer. You're far too valuable to us in Germany for the moment. We need you there. When your call-up papers arrive you come to pay your old uncle a last visit. You don't go back.'

'Fine,' said Rudi, 'but if there's to be war, do you think that we'll be content to sit here and do nothing?'

'Why do nothing?' said Mr Brown, quietly. He put his hand into his pocket and took out a silver cigarette case, opened it and lit up a Senior Service. He continued, 'Why not carry on with what you're doing now?' Rudi and Bruno looked at him. They were puzzled. 'This is what I was hinting at earlier. Why not come and work for us? Imagine how invaluable it'd be to have a group working for us in the heart of the Reich? It'd be bloody dangerous, but isn't what you're doing now dangerous? If I put my idea to Mr C. I'm sure that he'd jump at the chance. At the moment he can do nothing. My suggestion is this: when you finally have to leave Germany, you come to London. Leave all the arrangements to me. We can set up a German desk. It's perfect.' Brown's excitement was infectious.

'Now that's a brilliant idea,' said Bruno, beaming. 'I said that I'd be working for the English didn't I, Rudi?'

Rudi smiled, 'Yes, you did. You're right, it is a brilliant idea.'

'Claude, you never cease to amaze me. Have you discussed this with Churchill?' said Stefan.

'Well, let's say that it has been mentioned. However, at the moment this is just an idea. For now, let's leave things exactly as they are.' Brown took his watch out of his waistcoat pocket and glanced at it. 'My God, it's 3am. I must be off. I'm on the early flight to London tomorrow. Let me just repeat once more that Mr C. is grateful to you all. I promise you that he won't forget. When the time comes, we'll be contacting you, I'm sure.' Mr Brown got up and they all shook hands. Max helped him on with his coat and Brown said goodnight as he strode out of the room.

Major Claude Brown MC, of His Majesty's secret intelligence service, known as MI6, sat in his car. He gave a little smile to himself. He was very pleased with the outcome of tonight's work. Perhaps it would sow the seeds of a resistance group, which would operate in the heart of Nazi Germany. *Mr Churchill will be very pleased,* he thought, as he pulled away from the curb.

30

Max Adler knocked quietly on Stefan's study door and entered, carrying a pot of coffee. It was 10am. Stefan looked up, smiled, and said, 'Pour us both a cup, Max, and sit down,' Max did as he was bid. 'I think a trip to Berlin's a good idea.'

Max said, 'I'll go on tonight's sleeper. I'll be able to see that pig Nieper tomorrow afternoon.'

With a cold smile, Stefan said, 'Squeeze him hard. I want those exit visas within a week. You'll use the house as usual?'

'Yes, everything that I need's there.'

'It's essential that we keep the existence of this particular bolthole from the Altmann Circle. That includes both Bruno and Rudi. If ever the Black Cat is compromised, we have a second place that no one knows about. What did you think of Brown's idea last night?'

'It has merit. Everything's in place and we're as professional as any intelligence service that I know. A British group wouldn't last five minutes in a Germany at war. But, there are huge problems. Any group would be very isolated, a long way from help. They'd have to be self-sufficient and I don't have a great deal of faith in politicians.'

'Yes, but it's feasible. We'll have to put our heads together, Max, and see what we can come up with. One thing's for sure, Switzerland will stay totally neutral in any future war. The Swiss won't take kindly to any spy organisation operating on their territory; the frontier will be closed tighter than a drum.'

Max smiled. 'That shouldn't be a great problem, although I agree, the Swiss won't want to do anything to upset Hitler.'

Sighing, Stefan added, 'Anyway, as Brown says, let's leave it for the moment and see what happens. As things are, I've little faith in the British and we can't fight the Nazis alone.'

'Oh, I don't know, we're having a damn good try.'

'Max, go and sort that bastard Nieper out,' said Stefan, laughing.

Max looked at Stefan and asked, 'Do you think that it would be an idea to get rid of him … send a message?'

'It's tempting, I must admit. We don't, on the other hand, want to start acting like a bunch of Chicago gangsters. For that matter, we don't want to draw attention to ourselves. No, leave him alone, unless of course it's absolutely necessary.' Stefan finished his coffee, stood up and said, 'It's time those two young men were out of bed. Make them some breakfast, Max. I think it would be a good idea if they were to spend a few days touring our pretty little country. Rudi's only going to fret about his Rachel otherwise. Oh, and don't forget, Max, one week maximum!' Max nodded and left the room.

31

Leaning against the bonnet of the gleaming black Humber, the driver, Albert Perkins was reading that morning's edition of the Daily Mirror. He gave a contented sigh as he inhaled the smoke from the Woodbine stuck into the corner of his mouth, exhaling the smoke in two columns through his pinched nostrils. Albert was a small man, wearing a battered trilby and a large overcoat over a crumpled suit. It was said, by everyone who knew him, that the diminutive little cockney had no equal when it came to a knowledge of cars and their engines.

Looking up, he heard the sound of the approaching Imperial Airways aircraft and knew that the Major would soon come bounding out of the terminal with his usual energy, he not being subject to the usual customs formalities as ordinary mortals. Dropping the butt of the cigarette, he ground it out with the sole of his scuffed shoe, folded his newspaper and put it into his overcoat pocket. He'd seen a horse that he fancied in the 3.30 at Newmarket and hoped that he'd be back in London in time to place a bet. Fat chance, he thought to himself. Looking over to the entrance of the terminal building, he saw Brown push open the glass swing - door and emerge into the watery sunlight. Claud paused, looked over in Perkins direction, and strode over. Straightening himself up Albert walked over to the rear of the car and opened the back door, knowing full well that the Major would be in a tearing hurry as usual. As Brown arrived at the car, Albert held out his hand and took the battered suitcase offered by his master. He opened the boot, put the suitcase inside, and closed the boot with a click. Albert never slammed car doors. Walking round to the front, Albert could see that the Major had already settled himself comfortably into the luxurious, leather-upholstered interior and was absorbed with that morning's edition of The Times.

Opening the driver's door, Albert climbed in, looked through the rear view mirror and said, 'Down to Chartwell is it, sir?'

'That's right, Perkins, and get your foot down. I want to be back in London asap'

'Right you are, sir.' Albert enjoyed their frequent visits to the Churchill residence. Mrs B, the housekeeper, always made sure that he had a large slice of her famous cherry cake and as much tea as he could drink. In his dreams, Albert could see himself and the large, rosy cheeked housekeeper running a little B and B down in Brighton. The two men drove in silence, Brown absorbed in his newspaper. While Perkins concentrated on his driving, he hummed a tune under his breath that he'd heard only the other evening at the Palladium, the car's engine purring like a contented cat as they sped towards Chartwell. It was hard to imagine, reflected Albert, as they headed into the weald of Kent, that the beautiful old house was only 25 miles from the centre of London. As Perkins pulled into the drive, Brown stretched and put his newspaper to one side. He looked through the windscreen towards the house that was Churchill's home and sanctuary. The building had windows stretching along the whole length on two floors. At each end, jutting out from the house were two wings, the right hand one being partially covered in ivy. The front door was set in the centre, with two knee-high balustrades on either side stretching the length of the building. On the roof were four large chimney stacks. From a distance you could see a small spire topped with a weather vane at the back of the house. On the left was an annexe on the ground floor with a doorway. Pulling up to the front door, the car came smoothly to a halt and the two men got out.

'I suppose that you're off to see Mrs B for some tea, eh, Perkins?' said Brown with a smile. 'I shouldn't be too long. See if you can scrounge some of that delicious cake for me, will you? Something to nibble on the way back to London, there's a good chap.'

'I'll see what I can do, sir,' said Perkins as he headed towards the back of the house.

Turning, Claud headed towards the front door. As he was about to knock, the door opened and standing there stood Clementine Churchill with an armful of flowers. Claud smiled and touched his hat respectfully.

Mrs Churchill's face lit up. 'Morning, Claud, I heard your car, I was just about to try my hand at some flower arranging. Winston's in the study; do go on through,' she said without pausing.

'Thank you ma'am, I'll go straight through,' he walked into the hallway, taking off his hat and coat.

'Oh, Claud, will you be staying for lunch?'

'Very kind of you, ma'am, but sadly I won't have time,' he said, glancing over his shoulder.

'Never mind, next time perhaps?'

Claud knocked and waited. He heard what sounded like a growl from the interior and entered the study through a studded oak door. This large room was in the oldest part of the house and was said to date back to 1086. He could see above his head the wooden beams of a high, pitched ceiling. The floor, also of wood, had two long carpets, one going from wall to wall and one stretching from the fireplace down the centre of the room. At intervals around the walls were bookcases filled with numerous volumes, oil paintings hung at intervals, and above the fireplace was a large, gilded mirror. Churchill was standing, his upper torso bent slightly forward, leaning over a desk looking at some papers. His reading glasses were perched on the end of his nose and his trademark cigar was jutting out of the corner of his mouth.

'Ah, Claud, what news of our friends in Germany? All is safe, I hope? Did you bring some interesting tit-bits for me?' Churchill straightened and removed his glasses. 'Come, sit and tell me of your adventures. First, however, some tea.' Churchill rang a bell and the two men sat down facing each other.

'Yes, sir, I've lots of news. I was in Basel with some of the group yesterday evening, and I must say that I'm impressed with both their dedication and professionalism. I was particularly impressed with two young men who've just joined the group. One is the nephew of Stefan Wagner.'

'Ah, Herr Wagner, I'd like to meet him some day. If only there were more like this group in Germany, eh, Major,' using Claud's rank for the first time. 'They face grave danger every day. The General continues to furnish us with excellent intelligence?' This was a question but sounded more like a statement. For two hours Claud Brown briefed Churchill on every aspect of the Altmann Circle, including the meeting the previous evening in Basel and his idea of having an anti-Nazi group working in the heart of Germany in the event of war. Churchill was enthusiastic.

Claud finished speaking. Churchill lit a cigar and blew a plume of smoke towards the ceiling and he sighed. 'At the moment Major, I'm in the wilderness, but, when war comes, and come it will, I hope for high office, and I promise you that I will do everything in my power to help our brave friends who risk their lives in that vile nest of vipers.' Churchill stood, bringing the meeting to an end, and the two men shook hands. As Claud walked towards the door Churchill growled, 'Keep me informed Claud. I want to know everything.' Claud Brown nodded and left.

32

Standing in front of the mirror in his luxurious apartment in Albert Court, Claud adjusted his black bow-tie. He left his dressing room and entered the lounge. Glancing through the window he could see the Royal Albert Hall lit by the street lamps. There was an Elgar concert on this evening, he remembered. It would have been nice to go but he had an important dinner engagement that night in his club. Putting on his dark overcoat he turned out the lights and left. Walking out of the entrance he headed towards Kensington Gore. He hailed a taxi and jumped in, gave the address of the club, lit up a cigarette, and settled into the seat.

Sitting in a battered, leather armchair which had probably been there since the Crimea, Sir Robert Albright, the head of His Majesty's Secret Intelligence Service, stretched out his legs and idly twirled the stem of his sherry glass. Wearing immaculate evening dress, the stocky ex-rugby player who'd been an Oxford blue, waited for Claud to arrive. Taking a sip of the dry sherry, Claud's boss looked around the reading room at the other occupants. The place was quiet this evening, with only a few members present. From time to time you could hear a discreet cough or the rustle of a newspaper. Albright smiled to himself — *a bit like an elephant's graveyard* he reflected. The door opened on the far side of the room and Brown entered, spotted Albright, strode over and sat down. A steward discreetly walked over, took their drinks order and left as quietly as he'd come.

'Well, Claud, did you see the great man?'

'I certainly did, and he's really excited about our German friends. I spent about two hours telling him everything.'

Albright, grunted, smiled and said, 'Winston's got his own private intelligence service. It's amazing the number of people in high places who spend hours at Chartwell passing on top secret and classified information. As if the official secrets act didn't apply to him. Our dear Winston's sources of information are better than the whole S.I.S. put together.'

'There's a lot of truth in that. He commands the most incredible loyalty. However, "Cometh the hour, cometh the man" and I think Winston's hour is fast approaching.'

'God, I hope you're right. The stuff you brought out yesterday shows us which way the wind's blowing. The General's sure that Hitler will occupy the rest of Czechoslovakia within the next six months, but what will he do after that I wonder? I was over at the War Office this morning and passed on the latest info' to army intelligence,' Sir Robert smiled. 'Our friends would love to know where we're getting our information from, but the General and his group belong to us.'

'Will you use them in case of war?'

'Damn right I will. This idea of having a group inside Germany working for us is a bloody good one; we'd be fools not to use them. Our masters in Whitehall may have their heads stuck in the sand and their arses stuck in the air, but I don't. Anyway, the General's been passing solid gold information to us for years. We'll just keep it running and pray that they don't get rumbled.'

'These two young men, Rudi and Bruno, are impressive; a little green perhaps, but none the less, I took the liberty of promising them that we'd use them when they have to leave Germany. They're expecting to be called up after they leave university and they have no intention of serving Herr Hitler.'

'That's alright, we don't have to put them on the payroll, at least not officially. Don't worry, Claud, I know a golden opportunity when I see one. Now, when are you going back to Switzerland?'

'The day after tomorrow.'

'Good. Now let's go and have some dinner.' Sir Robert rubbed his hands, smiled and stood up. 'You know Claud,' he said, putting an arm around Brown's shoulder, 'the heavens have smiled on us with the Altmann Circle, I can feel it in my bones.' Claud smiled and nodded as they both headed towards the dining room.

33

'That's it,' murmured Max half aloud, addressing the silent room. Reaching into the large solid wardrobe he took out a long leather overcoat, a button-sized Nazi party badge on the left lapel catching the light. Anyone looking into this wardrobe could be forgiven if they thought that they'd wandered by mistake into a military tailor's shop. Along the whole length, there was a row of immaculately-tailored uniforms: Army, Navy, Airforce, SS, Brownshirt — each having the epaulette of a middle-ranking officer and all were tailored to fit Max. Stepping back, Max threw the coat onto the bed and closed the wardrobe's massive doors. The room had a slight chill in the air and a musty smell, suggesting that it'd been empty for some time, which it had. The house was situated outside the centre of Berlin, on one of the many lakes that could be found in that city. Its situation was ideal, being quiet and secluded, which suited Max perfectly. The house itself was built in the style of a Swiss chalet and had been constructed entirely of wood. A path led down to a jetty on the lakeside, where a large motor launch was moored. Stefan had bought this particular house and he'd presented the deeds to Max a few years previously as a gift for his service and loyalty. The houses along this stretch of lake were generally owned by rich bankers and industrialists, along with a few high ranking Nazis. The owners of these properties had bought them for the very reason that they were secluded — a good place to take their mistresses and lead their lives out of the spotlight. Walking down the staircase, Max entered the open-plan living room. He paused, trying to decide whether or not to light the log fire and bring some warmth into the house. No, better to do it when I come back, he decided. Anyone looking at the way he was dressed now would automatically assume that he was Gestapo, which was just as he wanted it. He wore a trilby, a dark suit and the long, black leather coat. Tucked into a shoulder holster under his left armpit there nestled a gleaming, black Mauser pistol. Slipping the letter from Stefan into his inside pocket he left the house and climbed into a powerful Mercedes saloon. He turned the ignition and the engine came to life with a throaty roar. Right, Herr Neiper, time to pay you a visit, he thought as he pulled away from the chalet.

Driving under the Brandenburg Gate he turned right into the Wilhelmstraße, *the centre of the web*, he thought to himself. Pulling into the curb, he saw on the left-hand side, wedged between the Justice ministry and the Propaganda ministry, Nazi party headquarters. Turning off the engine, Max took a deep breath and opened the car door. He stood looking up at the building for a moment and then walked towards the entrance. As he entered, he saw a group of four Brownshirts talking quietly together. He approached them and they fell silent, eyeing him suspiciously.

Smiling inwardly to himself, he thought that his disguise seemed to be working. Raising his right arm casually he murmured, 'Heil Hitler.' The four men nodded and gave the required response. 'I'm looking for the office of Deputy-Gauleiter Nieper,' Max said quietly. He raised an eye, looking from one to the other.

The oldest of the four responded, 'If you go up to the first floor, it's the door directly in front of you.' Nodding, Max headed in the direction indicated. The men watched his retreating back, 'I wonder what the Gestapo want with Rudolph?' murmured one of the Brownshirts. He walked over to the nearest telephone, lifted the receiver and dialled. The phone was answered immediately. 'You have a visitor on the way up, he looks like Gestapo,' there was a murmur from the other end and the Brownshirt quietly put down the telephone.

Directly in front of Max was a door with a gleaming brass plaque which said *Deputy-Gauleiter R. Neiper.* Max knocked and, without waiting for a reply, walked in. The man sitting behind the desk facing Max was wearing the brown uniform of the SA, with gold leaves on his collar indicating his high rank. At one time he'd obviously been large and muscular, but now the muscle was rapidly giving way to fat. *'Too many sausages and too much beer,'* Max thought to himself as he looked over at his adversary. Nieper's totally bald head gleamed in the overhead light that filled the room on this dark, dull October day.

He looked at Max suspiciously through small piggy eyes and said, 'Who are you and what do you want?'

Max gave a cold smile, said nothing and walking over to the desk, pulled out a chair and, without being invited, sat down. 'I think that you're expecting a visit from me. Herr Wagner from Basel asked me to come and see you.' Slowly putting his hand into his inside pocket he withdrew the letter from Stefan and handed it over.

Neiper relaxed visibly and at once became jovial. 'I'm so sorry Herr … I didn't catch your name.' Without waiting for a reply, he continued, 'How is Herr Wagner? Well, I hope?' He took the letter and picked up a paper knife, slitting carefully along the top of the envelope. Neiper looked over at his office door as if to make sure that it was closed properly and took out the letter. Opening it up he began to read. Max said nothing; he just sat there watching him.

Neiper's face visibly altered as he began to read, going from white to red and back to white again. 'This is fucking blackmail,' he spluttered, his face puce and his hands shaking with anger. 'How dare you come into this office and try to put this shit over on me!'

'Tut,tut, Neiper,' said Max quietly. 'Slow down, you'll give yourself a heart attack. I suggest that you start using whatever brain you have. For a start we've got you by the balls. Now, Herr Wagner's not asking too much of you. Only that you help our Jewish friends to get out of here without any problems.' Max stopped and gave a cold smile. It was obvious that Neiper was beginning to realise his predicament. 'It's very simple,' he continued, 'You have a choice; either you do as you're told or we send a fat, juicy dossier over to our friends in Prinz-Albrecht-Straße. Now, what's so difficult about that?'

Neiper visibly wilted in front of Max's eyes and he knew that he was beaten. He growled, 'You bastards. Who are these fucking Jews anyway?'

'That's not your affair. I think that Herr Wagner's being particularly generous to you. After all, he's offering you a substantial amount of money for this small favour, which is more than I would do you slimy piece of shit!' said Max, with ice in his voice. 'I'm sure that our friends in the Gestapo would love to get their hands on your fat carcass for a few hours. Now, if Herr Wagner doesn't hear from you within a few days, you know what to expect. There's no discussion Neiper. We don't care how you do it. If you have to grease a few palms, that's your problem. Just fucking do it.'

Neiper was boiling with anger. This man sitting in front of him was right. He was well and truly caught. The thought of ending up in the Gestapo's torture chambers filled him with dread. He had no allusions to his fate; after all he'd sent enough people to the Gestapo himself. Sighing, he looked at Max and said quietly, 'Alright, leave it with me, I'll make sure your fucking Yids get out, and good riddance.'

'Now that's very sensible. You have their names and details so see to it. Oh, and one other thing: we don't want our Jewish friends to have any problems at the airport. They intend to take the morning flight from Tempelhof on the first of November. Make sure that no Nazi bureaucrat causes them any trouble at passport control. Herr Wagner wants their exit from this benighted country to be smooth and trouble free.' Max stood up and bent forward placing his hands onto the desk. His craggy features inches from Neiper's face, his eyes cold, he added menacingly, 'Don't forget, a few days, no more.' Straightening up, Max walked over to the door. He stopped, turned, and looked over at the dazed Deputy-Gaulieter. 'Neiper, you should pray that our paths don't cross again.' Max opened the door and left as quietly as he'd arrived.

34

Driving into Savignyplatz, Rudi pulled up outside the Goldmann's shop and jumped out of the car. He saw Otto behind the counter serving a customer and pushing the door open he walked in.

A smile of pleasure passed over Otto's face as he saw the young man and said, 'Good evening, Rudi, go on up. I'll just finish serving this lady and then I'll close up.'

'Evening Otto, I'll see you upstairs.' Running up, he walked in, saw Rachel and strode over, his face lighting up with pleasure. She smiled too as she saw him, and soon they were embracing, their lips meeting each other in a long lingering kiss. 'Hello, darling. God, I've missed you.'

'Hello, Rudi. I've missed you too. Things have happened so quickly since you've been away,' she said excitedly. 'Papa will tell you everything.' They both turned as Otto entered, closely followed by Sam.

'Rudi, my boy,' said Otto, embracing the young man, 'Your Uncle is a very efficient man— since yesterday, I no longer own this shop. I must say what a relief it is. I didn't say anything at the time but I was worried and didn't think that I'd have any chance of selling it.'

'I know Otto. That's why Uncle made the offer. Now that the shop's, shall we say, German owned, there'll be no problem having the furniture shipped to Switzerland after you've left. Apparently, there are a lot of formalities involved and we want to make your leaving as simple as possible. God knows it's complicated enough, without making it more difficult.' Looking over at Sam, Rudi gave a big smile. 'Hello, Sam, excited?'

'I'll say, Rudi,' replied the boy, smiling.

'I'll make some coffee,' said Rachel, 'and then we can talk.'

'Yes, we must have a council of war; we've a lot of things to sort out.' As Rachel busied herself in the kitchen, the two men and the boy talked about Switzerland. Sam was obviously very excited. Very carefully pushing open the kitchen door, Rachel entered, balancing the tray of coffee in one hand. 'Right,' said Rudi, 'tomorrow we start the business of getting you all out of here. Firstly, do you have your ID cards and passports stamped with the 'J'?'

'Yes,' said Otto. 'Is there no end to the humiliation that these Nazi barbarians will heap on us?'

'Do you know, Rudi,' said Sam, 'the bastards made Papa pay five marks for each stamp.'

'Mind your language Sam,' said Otto. 'The boy's right. I had to pay them for the privilege of being humiliated further. Since we all had to have the names Sara or Israel put onto our papers in August, I didn't think that they could do anything else, but it never stops.'

Rudi nodded. 'I fear that it'll get worse. They're beginning to wage war on you in earnest and that's why we must get you out as soon as possible. Now, I had a call from Uncle when I got back this afternoon and he's heard from this Nazi. You should have no problems when you go to the various departments that you need to visit, that is, if this man's done his work properly. It's going to take some time, however. The three of you will probably have to go to your local police station. You must then go to the tax office and get the *Steuerliche Unbedenklich-keitsbescheinigung,* certifying that you've paid all of your tax. You then need a document stating that you've paid the *Reichsfluchtsteuer,* that is a twenty five percent tax on all of your combined assets. You'll have to visit the bank tomorrow. The swine insist on that in cash. The balance you can then transfer to Uncle's bank.'

'Otto sighed, 'Is there no end to it?'

'I'm afraid not, but it'll be worth it in the end.' Looking across at Sam, Rudi continued, 'At least you won't need the certificate releasing Sam from military service, he's too young. Otto, I'm sorry, but you may need special permission to keep your wedding ring.'

'What! That's monstrous! It hasn't been off my hand since the day I married,' snarled Otto, showing real anger.

Nodding, Rudi said, 'I'm sorry.' He continued, 'You'll certainly have to go to the *Devisenstelle,* the office that deals specifically with emigration, and finally to the Swiss Consulate and Embassy, at 4. Fürst-Bismarck-Straße. That, I think, will be about it, but you can be sure that the beaurocrats will point you in the right direction. As I said, if this Nazi's done his job, God willing you should have no real problems.'

Otto looked at his two children and then at Rudi, 'We owe your uncle a great debt. It's all so daunting the obstacles that they put in our way.'

'They certainly don't intend to make life easy for you, that's for certain, however, I don't intend to be far away. I'll come with you, not actually inside, but not far away. If you run into any problems let me know immediately. Max is in Berlin. I have a number for him and will contact him. I think that's everything. Tomorrow morning we'll start doing the rounds of the various departments. Oh, one other thing, we've booked five seats on the morning flight to Basel on the first of November.'

A few days later, standing outside the Swiss Embassy, Rudi rubbed his hands together. It was starting to get cold. It had taken three days, but now the worst was over.

He looked up and saw the Goldmann's coming out of the main entrance. As he studied their faces his heart soared. Their faces were wreathed in smiles. He could tell that they'd been given their coveted entry visas.

Forgetting where she was, Rachel ran over and flung her arms around Rudi. 'We've done it darling,' she cried, 'We now have everything that we need.'

Lifting her up, he twirled her around and gave a whoop of joy. 'At last! Do you know, this has been the longest three days of my life. Come on, let's find the nearest bar and have a drink.' They all walked away, talking non-stop, happiness radiating from their faces.

Looking at Rudi, Otto said, 'Your uncle must be a very powerful man. It was almost as if those Nazi officials were expecting us and most of them were polite. We had no real problems. The other Jews were being harassed, but us? As soon as they knew our name, things went smoothly, Oh, and I managed to keep my wedding ring.' He shook his head and murmured, 'Incredible, just incredible.'

'Yes Otto, Stefan Wagner is truly an incredible man. If only you knew just how incredible he really is.

35

Hans Erhard the Blockwarden sat down at the kitchen table, opened a bottle of Dortmunder beer, took a swig, and lit a cigarette. The lowest form of Nazi official, Erhard was both hated and feared in equal measure by the local people, not that he cared. It was unfortunate that his apartment was in the same block as Alex's. Erhard was a very dangerous man indeed. In his mid-fifties, he was small in stature with pinched features and a long, thin nose. Lifting the bottle of beer with his large, strong, hands, he took another swig and belched. Erhard had served in the German navy during the 1914 war and had gone on to work as a steward on the German liners after the war. He loathed Jews, envying them their money: the wives with their diamonds and furs, and the men flaunting their wealth. He'd seen many like that on the numerous cruises over the years, having to be at their beck and call every five minutes, and to call them 'Sir' and 'Madam'. In fact, Erhard was jealous of everyone who had more money, better looks, or any sort of talent than himself.

Spread in front of him on the kitchen table was the Nazi party newspaper. He looked down at it, not really seeing the printed words in front of him.

His mind wandered back to November 1925.

The docks in Hamburg had been shrouded in fog. Erhard stood at the top of the gangway and looked down at the quay far below. Fingering a length of knotted, red silk cord that nestled in his pocket like a dormant snake, he shuddered and turned up the collar on his thick, seaman's jacket. The last passengers had long disembarked and were by now heading towards home or the nearest luxury hotel. The crew had two days before the start of the next cruise. Most of them had already headed towards the numerous bars and brothels that Hamburg had to offer. Descending the gangplank, Erhard walked through the dock gates and headed towards a bar that he knew, his heart beating with anticipation and excitement. Lengthening his stride he hoped to find exactly what he was looking for. The fog swirled around him and there was a damp chill in the air, not that he noticed.

Walking into a bar he was immediately engulfed in the smog of smoke from a hundred cigarettes. It was warm in here, the large bar almost full. Spread around the room in various states of drunkenness were a mixture of men and women, laughing and joking; many of the women were prostitutes. That wasn't what Erhard was looking for. He spotted the boy almost immediately and stood in the entrance studying him. The boy was tall and slim with long, floppy blond hair and he was wearing a short jacket and tight trousers which showed off his small, rounded buttocks. His face was almost angelic but, at the same time, there was a hardness about it. This young angel was worldly wise and had almost certainly been around.

Walking over, Erhard stood next to the boy who looked up at him, smiled and nodded.

'Would you like a drink?' said Erhard, taking out a packet of cigarettes and offering the boy one. The boy nodded, took a cigarette and put his hand around Erhard's as he accepted the offered match, an unnecessary gesture as there was not a puff of wind in the bar.

'I'd love a beer please,' said the boy. 'Just off a ship?' he enquired.

'Yes.' Erhard ordered two beers, 'Shall we go and sit down?' They waited for the beers to arrive and found an empty table. The boy lifted his right hand and casually pushed a lock of blond hair that had fallen over his right eye out of the way. He had looked Erhard directly in the face, smiled and licked his top lip from right to left with his moist, pink tongue, giving Erhard a clear signal that he was available, if the price was right. 'What's your name?' Erhard asked, his voice hoarse.

'Oh, you can call me Peter if you like.'

'How much, Peter?'

The boy laughed. 'You don't waste any time do you? Well, that depends on what you want and for how long.'

Erhard had felt his huge erection trying to force its way out of his trousers. 'I want everything,' he answered, looking the boy up and down.

'Everything will cost you fifty marks. You pay for the hotel of course. Is it a deal?' Erhard nodded, not trusting himself to speak. 'I know a hotel just around the corner where they don't ask any questions.' The boy held out his hand, 'Sorry, but money in advance. The hotel will be extra, twenty-five marks.'

Putting his hand into his inside pocket, Erhard took out his wallet and handed over the money.

'Thanks. I can promise you a good time.'

The two men finished their beers, stood up and walked out of the bar.

Stepping into the cold foggy night Peter turned right and Erhard followed, eyeing the young man's slim body, excitement pulsing through him. They entered a dingy, ill-lit hotel foyer, Erhard purposely keeping to the shadows. The proprietor obviously knew the boy. Peter said something to him, the man nodded without interest, and then handed over a key. Peter walked over, smiled at Erhard and led him up to the first floor.

Turning the key in the lock, the boy pushed open the door, walked over, closed the curtains and turned on the bedside lamp. Pushing the door closed behind him, Erhard locked it and put the key into his pocket. 'Get undressed,' he said. Smiling, the boy did as he was told.

'Aren't you going to join me?' he asked coyly. Erhard removed his clothes with haste and the two men soon stood facing each other, naked. The boy, looking down at Erhard's groin exclaimed, 'You're certainly ready, aren't you.' Without saying a word Erhard walked over, put his two hands on the boy's naked shoulders, turned him round and pushed him face down onto the bed. He slipped the length of cord out of his pocket and looked down at the boy's prone, naked body.

Erhard's hips started to move with greater speed and urgency as he approached his climax. Giving a huge groan he ejaculated, sending great spurts of semen, which seemed endless, into the boy beneath him. He sank down, covering the boy's back with his upper torso. 'God you must have needed that!' said the boy. They were the last words he was ever to say. A feeling of overwhelming hate and loathing had come over Erhard. Hate and loathing for himself and for the boy still pinned beneath him. 'You dirty little bum-boy,' Erhard muttered hoarsely. Peter, sensing his grave danger, had tried to struggle free, but it was too late. Slipping the cord around the boy's slim, pale neck, Erhard very slowly pulled and tightened. Wanting the boy's death to be as painful as possible he twisted the garrotte, the act of slow strangulation sexually exciting him. Before the boy finally died, Erhard achieved orgasm two more times, shooting streams of semen over the boy's naked back. It took a long time for the boy to die and Erhard had savoured the boy's agony. Finally he lay still, his tongue protruding grotesquely from the corner of his mouth, his face blue. Erhard climbed off the lifeless body of the boy who only a short time ago had been a living, breathing, human being. He looked down at this once beautiful young man who now lay twisted and grotesque in death. 'Dirty little queer, dirty little queer,' Erhard repeated time after time as he quickly dressed. Looking for one last time at the corpse on the bed, he had quietly unlocked the door, peered out and left the room, locking the door behind him. He went quietly down the stairs. The proprietor seemed to be dozing over the newspaper. Erhard had slipped out of the front door and walked quickly away.

The boy's body wasn't found for several hours. The police came but of course had nothing to go on. Peter became another statistic, a prostitute murdered, one of many killed in that part of the city of Hamburg, for one reason or another.

Hans Erhard had left a trail of such bodies over the years in different parts of the world.

The front door opening outside his apartment brought Erhard back from his thoughts with a start. He heard Paul and Alex laughing and joking as they climbed up the stairs to Alex's apartment. 'Laugh while you can, you spoiled little queers. Your time's coming. You'll have nothing to laugh over when you're inside a concentration camp,' said Erhard to himself. On numerous occasions over the past few months, Erhard had gone quietly up the stairs and stood outside the apartment door, listening, trying to hear some sound that would give a clue as to what was happening inside. He could guess, and was filled with a mixture of jealousy and hate. Now it was time to make his report to his superiors. He smiled with great satisfaction.

At 8am the next morning, Paul and Alex came down the stairs on the way to a rehearsal. Spotting Erhard standing by his apartment door, Paul almost missed his footing. Alex was chattering away as usual. Paul loathed Erhard and could feel the man's eyes following his every move. Paul guessed what was going through Erhard's mind and it made his skin crawl.

'Good morning, young gentlemen,' said Erhard. 'Going to play some music, are we?' Paul nodded.

Alex, who never saw the bad in anybody, was more forthcoming. 'Good morning, Herr Erhard. Yes, we have an important rehearsal this morning. Sorry, can't talk now, we're already late. Goodbye.' A cold smile played over Erhard's face. Paul saw it and an icy chill passed down his spine. For the first time, Paul sensed just how dangerous this man was and the fear that he felt in the pit of his stomach was very real. It was a cold, persistent fear which lingered and wouldn't go away.

Looking at Paul's shapely buttocks as he and Alex walked away, Erhard felt a thrill of sexual longing. Crushing the thought instantly, he muttered to himself, 'Fucking queers.' Erhard turned, walked into his apartment and quietly closed the door. Sitting down, he started to write a report about the two homosexuals for his masters.

36

The long, heavy, grey staff car pulled out of German army headquarters, turned left into Bendlerstraße and headed towards the Tiergarten. Sitting in the car were four men. Three of them were wearing the field-grey uniform of the German army, the fourth was dressed in civilian clothes. The driver was a young, darkly handsome lieutenant who worked for military intelligence, the Abwehr. His name was Axel Weinburger. Next to him, in the passenger seat, sat Major Werner Koenig. Behind him sat the upright figure of General Frederick Altmann, and next to him, the civilian. Inspector Wolfgang Weinburger, a member of the Berlin criminal police and father of the young driver, slouched as he glanced idly out of the window. Many a criminal had foolishly underestimated this untidy little man, who had a mind as sharp as a razor and was certainly not a person to be taken lightly. The four men all had one thing in common: their membership of the Altmann Circle. The man who gave the circle its name sat staring straight ahead, saying nothing. The Iron Cross, first class, with oak leaves and swords, gleamed at his throat, testament to his gallantry in a past war. He was very much a soldier of the old school and to his new masters, had they known it, a traitor!

Glancing to his left, Werner briefly eyed Axel, his mind going back to 1932 when he'd been an instructor at the officer training academy. He'd been impressed with the nineteen-year-old cadet from the beginning. The boy had a sharp mind and was determined to get into military intelligence, a dream that Werner knew would soon be realised.

Inviting him for a drink one evening, Werner, then a captain, had taken him to a beer hall in a rough area of Berlin. He did this purposely, wanting to see his reaction to the numerous Brownshirts that called this bar their own. Entering, the two were immediately engulfed in sound. The hall was huge, with a wooden floor covered in sawdust. Hanging from columns around the room were swastika banners. A smell of stale beer and cigarette smoke hung in the air. The place was a sea of brown uniforms, jackboots and swastika armbands. A brass band played military and Nazi songs to the accompaniment of a group of men hitting the tables with the palms of their hands in rhythm to the music. Waiters, wearing black waistcoats and long white aprons, scurried amongst the clientele weighed down with trays full of foaming steins of beer. The field-grey of their army uniforms stood out and the two were immediately noticed. Their reception was very welcoming, a number of the Nazis giving a cheer and slapping them on the back as they pushed their way through.

Finding an empty table Werner and Axel sat down. Looking towards their nearest neighbours, Werner nodded and smiled.

Turning to Axel, he said into the younger man's ear, 'I want you to use your powers of observation. Look around and take it all in. I want to hear your impressions when we leave here.' Axel nodded, bemused by all of the noise and the undertone of suppressed violence that was in the air.

Detaching himself from a large group standing by the bar, a large man approached the table carrying a litre stein of beer in each hand.

Smiling, he put a beer each in front of them and said loudly, 'Here you are gentlemen, have a beer on us.' Underneath his smile there had been something menacing that was difficult to put a finger on. He continued, 'It's nice to see the army in here. You're welcome.'

'Thanks comrade, much appreciated, I'm sure,' said Werner.

The Brownshirt had glanced at the young cadet. 'You're at the officer training school at Potsdam, are you?' Axel nodded. 'I'll make you a promise young man. When we come to power, the Führer will burn that piece of shit paper, the Versailles treaty. Then we'll have an Army we can really be proud of, not the fucking 100,000 that we're allowed now.' The man's face was flushed with drink and although not drunk he'd obviously had his fair share that evening. He looked around the room and then back at Werner and Axel, 'We were stabbed in the back in '18,' he said, becoming maudlin. 'Those fucking Jews will pay a heavy price for that. Just you wait until Hitler's in charge, things will change for the better. The Yids and the communists had better look out then. We'll wring their fucking necks, and anyone else's who stands in our way. There are going to be big changes in this country very soon.'

Werner had smiled and nodded, 'You're quite right, comrade. Once the Führer's in power, we'll have a country to be proud of.' Axel had looked at Werner in surprise. Werner frowned, quickly warning the boy.

The Brownshirt leered, stood unsteadily and said, 'I'm going to join the comrades over there for a singsong. If you want anything give me a shout. Stay as long as you like. You Army boys are always welcome, Heil Hitler.' Walking away unsteadily the man had headed in the direction of the band and group of Brownshirts in the corner. The captain and the young cadet stayed in the beer hall for a further two hours, friendly Nazis making sure that their glasses were constantly filled. At about 11 p.m., Werner put his hand on Axel's elbow and nodded towards the exit. Getting up, the two men made their way to the door, their ears ringing with the well wishes of their new brown shirted friends.

When they got outside, the two men had taken huge lungfuls of air, breathing in and out deeply. 'Thank Christ that's over. Are you alright, young Axel?'

Axel nodded and replied, 'Yes, thank you, Sir. A bit pissed though.'

Laughing, Werner said, 'You're a soldier, I'd get used to it if I were you.' He suddenly became serious. 'And what did you make of our Nazi friends? Did you do as I told you and keep your eyes and ears open?'

'Oh yes,' said Axel, becoming equally serious, 'To be honest, they frightened me. They seem to hate everyone who's not like them. I don't understand this hatred of the Jews, and what do they mean by us being stabbed in the back? Surely we lost the war fair and square?'

'Yes we did, and as for the Jews, the Nazis need a scapegoat, the Jews are it. If those barbarians get into power, may God help Germany and the Jews because no one else will. I wanted you to come with me for a very good reason this evening Axel. You haven't disappointed me.' The two men walked along in silence for a while, each occupied with his own thoughts. After a few minutes, Werner had said quietly, 'You'll soon be graduating from the academy and going into the Abwher. It's possible that in a few month's time I'll come and see you with a request. If I do, I want you to remember what you saw and heard tonight.'

Axel had nodded and said, 'Very good, Sir.'

Then early in 1934 Werner had been to see Axel and had invited him to dinner. They had a long talk and he explained, without mentioning any names, what he was doing. 'You see, Axel, we need someone's eyes and ears in the Intelligence Service. If they begin to suspect what we're doing, we'll need to know quickly. Someone very high up is risking their life to do this. Will you help us?'

'Sir, I've never forgotten our night out. Everything that you said that night has happened. It would be an honour for me to be your eyes and ears. In fact, I can do better than that, if you'll allow me. Anything that I hear that I think will be useful to you and your group I'll pass on to you. Please let me explain. When I was at school I had a friend who was a Jew. Late last year he was attacked by a group of Brownshirts. He stood up to them and so they kicked him to death. His face was so badly damaged that his parents could hardly identify him. Did you know that my father was a policeman?' he asked. Without waiting for a reply, he continued, 'My father tried everything to find the people responsible. One day he had a visit from the Gestapo and was told that if he knew what was good for him he'd better drop the matter. Now, my father's a good policeman, but he knew that if he carried on he'd lose his job or worse and so, reluctantly he had no choice but to let it go. I suggest that you have a talk with him. I'm sure that he'd love to be given the chance to help you and your group. You see we both have very good reason to hate those bastards!'

Nodding, Werner had shaken hands with the young Axel. From the beginning of 1934, the General and Werner had begun passing on information on the Army and the rapid re-arming of the German armed forces. From time to time, Axel was able to pass on small pieces of intelligence which would possibly be of some use to the British. This was all done through Stefan in Basel. Thus, what was to become known as the Altmann Circle was born.

Werner came out of his reverie as the staff car pulled silently up outside of Max's secluded house, facing the river Havel.

37

Standing with his back towards the roaring, log fire, the General looked at the four men sitting around him. The light of the fire reflected off his gleaming, black jackboots as he stood with his legs slightly apart, his very presence dominating the room. A tall man with a rigid stance and iron-grey, clipped hair, the general looked every inch the Prussian soldier that he was.

'Thank you for inviting us all here this evening, Max, and I think that it's a good idea for us to meet from time to time if it's safe to do so.'

Nodding, Max replied, 'You're all very welcome.'

'Looking back over the past four years since our group was founded,' continued the General, 'I've found no reason to regret my decision to help to do everything in my power to bring down Hitler and his gang. Those of you who know me well, know that it wasn't a decision taken lightly. Look at our country today. People walk in fear of the Gestapo and we all know what's happening to the Jews. Anyone who's deemed a threat by the regime is imprisoned without trial. I've heard numerous reports about what's happening in places like Dachau and Sachsenhausen. Don't forget, all of these crimes are being committed in our name.' Altmann paused, lifted his right hand and touched the iron cross at his neck. 'Make no mistake, Hitler will eventually bring this country to ruin. If, by my actions, I can shorten his stranglehold on our beloved country, it will all have been worthwhile. However, we must all be realistic, getting rid of this man is not going to be easy. There are too many of our countrymen who see him as our saviour and that includes many of my colleagues on the General Staff. They seem blind to what's happening around them. Make no mistake, at the moment, groups like ours are few and far between.' He lifted his hand and extended his first finger. 'Don't any of you be under any allusions about what will happen to you if you're caught. You don't need me to tell you what your fate would be. Now, to the military situation. Within one year, I prophesy that Germany will be at war, a war that we will eventually lose. The little Corporal has great military ambitions and is determined to have his way. I don't have a crystal ball, but I'm sure that he'll turn his attentions towards Poland. Britain and France will not stand by and do nothing this time, although what they could do to help the Poles I don't know. Hitler will attack Poland and I tell you gentlemen that the SS death squads won't be far behind. To Hitler, the Slav peoples are *Untermenschen,* subhuman. He'll have no mercy and will destroy them. Also, don't forget he talks about *lebensraum,* living space for the German people. I believe that eventually the madman will attack Russia, and that will be the beginning of the end for us. Russia has an almost unlimited supply of men to range against us. The country is limitless and terribly unforgiving in winter. If, as happened in the last war, the Americans were to join in against us we would be doomed. Look at the facts. America is a vast powerhouse with huge resources and manpower. If they were to take to the field along with the British Empire and Russia we would eventually be overwhelmed. Believe me when I say that the reckoning, when it comes, will be terrible for us all. Germany will pay a high price.

'What about assassination, General?' asked Max.

'That's a possibility, of course, but not anytime soon. The scenario that I've just mentioned won't happen overnight. The German Army is probably the best in the world today and I should know. I believe that this country, at the beginning, will have great successes and that the German people will be behind Hitler. However, when we start to lose, then possibly a group may try to get rid of him, but not in the foreseeable future. You can pass my views onto our British friends if you like, Max. Of course, it's possible that I may be wrong but somehow I don't think so. When I get anything concrete I will pass it over in the usual way.'

Max looked from the General to the other members of the group and said, 'The British are certainly doing a good job keeping our identity secret. Claude Brown and the head of the SIS are keeping their cards very close to their chests with regards to our group.'

'Let's hope it stays that way for all our sakes,' said Werner.

Axel lifted his hand, rather like a schoolboy in a classroom. He was very aware of his junior status within the group. Looking across at the darkly handsome, young man Altmann nodded. 'There is one thing: I'm sure that no one in military intelligence knows or even suspects of our existence. However, let's not forget the SD. There's no co-operation at all between the two security services. It's madness of course. Canaris and Heydrich are, on the surface, good friends. In fact, they live close to each other and often socialise, going riding together in the Tiergarten on a regular basis. That said there's no way that either would share intelligence with the other. That could be very dangerous for us in this group. If the SD were on to us there'd be no way of knowing.'

'A very good point, Axel,' said Werner, 'but short of having someone in the SD working for us, and there's not much chance of that, there's nothing that we can do.'

'The lieutenant has a good point nonetheless. All that we can do is to remain vigilant,' said the General.

'There's one other thing which is important,' continued Axel, 'and you should pass it on to our British friends. A few days ago I saw a document marked "Top Secret". I took a quick glance and inside I found some interesting information. It seems that we have over 250 agents in place in Britain, many of them working as domestics in the homes of British officials. Also, we have most British airfields and coastal installations mapped, including oil-storage depots.'

There was a collective gasp. Wolfgang beamed and thought, 'Well done my boy'.

'Can you give me names of any of these people?' asked Max urgently.

'Sorry, Max, I wish I could, but there was nothing in the file like that. I suspect that that information is known only to a few. I could try ... '

'No, too dangerous, but thanks anyway Axel,' said Max smiling. He continued, 'It's nice to know that our man inside Tirpitz-Ufer, Abwehr headquarters, is able to give us such sensitive information. You're very useful to us there.' Axel shrugged, as if to say, 'It's nothing'.

The General smiled, glanced at his watch and exclaimed, 'The time! We really must go. There's just one thing. The Nazi regime is, in my opinion, so evil that eventually it will fall. However I fear that we may have to wait a very long time until it does.' Picking up his cap, the General started to make a move. Looking at Max he said, 'Give my best wishes to Stefan and I promise to pass on to him any information that comes my way.'

Max nodded, and the other three rose to leave.

'Wolfgang,' said Max, 'why don't you stay a while and have some supper with me? I can run you back to Berlin later.'

'A marvellous idea, Max. Thank you.'

The three army officers put on their peaked caps, said their farewells and left. Standing in the doorway, Max and Wolfgang watched the red tail-lights of the staff car disappear down the lane and turn onto the main road to central Berlin.

The two men returned to the warmth of the sitting room.

'What a man he is,' said Max.

'Yes, if there were more like him then perhaps Germany wouldn't be in the mess that it's in today. You know, Max, if I could I'd leave the police tomorrow. He's right you know, there's no justice in this country anymore.'

'Come on, Wolfgang. People like you are needed, if only to keep your eye on them.' Clapping his two hands together Max continued, 'Now, what's it to be, scotch?'

'Yes, wonderful, what's for supper? I'm starving.'

'I've a very nice, wild boar stew on the stove, ideal for this weather.'

'Sounds good, Max. Come on I'll give you a hand to lay the table.'

Sitting together after consuming an excellent supper, Wolfgang lit a cigar and gave a contented sigh. 'That was wonderful Max, thanks. You know, after Axel's mother died the most difficult thing I found was how the evenings seemed to be so endless.'

'What was it?'

'Breast cancer.'

'Well, at least you had someone. Sadly I never met a women that I wanted to spend the rest of my life with. Perhaps it's just as well, when you consider my line of work. Talking of that, have you ever come across a man called Rudolph Neiper?'

Coming out of his reverie with a start, Wolfgang looked at Max with surprise, 'Do you mean the Deputy-Gaulieter?'

'The very same.'

'Now there is a name from the past.'

'What do you know about him?'

'I'll tell you,' said Wolfgang. Gathering his thoughts, he continued, 'In 1930 I was a sergeant in the Criminal Police Department in Wedding, as you know, a communist stronghold. One evening, we received a report that a body had been found in an alley. Leaving my office I went straight to the scene. As I arrived a young, uniformed officer told me that the body was that of Conrad Meyer, a local communist leader. He'd been shot in the back of the head at very close range, execution style.'

Sitting on the edge of his seat, Max looked keenly at the police inspector, 'Bruno's father,' he murmured.

'Now, the interesting thing is that pinned to the front of his jacket was a piece of paper with a Swastika drawn on it, a calling card so to speak.'

'This is incredible. You don't know it, but Conrad's son Bruno is a member of our group. The General, Stefan, myself and Conrad all served together in the trenches: Conrad and I were great friends.

'It was Wolfgang's turn to be surprised. He continued. 'We had no clue to the killer's identity, except of course that he or they were Nazis. The news spread through the district like wildfire and for weeks after there was trouble between the two groups. Conrad was very high up in the German Communist Party. The killing, in my opinion had been ordered from the very top.'

'Where does Neiper come into all of this?'

Lifting his hand, Wolfgang murmured, 'Patience my friend.' Taking a sip of his whiskey he continued, 'We had no clue to the identity of the killer until I received a phone call one night from an informant. A particularly odious but useful low-life called Krammer. He'd been very useful to me in the past and continued to be for some years afterwards. He's now serving time for armed robbery in Spandau. Anyway, we arranged a meeting in a bar and he told me that he'd heard talk around the district that Neiper and two others had carried out the killing. The order had come from Röhm himself and he'd been instructed by Hitler who wanted to send a clear message to the communists.'

Giving a whistle, Max said, 'So what happened?'

'A big fat zero! Oh, we had him brought in for questioning. The bastard was able to produce at least a dozen of his Nazi friends who swore that he'd spent the night with them in a beer hall playing cards. In the end we had to let him go. No evidence you see. However, I'm one hundred percent sure that he was responsible and I'll tell you why. Over the years a number of other communists were murdered in similar fashion, right up until the time that the Nazis took power, and Neiper's name always came up. Of course, after 1933 the Nazis were able to murder the communists, and anyone else who stood in their way, with impunity. I could never get enough evidence against him. Let me tell you, it was very frustrating. Anyway, why do you ask me about him?'

Smiling coldly, Max explained what had happened a few days previously and why.

'That sounds about par for the course. I think that our friend Neiper managed to get so high in the party because of all of the killings he carried out for his bosses. You say that Conrad's son works for us?'

'Yes. Stefan looked after him from a distance after his father was killed. Let me tell you, he's a big, very tough character just like his father. Do you know, Wolfgang, I'm very tempted to pass on what you've just told me to Bruno. I'm sure that he'd be delighted to know who killed his father.' Smiling, Max continued, 'Don't be surprised if our friend doesn't end up with a bullet in his head, will you?'

'Don't worry I won't lose any sleep over it. That's one crime that I won't try to solve.'

'Good. You know Wolfgang, I'd really like to spend a couple of hours in a night club tonight, what do you say?'

Giving a huge grin Wolfgang said, 'That's a very good idea. Come on, let's go.'

The next day Max took the afternoon Lufthansa flight to Basel. By the evening he was ensconced with Stefan and Claude, the meeting going on until late into the night.

38

On the stage at the end of the large hall stood a gleaming, black, Bechstein grand piano, to the right of which were four music stands and chairs. Exclaiming with delight as he spotted the piano, Alex hurried down the length of the hall to take a closer look. Looking from one to the other, Paul and the three Jewish musicians grinned at Alex's boyish enthusiasm. There were row upon row of chairs going from the front to the back of the hall. Alex had already climbed up to the stage and was quietly running his fingers lovingly over the keys.

Papa looked at Paul, chuckled, and said, 'There won't be an empty seat in here this evening. We estimate that there'll be at least three hundred in the audience. The Rabbi's delighted. We've raised a lot of money.' As Papa had been talking, they'd been slowly walking towards the front of the hall. The four men climbed up onto the stage and began to take their instruments from their cases, all except the bass which was lying on its side next to the music stand.

Alex stopped playing and said, 'What a programme we have for tonight. There's enough to take us up until midnight. I'm looking forward to this so much.'

'So am I,' said Paul enthusiastically. 'We'll give the audience a night to remember, eh, Papa?'

'I certainly hope so. We can all forget our troubles for a while.' The four string players seated themselves.

Looking over at Alex, Paul winked and said, 'Would the *Wunderkinder* please give us a tuning note?' Alex pulled out his tongue and played an A, and the four string players started to tune their instruments.

'Shall we rehearse the 'Trout' first and then the Brahms?'

'A good idea,' said Isaac. 'Don't forget that I have to swap from bass to viola.'

Papa said, 'I've an idea. Why don't you and Alex play the Mozart sonata in between the two pieces, Paul, because I have to change instruments too?' Robert, sitting with his cello in between his legs, said with a grin, 'It's like playing musical chairs.'

The four others laughed and Paul said, 'That's a good idea Papa. That is if Alex isn't so tired by then that he won't be able to carry on.'

Alex gave a little scowl. 'Don't you worry about me, just concentrate on the notes and try not to make too many mistakes.'

Smiling, Paul said, 'Come, the Schubert.' The five became serious and readied themselves, looking towards Paul as their leader.

Felix and Sarah Goldbaum had been very happily married for sixty-five years and were now in their mid-eighties. Walking slowly towards the front of the hall, the old couple nodded to various friends and acquaintances as they made their way to the seats that had been especially reserved for them. They were very highly thought of in the Jewish community. They had raised six children and now had numerous grandchildren and great grandchildren, all of whom were present this evening. There was a buzz of conversation as the hall started to fill up. Many of the younger children were sitting on cushions at the front.

At the back of the stage, Rabbi Steen looked at his watch and glanced over at the five immaculately dressed musicians. All were wearing white tie and tails, the universal uniform of musicians everywhere.

'I think we'll give it another ten minutes. Look the hall's almost full. In my thirty years as Rabbi, I've never seen so many people here. Thanks to you, Paul and Alex we've managed to raise thousands of marks. I can't say how grateful we all are.'

'Thank you, Rabbi,' said Paul, as Alex nodded his agreement, 'but please don't forget Papa, Robert and Isaac.'

The Rabbi raised his hands and continued, 'Please don't misunderstand me. I know that Papa and the others agree with me. These are difficult times for us and we feel that, under the circumstances, it's brave of you to agree to come here tonight. We wouldn't want you to have any problems with the government because of us.'

'Please don't worry on our behalf, Rabbi,' said Alex. 'It's an honour for us to be here, and if we've been able to help you raise a lot of money, so much the better.'

Nodding his thanks, the Rabbi looked once more at his watch. 'It's time to start if you're ready?'

Alex smiled, and nodded.

'I'll just go and make a short announcement then,' said the Rabbi.

Walking onto the stage, Rabbi Steen could see that the hall was completely full, with people standing at the back and around the sides. As he came into the light a silence fell throughout the hall.

'Good evening, Ladies and Gentlemen. Thank you all for being here tonight, a night that promises to be one of wonderful music. We are very lucky to have two of the most promising young musical talents that have been seen in this country for many years here tonight. I mean of course, the young violinist Paul Lindmann, and the young pianist, Alexander Kraus. Our dear friends, Papa, Robert and Isaac will be playing with the two young musicians later on in the evening. Let us forget for a short while the problems that beset our community and enjoy the beautiful music that's on this evening's programme. Thank you.'

The Rabbi walked down the side of the stage and sat down on a seat next to the Goldbaums.

Alex, looking immaculate in his evening dress, came out onto the stage, stood by the side of the piano and bowed. The hall erupted in thunderous applause, the young women in the audience falling instantly in love with the handsome young man, while the older ones just wanted to mother him. Giving a boyish grin, Alex sat at the piano. There was a silence in the hall that you could almost feel. Even the young ones sitting at the front on their cushions looked on in silence. He sat looking into space for what seemed an eternity, but was in fact only a few seconds. You could have heard a pin drop as he collected his thoughts, thinking only of the music that was inside his head. Lifting his hands to the keyboard, he started to play the haunting melody of Beethoven's 'Moonlight sonata.' He played one more sonata after the 'Moonlight' to rapturous applause then left the stage, returning a short time later with Paul.

The tall, slim, handsome violinist bowed, looked out at the audience, and said, 'Good evening, Ladies and Gentlemen. For my first piece this evening I would like to play the Sonata no13 in B flat major, by Mozart.'

Looking at her husband, Sarah Goldbaum said in a stage whisper, 'Oh, Felix, aren't they handsome? And so young.' The old man nodded in agreement as members of the audience laughed.

Paul looked down at the old, Jewish couple, smiled and said, 'With your permission, Madam, I would like to dedicate this performance to you; without doubt the most beautiful woman in the hall tonight.'

Putting her hand to her mouth, Mrs Goldbaum tittered and there was wild applause from the audience. Putting his violin under his chin, Paul looked at Alex and gave a little wink, indicating that he was ready. The two started to play. After the Mozart, they played the Schubert Rondo. The audience stood as one and clapped at the end of this performance,

Paul and Alex having to return to the stage time after time. They had a break of half an hour for the interval and then it was time for the three other musicians to join them.

Walking on to the stage the five, to great applause, sat and readied themselves for the 'Trout' quintet. The second half of that wonderful evening went as well as the first, the audience wanting to keep them there all night. After the last chord of the Brahms quintet had died away, the audience went wild, giving the five musicians a standing ovation. Papa looked over at the other two players. Understanding immediately, the three moved quietly to the back of the stage. Paul and Alex were left standing alone at the front. Seeing this, the audience clapped even louder. Turning his head Paul said something to Alex. Alex nodded and went to sit down at the piano.

Raising his hands for silence, the applause started to die away. After a short while it became quiet again. Paul, looking out at the audience said, 'Ladies and Gentlemen, I know that I speak for Alex when I say thank you from the bottom of my heart for the reception that you have given us this evening. If I were given the choice of playing at the opera house or playing every week here for you, I would choose here. It should not be necessary for us to come here to raise money for your dispossessed people in a civilised society. How can we, who produced the genius of Beethoven, have sunk so low that we treat our fellow countrymen in such a fashion? Please believe me when I say, not all of us in Germany today are the same as those who wear brown and black uniforms.' Immediately, the audience rose to its feet, giving more applause. Paul raised his hands once more and waited for quiet. He continued, 'A few weeks ago, when my good friend and mentor, Papa, asked us if we would be prepared to do this concert, I perhaps foolishly played a few bars of a piece that they have banned. He said to me how sad he felt that I would never in his lifetime be able to play that piece in Germany. I would like to prove him wrong this evening. Ladies and Gentlemen, the slow movement to Mendelssohn's Concerto in E minor.'

Accompanied by Alex he played the hauntingly beautiful melody. The audience, many with tears in their eyes, remained standing, almost as if he were playing a national hymn which, in a way, he was. As the final chord died away there was complete silence in the room.

Mr and Mrs Goldbaum, with tears streaming down their faces, stepped forward holding hands. Mr Goldbaum looked up at the two young men and said. 'To say thank you to you is not enough but I have no other words to use and so I can only say on behalf of my community, thank you, both.'

With tears in his eyes, Papa walked to the front of the stage. Putting a hand on each of Paul's shoulders, he kissed him on both cheeks, then turning to Alex, he did the same. And so ended a wonderful evening.

39

The long, slim, white envelope was pushed through the letterbox and fluttered to the floor. Walking out of the lounge, Greta saw it lying there and went over to pick it up, noticing immediately the typed name and address. It was addressed to Klaus.

She walked back into the lounge, looked over at her husband and said, 'You've received a letter Klaus; it looks official.' She didn't know why but she had a feeling of unease in the pit of her stomach.

Looking up, Klaus smiled and took the letter. 'Thank you, my dear,' he said. Using his finger, he slit open the letter and began to read. Watching him closely, Greta saw his reaction instantly and her heart gave a lurch. His face went the colour of chalk and his hands began to tremble as if afflicted with palsy.

'Klaus, what is it?'

Klaus looked up and said, his voice trembling, 'It's from the Gestapo. I have to report to Prinz-Albrecht-Straße next Monday at 10am'

Her hand flying to her mouth, Greta exclaimed, 'Oh my God, why?'

'It doesn't say. Just to report. It's signed by SS-Colonel Langers. I remember him from the night Robert and I were picked up.' Klaus felt a sense of nausea as if he was about to vomit.

'Klaus, what have you done? You have been reporting to the Police regularly, haven't you?' The fear in her voice was audible. 'What do they want? Why can't they leave us alone? Haven't we suffered enough?'

Looking at Greta, Klaus started to calm down a little. Common sense took over. 'Wait a moment, Greta. Why would the Gestapo send me a letter? Let's face it, they know where I am and they can pick me up at any time if they want to.'

Her heartbeat starting to return to something like normal, Greta replied, 'Yes, that's true, but what on earth do they want?'

'It's a mystery to me, but I know someone who might be able to throw some light on the matter. I think that we should keep calm, at least for the moment.' Standing, Klaus went into the hall and put on his hat and overcoat. 'I'll be back shortly, try not to worry too much.'

'Where are you going?' she asked.

'To the police station,' he replied as he headed for the front door.

Over the months since he'd been released from the camp, Klaus had had to report once a week to the police. He'd got to know the desk sergeant well. Sergeant Willhelm was in late middle age and a decent man. Although he hadn't said it in so many words, Klaus had the impression that the man had a great deal of sympathy for him. Always polite, the sergeant treated him decently and would sometimes offer him a cup of coffee. Pushing open the door, Klaus entered and walked over to the desk, spotting Willhelm immediately.

Frowning as he saw the professor enter, Willhelm walked over and said, 'Good morning, Professor, what can we do for you? It's not your day to report,' he said raising his eyebrow.

'Good morning, Sergeant, I wondered if I might have a word in private? It won't take a moment, but I'd be grateful.'

'Of course, come on through.' Looking over to the young policeman sitting at a desk at the back of the room, Willhelm called, 'Keep your eye on things for a while.'

'All right, Sarge,' the young man replied.

'Come on in, Professor. Would you like some coffee?'

Nodding, Klaus replied, 'Thank you, that would be nice.'

Pouring coffee into two cups, Sergeant Willhelm handed one to Klaus, sat down and said, 'What can I do for you, Professor? You look worried.'

'I am a little. I received this letter from the Gestapo this morning. Please read it.' Klaus handed it over.

Putting on a pair of spectacles, the sergeant took the letter and began to read. After a few minutes, he handed it back. 'Interesting, I've no idea what they could want but it can't be too serious. If it were, they wouldn't have sent you a letter, that's for sure. They'd have just come knocking on your door. You know the procedure. Anyway, if it had been anything serious I'd know about it. I think that it must be something administrative; try not to worry.' He hesitated and then continued, 'As it's you Professor, I'll tell what I'll do. I'll make some enquiries I have contacts over there. You go on home, I'll see what I can do and phone you.'

Standing up Klaus extended his hand and said, 'Thank you, Sergeant, I'm grateful. You're a good man.'

'These are difficult times for all of us, Professor,' he said quietly. 'We must all take care. I'm due for retirement soon and believe me it can't come soon enough. Go home. I'll phone you.'

After their conversation, Klaus felt a lot better. However he couldn't altogether suppress his fear. Anyone who'd spent any time in a concentration camp would have understood this perfectly. Putting his key in the lock, Klaus entered the house and walked into the lounge.

Greta was sitting with a magazine in her lap staring into space, a worried expression on her face. She jumped up as he entered and rushed over to him, taking his hands in hers. 'What happened?' she said with fear in her voice.

'I spoke to Sergeant Willhelm and he seemed to think that there was nothing to worry about. He's going to make some enquiries and contact me. We'll just have to be patient. Try not to worry, my dear.'

At that moment, the shrill ringing of the phone could be heard in the hall. Rushing through the door, Klaus picked up the receiver with shaking hands and said 'Hello?' Looking on, Greta could hardly contain her impatience and paced up and down, the call seeming to go on forever.

Klaus gave the occasional grunt as the person on the other end of the line talked. Finally he said, 'Thank you very much Sergeant, I'll always be grateful to you.' He quietly replaced the receiver and looked at Greta.

'Well?'

'It's mysterious. All he could find out was that I'm to have an interview with an SS-Lieutenant who works for the SD, the SS security service.'

'Whatever it is, Klaus, I intend to be there with you.' He was about to say something but she raised her hand, 'I mean it, Klaus.' The tone of her voice warned him not to argue.

40

At 9 45am on the day that he'd been ordered to report, Klaus and Greta stood in front of Gestapo headquarters on the Prinz-Albrecht-Straße. Klaus's mind was a whirl of emotion, going back to the night four years previously when he and Robert had been brought here. Klaus gave his wife's hand a squeeze and managed a little smile, as if to say, 'come on, let's get this over with'. The two walked through the entrance and, looking to the left, they saw an SS sergeant sitting at a desk, and walked over. His heart fluttering in his chest, Klaus fixed his eyes on the black uniform, memories of the camp flashing through his brain.

As he approached, his reaction was automatic. Standing in front of the desk, at attention, he respectfully removed his hat and said, 'Good morning, Herr Sergeant, I've been told to report here this morning at 10am. My name is Hoffmann.' He waited for the man's response, a film of sweat beading his brow.

The SS man looked at Klaus and then turned his attention to Greta. 'And who's this?' he asked, looking Greta up and down.

'My wife, Herr Sergeant'

The man grunted and looked down at a list on the desk in front of him. 'It says nothing about your wife here, Hoffmann.' He paused. 'Go and sit on the benches over there. You'll be called for when you're wanted.'

'Very good, Herr Sergeant.' Taking a step backwards, Klaus turned and, followed by Greta, walked over to the place indicated by the sergeant and sat down. His hands shaking, Klaus took a handkerchief out of his pocket and wiped his brow.

'Are you all right, Klaus?' said Greta. He nodded, saying nothing. Greta had never seen her husband like this. Servile was the first word that came to her mind, and she began to understand, really understand for the first time, how much fear these men in black engendered. She, of course, had never seen the inside of a concentration camp. If she had, she would have understood her husband's behaviour completely.

At this time in the morning, the headquarters was a hive of activity and the place had an urgency all of its own. Black and field-grey uniforms were predominant, with the occasional civilian-clothed Gestapo officer going about his unknown business. Klaus sat nervously, his eyes downcast, saying nothing. The hands of the clock on the wall opposite moved around slowly, remorselessly, and for the two people waiting, time seemed to have stood still. They sat on the benches for one and a half hours before they were finally sent for.

The telephone sitting on the desk by the SS sergeant's elbow gave a shrill ring. Nonchalantly, he leaned over and picked up the receiver. Listening for a few moments, he murmured something and replaced the 'phone back in its cradle. Coming from around the desk he approached Klaus and Greta.

'Come with me you two,' he said abruptly, looking at Greta. They followed him along a corridor and into an office, both failing to see the name plate on the door. Two chairs were placed in front of a large desk. Indicating the chairs, the SS man told them to sit down. He left the room, leaving them alone once more. This time they weren't kept waiting long; a side door opened and both Klaus and Greta looked in that direction.

Standing in the doorway, dressed in an immaculate black SS officer's uniform stood the man who'd summoned them here. At first there was no recognition. Then the young officer moved into the interior of the office, the light falling full on his face. It was Greta who recognised him first and her hand flew to her mouth as she gave a cry. In the split second that it took for her to recognise her son, Klaus also realised who was present in the room with them. In the four years since they'd seen him last he'd filled out; he was no longer a boy but a man. The parents of this young man sat there with mouths wide open, too shocked to speak.

Walking over to the desk, Dieter sat and eyed his parents. There was a cold distant look on his face with no sign of nervousness. 'Good morning, Mother, Father. I'm sorry that you've been kept waiting but I had urgent business to attend to.' His mind went back to a few minutes previously, when he'd been down in the cellars supervising the torture of a prisoner for the past two hours. The man had died just before he'd left the cell.

Coming back to the present, Dieter said, 'Can I offer you coffee?'

Klaus was the first to recover. Even though he would have dearly loved a drink, he shook his head and said, 'No thank you, Lieutenant.' Without pausing he continued, 'I see that you got your wish after all.'

Nodding his head towards Dieter's uniform and seeing the look of puzzlement on Dieter's face, he said, 'The SS, or should I say, SD?'

Dieter smiled, the smile not reaching his eyes, 'Of course, I knew that I would.'

For the first time Greta spoke, her voice filled with repressed anger. 'Was it worth it, the price that you paid for getting your wish?'

Dieter lifted his two hands and said, 'Price, what price?'

'The betrayal of your father and the death of Robert Wagner.'

'Betrayal? I betrayed no one. I did my duty, no more or less, and as for Wagner, like you Father, he brought his misfortune down on his own head. Do not expect any sympathy from me.'

'Why did you send for us today?' asked Greta. 'It was inhuman of you to send us a letter and then keep us waiting for one and a half hours. Not knowing why we were here and why we'd been sent for. Do you get so much pleasure from inflicting such fear on innocent people?'

'Mother, if you're innocent, then you have nothing to fear.'

'Tell me,' said Klaus, 'do you know what it's like to be inside one of your concentration camps?'

'Of course. I paid a visit to one only last week. I repeat, if you're an innocent, decent German, then you have nothing to fear. It's only our enemies who have anything to be frightened of.' Leaning forward, Dieter lifted his finger and, pointing at Klaus, said icily, 'I hope that you haven't forgotten what it's like. I can arrange for you to be returned. Do you want that? The second time around is likely to be fatal.'

Klaus felt a chill of fear course through his body. 'No, Lieutenant. Once was enough, believe me.'

Nodding, Dieter said, 'Yes, I thought so. Understand something, we are all servants of the state and I represent the security of the state. If you're not with us then you're against us. There's no half way. Remember that and you won't go wrong.'

Klaus wanted to say more but if he was honest he was too frightened. Anyway, he realised how futile it would be to try and argue with the young fanatic sitting in front of him. This person who'd once been the son that he'd loved dearly and whom he now despised.

'Now, to answer your question, you were sent for because it's been decided by my superiors that the original order imposed on you when you left the camp has been suspended. You no longer have to report to the police and any travel restrictions that were placed on you have now been lifted. However, a word of warning from me, Father, be very careful of your actions in the future; stay out of politics and guard your tongue. As I said before, if you're returned to a camp you'll never see the outside again.'

'Should I be grateful, Lieutenant?' asked Klaus.

Leaning forward in his chair, Dieter said, very quietly, 'You should be very grateful indeed. You've been given a second chance. I promise you, you won't be given a third. Oh, by the way, if you wish, you're now free to apply for your old post at the university. I think that if you do, your application will be treated sympathetically.' He shrugged, as if to say, 'Try if you like'.

Klaus nodded, saying nothing.

'Can we leave now, Lieutenant?' asked Greta, realising that she'd not once called her son by his first name.

Leaning back in his chair, he yawned and said, 'Of course, if you wish, I was going to offer you lunch, but ….'

'Thank you, but that won't be necessary,' said Greta, rising. She looked down at Klaus, a look of infinite sadness on her face. She realised that the son she had once nursed and loved was gone forever. Klaus stood and without speaking headed for the door, standing to one side to usher his wife out. She shook her head, indicating that he should go first. He walked through the door. Turning, she looked at Dieter and said quietly, 'You know, Dieter,' using his name for the first and last time, 'if I had known the hell that you were going to put your father through, I'd have drowned you at birth.'

'Goodbye, Mother.'

Giving him a look of contempt, she walked out closing the door quietly behind her.

Looking at the closed door, Dieter, for the first time, felt a sense of sadness overwhelm him. 'Oh, Mother, why can't you understand that I was only doing my duty?' he said aloud.

Hurrying as fast as they could, Klaus and Greta left Gestapo headquarters. Outside they took long deep breaths of air as if to cleanse themselves of the place.

'Come on Greta, I need a stiff drink.' Nodding her agreement, the two headed towards the nearest bar. Finding a quiet table, Klaus ordered two large brandies. When they arrived, he drank half in one go. Giving a shudder, he said, 'I never want to go through anything like that again. I can't believe that that monster's my own flesh and blood. God, he was so cold; did you see his eyes?'

'Yes, although to be honest I'm glad that he sent for us. At least now I have no more illusions. I tell you Klaus, from now on I no longer have a son. Before we left I said to him, may God forgive me, that I wished that I'd drowned him at birth.'

Klaus gave a start, 'That was a dangerous thing to say, Greta.'

'I don't think so. He's become like a machine; my words meant nothing to him.'

Klaus looked at Greta and gave a sigh, 'Do you know, I felt real fear in there, just like in the camp. As soon as we went in and I saw the black uniform I felt emasculated, totally subjugated, something less than a man.'

'That's what they want. We cower before them, they rule by fear.' She put her hand across the table and placed it over his. 'For the first time, I think I understand a little of what it must have been like for you in that camp. I hope that we've seen the last of Dieter. I pray to God that we have. I never want to hear his name mentioned again. I can't believe that I feel such hate for my own son. Even after he betrayed you, I couldn't bring myself to hate him, but now …. Although I don't understand why everything's changed. Why?'

'I don't know; they make their own rules. I suspect that Langers is behind this, but don't ask me why.'

'What about the university, will you apply?'

'Oh my God, Greta, I don't know. To get back to teaching would be wonderful and we need the money. Perhaps I should swallow my pride. I'm so bored working in that office. Don't misunderstand me, I'm very grateful; we'd have starved without that job. The problem is that they still control everything; nothing's changed in the past four years. I'll think about it. Come, my love, let's go home. I feel drained.' The couple stood, and, holding hands like young lovers, they walked out of the bar and into the street.

41

Sitting together in the lounge, Rudi, Rachel and Astrid talked quietly amongst themselves. Playing quietly on the radio in the background was a Bruckner symphony. The shrill ringing of the front door bell interrupted them. Astrid stood, excused herself and went to answer it.

Rudi bent forward and kissed Rachel on the lips, saying quietly, 'How's our little son?'

Smiling, she replied, 'And how do you know that it'll be a boy? I know one thing: I'm suffering dreadful morning sickness.'

'You poor darling. Oh, I'm sure it's a boy, just you wait and see.'

She was about to reply when the door opened. Standing there was Professor Hoffmann, his face set and serious as he looked over at the young couple.

'Professor, good evening,' said Rudi, standing and offering his hand to the older man. 'You haven't met Rachel yet have you?'

The Professor seemed distracted as he took the young girl's hand, 'Good evening, my dear, it's so nice to meet you. Greta and I have heard so much about you.' Turning towards Astrid and Rudi, he continued, 'I'm sorry to burst in on you unannounced like this, but I have some important news.'

'Please sit down, Klaus. Would you like a drink?' said Astrid.

'Yes that would be nice. God knows, I could do with one.'

'Whiskey, Professor?' said Rudi, walking over to the sideboard and lifting the decanter.

'Yes, that's fine, Rudi, thank you.'

Turning towards the ladies, Rudi raised his eyebrows. 'What would you like, Mother? Rachel?'

'Sherry for me please, darling,' said Astrid as Rachel nodded her agreement. Rudi poured the drinks and sat down, looking at the professor expectantly.

'This is going to come as a shock. Greta and I were at Gestapo headquarters this morning.' Pausing, he looked from one to the other and seemed to be trying to find the correct words. 'Dieter is in Berlin.'

Both Astrid and Rudi gave a gasp of surprise, a look passing between the two of them. 'Dieter, at Gestapo headquarters, but how?' said Astrid as she furrowed her brow.

'I was sent for, to be interviewed. Greta came with me. I don't mind telling you I was terrified.' No one said a word, allowing him to continue. 'We sat in an office and who should walk through the door but Dieter, looking very smart in his SS uniform, or should I say SD uniform.'

'SS intelligence?' said Rudi.

'Yes, it was the most bizarre situation of my life. Can you imagine? My son standing there, the person who betrayed me and Robert. He looked so cold, polite but cold, and that awful uniform sent a chill down my spine. He was like a total stranger and I didn't once call him by his first name, just Lieutenant. They've taught him well, the last time that I saw that look was in the camp.'

'Well, I'll be damned,' said Rudi, 'but what did he want?'

'Oh, to tell me that I was no longer regarded as an enemy of the Reich. I'm now rehabilitated and can, if I wish, reapply to the university for my old post back.' He snorted and continued, 'Sadly, it's much too late for Robert.'

'Has he changed much?' asked Astrid.

'He's filled out, a man now rather than a boy, and very handsome. It was the way it was done that made it so cruel. I just received a letter telling me to report, no reasons. You can imagine how I felt. All of the memories of the camp came flooding back and when we arrived, we were kept waiting for one and a half hours. They, or he, were making sure that we knew who was in charge.'

Giving a sigh, Astrid said, 'Poor Klaus, it must have been awful for you. What I don't understand is why? Why have they decided that you're now no longer a threat to them?'

'I can't answer that question; they're so arbitrary these Nazis. Anyway I believe Langers must be behind this, but don't ask me why.'

'What will you do, Professor?' asked Rudi. 'About the university, I mean?'

'Rudi, I have no choice. When I was sent to the camp, Greta had to live on our savings and there's nothing left. Anyway, teaching is the only thing that I'm any good at. It's all I know. I was so grateful for the job in the office and God knows we couldn't have survived without it. To be honest, we need the money.' He looked at them, as if to say, 'Please try to understand my predicament.'

'Don't worry, Klaus, we understand,' said Astrid.

'I spoke to that odious swine the rector this morning and you should have heard him. "Of course you're welcome to come back, Hoffmann. We have your old post waiting for you.' said the Professor, mimicking the rector. He continued, 'At least mathematics is not political.'

'Yes, Professor, but you should be careful, the place is full of Nazis now. Keep your thoughts to yourself,' warned Rudi.

'Don't worry, my boy, I will. Anyway now you know that Dieter is a fully-fledged member of their exclusive society and I think a very dangerous young man.'

Rachel had been sitting quietly during the whole of the conversation, looking from one to the other. She, of course, knew the whole story.

Turning towards her, the Professor said with a smile, 'That's enough about me. I believe that you'll be leaving soon?'

'Yes, we're all leaving together in ten day's time, the 1st of November. Rudi's coming to spend a few days with us, aren't you Rudi?

'Good, good. I hope that at last you'll be able to find some happiness. I'm so ashamed at times to call myself a German. Do you know the saying "For evil to triumph all it needs is for good men to sit back and do nothing."? That's how I feel sometimes.'

Rudi knew that he should say nothing, but felt that if he couldn't trust this man he could trust no one. 'We're not all sitting back and doing nothing now, Professor,' he said quietly.

The Professor nodded, and replied, 'Rudi, if you ever need my help, all you need to do is ask, and I'll give it you willingly.' Standing, he looked around and said, 'It's time I was off. Don't forget to come and see us before you go, Astrid.'

'Of course, Klaus, the three of us can go out to dinner one evening. We have a lot to celebrate: you back at the university and me out of this benighted country.'

The Professor smiled sadly and nodded.

'I'll see you out,' said Rudi, heading towards the door. He stopped, turned and continued, 'By the way, Rachel and I will be married once we're safely in Switzerland. Please tell Frau Hoffmann.'

Beaming, the Professor said, 'Congratulations to both of you. May I offer you my most sincere best wishes.' Looking at Rudi, he continued, 'Now you have even more reason to be careful.'

Walking into the hall, Klaus turned and said, 'Oh, I must tell you, I've reinforced the back of that cupboard, the one in the attic. If you tap it now, it's solid. Rudi, I meant what I said in there. If you ever need help you know where to find me.' Turning, he walked into the cold, dark night.

42

Leaning his head against Paul's shoulder, Alex gave a sigh as he thought of the hard day's study that he'd just finished — eight hours of relentless practice on the Brahms' second piano concerto. He was, however, content with the result and thought that if the great composer could have heard it, he would have been, too. What he needed now, more than anything, was sleep. They were driving at speed past the Olympic stadium, heading towards Alex's apartment in Spandau and what they hoped would be a good night's sleep. Glancing at his watch, Paul noted the time, 11pm.

'Tired, little one?' asked Paul.

'Hmm, exhausted; I could sleep for a week. I hope that you're not feeling in the mood tonight.' Giving a little giggle, he continued, 'If you are, you'll just have to pleasure yourself.'

'Alex! Anyway, I'm not. You're not the only one to have had a busy day, you know. I spent this morning with Maestro Furtwangler discussing what concerto I was playing with the Philharmonic next month. We decided on the Dvorak. This afternoon I spent playing with the string section, which was great fun. That reminds me, young Alex, we have to give some thought to the gala concert in the opera house at Christmas time.'

'I know,' Alex replied, giving a yawn. 'I'm doing the Brahms. It'll be ready in time. What about you?'

'The Beethoven. Papa Stern loves it and so do I. Wasn't the concert that we did for the Jewish community super?'

'Wonderful! I haven't enjoyed myself so much for ages, and they were all so grateful, weren't they?'

The two young musicians lapsed into silence. Turning left off the main road, Paul took the first right into Alex's street. The lights of the Mercedes swept the opposite side of the road as he turned, briefly illuminating a small, black car parked on the other side of the road. Sitting inside were two men; it was possible to see the glow of their cigarette ends. Paul's heart started to hammer a tattoo in his chest as a feeling of danger overwhelmed him. Saying nothing to Alex, he was suddenly very much awake, sensing that something was very wrong. Parking the car, Paul and Alex got out. Paul resisted the urge to turn and look over at the parked car. Gestapo! His nerves screamed. He knew with the utmost certainty that the two men sitting in the car opposite represented danger to him and Alex.

Climbing the stairs, Paul was trying to work out the best thing to do. 'Think, think!' he said to himself. Alex was totally oblivious to their danger. Inserting the key, Alex pushed open the door and put his hand out to turn on the light.

Lifting his hand, Paul grabbed hold of Alex's arm, restraining him. 'Stop!' he said as his sense of urgency conveyed itself to Alex.

'What is it?'

'Shush! Close the door, quickly!' Striding over to the window, Paul cautiously pulled the curtain to one side and looked down at the car parked on the other side of the road. One of the men looked up in their direction. Paul hastily stepped to one side. Feeling remarkably calm, Paul turned to Alex and said, 'Turn on the light.'

Standing in full few of the window so that he could be seen from the street below, he closed the thick curtains and looked at Alex.

'What is it, Paul?'

'We've got visitors — Gestapo. Did you make the bed this morning?'

'No, but …'

'Go in the bedroom. Close the curtains before you turn on the light, make the bed, and do it properly.' Crossing the room in great strides, Paul opened a cupboard door, rummaged around and took out a chess set.

Alex came in from the bedroom closing the door behind him. Looking over, Paul said, 'Go into the kitchen and get two beers.' Alex hesitated. 'Do it Alex. Now!' Returning from the kitchen carrying two bottles of beer, Alex watched as Paul laid out the chess set.

'Right take your jacket off and sit down. We're going to have a game.'

'Well,' murmured the younger Gestapo man to his more senior colleague, 'It looks like our two love birds are at home. Shall we go on up?'

'You youngsters are all the fucking same,' replied the older man, 'Don't be impatient, take your time. Now, Heini, have another cigarette. Let's give them time to get stuck across each other.' The Gestapo man leaned back in his seat, pushed his trilby over his eyes and waited. The younger man shrugged and did as he'd been told.

Removing some pieces from the board, Paul looked at Alex and said, 'They could be here in five minutes or an hour. We must keep calm; our lives might depend on it.'

'But how do you know it's them?'

'It's a feeling. Someone's tipped them off about us, I can feel it. Maybe someone from 'The Black Cat', or, more likely, that bastard from downstairs, Erhard. Look, Alex, you can spot the Gestapo a mile away and why would two men be sitting out there at this time of night? No, it's too convenient.'

'But Paul, if you spotted them as we arrived, why didn't you just keep driving? We could have gone to your mother's.'

'No good, little one. They'd have just waited for another time. I'd rather get this over with now. If I'm wrong, all that we'll have lost is a night's sleep. Listen, when they arrive, we're just two friends having a game of chess. We're relaxing after a hard day's practice. We weren't tired so decided to have a game and when we finish I'm going home to my own bed. Do you understand? They may try to trick us. No matter what happens, keep your cool.' He glanced towards the clock on the shelf. It was almost 1am. 'Come on you bastards,' he muttered to himself.

Looking at his watch, the older Gestapo man stretched, glanced over at his companion, and said, 'Alright, Heini, let's go and see the two lovebirds shall we?' Climbing out of the car, the two men crossed the road and walked into the apartment block. Erhard's door was slightly open as he'd been told to expect them. Hearing the two men arrive, he went over and opened the door.

The older officer nodded, looked at the Block warden, and said, 'First floor?'

'Yes, number three.'

The two men headed for the stairs, followed closely by Erhard.

Reaching Alex's door the older man said, 'I'll do it.' Lifting his right leg he sent his right foot crashing into the door. The flimsy lock split, bursting the door open.

Rushing in, the younger officer, shouted, 'Alright, you fucking queers ...' His voice trailed off, not expecting to see the two young men playing chess.

As the door burst open, Paul and Alex jumped to their feet, knocking the chessboard onto the floor. 'Who the hell are you?' shouted Paul.

'Gestapo— stay where you are,' said the older man realising instantly that something wasn't quite right. 'Check the bedroom,' he said to the younger man. Doing as he was told, he walked over, turned on the light and looked inside. Seeing the bed made up and tidy, he turned off the light, looked at his colleague, and shook his head.

'Will someone please tell us what's going on?' said Paul, feigning anger.

Taking control, the older Gestapo man said, 'What's going on here?'

'We were having a beer and playing chess. Is that illegal?

'At this time in the morning?'

'Well, yes, Officer, we're musicians. I bought Alex home and as we weren't tired we decided to have a game of chess. Look, I think that there's been a mistake here. We're law-abiding citizens of the Reich. We've done nothing wrong.'

Doors were opening along the corridor as tenants in their night clothes started to peer out, wanting to see what was happening.

The two Gestapo men looked at each other. This was something that they didn't expect.

Paul, taking the initiative pressed on, 'When you burst in here, you said something about queers. Do you think that we're homosexuals? If so, that's a scandalous libel.'

Alex, seeing Erhard standing in the background, lifted his finger and pointed, saying loudly, 'Is he the one who called you here?' The two Gestapo men looked over at Erhard, who was by now looking very uncomfortable. 'If so, you might care to ask him who's queer around here. The way that pervert looks at me and Paul makes my skin crawl.'

'Yes,' said Paul, taking his cue from Alex, 'Every time that we walk into this building we can feel his eyes loitering on our bums!'

'Alright, that's enough,' said the senior man, 'You're musicians you say. What's your name?' he asked, looking at Alex.

'Alexander Kraus,' came the reply.

'The pianist?'

'Yes, and this is Paul Lindmann, the violinist.'

The senior Gestapo man visibly relaxed, the atmosphere in the room becoming lighter. 'My wife's a fan of you two. You're quite well known aren't you?'

'Well, yes, I suppose so,' said Paul.

Turning towards the open door, the older Gestapo agent seeing the tenants crowding around shouted, 'Alright you people, the show's over. Get back to bed. Move!'

Everyone scuttled away, except Erhard.

Sighing, the man looked at his young colleague, and said, 'I think that we've been misinformed here.' Turning he gave Erhard a look which spoke volumes. 'A word of warning though. We'll be keeping our eyes on you and on this place. I'd be very careful, because we could come calling at any time, day or night.' The threat was implicit. Turning towards the younger man, he said, 'Come on.'

They left the room, closing the shattered door behind them.

Outside, they took Erhard by the scruff of the neck, frog-marching him downstairs. At the bottom of the steps, the older officer smashed his clenched fist with full force into Erhard's face, breaking his nose. 'The next time you send a report to us, you piece of shit, make sure that you've got your facts right, or a fucking sight more evidence.' Loosening his grip on Erhard's collar, the two Gestapo men walked out, leaving Erhard lying in a pool of blood.

Standing by the car, in the cold night air, the younger man looked at his boss and said, 'Well, Chief, what do you think?'

'Heini, I don't know, but I'm not going to take anyone in for playing chess. I'd be the laughing stock of Gestapo headquarters. But like I said, we'll keep our eyes on them. If they are queer, we'll get them sooner or later. You see queers just can't get enough, they like to screw like rabbits.'

The two men got into the car and drove away.

Looking at the closed door, Paul went white and broke into a cold sweat. Trembling, he ran into the bathroom and was violently sick into the toilet bowl, retching until his stomach was empty.

Alex came in and put an arm around his shoulders, 'You were magnificent, Paul.'

Gasping, Paul said, 'You weren't so bad yourself. Now, put a few things together, we're getting out of here. I'm going to phone mother ... and Alex?'

Alex turned, 'Yes?'

'We've just had our last chance, we won't be getting another.'

Looking at Paul seriously, he replied, 'In that case, perhaps we should think about leaving Germany permanently.'

Paul nodded and walked over to the phone.

Securing the broken door as best as they could, Paul and Alex went downstairs and into the hallway. Erhard's door was firmly closed and there were smears of blood all over the floor.

Getting into the car, the two shaken young men drove away. 'Mother's expecting us. I woke her up. Alex, we're going to have to tell her the truth. You do realise that, don't you?'

'Yes, of course. It was a good job that you spotted them tonight.'

Giving a shudder, Paul replied, 'If I hadn't, we'd be sweating it out in a Gestapo cell by now. It's strange, but I've had a bad feeling in the pit of my stomach for some weeks now. Pulling into the driveway of the luxury apartment block, they got out and took the lift to Rosa's apartment. As they entered, Rosa was pacing backwards and forwards, puffing on a cigarette.

She stopped, looked in their direction and gave a gasp, 'My God, Paul, what's happened? You're as white as a sheet.'

'All in good time, Mother. Alex and I need a stiff drink,' he said, heading towards the small bar and pouring two large measures of whiskey. Turning, he handed one to Alex, took a large swig, and sat down on the settee with Alex next to him. Glancing up at the clock he noticed that it was 5am. He looked over at Rosa, who sat down facing them, and said, 'There's no easy way to tell you this, but we had a visit from the Gestapo tonight. They hoped to catch us in bed together. We were lucky. I spotted them as we arrived. They suspected that we were homosexual.'

Looking closely at her son and his friend, she asked, 'And *are* you homosexual? Because if you are, you're both in grave danger.'

'Yes, Mother, we are. Alex and I have been lovers for some time now. You don't seem surprised.'

'Oh, Paul, darling, I've known so many homosexuals in my time, in the theatre and art worlds. Most of them have had the good sense to get out of this country, thank God. As for you, you're my son, and I've suspected for a long time that you might be, and now I know. I'm glad that it's out in the open. Tell me, do you love each other?'

Alex looked at Paul and said, 'More than anything else in the world.'

'Good,' she replied, 'Now, we have to be practical. Firstly, Alex, you must move out of that apartment immediately, this morning. You must move in here with us. I'll telephone your father later this morning and tell him.' A look of alarm passed over Alex's face. Rosa smiled, 'Don't worry, I'm not going to tell him that you're my son's lover. I'll think of something.

Paul was amazed at his mother's reaction. He'd expected tears and hysterical recriminations, but instead, she was totally calm and in control. It was a side of her that he'd never seen before.

'Now, tell me everything in detail from beginning to end, don't leave anything out.'

Doing as he was told, he and Alex told her the whole story.

When they'd finished, she said, 'So, they were obviously tipped off by someone. Tell me, how many people know about you two?'

'A few,' admitted Paul, 'We haven't been exactly discreet.'

'Then that was very stupid of you both, if you don't mind me saying so. Don't you realise how much danger you're in now? That Gestapo officer said that they'd have their eyes on you from now on.' She paused and lit a cigarette, looking pensively into space for a moment and said, almost to herself, 'We must do something about that. I have an idea. Now, the safest thing for you both would be to leave Germany. As long as you stay here you'll be in danger. I also have some ideas on that, but that can wait for the moment.

'Yes, Frau Lindmann, I said the same thing to Paul. Perhaps we could continue our studies elsewhere?'

'Mother, I have to ask you… you're taking the news of my — our sexuality — very calmly.'

'My darling, you're my boy and always will be. Do you think that I love you any less? And I've gained another son in Alex.' Alex beamed, 'Alright, have some breakfast and then go and get all of your things, Alex. The both of you must now be discreet, even here in the apartment. The guestroom's right next door to your room Paul and there's a connecting door, as you know ….' She didn't say anymore.

'Thank you, Mother, for being so understanding. I don't know what we would have done if you'd have rejected us.'

She snorted as her eyes filled with tears, 'Rejected you indeed! You're my cubs and I'll do whatever it takes to protect you both. I promise you that later this morning I'm going to give the finest acting performance of my entire life. Now, run along. Oh, and one other thing. Keep away from any bars that you may have been frequenting, I'm sure that you know what I mean.'

43

At 10am that morning, Rosa drove into the magnificent grounds of the palace occupied by the second most powerful man in Germany. Reichsminister Hermann Göring. She was there to have morning coffee with her good friend Emmy, the wife of the Reichsminister. Emmy, an ex-actress, was often to be seen hosting social events for Hitler himself. Rosa hoped that by talking to Emmy she would be able to do something about the disaster that had befallen Paul and Alex in the early hours of this morning. Climbing out of the car, she approached the large double doors and rang the bell. Within seconds, a butler opened the door, bowed and said, 'Good morning, Frau Lindmann, Frau Göring is waiting in the library for you.'

Nodding, Rosa handed her coat to the man, said, 'Thank you,' and walked into the beautiful library.

'Rosa, darling, welcome,' said Emmy, 'You look very peaky this morning, is everything alright?'

'Good morning Emmy. No, I've had a dreadful night. It'll be a relief to unburden myself.' Her face was a picture of misery and worry and she looked close to tears.

'Oh, you poor darling, come and sit down and tell me all about it.' Stretching her arm out to an ornate table she pushed a bell, summoning the butler. 'But first, coffee.'

Sipping her coffee from fine bone china, Rosa told Emmy of the previous night's events.

'How awful, those Gestapo men can be barbarians sometimes. I know that they're very necessary, but really. Paul and Alex are the two finest young musicians in the country and to suggest that they're ... well, you know.'

Wringing her hands, Rosa said, 'But, Emmy, what can we do? The boys were only playing chess. They'd had a long day rehearsing and weren't in the slightest bit tired so they decided to have a game. Then those dreadful Gestapo men burst in and accused them of ..., well you know. It's scandalous!'

Making her mind up, Emmy, said, 'You must talk to Hermann. Fortunately, he's here today.'

'Do you think he'd mind? He's such a busy man and I wouldn't want to trouble him.'

'Of course not. My dear, when he hears about this he'll be very angry, I can tell you.' Emmy again summoned the butler, 'Would you ask the Herr Reichsminister to come and see me please.' Bowing, the butler said, 'Yes,' and left, closing the door quietly behind him.

A few minutes later, the fat, jovial Hermann Göring entered the room.

'Rosa, my dear, how lovely to see you. What's the matter? You've being crying,' he said as he embraced her and kissed her on the cheek.

'Hermann, poor Rosa had an awful night. Tell Hermann all about it darling.'

The Reichsminister, looking concerned, took Rosa's hand, led her over to the settee and sat down. She once more recounted the events of the previous evening, Göring nodding from time to time.

'And they were just playing chess you say?'

'Yes, nothing more, and to be accused of something so awful without a shred of evidence —it's scandalous!'

'Yes, I agree. Rosa you mustn't worry any more. I'll phone General Muller at Gestapo headquarters. It seems to me that those two Gestapo men were given false information.' Patting her hand, he said, 'I'll have this sorted out in no time at all.'

'Thank you, Herr Reichsminister, I'm so grateful. I phoned Alex's father early this morning and told him that Alex was moving in with me and Paul, where I can keep my eye on him. I didn't mention this morning's incident.'

'He's an industrialist, isn't he?' asked Emmy.

'Yes, he has pots of money. Why he makes Alex live in that dreadful place, I'll never know.

'Now, I'll leave you two ladies to it,' said Göring. 'Oh, by the way, will you be at the Goebbels dinner party next week?'

'Oh, yes, I wouldn't miss it for the world.'

'Good, my dear, We'll see you there. The boys are giving a gala concert at the opera house at Christmas time, aren't they?'

Rosa nodded, 'Yes, they're very excited about it.'

'Good, there'll be a lot of very important people there that night. Anyway, duty calls. Now don't worry about this business with the boys, I'll sort it out.' The fat Reichsminister gave his most jovial smile, stood and left the room. As he walked towards his office, he put his head around his secretary's door and said, 'Get me SS General Muller on the 'phone, I need to speak to him.'

An hour later, Rosa climbed into her car and drove away. There was a little smile playing at the corner of her mouth.

Almost before he'd sat down, the telephone rang in Göring's office. Lifting the receiver, he murmured, 'Göring.'

'Good morning, Herr Reichsminister, Muller here. I believe that you wanted to speak to me.'

'Yes, General, I've just been speaking to the mother of a young man. She's a family friend. Now, last night two of your men raided an apartment in Spandau. I'm very concerned and believe they were overzealous. A friend of his rents the apartment. When your men burst in they accused the two of having some kind of homosexual liaison. However, all that the two were doing was playing a game of chess.'

'Yes, sir, I'm listening.'

'Now it seems to me that your men were misinformed. I must tell you that these two are two of the finest young musicians in the Reich and have supreme musical ability. I've met them myself on numerous occasions and have no reason to believe that either of them is that way inclined.'

'Of course, sir, I know nothing about this, but will look into it urgently.'

'Do that General. If they'd been caught in a compromising situation that would be one thing. Playing chess, however, is not yet a crime as far as I know. These two, I've no doubt, will become musical ambassadors for this country. Here are their names.' He gave Muller the details. When he'd finished, he said, 'Now, I want this matter dropped and closed permanently. Today! I hope that I'm making myself clear, General.'

'Very, Herr Reichsminister. I'll talk to the two officers involved and find out where they got this information from. You can trust me to sort the matter out immediately.'

'Call me before the end of the day. See to it.' Without waiting for a reply Göring put down the phone.

Very carefully, SS General Muller replaced the telephone into its cradle. 'Shit!' he murmured to himself as he pressed the intercom to his secretary's office next door.

Two hours later, two very frightened Gestapo agents stood outside Muller's office. They'd both been summoned from their beds and told to get dressed quickly. Something that they usually told others to do, for them it was a first.

'Christ, Chief, what does he want?' murmured Heini out of the corner of his mouth.

'How the fuck should I know?' growled the older man whose name was Zimmermann. 'But I tell you what, it must be serious if the boss wants to see us. I don't think he's calling us in to offer us promotion.'

Suddenly, the office door opened as a senior Gestapo officer came out, looked at the two men, and said, 'He'll see you now. Be careful, he's in a foul mood.'

Quietly, the two men knocked and entered, fearing the worst. Standing in front of the general's desk, they waited, full of apprehension.

Muller totally ignored them for what seemed an eternity. Finally, he looked up and leaned back in his chair, eyeing them up and down. Suddenly he sat forward, and said, his voice dripping with venom, 'Would you like to guess who I had a telephone call from this morning?'

'No, Sir, I mean, yes, Sir,' stuttered Zimmermann.

'I'll tell you, shall I? No less a person than Reichsminister Göring. It seems that you two fucking clowns tried to pick up the son of a personal friend of his last night. Does it ring any bells? Let me jog your memory. He had a friend with him and they were playing chess. Apparently they're two of the most brilliant young musicians in Germany. Not only that, but their parents are very rich and influential and have many friends high up in party circles. Well, do you have anything to say?'

Fearing the worst, Zimmermann, who'd turned white, said, 'Sir, we were acting on a tip off. When we went in we expected to find them in bed together.'

'And were they in bed together?' said the general, sarcastically. 'No, they were having a quiet game of chess. May I ask, did you find any evidence to suggest that these two were queers?'

'No, sir, we didn't, but we'd received a report ...'

'Who from?' Muller asked.

'The Blockwarden, Erhard.'

'And on what premise did this Erhard base his evidence? Did he see them screwing or something like that?'

'Well, no Sir.'

'No sir? Don't you think that it's possible that for some reason this man might perhaps hold a grudge against these two?'

'Well, yes Sir, I suppose it's possible,' Zimmermann admitted uncomfortably.

'So, what do we have here? Two young men sitting playing chess together. Now, if you'd both had the brains to knock the door instead of kicking it down ... one of them would have answered it. Am I right?' Without waiting for a reply, he continued, 'If the person who'd answered the door was undressed, all that you would have had to do was go in and see if there was anyone else in the bed. There's only one bedroom I believe?'

'Yes, Sir.'

'If there had been, you'd have had enough evidence to arrest them. Am I right? If, as happened, they'd looked guiltless, you could have just had a nose around and left and I wouldn't be receiving calls from the second most powerful man in Germany. Anyway, as it happens, these two seem perfectly innocent to me. Let me put it another way; Reichsminister Göring insists that they are innocent and that this matter's dropped. Are you going to argue with him?'

'No, Sir,' the two men answered in unison.

Sighing, the General said, 'Very well, you were only doing your job and acting on a tip off, but next time be a little more subtle and don't go around like a couple of bulls in a china shop. This Blockwarden, Erhard, is he normally reliable?'

'He's a slimy bastard, Sir,' said Heini, speaking for the first time.

'Aren't they all?' said the General mirthlessly. Making a decision, he said, 'Get rid of him today and tell him from me to think himself lucky that he's not inside a concentration camp. Replace him with someone more reliable. This case is now closed. Do you understand? If I ever receive another call like that again from anyone high up in the government, you two will be in shit right up to your eyeballs. Now, get out!'

Almost running out of the room, the two men, visibly shaken, breathed a sigh of relief and went to pay a visit to Erhard.

44

Rosa entered the foyer, took off her fur coat and walked into the lounge. Sitting on the settee Paul and Alex were both looking nervous and worried. Paul was pale and wan, nervously smoking a cigarette, while Alex sat staring into space. It was obvious that the two young men at last realised the enormity of what had almost overwhelmed them the previous evening.

'Good afternoon, my two little cubs,' said Rosa, her heart going out to them both.

'Hello, Mother,' said Paul as Alex nodded a welcome.

'I have had a very interesting and busy day on your behalf and, I hope, a successful one. I spoke to Reichsminister Göring this morning and hope that his wife will call me back later this afternoon.'

Almost on cue, the telephone started to ring in the hall. Rosa got up and walked out. There was a murmured conversation which went on for a few minutes. They could hear Rosa laughing and talking.

Glancing over at Alex, Paul smiled and said, 'Thank God for mother's friends in high places, let's hope it's worked. Today's been the most nerve-racking of my life.'

'Yes,' said Alex, 'what a mess we nearly got ourselves into last night. I'll be having nightmares about it for years. One good thing though, at least I don't have to go back to that awful apartment. I'm so glad that your mother spoke to Father this morning,' he laughed. 'She's incredible and can wrap a man around her little finger. Father was almost benign when I spoke to him and said what a good idea he thought it was for me to stay here with you. If only he knew.'

They were interrupted by the return of Rosa, whose face was wreathed in a huge smile. 'Good news, my two little cubs: that was Emmy Göring. The Reichsminister spoke to Gestapo Muller this morning and the Gestapo chief has just called him back. Muller spoke to the two agents who raided the apartment last night and they confirmed that there was nothing untoward going on between you two. The matter is now officially closed. Oh, and that dreadful

Blockwarden's been fired. Apparently it was him who informed on you.'

'I thought it was,' said Paul. 'Do you know I'm sure that he's homosexual himself.'

'Yes, I wouldn't be surprised,' said Alex.

'Paul, darling, pour us all a drink and pass me a cigarette, would you please?'

Paul walked over to the small bar and poured everyone a large drink. He turned and handed the drinks around as Rosa lit herself a cigarette. 'I'll have one of those, please, Mother,' he said, taking one from the silver cigarette box and lighting it. 'Since last night, I feel the need for tobacco.'

'Now, on the subject of last night, we have a lot to talk about.' She became very serious. Taking a deep drag from her cigarette, she inhaled and blew a plume of smoke towards the ceiling. Looking from one to the other, she continued, 'The two of you were very lucky. If you, Paul, hadn't spotted those Gestapo men and had been caught in bed together I could have done nothing for you. I hope that this incident has taught you a lesson that will last you both for the rest of your lives. In Nazi Germany, to be caught out, as you very nearly were last night, is almost certainly a death sentence, but don't imagine for one moment that life is very much better for homosexuals anywhere else. Alright, they don't put you in a concentration camp in, let's say, England, but they do put you in prison. In just about every country that I know of, with the possible exception of France, homosexuality is illegal. The sad truth is, boys, most people despise homosexuals. All of my adult life, I've known homosexual men in the theatre and the arts. Even the so-called liberal and enlightened people that I know will only tolerate homosexuality as long as it's discreet and not flaunted in their faces. Once it becomes general knowledge, you can say goodbye to just about anyone that you once regarded as a friend. The truth is that life can be very sad and lonely for homosexuals; that's why you're both so lucky to have each other. If you do leave this country —I'll come on to that in a minute— you're both going to have to live your lives very discreetly. Do not imagine for one moment that because you're out of Germany things will be magically changed. You can both be the finest musicians in the world and have the world at your feet, but if you don't use discretion, you'll be finished. I don't believe that things will change in my lifetime and probably not in yours. So learn your lesson now. Love each other by all means, but be very discreet about it. Oh, listen to me, what a speech! Get me another drink, will you Alex, darling?'

Rosa smiled and looked over at the two young men and said, 'Thank you, Alex,' as he handed her a refill.

'You know, Mother, Alex and I have been incredibly stupid. It needed something like last night to bring us to our senses and I promise you that we will be very discreet from now on. However, no one will ever take the love that we have for each other away. This is not just about sex,' he smiled and continued, 'although that's great, but we love each other and have a bond that nobody can take away from us. We have our music and each other. We don't need anything else.'

'Good. I understand. Tell me, how would you both like to go to America?'

Both Paul and Alex's eyes lit up. 'America!' said Alex excitedly.

'You bet!' said Paul.

'I had lunch with Larry Holmes, the cultural attaché from the American Embassy today. We talked about you both doing a concert tour over there early next year. He thought that it was a wonderful idea and nearly jumped out of his seat with excitement at the idea. I hinted to him that you might like to stay. He said that if you were to apply on artistic grounds he could see no problem; in fact, he'd do everything in his power to help.

'Oh, Mother, America, that would be wonderful. We could play things that are forbidden to us here. Just think, Alex.'

'Yes, they have some fine orchestras and musicians there. We could both be very happy.'

'What about you though, Mother?'

'Oh, you don't have to worry about me, I can look after myself. The lovely thing about this idea is that the Nazis won't stand in your way. They'll think of you as being ambassadors for their precious Reich. They're not to know that you won't be coming back.' The two young men smiled, understanding her logic. 'I've had a brilliant idea — let's all get showered, put on our finest evening wear and go and find the most expensive restaurant in town. I want to show my two lovely talented boys to the whole of Berlin.'

45

The five people clambered out of the two taxis after they'd pulled up outside Tempelhof airport. Unloading a large number of suitcases, the three men, Rudi, Otto and young Sam, walked towards the entrance followed by Rachel and Astrid. Pushing open the large, glass-fronted doors, the five walked into the cavernous modern interior. Looking around they saw the Lufthansa check-in desk and walked over to it.

Taking out their tickets, they stood in line and waited. Rudi looked to his left in the direction of the immigration and passport control. 'Well, there it is, Otto,' he murmured, 'the last barrier.'

Following his gaze, Otto nodded. 'Yes, I admit to being very frightened at the moment.' Overhearing them, Rachel and Sam looked over too. As their eyes met for a brief second, a worried look passed between them. The luggage was taken and weighed, and their flight tickets were checked with forty-five minutes to spare before the flight would be called.

'Let's all go and have a coffee,' said Astrid, heading in the direction of the cafe, with the others following close behind.

The man spotted them as soon as they entered. Ludwig Klaus was the senior immigration officer on duty. 'The Goldmann family, I believe,' he murmured to himself as he saw them arrive. He'd been waiting for them. Putting his hand into his grey-green uniform jacket he could feel the thick, bulging envelope of Reichsmarks that had been handed to him by Neiper the previous evening. Giving a smile of satisfaction to himself, he wondered what it was that these Jews had over the Deputy-Gauleiter. He shrugged. *Not my affair; I've been well paid for my little contribution. However, I do hope that their papers are all in order, or they don't get through.* he thought to himself. With a sudden gesture of his right hand, he motioned to one of his subordinates to come over.

When the younger man arrived, Klaus said, 'Get on the tannoy and tell the Goldmann family to come to the passport control immediately.'

'Very good, Sir. The Goldmann family?'

'Yes, that's it.'

Nervously, Otto and the others were sipping coffee, saying little to each other when the tannoy system suddenly crackled into life. 'Would the Goldmann family go to passport control immediately, the Goldmann family,' The system went dead. Nearly dropping his coffee, Otto half stood in fright, as Rachel and Sam looked on, fear etched on their faces. 'Don't panic, Otto. The three of you go. Remember, your papers are all in order,' said Rudi.

'Yes, go, we're not far away. Good luck,' whispered Astrid, as Otto and his two children headed for the cafe entrance. Astrid looked at Rudi, saying nothing, her brow furrowed with worry.

Otto, Rachel and Sam walked over towards the passport control desks. A young officer was sitting behind one, with an older, more senior man standing behind him.

'Goldmann?' asked the younger man, raising an eyebrow.

'Yes, sir,' said Otto, with a tremor in his voice, his heart beating so loudly he thought that everyone in the building could hear it. Rachel and Sam stood close by his side, unable to conceal their fright.

'Your papers!' snapped the younger officer. Otto gave all three sets to the young man, who in turn handed them over his shoulder to the more senior officer.

Taking the papers, Klaus said abruptly, 'All of you follow me.'

The Goldmanns complied, walking around the desk and following the man into an office. 'Close the door,' he ordered, sitting down behind a desk and leaving the three Jews standing in front of him. Very slowly and deliberately he leafed through each set of documents, saying nothing. He raised his eyes, looking from one to the other and back down to the documents again. Otto had a sudden urge to urinate. His bladder felt as if it were about to burst. Rachel's face was white and Sam nervously twisted his hands, wanting to scream, *'Come on you bastard! Hurry up.'*

With a sudden movement of his right arm, the customs and immigration officer picked up a stamp. Thud— thud— thud. He stamped each set of papers, and said, 'All is in order. You may go and wait in the departure lounge.' The three turned, feeling the eyes of the man on their backs as they walked out of the office.

Rudi and Astrid presented their passports at the desk and were waved through. 'Where are they?' he muttered to his mother as they turned the corner into the departure lounge. Standing there, their faces wreathed in smiles, stood Otto, Rachel and Sam.

'The Berlin flight is due in ten minutes, Major,' said the elderly Swiss customs officer. Nodding his thanks, Major Weiss walked through the door and out of the office. There was a cold wind blowing across the airfield as he buttoned his greatcoat and waited for the plane to land. It circled overhead and made a perfect landing, taxiing slowly to a halt. The major waited for the passengers to disembark, recognising Rudi instantly. Walking over, he raised his right hand to the peak of his cap in salute, smiled and said, 'Welcome to Basel. It's nice to see you again, young man.' Turning to Astrid, he continued, 'You must be Frau Wagner. I'm pleased to meet you at last.' Finally, he looked at the Goldmanns, and said, 'A very special welcome to you. Now, if you would follow me, I'll personally see to your immigration formalities. You, Frau Wagner and you, Rudi, can go through the normal channels.' The Goldmanns followed Major Weiss into an office very similar to the one in Berlin. 'Please, sit down,' said Weiss, jovially. 'This shouldn't take long. If I could please have all of your documents.' The three sat, looking from one to the other.

'Did you have any problems in Berlin?' asked the Major.

'No, but it was a bit nerve-racking, nonetheless,' admitted Otto.

'I promise that this won't be in the slightest bit nerve-racking, Herr Goldmann,' said Weiss as he sifted through their papers. After scrutinising the documents carefully for a few minutes, he smiled and stamped the papers in front of him. 'Perfect,' he said, 'On behalf of the Swiss government, I welcome you all to your new home and hope that you will be truly happy in our little country.' Standing, he solemnly shook hands with each of them.

The gleaming, black Daimler stood at the curb in front of the airport entrance, its doors open. The Goldmanns walked through the entrance. Standing there were Stefan, Max, Rudi and Astrid, their faces showing both delight and happiness. Dropping her bag, Rachel ran and flung herself into Rudi's waiting arms, tears of joy streaming down her face. For the first time, they were able to truly show their love for each other.

46

A fine powdering of snow dusted the Münsterplatz as the wedding party pulled up outside Stefan's luxury house. Jumping out of the car, they rushed indoors out of the cold wind that swirled around the square, laughing and joking. The table in the dining-room seemed to be groaning under the weight of food and champagne that had been laid out before they'd left for the town hall.

'Come on everyone, let's have a drink and toast the happy couple,' said Stefan in great, good humour.

'Yes, a good idea!' laughed Otto, walking over to the table and opening a bottle of the vintage champagne as the others crowded into the room. The civil wedding ceremony at the town hall had been simple but moving, the young couple obviously totally in love. Filling their glasses, Otto and Max handed them around. Rudi and Rachel stood in the centre of the room holding hands, their gleaming gold wedding bands sparkling in the firelight.

'A toast to the happy couple,' said Stefan raising his glass.

'The happy couple!' everyone responded, lifting their glasses.

Otto said, 'I'd like to welcome you, Rudi, to our family. For me, it's an honour to have you as my son-in-law. May God be with you both. The debt that my family owes to you can never be repaid, and we owe you our freedom. For my daughter to have the name Wagner is for me a very great pleasure. His eyes filled with tears and he brushed them aside. 'Thank you.'

'No, Otto, thank *you* for having such a beautiful daughter,' said Rudi. Turning to Rachel, he continued, 'Thank you my darling for having me. Shall we tell them?'

Rachel blushed slightly and said, 'Well, yes, I suppose that we should, don't you?'

'Ladies and gentlemen, my wife and I,'—everyone laughed —'have an announcement to make. It's especially important to you, Mother and you too, Otto. We've rather put the wagon before the horse.' He hesitated slightly, not quite sure how they would react to the news. 'You're both going to be grandparents in April.' He continued.

There was silence for a second. Sam piped up, 'Oh, I know what you two have been doing.' There was a roar of laughter as the ice was broken and everyone crowded around, kissing Rachel and slapping Rudi on the back.

Astrid, standing next to Otto said, 'These are incredible times that we live in. I for one don't blame any young couple for living life to the full. None of us knows what's around the corner or where we'll be in one year's time. Let's not forget that we are the lucky ones. We're now free of the Nazis. There are many others who are not so fortunate and so I say a double congratulations: firstly on your marriage, and secondly on the coming birth of our first grandchild.'

Otto smiled, 'Young people nowadays — so impatient. However, Astrid is right. Congratulations! I hope that you go on to give us many more grandchildren.'

'Can we eat now? I'm starving,' said Sam.

Everyone gathered round the table and helped themselves, laughing and joking. 'Not long now. We'll soon be on our way to Lucerne,' said Rudi, squeezing Rachel's hand.

'Yes, I can't wait. Two whole weeks. I must say that they took our news remarkably calmly. I must be honest, I was a bit nervous at first.'

'Yes, so was I. You know, darling, I can't believe this. I must be the luckiest man alive. When we first met in August I wondered if we would ever be able to overcome our problems. Now, here we are, in early November, married in a new country, with a new life.'

For a moment, Rachel's face clouded, 'Yes, but you have to go back.'

'It won't be for long, I promise. Anyway, don't let's think about that now sweetheart. I can't wait for us to be alone tonight.'

She giggled, 'Neither can I, Herr Wagner.'

The small group stood at the front door waving as the car turned out of Münsterplatz.

'Come on let's go inside, it's freezing,' said Stefan. As they entered the library, they all sat by the fire, happy and content. Sam excused himself and walked upstairs to his room, feeling the need to be alone for a while.

'What a lovely day for them both,' said Astrid, giving a little smile. 'You're right, Otto — young people nowadays! But you can't blame them for trying to find a little happiness while they can. I just thank God that we were able to get you all out. I have a bad feeling that I can't shake off and I don't know why. After all, we're safe here in Switzerland.'

'Yes, but as you say, we're the lucky ones,' replied Otto. 'I meant what I said earlier — the debt that we owe you we can never repay.'

'Otto, think nothing of it. All we did was smooth the way,' said Stefan. 'Now that your capital has been transferred, you can think about buying a little business for yourself.'

Nodding, Otto said, 'Do you know my father, may he rest in peace, was both a watchsmith and a very talented draughtsman. His drawings were magnificent and he taught me everything that I know. The drawing side I haven't done for years, of course, but I haven't forgotten. It's something that you don't forget. In fact, at one point I nearly took up draughtsmanship as a profession. '

Max glanced at Stefan, their two minds fixed on the same point.

Almost as if he could read their thoughts, Otto said, hesitantly, 'If you don't mind me asking, this work that Rudi's involved in, is it dangerous? If it's secret or anything ...'

Stefan raised his hand, 'Yes, it's very dangerous. I'll tell you all about it over dinner. Now that you're safely out of Germany, I feel that you have a right to know.' Turning to Astrid, Stefan asked, 'Would you mind taking Sam out for a spot of dinner this evening and then perhaps to the cinema? It's better that he knows nothing about the Circle. He's a bit too young at the moment and the three of us can have a long talk.'

'Yes, that's a good idea. I haven't been to the cinema myself in a long time.'

'Tell us more about your drawing ability, Otto,' said Max.

'Well, it's not drawing pictures — more technical, plans and things like that. It was more of a hobby really. As I say, I trained as a watchsmith.'

'Tell me, seriously, could you copy documents, ID cards, things like that?' asked Max.

'You mean forgery?'

'You're catching on, Otto,' said Stefan.

Otto chuckled, 'It's funny that you should say that, but when I was young I often thought it would be a good idea to try my hand at something along those lines. You know, make a bit of extra cash ... times were hard but I suppose that I was too law-abiding.'

'For instance,' persisted Max, 'if you had the right paper, you know, the genuine article, could you forge, for example, an ID card?'

'Well, I'd be a bit rusty at first, but yes, I probably could. What do you have in mind?'

'We have many contacts in Germany and getting the correct paper and blanks wouldn't be a great problem. It's often occurred to me on my various journeys into the country that a set of false documents would be very handy. The problem is, that I'd be reluctant to approach the criminal fraternity … someone might get too nosey and that's the last thing we want. However, if you could do the job for us …' Max's voice trailed away.

Otto smiled, 'If you can get me the correct things that I'd need, with a little practice I'll guarantee that you'll get very good forgeries. Now, I don't know the details. I expect that I'll learn that tonight. If it means my being able in some small way to get back at the tormentors of my people, then I'll gladly do anything that I can to help you.'

'Alright, Otto,' said Stefan, 'what you need is a small business in the town, watch making, jewellery. Things like that. At the same time you can do a little work for us on the side. You see, Max is right. Rudi, Bruno and Werner need sets of false documents, all kinds of documents. With good forgeries they can bluff their way out of a lot of difficult situations.'

'Don't forget me,' said Max. 'We have the uniforms. If we have the correct papers to go with them, there's nothing that we can't do.' There was a sense of excitement in the air.

'Oh, you don't know how wonderful it would be for me to fight these vile Nazis. I'm not the stuff of heroes, I know, but I can make a contribution, really do something to help. Yes! Please count me in.'

Stefan chuckled, 'Rudi has a new wife and the Altmann Circle has a new member. Welcome to the club, Otto.'

47

The murmur of voices suddenly quietened, and finally stopped as newly-promoted SS-Brigadier Langers entered the conference room. Walking to the head of the table, he looked around and casually lifted his right arm, saying, 'Heil Hitler.' Everyone in the room responded. Dieter was sitting to Langers' right. Around the table were representatives of the SS, SA and Gestapo.

'Alright, Gentlemen,' said Langers, 'Most of you, I've no doubt, are aware of the reasons for this meeting. For those of you who are not, I'll bring you up to date on the events of the past two days. Yesterday, the 7th of November, a young, Polish Jew went to our Embassy in Paris and shot and mortally wounded the third secretary, Ernst Vom Rath. His name was Herschel Grynspan and he had some bee in his bonnet about the treatment of his family. They, along with a few thousand other Jews, were deported to Poland apparently. The problem is that the Poles didn't want them either. I mean, let's face it, who does?' There was a laugh from around the room as Langers continued. 'This young Jew has done us a big favour as we now have a good reason to teach these Yids a lesson that they won't forget in a very long time. The order is at this moment going to different offices around the Greater Reich. There's to be, and I quote, 'A spontaneous uprising of the German people.' He sniggered, 'So spontaneous that it's not planned until tomorrow night, that is, the 9th. The instruction has come from Dr Goebbels and he's been given the nod by the Führer. At the moment, both General Heidrich and Himmler are in Munich. The target is the Jews; their property: shops, houses and, most importantly, the Synagogues — they're to be destroyed.'

A Brownshirt officer lifted his hand and enquired, 'You say that this will be happening all over the Reich, Brigadier?'

'Yes, every city, town and hamlet. Now — this is important — you must instruct your men that they are not, under any circumstances, to touch Aryan-owned property. We don't care what they do to the Jews, and that includes the Jews themselves, but, I repeat, they're not to touch German property.'

'At what time will this start, Sir?' asked a young SS man.

'Late tomorrow evening. It'll be the SA who'll do most of the work and they'll need pickaxes, crowbars, sledgehammers and cans of petrol. Remember, the Synagogues are to be primary targets. Where possible, of course, your men should wear civilian clothes. Any questions?' No one spoke. 'Alright, your local offices will be given further instructions, including names and addresses, to make sure that you know where to find our Jewish friends. Gentlemen, let's make this a night to remember, or should I put it another way, a night that they'll never forget. I'll tell you something, after tomorrow the fate of the Jews will be in the hands of a far more efficient organisation than the SA. Let the Brownshirts have their final fling, because after that the SS will be responsible for the Jewish problem. By the day after tomorrow, I want to see the streets of this city littered with broken glass. That's it, dismissed.'

48

Old Felix Goldbaum sat in his favourite armchair, the newspaper covering his knees as he dozed after his supper. His wife, Sarah, looked over at the eighty-five-year-old man that she loved as much today as she had on the day that they'd married some sixty- five years previously. She smiled. The two of them were still talking about the concert that the two young musicians had given a few short weeks ago. Contentedly knitting, she sat facing her son and daughter-in-law as they sat at the table, Philip reading and Clare looking through a catalogue. They had a large apartment above their shop, a delicatessen, on the Kurfürstendamm. Glancing at the clock on the wall, Philip noticed that it was approaching 10pm.

His ears pricked up as he heard a faint sound, like a low roar. 'What's that?' he murmured to himself. By now, Clare and Sarah had heard it, too. A little further down the street they heard a loud crack as a window shattered. Jumping up, Philip raced to the window and looked out. In the distance he could see a red glow in the sky. 'What's going on?'

By this time Felix had begun to stir. 'What's that noise?' he muttered. Another window smashed and then another — all the time getting closer.

There were shouts coming from outside, 'Fucking Yids! Come on, it's time to teach them a lesson.' Another window broke with a resounding crash. Sarah and Clare were by now both standing, shaking with fear as the noise approached.

'Here's another!' a man shouted, just outside. There was a huge explosion as the shop window caved in and the door downstairs was broken open. Shards of glass were scattered everywhere, covering the display of food and delicacies that decorated the front window. Philip started to run towards the door of the lounge. As he reached it, it was kicked open, smashing into his face. Dazed and in great pain, he staggered back and fell.

Standing in the doorway were three men, grinning at each other. 'Well, well, look what we have here, four of them. Evening Israel, evening Sarah,' he said giving a mock bow. Downstairs were the sounds of other people and the crunch of broken and smashed jars being trampled underfoot. The three men entered the room, pushing past Clare as they saw the collection of family silver displayed on the sideboard.

'Oh, very nice. What are you fucking Yids doing with this, eh?' said one of the thugs.

Philip managed to stand, his face covered with blood. 'Leave that alone! You have no right ...'

'Shut the fuck up, you Jewish turd,' said the third man, turning and smashing his fist into Philip's face, knocking him down again. He turned and pocketed a silver snuffbox that had belonged to Felix's grandfather. The two women were quivering with fear as the three men started to help themselves to the smaller pieces of silver.

Another man appeared at the head of the stairs carrying a large container in his brawny arms. 'I've got a present for you, fucking Jews,' he snarled. He saw Philip struggling to rise and walked over, kicking him in the head as he upended the container over his prone body. 'Here you are, some pig's blood — just what you need!' he shouted as the blood cascaded onto Philip and over the floor.

Felix, shaking with rage as he saw his home defiled in such a way, shouted, 'You filthy animals! You're not human beings! You're not fit to be called members of the human race! Get out, get out!'

The brawny man turned, threw the container on the floor, and said, menacingly, 'Not fit to be members of the human race, eh? You shrivelled old Jew.' Bodily lifting the frail old man, he raised him above his head and threw him with all his force through the plate glass window. As the body hit it, the glass exploded outward. Turning over and over, Felix's body flew through the air, his head making contact with the pavement below, smashing his skull. Sarah gave an ear-piercing scream and fell to the floor. The four Brownshirts, without looking back, walked down the stairs, through the ruined shop and into the street.

49

The black staff car drove slowly down Budapester Straße and past the Kaiser-Wilhelm memorial church. Sitting in the back were Dieter and Langers. Just in front and to the right, they could see a red glow in the sky as they approached the Kurfürstendamm. A policeman suddenly appeared in front of the car and lifted his hand signalling for them to stop. Looking inside as Dieter rolled the window down, the policeman saluted and said, 'Good evening, Sir. I wouldn't drive any further if I were you, you'll just rip the tyres to shreds. The whole of the Kurfürstendamm's covered with broken glass. It's chaos out there.'

Langers nodded. 'Thank you, Officer.' Turning to Dieter, he said, 'Come on, it's a lovely evening for walk.' The two men, wearing calf-length greatcoats over their uniforms, got out and put on their peaked caps at a jaunty angle, the death's head badge gleaming in the overhead light. Looking at his driver, Langers said, 'Wait here, we won't be too long.'

Dieter glanced at his watch. It was 1am as he and the brigadier walked down the wide street, broken glass crunching under their jackboots. Shouts and cries filled the night and the sound of breaking windows was all around them. People seemed to be flitting in and out of the shadows everywhere, some carrying the looted possessions of their unfortunate victims. They turned right into Fasanenstraße and looked down at a mob that had congregated in front of the Synagogue. The night sky was filled with black, choking smoke as the fire devoured the building. The crowd, their faces illuminated by the raging fire, gave a collective shout as the windows exploded in the intense heat. At the front of the building, someone had lit a secondary bonfire. Some of the men in the crowd were throwing prayer books onto it and had managed to get hold of the sacred Torah which they were tearing to shreds and feeding into the flames with shouts of glee.

There was a fire engine standing at the curb, the crew looking on with their hands in their pockets as the synagogue devoured itself. Walking over, Langers said to the senior fireman, 'What are your instructions?'

Seeing the brigadier's uniform, the man stiffened and replied, 'Just to make sure that the buildings either side don't catch fire, Sir. As for the church, or whatever you call it, we're just going to allow that to burn to ash. By the morning it'll be no more than a smoking ruin.'

'Good, thank you.' Turning to Dieter, Langers said, 'Come on Dieter, let's drive over to the SS barracks at Lichterfelde. I could do with a brandy.' Surveying the damage around them as they slowly made their way back to the car, Langers smiled. 'Dieter,' he said, 'I think tonight's little effort's been a great success. The reports coming in from all over the Reich are the same: destruction on a massive scale. Tonight will go down in history. Don't you think that's it's wonderful to be the makers of history, my boy?' The two men were slowly walking along as if out for a Sunday stroll; Langers, dragging on a cigarette and Dieter walking by his side, hands clasped behind his back. Langers looked at Dieter and suddenly asked, 'Have you ever met Colonel Eichmann?' Without waiting for a reply, he continued, 'He's our Jewish expert you know. He's in Vienna at the moment, sorting them out there. An incredible man, even speaks a little Yiddish. He's spent years studying them and is wise to their ways — very efficient. I think that we'll hear a lot of him in the future. I meant what I said, you know; after tonight we will be in charge of the Jew's future and may their God help them.

'There's something that I'd like to know, Sir?'

'What's that?'

Dieter chuckled, 'Who's going to pay the bill for tonight's little exercise? I mean, this damage will cost a fortune to put right.'

'The Jews of course. After all, it was they who provoked this incident. Don't you worry, Göring will make sure that the bill's paid in full with a bit left over.' As the two men approached the staff car, the driver jumped out and opened the back door. Langers looked at Dieter, a twinkle in his eye as he turned to get into the car. He paused, and said, 'By the way, your promotion came through today. Congratulations, Captain Hoffmann, you must be the youngest Captain in the SD, probably even the whole SS. Come on, you can buy me that drink.' Dieter's heart soared as he climbed into the car. 'Yes! Onwards and upwards,' he said to himself as they drove away, leaving the carnage behind them.

50

Papa Stern paced up and down. The old Jewish musician was frightened and agitated. He'd been thinking of going to bed when he'd heard the shouts and strange noises in the distance. Looking out of the window he could see a red glow in the sky and he didn't understand it; it terrified him. As he walked, muttering to himself, he heard a car pulling up in his drive with a squeal of tyres. The car door was opened and he heard hurried footsteps approaching the front door. He stopped his pacing as the front doorbell rang again and again, giving it a sense of urgency.

Walking into the hall, the old man called out with fear in his voice, 'Who is it? What do you want?'

'Papa, open the door. It's me, Paul. Hurry Papa!'

Giving a sigh of relief, he went to the front door, fumbling with the lock in his haste to open it.

Paul was standing in the doorway, his overcoat draped over his shoulders. Behind him Papa could see the car, its doors wide open and engine running. 'Thank God you're here. There are terrible things happening in the city tonight. Papa, get your coat and come with me. Hurry!'

Sensing Paul's urgency, the old man turned quickly and took down his overcoat. 'Wait, Paul, my violin.' Hurrying into the lounge, he picked up the precious two hundred and fifty year old instrument and, turning off the lights, left the room. 'I'm coming now,' muttered Papa, as he walked out of the front door, locking it behind him. As he climbed into the front seat, he demanded, 'What's happening, Paul?'

'The Jews are being attacked. It's chaos in town, smashed shops, burning buildings, everyone's gone mad,' he said as he pulled away at speed. 'I said to mother and Alex that I was coming over. You must stay with us for the next few days. Listen, I'm going to take the long way around and avoid the city centre.'

Pushing open the front door, Paul ushered Papa in.

'Come on through.' The two men entered. Standing there were Rosa, Alex and a man that Papa had never seen before.

'Oh, thank God you were in, Papa,' said Rosa, embracing the old man. Alex kissed Papa on each cheek.

'We were very worried about you, Papa.'

'This is Larry Holmes, Papa. He's the cultural attaché at the American Embassy.'

'I'm pleased to meet you,' said the old man in perfect but accented English.

'No, sir, I'm pleased to meet you. I've heard a lot about you.'

'Come, sit down, pour us all a drink Paul darling, would you?' said Rosa, 'The whole world's gone mad. Larry and I were just leaving the restaurant when it started.'

'Yeh, all hell was let loose. These goddamned Nazis have gone crazy. I tell you, when the world's press gets to hear about this, there'll be big trouble.'

Papa nodded as Paul handed him a drink,

'Mr Holmes, we Jews are beginning to get used to treatment like this. I fear for our future more and more each day.'

'Mr Holmes,' said Alex, looking keenly at Papa, 'after the news that you've given us tonight, isn't there perhaps anything that we can do for Papa? After all, he's been Paul's teacher since Paul was five.'

Looking from one to the other Papa asked, 'News, what news?'

Paul responded, 'Mr Holmes has just told us that Alex and I are to be invited to do a concert tour of America, starting in January.'

Despite the circumstances of his being there that night, Papa's eyes lit up, his face radiating joy. 'But that's wonderful, just wonderful news. I'm so happy for you both — congratulations!'

Looking at Alex, Holmes said, 'What do you have in mind son?'

'Well, as Paul's teacher and mentor, surely he should be invited too?'

Paul looked hopefully towards Holmes, as he replied, 'You have a good point, and it's not as if you're asking to emigrate, at least not officially. A visitor's visa could be arranged for Mr Stern, no problem.'

'Well, Papa?' said Paul.

'That would be wonderful. Could you really arrange it, Herr Holmes?'

'Sure, and after tonight I can't see the Nazis standing in your way. After all, you're the kid's teacher and it's really good propaganda for them.'

'Papa,' said Paul, 'I must tell you this. Alex and I have no intention of returning. We'll ask for leave to stay on artistic grounds and Mr Holmes assures us that there'll be no problem. If you come with us, are you prepared to leave everything that you own behind? The Nazis must think that we're coming back.'

'Before you answer that question,' said Holmes, 'I'd take a look out of that window. As you yourself have said, things are going to get a lot worse for the Jews in this country. After what I've seen tonight, it seems these guys are capable of anything and I mean anything!'

Looking around, Papa replied, with a sigh, 'You're right of course, they want us all dead. If I can just take my violin, then yes, Mr Holmes, if you can arrange it for me, then I would love to go to America.'

Giving a broad grin, Holmes said, 'Consider it done.' As Paul and Alex jumped up and started to hug the old man.

51

arah Goldbaum stared into space. The doctor turned to Clare and Philip, whose hair was still streaked and matted with pig's blood. 'She's in a catatonic state, I'm afraid. Get her to bed and keep her quiet. I've prepared a sedative.' The doctor stood up, nodded and left the room. The air was cold as it poured in through the smashed living room window. Outside, as the dawn was breaking, all was now quiet.

'Come on Mother,' said Clare, helping the old lady to her feet and leading her into the bedroom. After a while she came back and looked at Philip. 'She's sleeping,' she said as she walked over to her husband and put her arms around him, tears streaming down her face. 'What's to become of us, Philip?' Philip had no answer.

A little later Philip went to check on his mother.

'Clare, come here, quickly!' said Philip. The old lady was lying in the bed that she'd shared with the man she'd loved for more than sixty years. Her eyes stared sightlessly at the ceiling. Clare walked in as Philip gently pulled the cover over his mother's head.

The young couple clung onto each other in their grief, and sobbed until it seemed their hearts would break.

Philip stood with his arms wrapped around his torso trying to keep warm. Standing in a column were about one hundred Jewish men and boys. The police had arrived just after his mother had died and taken him away.

A young lad of about seventeen asked fearfully, 'What are they going to do with us?'

'I don't know,' replied Philip, his hair still matted with the pig's blood from the previous evening. Walking up and down menacingly were a number of SS men and Brownshirts. Everyone looked up as four or five army lorries turned the corner and pulled up alongside the column.

'Right! Get on board. Move!' shouted one of the SS men, 'Come, *Schnell!*'

The column quickly dispersed as the men and boys hurried to do as they were ordered and clambered aboard the waiting lorries. Pulling away, the transport headed north out of the city. After travelling for a while Philip looked out of the back of the lorry and noticed a sign which read: SACHSENHAUSEN 5 km.

52

The mid-December sky was overcast, threatening more snow. Berlin was covered in a blanket of white as the afternoon traffic drove carefully down Unter Den Linden. A double-decker Berlin bus went chugging past as Alex, Paul and Papa Stern walked up to the entrance of the American Embassy and entered. The three were soon ensconced in Larry Holmes's office, drinking coffee, the warmth enveloping them after the cold outside.

'Well, you guys, everything's finally arranged,' said the tall, gangly American. He continued, 'I've had your passports stamped for entry into the States as visitors. They're good for six months. Here are your official invitations from the American State Department. One for you too, Herr Stern. Your Propaganda ministry has been officially informed by the Ambassador.' Larry chuckled, 'Boy, after last month's incident, they sure do need some good publicity and they're delighted with this invitation.'

'What about me, Herr Holmes?' said Papa anxiously.

'No problem. They tried to be a bit difficult, I believe, but the boss twisted a few arms and in the end they agreed. You'll probably be receiving an official letter from them, but don't worry. I've two documents here for you, Papa — you don't mind if I call you Papa, do you?'

Papa grinned, 'Not at all, everyone else does.'

Holmes continued, 'One's in German and the other in English stating that you have the right to enter the States. Don't forget, as far as they're concerned, you're coming back.'

'Yes, Larry, what about that?' said Paul, 'Will we have any problems? I mean what should we do?'

'Well, I'll tell you. After about three months, ask to see one of the officials who'll be organising everything for you. You know, your concert schedule and things like that. Explain what you want, lay it on a bit thick, how you have no artistic freedom and your musical talent's stifled in Germany. I can promise you, the State Department will agree; in fact, it's already been arranged. Don't forget there are many fine artists already living in the States, who left Germany for those reasons when the Nazis first came to power. Now you, Papa, are a fine musician in your own right, also you're a Jew. All that you have to say is that you fear persecution. Let me tell you, we have a very large Jewish community back home and they're spitting fire after what happened here last month. I tell you, they shot themselves in the foot; world opinion was outraged.'

Alex gave his boyish grin. 'Wow, you yanks are efficient,' he said, in his best American accent.

'We do our best, you guys, we do our best. By the way, I can tell you that your first public appearance will be at Carnegie Hall in New York City at the end of January.'

Everyone smiled.

'Oh, wonderful!' said Papa. 'I played there with the Vienna Philharmonic Orchestra in 1920.' His face took on a faraway look for a few seconds as he remembered the experience.

'Do you know what I'm going to play for that first concert?' said Paul, excitedly. 'The Mendelssohn E minor concerto.'

'I think that I'll play the Greig,' said Alex. 'I love that concerto.'

Larry laughed, 'You guys can play anything you like. Believe me, you'll be a smash hit stateside. I believe that you're leaving on the *Bremen* at the beginning of next month?'

'Yes, that's right, all booked. We can't wait, can we?' said Paul as the others grinned and nodded their agreement.

'Okay, you guys, thanks for coming by. Paul, tell your mother that I'll call her later this week, and of course I'll see you at your gala performance. Don't be surprised if Dr Goebbels comes over to speak to you about the tour, will you?'

'Oh, Dr Goebbels,' said Alex, 'My hero.'

Laughing, the four men stood and Larry ushered them out.

After leaving the Embassy, Alex insisted on buying them all coffee and cream cakes at Kranzler's. Papa was in such good humour that he forgot any fear that he would normally have had.

'Now listen, Papa,' said Paul, 'this gala concert that we're doing — how would you, Robert and Isaac like to sit in with the rest of the orchestra and play?'

Papa nearly dropped his coffee cup with surprise, 'Are you serious?'

Yes, I spoke to Anton Bruch, the orchestra's leader, and he thinks that it's a great idea. He spoke to the other members and they would be delighted. In fact, they think that it's a huge joke; to be able to get one over on the Nazis like that, what a laugh!'

'Yes, but what about maestro Furtwangler?'

'Anton's spoken to him and he's happy to turn a blind eye. In fact, I think that he thinks that it's a good joke too. Although he'd never admit it.'

'Oh, to be able to play with the Philharmonic just one last time,' said Papa, 'Yes! We'll do it.'

'Alright, the first rehearsal's at 11am, the day after tomorrow.'

Chuckling to himself, Papa said, 'Come, more coffee and cake everyone.'

Paul looked at Alex and winked, his face creased in a huge smile as it started to snow again outside.

53

As Adolf Hitler and his party entered what had once been the royal box, the audience rose almost as one. Turning and facing the Führer they lifted their right arms. Hitler nodded, returned the salute and sat.

The hum of voices started to die in the packed auditorium as the house lights dimmed. People looked towards the stage expectantly as the members of the large Berlin Philharmonic Orchestra waited quietly for the great Wilhelm Furtwangler to walk out. Standing in the wings with the conductor were Paul and Alex looking immaculate in their evening dress. Furtwangler smiled, nodded, and walked out onto the stage. Immediately the air was filled with the sound of applause. Mounting the rostrum, the conductor turned, bowed and faced the orchestra. Bringing the baton down, the strains of the German national anthem filled the hall, accompanied by the voices of the large audience, singing with all their pride in the new Germany. Furtwangler started the concert proper, the opening bars of Wagner's overture 'Tannhäuser' filling the auditorium. Paul and Alex looked across the orchestra at Papa sitting with the first violins, a look of absolute joy fixed on his face. Both Robert and Isaac were amongst the players and were equally as happy.

'That's where he belongs,' whispered Paul as Alex nodded his agreement.

'When we're in America he'll be allowed to start again, Paul.'

The two young musicians fell silent, listening to the undoubtedly beautiful music of Wagner as it reached its climax and came to a triumphal end. Furtwangler left the stage to loud applause then turned and walked back out, taking another bow. As he returned for a third time, Paul picked up his violin in preparation and looked Alex straight in the eyes, mouthing, 'I love you.' Alex smiled and winked. Furtwangler came back as the applause started to die down.

'Are you ready, Paul?' he said, smiling.

'Certainly, Maestro,' said Paul.

'Then, after you.'

Leading the way, Paul walked out onto the stage. Immediately, there was the thunder of applause as the young violinist went up to the leader of the orchestra and shook hands. He looked over at Papa, smiled and raised his hand. Turning to face the audience, he bowed low. In front of him was a sea of faces, the men in evening dress or uniform, the women wearing evening gowns, their jewellery glinting in the subdued light. Looking over at Paul from the podium, Furtwangler smiled and raised his eyebrows as if to say, 'Are you ready?' Paul nodded as a complete silence descended over the concert hall. The conductor raised his baton and brought it down, the timpanist beating out the first *pianissimo* four beats of the opening bar, boom-boom-boom-boom. The beautiful sounds of the Beethoven concerto filled the hall as Paul tucked the violin under his chin and prepared to play.

The concerto was reaching its climax, the notes seeming to fly effortlessly out of the instrument. There was a fine film of sweat on Paul's brow and upper lip as every sinew of his being was given to the great composer's music. As the piece came to its wonderful conclusion, Paul slowly lowered his bow. For a few seconds there was a total silence in the hall, and then the audience erupted with applause as people started to stand and give an ovation. Paul bowed and left the stage, returning five or six times as the clapping continued. 'More! More!' shouted people from all over the auditorium. The members of the orchestra were standing, the string players tapping their bows on the music stands, enthusiastically adding their praise for his performance.

Tears were streaming down Papa's face. 'That was the most wonderful performance that I've ever heard, Paul. You are truly a musical genius,' he murmured with awe in his voice.

Lifting his hands for silence, the applause started to die down as Paul put his violin once more under his chin and lifted the bow. In contrast to the Beethoven, his encore was a hauntingly beautiful piece by Bach. When he'd finished, he bowed and left the stage, resisting further calls for an encore.

The second half of the concert was as incredible as the first. The darkly handsome young Alex walked on to the stage, again to rapturous applause and sat in front of the keyboard. Flexing his fingers, he looked over at Furtwangler and nodded. The introduction from the orchestra of the Brahms Second Concerto filled the concert hall, the audience holding its breath in anticipation of Alex's entry.

The concerto came to a climax, finishing with a *fortissimo* chord. Lifting a handkerchief, Alex mopped the sweat from his brow as again the auditorium erupted into applause. Alex stood and bowed, shaking hands with the leader and Furtwangler before leaving the stage, returning again and again, the last time with Paul carrying his violin.

The audience went wild as Alex sat again at the piano and Paul raised his hands asking for quiet. The applause died away and people began to sit in anticipation of the encore that they knew was to come. 'My Führer, Ladies and Gentlemen, thank you all for your wonderful reception this evening. The people of Berlin will always be in our hearts.'

'Hear! Hear!' said Alex, a cheeky grin all over his face, to loud laughter and applause from the audience.

'If you have time, do you have the time?'

'Yes!' roared the whole auditorium.

'Very well, we'd like to play for you the violin Sonata Number 10 in G Major, Opus 96 by Beethoven. Thank you.'

The two virtuoso musicians played sublimely, the Beethoven finishing with a glittering cascade of notes.

The air was filled with the hum of conversation and the clink of Champagne glasses as white-jacketed waiters circulated carrying trays of drinks and canapés. People were continually coming across to congratulate Paul and Alex on their performance as they stood with Rosa, Larry, Rudi and Bruno. Suddenly, a hush descended on the large reception room as people almost came to attention, some hastily extinguishing their cigarettes. Standing with his entourage in the large double doorway stood the Führer of all Germany, Adolf Hitler. All around the room, people raised their right arms in the Hitler salute, which he casually acknowledged. Accompanied by Reichsminister Hermann Göring, Dr Joseph Goebbels, their wives, and a bodyguard of SS, he walked over towards the two young musicians, a smile on his face. As he approached, the crowd parted respectfully.

Paul and Alex straightened, both raising their right arms, 'Good evening, young gentlemen,' said the most powerful man in the Reich as he extended his right hand and shook first Paul's hand and then Alex's. 'May I congratulate both on a wonderful performance,' his piercing eyes moved from one to the other, 'You are both a credit to the Reich.'

'Thank you my Führer,' said Paul and Alex simultaneously, totally mesmerised by the man's stare.

'I believe that you are to represent us on a tour of America soon?'

'Yes, my Führer,' answered Alex, 'We're both looking forward to it very much.'

'Good, good,' answered Hitler, 'Do not forget that you are envoys of the greater German Reich. You are both my personal representative and that of the German *Volk*.' He paused, smiled, and then continued, 'I'm sure that you will both prove to be great ambassadors for our nation. I wish you both a successful tour and when you return I would like to hear a full report of your time in that great country.'

'You certainly will, Sir,' responded Alex.

Hitler nodded and turned, abruptly heading in the direction of the doors, closely followed by his retinue. People again came to attention and raised their right arms in salute, the hush followed by a babble of conversation as the Führer left the room.

'God, I don't believe that that just happened,' murmured Bruno to Rudi. Lowering his voice even further, he whispered, 'I could have throttled the bastard.'

'Shush! You idiot,' hissed Rudi, 'We'll never have him so close again, worse luck.'

Both Paul and Alex looked dumbstruck, 'I should have played some variations on a theme of Wagner tonight, shouldn't I?' said Alex as everyone roared with laughter and the tension was broken.

Standing over to one side of the room, were two SS officers who'd stayed behind after Hitler had left. They wore the black number one dress, the blood red of their swastika armbands adding a splash of colour to the darkness of their uniforms.

Rudi glanced across at them and immediately froze as he recognised Dieter. Their eyes met for a fleeting moment, before Dieter turned towards his companion and said something. Langers looked over at the little group surrounding Paul and Alex, as if searching for Rudi, before he too turned away.

Rudi's heart started to beat a tattoo in his chest as he looked at his old friend and the person he held responsible for his father's death. Saying nothing to the others, he walked over in the direction of Dieter, his face cold and set. Seeing him approach, Dieter said something to his companion and walked towards Rudi, his black jackboots gleaming in the overhead light.

The two young men stopped and faced each other.

'It's been a long time, Rudi,' said Dieter holding out his hand.

'Four years,' replied Rudi ignoring the proffered hand and looking coldly at this black uniformed young man who stood in front of him.

'Tell me, what does it feel like to know that you're responsible for a decent man's death? A man who gave you nothing but love and friendship as you were growing up. A man who sat you on his knee when you were very little, and took us both fishing.' Rudi's voice was icy but controlled as he stared Dieter in the face and said, 'Well?'

A cold smile passed over Dieter's face. 'You conveniently forgot to mention that this man turned out to be a traitor just like my father. I do not have to justify myself to you, Rudi, but I'll tell you this, I'd do exactly the same again if necessary. I would advise you to remember that.'

'Advise me! Listen, I have nothing but contempt for you or the uniform that you so proudly wear.'

Dieter stiffened. 'Once, just this once, I'll forget that you said that, for old time's sake, but if you ever dare to say anything like that to me again I promise you a one way ticket to a concentration camp, just like your father.'

Giving his old boyhood friend a look of utter contempt, he replied, very quietly, 'I'm going to make you a promise, Dieter — if I'm ever given the opportunity, I'll kill you. I swear that on my father's grave.'

Dieter snorted, 'I doubt very much that you'd have enough courage to pull the trigger. The problem with you is that you are weak and always have been; you're not committed enough to anything. But be very careful. You've been warned, don't ever cross my path again because, if you do, I promise that there'll only be one winner, me!'

Rudi smiled and spoke looking Dieter directly in the eye, 'No, Dieter, you can't see it yet but it's you who've been warned.' Turning on his heel, Rudi rejoined the group who were standing around Paul and Alex.

Bruno looked at Rudi and said, 'Who was that black-uniformed piece of shit?'

'Remember that face, Bruno, he's our enemy,' replied Rudi, coldly.

54

Covering the table the snow-white damask cloth gleamed in the candlelight, the silver and crystal sparkling in the diffused light as the jovial company sitting around the table talked amongst themselves. Pushing his chair back, Rudi stood and raised his glass, saying, 'Rosa, Gentlemen, I'd like to propose a toast to Paul, Alex and Papa. May you have a successful tour and a long stay in America.' Lowering his voice, he continued, 'Longer than anyone expects.'

They all raised their glasses and said, 'Paul, Alex and Papa.' Robert and Isaac looked at each other with a mixture of both fear and happiness; happiness for Papa and the boys, fear for themselves and their future.

Standing, Alex looked around the table and said, 'This morning, Madam, Gentlemen, I received a telegram from my father. He's too busy making another million to be here in person to say *bon voyage*. Do you know? I don't care. Sitting around this table with me tonight are the finest friends that anyone could ask for.' He paused, looked at each of them and continued, 'To you Rosa, I can only say from my heart, thank you. If the others sitting around this table tonight only knew what you did for Paul and myself recently. You showed us both a love which can never be repaid. We'll both be grateful to our dying day.'

'Yes Mother, thank you.'

Alex continued, 'It would be a very great honour for me if you would allow me the privilege of calling you "Mother".' Everyone around the table was a little puzzled about exactly what Alex meant, but all realised that something important had just been said.

Rosa, her eyes filling with tears, said, 'Dear, dear, Alex, I'd be delighted to have such a handsome and talented young man as my second son. Yes, you may call me 'Mother', anytime.'

Bruno, not to be outdone, said, 'As everyone seems to be adopting everyone else around here, who would like to adopt me?'

There was laughter around the table and Rudi said, 'Bruno, no one in their right mind is going to adopt you, so I suggest that you shut up.'

'Well, I was only asking; it's time that my luck changed.'

'Okay, you guys,' said Larry, 'now seems like a good time to make an announcement. At dinner last night, I asked Rosa if she would do me the honour of being my wife. I'm very happy to say that she accepted.' There was loud applause from around the table. Paul looked at his mother, grinning from ear to ear.

'Well, darlings, it was time someone made an honest women out of me,' drawled Rosa. 'How could I resist this handsome American?'

Trudi came bustling from the kitchen, 'The caterers are just leaving, Frau Lindmann,' she said breathlessly.

'Thank you Trudi. Now, come and sit down and join us for a drink. Paul darling, pour Trudi some wine, will you?'

'Oh, thank you Madam, Master Paul.' Trudi looked at Paul sadly. 'What will I do without you and Master Alex to look after?' she said her eyes filling with tears.

'Trudi my love,' replied Paul, 'it's not forever. Anyway, you can come and visit us in America. Would you like that?'

'Oh, I'm not sure, all those gangsters …' everyone at the table roared with laughter. 'Now, I must go back to the kitchen, I don't trust those caterers,' she said, hurrying back towards the kitchen entrance.

Standing together in the foyer at the end of the evening, Paul and Alex embraced Rudi and Bruno. Looking shrewdly at Rudi, Paul said quietly, 'I don't know what you two are involved in. Both Alex and I love you like brothers so please, whatever it is, be careful won't you?'

'Don't worry, Paul, we both intend to tread very carefully, don't we Bruno?'

'Yes, we certainly do and you two, be happy and look after each other. We're going to miss you both. I for one will never forget our time together in the labour camp.'

'Yes,' said Paul, 'an awful lot's happened to us all since then; it seems like an age and yet it's only a few months.'

Papa looked at Isaac and Robert and there were tears in the eyes of all three men. They hugged each other, not wanting to let go, a feeling of absolute dread overcoming Papa as he looked at his two oldest friends. He feared for their future, 'Goodbye Isaac, Robert. May God guard and protect you both. Remember all the good times that we've had together and all the wonderful music we've played. They can't take that away from us, can they?'

'No old friend, they can't,' said Robert, quietly, 'You'll be in our prayers. Tell our fellow Jews in America what life is like for us here in Germany, won't you?'

'Yes, I will. I promise.'

55

The luxury liner *Bremen* pushed her way through the rough seas with ease as she headed out into the Atlantic Ocean. Paul and Alex were dressing for dinner in their luxurious stateroom, both feeling happier than they had for a very long time, a sense of absolute freedom overwhelming them as they readied themselves for their first evening on board. Walking over to Alex, Paul took him in his arms and gave him a long and leisurely kiss. 'Happy?' whispered Paul.

'I don't think that I've ever been happier,' murmured Alex, 'Do you think that it'll be safe to make love tonight?'

'Oh, yes, that's a very good idea.'

'Paul? Do you think that we should tell Papa about us?'

'No, Alex. He wouldn't understand, better to say nothing.'

At that moment there was a knock at the door. Paul went to answer it. Standing in the doorway was a ship's officer who saluted and said, 'Good evening, Gentlemen, the Captain sends his compliments and would like to invite you both to join him for dinner.'

'That's very good of him. Tell me, is my teacher Herr Stern invited too?'

The Purser looked embarrassed as he replied, 'No, sir, I don't think so.'

'In that case, tell the Captain that we decline his most generous offer.'

'Very good, sir, I'll tell him.'

'Thank you,' said Paul closing the door.

'Good for you, Paul,' said Alex.

'This is very much a German ship, isn't it? We're still on Reich territory. Ah well, it's only a few more days,' murmured Paul thoughtfully.

They were interrupted by another knock on the door. Standing there with a gleam in his eye and a smile that stretched from ear to ear, stood Papa, looking very suave in his evening dress.

Tucked underneath his arm he carried a bottle of champagne. 'Good evening my two *Wunderkinder*,' he laughed as he entered and continued, 'Close the door, quickly, I've something to show you.'

'What is it, Papa?' said Paul seeing the excitement on the old man's face.

'What is it? I've fooled the Brownshirts.' To Papa all Nazis were Brownshirts. Putting his hand in his jacket pocket, he took out a small but bulging leather wash-bag. Walking over, he opened it and poured the contents out on to the table, looking with satisfaction from one to the other.

'My God!' said Paul, as he and Alex looked down at the table unable to believe their eyes. Lying in front of them was a small mountain of sparkling diamonds. 'Where did you get those, Papa?' said Paul with an air of bewilderment.

Chuckling, the old man replied, 'Ever since I was a young man, whenever I've had some money to spare, I've invested in these. Over the years, as you can see, they've mounted up.'

'There must be a fortune there,' said Alex.

'Oh, yes,' replied Papa, 'I'm sure there is. I've been collecting them for twenty-five years. You see, I've never liked stocks and shares, I don't like paper, and gold's too heavy.' He smiled. 'And so I decided on diamonds. My father taught me to always be prepared for a rainy day and so here we are. These, my young friends, will insure my old age. Now, Champagne's in order, I think.'

Paul opened the bottle and poured three glasses, handing them around, 'A toast to our freedom; may it last for a very long time.'

'Our freedom,' replied Papa and Alex.

Turning to Paul, Alex said with a wide grin, 'I don't suppose we'll get that invitation from the Captain now.'

'Fuck the Captain!' replied Paul as he started to laugh, joined by Alex and then Papa and soon there were howls of laughter from all three of them. They were all unable to stop as they rocked with laughter, cried and slapped each other on the back until they could laugh no more.

The little mountain of diamonds glinted at them from the centre of the table.

56

Max stood underneath a street light, looking through the cold clammy fog at the entrance to the bar. The street was quiet at this time of the evening; Wedding seemed to be in hibernation, the occupants asleep. Crossing the road, Max pushed open the door and went in, a smell of stale beer and cigarette smoke hitting him in the face. There were a number of empty tables around the dingy room, as it was still too early for the regular clientele, most of them still at work. Standing behind the bar, polishing a glass stood an enormously fat man wearing a stained and greasy apron, the light reflecting off his bald head.

Walking across the room Max approached the bar and said, 'Good evening, Comrade, a beer and schnapps please, and have a drink yourself. Looking around, Max noticed two old men sitting in the corner playing cards.

Nodding, the man turned and poured two glasses of schnapps, pushing one towards Max while pouring the beer.

'A filthy night,' muttered the fat man in a gravelly voice, the result of twenty years of strong cigarettes.

'Yes, I'm hoping that you'll be able to help me.'

'Oh, yes,' said the man raising an eyebrow, 'and what do you want?'

'Well, I'm looking for someone. Fritz Krant. Do you know him?'

The fat barman eyed Max suspiciously. 'Who are you, Police? Gestapo?'

Max lifted his hands, 'No Comrade, nothing like that. Fritz and I served in the war together. I'm just looking up an old friend.'

Nodding, the man turned and shouted, 'Kurt! Come here, quickly.' A curtain parted behind the bar and a young boy of about twelve years, almost as fat as his father and with a mop of black hair, entered.

'Yes, Papa, what is it?'

'Go around to the Krant's. Tell Fritz that there's an old comrade waiting to see him. Go on run along quickly.' The boy looked at Max as suspiciously as his father had done and went over to the entrance, closing the door behind him.

'He's got a job as a night watchman so should be at home at the moment.' said the barman.'

'Thanks. I'll have another beer while I'm waiting and have a read of the paper.' Picking up his beer Max went and sat down, taking a newspaper from his overcoat pocket. The fat barman said nothing as he lit up a cigarette and inhaled deeply.

Glancing up as the door opened about ten minutes later, Max saw his old friend walk in. Fritz Krant was about forty years of age, of medium build with light brown cropped hair. The empty sleeve of his old and patched jacket was tucked into the coat pocket where his arm should have been, a muffler was wrapped around his throat and his sightless left eye was covered with a black patch. The barman nodded in Max's direction and Fritz looked over, a frown of puzzlement creasing his face for a second until his eye lit up in recognition and a smile passed over his handsome face.

Standing in front of Max he extended his right hand. Max stood and shook it, saying quietly, 'Evening, Fritz, it's been a very long time.'

'Good evening, Sergeant Major, yes, 1917 wasn't it?'

'That sounds about right, the Tommy's tried to blow you up as I remember.'

'Yeh, the bastards nearly succeeded too.' he said, with a grin.

The fat barman waddled over and placed two beers on the table and walked away. Carefully looking around, Max noticed that the place was beginning to fill up, a number of working men having entered the bar, their shifts over for the day. Kurt, the barman's son, was going from table to table taking orders from the men and giving them to his father at the bar.

'So, tell me Sergeant Major, what brings you here? Don't tell me that this is a social visit after all these years.'

Without giving a direct reply, Max said, 'Tell me about yourself, Fritz. What's life been throwing at you?'

Giving a bitter laugh, he replied, 'Life, well let me tell you, there's not much going for a one-armed, one-eyed Jew like me, and I don't see things getting any better, not in the foreseeable future. I've got a job, if you could call it that, as night watchman at the steel works. How long that'll last is anybody's guess.'

Nodding, Max asked, raising an eyebrow, 'Married?'

'Yes, Sophie, and I have a son, Theo.'

'Well, Fritz, tonight things might start to get better. I've a proposition to make to you. First, though, I'm going to ask you a stupid question. What do you think of our new masters?'

Fritz gave a huge snort and scowled, 'That, Sergeant Major, if you don't mind me saying so, is a stupid question. I'm a Jew so what do you think I think of the bastards?'

'Sorry, but it had to be asked. I'll tell you why I'm here tonight. I'm looking for a trustworthy man to come and work for me. Now I know that you can be trusted because of the time that we served together in the war, hence the visit. You weren't that difficult to find.'

Smiling, Fritz asked, 'Is it legal?'

'You tell me if anything's legal nowadays. Look, I'll put my cards on the table; if you don't like what I have to say just say so and I'll get up and walk out into the night and you'll never see me again.

'Go on, Max,' he said, using Max's name for the first time, 'I'm interested.'

Looking over towards the bar, Max caught the owner's eye and lifted two fingers, indicating that he wanted two more beers. The man nodded, 'You ask if it's legal? Well, yes and no. I own a large place down on one of the lakes and I need someone that I can trust to generally look after the place, a caretaker. There's a small cottage in the grounds that goes with the job and the pay's good. Tell me, does your wife drive?'

'Strangely enough, she does. She drove a coal lorry around Berlin during the war.'

'Good, there's a small car that goes with the job as this place is pretty isolated. That's the legal bit. However, I'm not going to lie to you, Fritz, I'm part of an organisation that'll do anything to bring these bastards down. From time to time, there'll be certain people coming and going and you'll need to keep your good eye closed. Do you follow me?'

'Certainly. This group, tell me more.'

'If I were to mention certain names you'd know at least two of them from our past. I'm not going to mention anyone for the moment, better that you don't know. Look, Fritz, this could be very dangerous; anyone working for us can expect no mercy if they're caught. Now, you have a family to think of. I think that you should talk it over with your wife first. You say you have a son?'

His face lit up, 'Yes, Theo, he's a good lad, 15 years old now and very bright indeed.'

'What about school?'

'School? He's a Jew, remember, so no, he's left.'

'Good, we can put him on the payroll too; if you decide to take the job, that is.'

'Max, it seems to me that we've nothing to lose. I don't know what those bastards have up their sleeves for us but you can bet your life that it won't be pleasant.'

The bar was by now almost full, men talking and laughing, a smog of cigarette smoke filling the air, no one taking any notice of the one eyed man and his companion.

'Well, on that subject, I've good news. If you take up the offer, you'll have to be prepared to disappear completely and keep totally away from your old haunts, and I mean completely. Our group will give you all a totally new identity, new papers, passports everything that you'll need to make a new life. In effect, you'll cease to be Jews.'

'Christ! Can you do that? Because if you can, my minds already made up,' he sniggered, 'I just hope that nobody asks me or Theo to drop our trousers! Tell me Max, why me?'

'Fritz, you were about an inch away from death the last time that I saw you in the military hospital. I remember thinking at the time what a brave bastard you were and you never once complained. You're just the kind of man that we need, and the added bonus for us is that you're a Jew. Talk to your wife. I'll meet you in here at the same time in two day's time and you can give me your answer then. If you accept my offer be prepared to disappear in about a week's time. Oh, just one other thing, I suppose that you must know a lot of very angry young Jews? I mean, young and fit, and who, if given the chance, would be prepared to fight this Nazi shit?'

'Oh, yes, they're frustrated and very angry, but what can they do?'

'That, my friend is something for us to talk about, something for the future.' Max nodded, threw some money on the table for the drinks, and said, 'I'll see you in two day's time.' He stood and walked towards the entrance. Felix's eyes followed him all the way out.

57

Rudi was sitting reading "Oliver Twist" when the telephone rang in the hall. It seemed to echo as if to highlight the emptiness of the house. Since his mother had left he felt as if the whole place was going to swallow him up, and how he missed his beloved wife, Rachel.

Giving a sigh, he stood and walked out to answer the phone. 'Hello,' he said.

'Hello, Rudi, Joseph here. Max has called for a big meeting with everyone. Tomorrow night at eight, the usual place.'

'Alright, Joseph, thanks. Are you going to contact Bruno?'

'Yes, leave that with me. See you tomorrow.' Replacing the receiver Rudi walked back into the lounge, picked up his book and continued to read.

They arrived at the Black Cat in ones and twos, Joseph arriving first and going directly to the upstairs apartment. Werner and Max came next, closely followed by Bruno and Rudi.

When they had all settled and helped themselves to drinks, Max took centre stage and said, 'Good evening, Gentlemen. Stefan and the General thought it a good idea to have this meeting tonight. They feel that this year will be decisive. We already know that Hitler plans to take over the rest of Czechoslovakia early this year, about March time I believe.' Max glanced over at Werner for confirmation. Werner nodded. 'After that we believe that he'll turn his attention towards Poland and then the balloon will really go up. We have to give a lot of serious thought about the Altmann Circle and think through a plan of action in case we find ourselves in trouble. If for any reason we're compromised, we have to be able to get out of Germany, but not necessarily quickly.'

Raising his hand, Rudi said, 'But surely, if we need to get out we should do it as quickly as possible?'

'Yes, Rudi,' said Max. 'But that may not be possible. What's the first thing that they'll do if they're on to us?'

'Put a close watch on all of the exit points — railways, airlines, things like that,' said Werner.

'Exactly. I've come up with a plan of escape which may not be quick but is, I believe, the safest way out. A route that I hope they won't think of. For example, did you know that it was possible to get from Berlin all the way to Basel by boat?'

There was a lot of shaking of heads as Bruno said, 'Now, that's one method that I'd never have thought of. Do we have a boat, though? I'm an awful sailor and I can't swim,' he said, with tongue in cheek.

'Don't worry, Bruno, I'm sure that we'll be able to find you a life-jacket,' said Joseph.

'To answer your question, Bruno, replied Max, 'yes we do have a boat, in fact we have three.'

'Three!' exclaimed Rudi.

'Yes, three, Bruno pass me my brief-case will you?' answered Max.

Bruno leaned over, picked up the case and passed it over.

'Thanks,' said Max opening the case and taking out a map of the waterways. 'Gather round and take a look.' Putting his finger on the map, he traced the route. 'We leave Berlin and go down through Potsdam to just before Magdeburg. We go up and along the Weser-Elbe canal, through Hannover and into the Ems-Weser canal, through Münster and down into the Rhine. We'll have another boat moored in Cologne in case of emergencies. Further down-river at Mannheim we'll also have a boat. If we lose one boat we have two backups just in case. Not only that, but we can use the waterways for many clandestine things as they're not as closely watched as railway stations or airports. There are, however, the river police to keep in mind. Don't underestimate them; they're very good at their job and are of course under the control of the Gestapo.'

'My God! You think of everything. This is brilliant!' exclaimed Rudi.

'We do our best, although I'm praying that we never need an escape route. Better to be safe than sorry though.'

'One question,' said Bruno, 'where's the boat moored in Berlin?'

'I was coming to that. For the next few months, I'll be staying here in Berlin. For security reasons it's better that you don't know where. Werner knows the location and before we leave tonight I'll give you a telephone number to ring in an emergency. There is, of course, Stefan's number in Switzerland and he always knows where to contact me. If you get into trouble, go to ground, here if possible, and contact me. I'll come and get you. If you're taken prisoner of course, there's not much that anyone can do for you. It's for that reason that I don't want you to know where our other hideout is. What you don't know, you can't tell.'

'That seems sensible. One question though,' said Rudi. 'Are we still going to use the code word "Pickwick"?'

'Yes, as discussed by us in Basel,' said Max.

'I've never mentioned this,' said Rudi, 'but if the Black Cat is ever compromised we do have another bolthole. However, I'd only use it in an extreme emergency. I'd hate to put the owners into any danger, but it's there if needed.'

'Good,' said Max. 'Now, our forger, Otto, has proved to be invaluable. The man's a genius and I defy anyone to tell the difference between his work and the real thing — it's brilliant. I have a set of false papers for each of you. Learn your new identities by heart. Of course you must only use them if your true identity's compromised.'

'So that's what you wanted our photographs for,' said Bruno.

'Yes, Bruno. I can't think of any other reason for wanting your photo'.' He smiled, and asked, 'Are there any questions?' There was silence around the room. 'Very well, I'll keep in touch and here's the number to contact me. Don't worry if you can't recognise the voice on the other end of the line. You can trust these people one hundred percent. Just leave your message and I'll get back to you. They've been briefed.' Everyone stood to leave. Max looked across at Bruno, made a decision, and said, 'Bruno, will you stay behind? I have something that I need to discuss with you.'

Bruno looked puzzled and said, 'Of course, Max.'

'Good. Rudi, I wouldn't wait if I were you as this might take some time.'

Everyone left The Black Cat as quietly and unobtrusively as they'd arrived

After everyone had left, Max looked at Bruno, a smile flitting for an instant across his face, his eyes full of sorrow, and said, 'Come, Bruno, pour us both a drink and join me.' Bruno nodded and poured two glasses of whisky, handing one to Max as he sat facing him. Lifting his glass, he said, 'Cheers!' and waited for Max to begin, sensing that he was about to hear something important.

'How old are you now, Bruno?' asked Max.

'Twenty-one. Why do you ask?'

'Twenty-one,' mused Max. 'Do you know your father and I were fighting for our lives at your age? Now, here we are again, preparing for another war. In fact, you, I and the others have already begun our war, haven't we?'

'Yes, I suppose we have, but this is one worth fighting, don't you think? Look what these Nazis have already inflicted on our country and in our name. Can we just stand by and do nothing? Do you know, Max, it frightens me. I know that sometimes I come across to the others as a joker, but believe me, when it comes to our fight, I'm as dedicated and committed as any of the group. It's just my way. Believe me, I'm as scared as anyone.'

'My boy, you'd be a fool not to be scared and there's no one in the group that thinks otherwise. Do you know, we all love your image as the joker and wouldn't want you to change; if only you knew how much like your father you are. He was taken from you at too young an age. He didn't deserve that and neither did you.' Max looked Bruno directly in the eyes, his stare penetrating. 'What would you say if I told you that I knew who killed your father?'

Bruno stiffened, and said, very quietly, 'Then I would ask you to give me his name so that I could go and kill him!'

Nodding, Max said, 'I only discovered his identity recently and then almost by accident. There's a member of our group you've not yet met. He's a police inspector and investigated your father's murder at the time. He tells me that they knew who his killer was but didn't have enough evidence to arrest him.' He smiled and continued, 'You see in those days we lived in something like a democracy, unlike today.'

'Who is he, Max?' There was a note of cold anger in Bruno's voice.

Lifting his brief case, Max took out a large photograph and handed it over, all the time looking at Bruno. 'His name is Nieper. He's now a Deputy-Gauleiter. At the time of your father's death he acted as a hit man for the party. Anyone that they wanted eliminated, he did the job for them. Your father wasn't the only one by any means.'

Bruno studied the photo in front of him, memorising the face. 'I'm going to kill him, Max. The first day that I saw you was at father's funeral. As you know, I didn't have any idea who you were until many years afterwards. I swore an oath, standing at that graveside that if I ever found out who'd killed him, I'd have my revenge and I promise you Max, that I will kill this man.'

'I never doubted that you would. Let me tell you something about Nieper. He's a thug, a low life. Although he's now high up in the party, he still likes to mix with his friends from the old days. Each Saturday night he goes to a large beer hall down by the zoo, arriving at about eight and leaving at about midnight. Now, for some reason, he never takes his chauffeur, preferring to drive himself.'

Bruno nodded, 'Go on, I'm listening,' he said coldly.

'He's of course always dressed in uniform. The time to hit him is when he leaves and goes back to his car. By that time he's usually had a few beers and schnapps, not drunk exactly, but …'

'I understand. All I have to do is wait.'

'Oh no, Bruno. Take some advice from an old hand, always blend into the background and never ever stand out. I'll give you an example. Sometime ago, I paid a visit to Nazi Party Headquarters. I purposely dressed to look like a Gestapo officer. You know how you can always spot them? Anyway, when I walked into the place everyone assumed that I was Gestapo. I didn't do anything to disabuse them of the idea and it worked, everyone kept their distance. It might surprise you to know that I've been a fully paid up member of the party since 1930.'

Bruno's eyes shot up. 'What!'

Max laughed. 'Oh, yes, that little party badge and card can sometimes be a great advantage. If you're wearing the badge in your lapel, in certain circles you're welcomed with open arms, no one ever thinking to question you. Blend, Bruno, always blend.'

'So what exactly are you suggesting?'

'It's really very simple: you go dressed as a Brownshirt then go to the cellar, mingle, have a few beers, and watch. When he leaves, you follow him and blow his fucking brains out! Believe me, you'd be doing the world a favour.'

'Where will I get the uniform from?'

'Why, from me, of course. Bruno there's still a lot that you don't know about our organisation and I can get you just about anything that you're ever likely to need. I have a place full of uniforms, weapons, ammunition and explosives.'

'This is the place that you mentioned earlier on this evening?'

'Yes, that's the reason we don't want you to know about it for the moment. In good time, when we feel that you need to know, we'll tell you, but not just yet. You see, Bruno, I've big plans for the Altmann Circle and hope to expand it greatly. We're going to war on this filth. They just don't know it yet. Be patient. Eventually, when the time's right, you'll learn everything.'

Bruno grinned, 'You know, Max, you really are incredible. I would have loved to have seen you and my father in action — what a team!'

'My boy, you better believe it. Now, that uniform. I know your size and I'll leave it here for you to pick up along with a pistol and holster. When will you do the job?'

'This Saturday, of course.'

Max smiled and said, 'Good luck.' He lifted a finger and continued, 'But be very careful, you're far too valuable to us to lose.'

'Don't worry, Max, I want a long war,' he said, raising his glass.

58

D riving past the Kaiser Wilhelm Memorial church and up
Budapester Straße, Bruno took a right turn into
Wichmannstraße and pulled into the curb, turning off the
engine. The entrance to the beer cellar was just around the corner in
Landgrafenstraße. Although within easy walking distance of The Black
Cat, Bruno wanted the car in case he needed to get away quickly, as he
knew that anything could happen within the next couple of hours.
Feeling very calm, he sat in the darkness of the car's interior and reflected
on his course of action this evening. The SA uniform that he wore felt
strange. Nestling in the right-hand jacket pocket was a small, compact
.22 pistol; much more useful than the large calibre Luger automatic that
he carried in a leather holster on his left side. The .22 was as effective at
close range as the Luger and much quieter. Opening the car door, he
stepped out and put on the brown SA kepi as he walked in the direction
of the hall. He arrived at the entrance and stood at the top of the stairs.
Glancing at his watch he noted the time: 10pm. The noise coming from
the cellar even at this distance was loud, the thump, thump of martial
music almost deafening. Squaring his broad shoulders, he walked down
the steps and into the hall. As he entered, the cigarette smoke and heat
of the place immediately engulfed him. The first thing that struck him
was how large the hall was. In front of him was a sea of brown uniforms
and swastika armbands. He realised straight away that Max was right;
dressed as he was he blended in perfectly with his surroundings. The SA
band was playing the march "Berliner Luft" as he forced his way through
the crowd to the bar. No one took any notice of him. He ordered a beer
and went and stood by a large pillar, looking around at the Brownshirts,
some with their wives and girlfriends. The band finished playing and loud
applause erupted from the crowd, some shouting, 'More! More!' Bruno
looked around, searching for his quarry. At first he couldn't see him
anywhere, but at last he spotted him sitting at a table on the other side
of the room. It was impossible for Bruno to mistake him, as he sat
laughing and joking with his cronies, his rank clear for all to see as he

took a swig of beer from a foaming tankard in his hand. All of the men sitting with him were middle-aged, their seniority obvious as they, too, drank and talked amongst themselves.

Spotting a table nearby, Bruno walked over towards it. There were three young SA men sitting there. Taking a deep breath, Bruno approached and with a big smile on his face, said 'Good evening, Gentlemen, Heil Hitler! May I join you?'

'Of course, Comrade, sit down, you're welcome,' said one of the young men.

'It looks like we could all do with a refill,' said Bruno, calling over a waiter, 'What's it to be? Beer? Oh, by the way, they call me Sepp.'

'How do you do, Sepp? I'm Frederic, this is Wolfgang, and this is Rudolph, on account of his red nose.'

'Piss off!' said Rudolph, taking a swing.

Just as Wolfgang was about to say something, the band struck up the Horst Wessel song. The whole room started to sing, thumping their beer tankards on the tables in rhythm with the music. Bruno sang along lustily with the others.

When it had finished to great cheers, Frederic said, 'Great music, eh, Sepp?'

'Wonderful!' said Rudi, thinking to himself, *'You fucking moron.'*

'We were just talking about our military service,' said Wolfgang. 'It's the army for me next month, I can't fucking wait.'

'Don't worry,' said Rudolph, 'we'll all be in uniform before too long. What about you, Sepp?'

'I fancy the submarine service, myself,' said Bruno.

'Fuck that, too dangerous,' said Frederic, 'I'll keep my feet on dry ground thank you very much. You know that it's the Führer's fiftieth birthday in April? I hear that there's going to be a massive military parade through Berlin. That should be good.'

'Yes, we can show the world just what German strength is,' said Wolfgang.

'Do you think there'll be war?' Rudolph asked the table in general.

'Yeh, course there will, the sooner the better for me. I want to kill some *Untermensch* — fucking bastards! It's time we Germans showed that we're no longer prepared to be kicked around,' said Frederic, with some heat.

'Do you think that the English will go to war against us?' asked Wolfgang.

'I hope not,' said Rudolph. 'We should be friends with the English, not enemies; they're the most like us after all. Come on, let's have another beer,' replied Frederic.

From time to time Bruno glanced across at Nieper's table. At one point his heart missed a beat as he realised that his seat was empty. 'Shit!' he murmured to himself, but then gave a sigh of relief when he saw him coming back from the toilet. The conversation passed back and forth for another half an hour. Bruno was starting to get restless when he saw Nieper stand as if getting ready to leave.

Bruno looked at his watch and said, 'Well, Gentlemen, it's time that I left. My girlfriend's working in a bar on the Ku-Damm and she should be finishing soon.' He winked and continued, 'I'm on a promise tonight and that's something I have no intention of missing, much as I like your company.'

'Lucky bugger,' muttered Frederic.

'Ah well, Frederic, you've got your right hand,' said Wolfgang.

'Fuck off! Anyway, you still think it's just for pissing out of,' said Frederic.

They all laughed. Bruno said, 'Goodbye, my friends, until we meet again.' He thought to himself, '*And I hope that I'm carrying a machine gun.*' He smiled, said, 'Heil, Hitler!' stood and walked towards the door, just in time to see Nieper's back disappearing through it.

Quickly climbing the stairs, Bruno saw Nieper walking down the street into the cold night air. He followed, keeping his distance. The side streets were quiet. Bruno saw Nieper approaching his car and quickened his pace, arriving just as the Deputy-Gauleiter inserted the key into the lock.

'Good evening Herr Nieper,' said Bruno, just as Nieper opened the car door.

Nieper swung around, a look of surprise on his face. He visibly relaxed when he saw Bruno's uniform. 'Good evening, young comrade, what can I do for you?' he said as he climbed into the driver's seat.

Putting his hand out, Bruno stopped the man closing the car door. Bending down, he came face to face with his father's killer, 'It's not what you can do for me, but what I can do for you.'

'Who the fuck are you?' said Nieper, beginning to feel real fear, although he couldn't explain why.

'I have a present for you. Something that I've wanted to give you for a very long time,' said Bruno quietly as he slipped the .22 pistol out of his pocket.

Nieper's eyes widened as he saw the dull glint of the gun held in Bruno's hand.

Bruno pushed the tip of the barrel into Nieper's temple, and said, 'This is for my father,' as he squeezed the trigger. The report was a sharp crack. The bullet penetrated the victims left temple, exiting the other side, spattering blood and brain tissue. Nieper slumped into the passenger seat. Looking down at the body, Bruno said, 'I hope that you rot in hell, you piece of Nazi shit. He closed the door and walked away humming the Horst Wessel song.

59

Standing side by side looking out across the lake, Max, Fritz and Theo watched the swans gliding across the icy water on this cold January morning.

'Have you settled in alright?' asked Max.

Turning towards him, Fritz replied, 'Yes thanks, it's like a five star hotel after our place in Wedding.'

'How about you, Theo?' said Max to the muscular, young fifteen-year-old Jewish boy, who had deep blue eyes and almost white blond hair. '*He's their ideal of an Aryan,*' thought Max, '*and yet he's a Jew — ironic!*'

The boy looked over at Max and replied, 'Yes, thank you, sir. It's beautiful here.'

'I'm glad that you like it. One of your jobs will be to keep the grounds in good order. As you know, I'll be away from time to time and I don't want the place to become neglected. Once a place falls into disrepair it starts to attract attention and that's the last thing we want. Tell me, are you all familiar with your new identities?'

'Oh, yes, we can give you the whole family history,' said Fritz with a smile. 'Sophie's been testing us night after night.'

'Good.' Max looked from father to son and continued, 'As you're as involved as anyone now, there are a number of things that I want to show you both. I'm including you, Theo, as it's your hide at risk as much as the rest of us. Anyway, you're not a child, and from time to time you may be asked to do certain little jobs for us. How do you feel about that?'

'Sir, I'm willing to do anything to help, especially anything that will hurt our tormentors.'

Max smiled. 'Young man, I like you and think that you'll be very useful to us in the future.'

'Alright, come with me.' Leading them into the large rustic house, Max opened a door which led down some stairs to a spacious wine cellar. There were rows of racks full of wine. At the far end of the whitewashed room, there was another rack stretching the length of one wall.

'Look at this,' said Max, walking towards the wall. He took hold of the left-hand end of the rack and pulled. The whole rack started to move slowly away from the wall, revealing a small door. Both Fritz and Theo gave a gasp of surprise.

'Follow me,' said Max, leading them to the door and opening it. Turning on the light, Max ushered them inside. Down the side of one wall were five military bunk beds with mattresses and blankets. It was warm in the room. At one end there was a toilet and shower cubicle. Facing the beds were two large metal cabinets. Next to them, piled to the ceiling, were a number of metal ammunition boxes. Walking over to one of the cabinets, Max opened it. Inside were row upon row of military uniforms, most of them army or SS. Turning to the next cabinet, he opened the two doors. Inside were a number of the most up to date rifles, all gleaming with oil, a number of machine pistols and automatic hand guns.

'My God, Max, are you going to start your own private war?' asked Felix.

'We might do just that,' he answered. 'That's not all, look at this.' Walking to the far end of the room, he picked up a torch from a shelf and turned to another door set in the wall. Turning the handle, he walked into a rough-hewn passage and switched on the torch shining it along the whole length. It was about fifty metres long and came to a dead end. A faint light coming from a grill set in the roof of the tunnel at the far end illuminated the passage. The three men walked along and looked up at the metal grill, the watery winter sunshine coming through.

'This comes out in the garden behind your cottage; there are some bushes surrounding it so it's difficult to spot. This of course gives access to the secret room without anyone having to enter the house.'

Giving a whistle, Theo said, 'Sir, you really are well organised. How did you manage to do all this?'

'A very good question,' said Max. 'Let's go back and I'll tell you.' The three walked along the passage and into the cellar, Max closing everything behind them. They climbed the stairs back up into the living area. Turning to Theo, Max said, 'Go and get us three beers from the kitchen, will you Theo?' The boy nodded and left the room, returning with the three bottles.

'Sit down and I'll tell you. I bought this place in 1935. Our group has its main base in Switzerland. During the summer of that year I brought in some men, all of them builders, electricians, plumbers. In the wine cellar, they built a wall about two thirds of the way down, put in the door and covered it with the hinged wine rack. They installed the electricity and water supply, then we excavated the tunnel and you can now see the result. We have a secret and reasonably secure base from which to operate if the need arises. This place is pretty isolated, but very near to the capital city of Germany, Berlin.

'Yes,' said Felix, 'but what exactly is your plan?'

'On that I have to be a bit vague. Look, it's only a matter of time before that madman Hitler plunges this country into war. Only months I think. He's determined to have his war and we're equally determined to do everything that we can to make things as difficult as possible for him and his gang. Just think of it, a clandestine group operating in the heart of the Reich. We already have contacts with the secret service of a foreign power and to them we'd be invaluable. If they tried to infiltrate a group in this country the Gestapo and SD would have them within five minutes. We're Germans and are already here. If we're very careful no one should be very interested in us as we blend in perfectly.'

'May I ask, sir,' said Theo, 'does the group already exist?'

Max smiled and said, 'Theo, I think that you should call me Max.'

'Theo nodded and said, 'Thank you.'

'To answer your question, yes, the group's been in existence for a number of years now. However, before war's upon us, I'd like to expand it.'

'Ah,' said Felix, 'now I'm beginning to understand why you asked me the question about angry young Jews.'

'Exactly! Which is the one group in Germany today who have the most to fear from the Nazis? That's right, the Jews. I'm sure that there must be very many young Jewish people out there who'd love to work against their oppressors. In my opinion things can only get worse for the Jews, much worse. Do you understand my thinking? I'd be glad of your advice.'

Felix looked at Max and said, 'I think that there may be a problem that you haven't thought of, Max. As you rightly say, things are bad for us Jews and getting worse. I don't think that any young person would consider leaving their families at such a dangerous time to join us. I say us, because we're now very much involved.'

'Of course,' answered Max.

'I assure you, Max,' went on Felix, 'that we're glad to be part of the group. We loathe the Nazis as much as any other Jew, but we're not talking about a job in an office. I assume that anyone joining us would have to disappear, go underground?'

'Most certainly,' answered Max.

'So, there's your problem. I don't believe that anyone would be prepared to abandon their loved ones at such a time as this.'

'Yes, I see what you mean,' said Max, thoughtfully.

'Wait a moment,' said Theo, 'Simon.'

'Simon?' repeated Felix, quizzically, looking at his son.

'Yes, Papa, don't you remember him? He lodges with Frau Rheinhard in the next block to ours.'

'Oh, yes,' replied Felix.

'Tell me about Simon,' said Max, quietly.

'Well, he's about nineteen and an orphan. His parents were killed in a car crash when he was a child and he was brought up in the Jewish orphanage. There must be many young people like him in Berlin. If anyone knows, it would be him. He loathes the Nazis. Some SS men beat him up. Don't you remember, Father?'

'Of course, Simon, yes, I know him. Well done, my boy. I told you that he was bright, didn't I Max?' Theo beamed.

A smile passed over Max's face. 'Now there's the perfect answer — orphans. They have no families to think about. Can you arrange for us to meet?'

'Certainly,' said Theo, 'I know him well.'

'That's a good idea,' said Felix, 'Let the boy do it. He knows him better than I do.'

'Very well, Theo. Go into Berlin and arrange it, but be careful and don't say what it's about, and don't under any circumstances mention this place or what you're doing here.'

'Don't worry Max,' said Theo, his voice both mature and confident, 'Leave it to me.'

Max just nodded, a smile of satisfaction playing at the corner of his mouth.

60

The two men and Theo walked through the entrance to the tenement building, a smell of stale cabbage and urine pervading the air. Climbing up the dimly-lit staircase to the third floor, Theo stopped in front of a dingy door and knocked. The door was opened almost immediately. Standing there was a tall, slender young man of about nineteen with dark brown hair, brown eyes and an olive complexion. Although slender, he was in no way skinny and showed a hint of muscle.

He gave a crooked smile, showing even white teeth.

'Good evening, you'd better come in,' he said, standing to one side. Max, Fritz and Theo entered a dark kitchen-cum-living room. Sitting at the table was an old woman knitting. She looked up as they entered, gave a nod and carried on with what she was doing.

'Let's go through here,' said Simon, leading them through to a small bedroom. Inside, there was just a single bed, a small table and a battered wardrobe. 'Please make yourselves at home,' he said with a hint of self-mockery. 'Now, I'm intrigued. Just what can I do for you?'

Max and Fritz sat down on the bed.

Looking at the young man Max said, 'Simon, I'm here tonight to offer you a job, if you can convince me that you're the person that I'm looking for. First, tell me, what do you think of the Nazis?'

'Mister,' replied Simon, with a hint of anger, 'Do you ask every Jew that you meet that question? Who is this, Fritz?'

I'm sorry Simon, my name's Max and I didn't mean to insult you.'

Mollified a little, Simon said, 'A few weeks ago I caught a Brownshirt on his own down town. I took him into an alley and beat the shit out of him. You see, they're not so brave when they're alone. Does that answer your question?'

'Admirably,' said Max with a smile. 'You're an orphan I believe?'

'That's right, yes.'

'So you're all alone in the world?'

'I don't have any family, no, but I've lots of friends,' he said, almost defensively.

Max nodded, 'Tell me, your friends, do you trust them?'

Simon smiled and replied, 'Max, believe me, some I'd trust with my life, others I wouldn't trust with yours and I don't know you. Why do you ask?'

'We'll come to that later. Do you have a driving licence?'

'Yes, I do. I learnt during my last year at the orphanage. They were good like that and tried to help us with life after we left.'

Max looked closely at the young man. He was impressed with the boy's self- confidence and obvious courage.

'Tell me, would you like to come and work for me? You'd be living with Felix and Theo and the pay's not too bad. Also, eventually, you'd be given the chance to get back at your enemies. I might even be able to use some of your friends, that is, the ones you trust.'

The boy replied, 'As I'm sure you already know things are very tough for us. I don't have, and can't get, work, so yes I'd like to work for you but doing what exactly?'

Before replying, Max looked at Felix and said, 'Well, Felix, you always had good instincts. What do you think? Can we find work for this young man?'

'Max,' replied Felix, 'I'd certainly like to have him on the team, eh, Theo?'

'Definitely!' replied Theo.

'Alright, Simon, here's the deal: take it or leave it. You get a job, a new home and a new identity. You disappear completely and keep away from your old haunts until I tell you otherwise. Sometime in the near future, I'll ask you to contact some of your old friends; hopefully we'll have some work for them. One thing though — like you, they should have no ties with anyone. Do you accept?'

'Max, let me tell you, half an hour ago I was almost ready to go down to the Anhalter station and sell myself. Now I've got a job, although I'm still not sure what it is. Yes, I accept.'

'Good, now the old lady next door?'

'Oh, she'll be glad to see the back of me. I'm a Jew you see, she's not.'

'Good. Felix and I will wait downstairs by the car. Pack your things and come down with Theo when you're ready. Come on Felix. The two men stood and went into the shabby living room. The old woman was still knitting. Putting his hand into his inside pocket, Max took out his wallet and handed over a wad of Reichsmarks, saying, 'Here you are, mother, something for your trouble.'

She nearly fell out of her chair in her haste to take the money, and said, 'Oh, thank you sir, thank you!'

'Oh, just one more thing. We haven't been here tonight. If I hear that you've been talking about our visit in the local bar, I'll come back and cut you're fucking throat! Do you understand?'

'Oh, yes, sir, don't worry I won't breathe a word, honestly.'

'Just make sure that you don't. Come on Felix.' The two men walked out.

Standing by the car, Max turned to Felix and said, 'A good night's work, I think. I'm impressed with the boy. He's going to be invaluable to us and we can recruit some of his friends later. For the moment we'll leave things as they are.'

'Yes, Max, I agree. He seems like a good lad; very useful in a tight spot with the right kind of training.'

'I'm glad that you said that. Tomorrow, get the lads to fill some sandbags and put them in the cellar. I want you to set up a firing range and teach them how to use a pistol. If I remember you were a bloody good marksman. I trust you haven't forgotten?'

'No chance, although I'm a bit rusty by now.' replied Felix. 'It's a good job I've still got my right arm.'

'Simon and Theo walked out of the apartment block, Theo carrying a battered suitcase. The two men turned towards them and Max threw his car keys towards Simon. He deftly caught them as Max said, 'You drive; you're my chauffeur now.'

Simon's eyes nearly popped out of his head as he looked at the long, sleek, black Mercedes Benz.

61

The Company-Sergeant-Major came to attention, about-turned and saluted. Lieutenant Johann Klein returned the salute and said, 'Good morning Sar'nt-Major, we have a fine day for it.'

'Good morning, Sir, yes. Would you like to inspect the Company?'

'Most certainly. Bring them to attention.'

Turning, the CSM barked the order, the men coming to rigid attention, no one moving a muscle. All around them young officers were doing the same, each wanting to have the most well turned-out men on this most important of days. Today was to be one of the biggest military parades ever seen in Berlin. Adolf Hitler was celebrating his fiftieth birthday and intended to show the world Germany's military might.

Lieutenant Klein walked slowly down the ranks. Stopping in front of each man he eyed them from the tops of their steel helmets to the soles of their gleaming, black, jackboots. The parade martial, a colonel, walked up and down glancing at his watch from time to time as he looked towards the direction of the huge column of men and machines stretching back into the far distance. Every part of the German armed forces was on parade, including tanks and huge cannon pulled by large-tracked troop carriers. The massed bands, their brass instruments gleaming in the weak sunlight, stood talking amongst themselves as they waited for the start of the parade, the drum majors strutting up and down twirling their maces. Klein came to the end of his platoon, satisfied with their turn out. He asked the CSM to inspect him, in turn doing the same for the senior NCO, the two looking each other up and down with a critical eye.

'Well, Sar'nt-Major, this is to be my last time on parade with the platoon. Next week it's off to the Bendlerstraße for me.'

'Yes Sir. It's a good career move for you. Secretary to General Altmann, I believe?'

'That's correct. Although in a way I don't want to be stuck behind a desk, especially at this time. Look at it Sar'nt-Major, all these men and this equipment, doesn't it make you feel proud? This is the finest army in the world and I'm proud to be a part of it.'

'Me too,' replied the older and more experienced soldier.' A loud whistle interrupted the two men as the parade marshal signalled the start of the parade. The regimental standard bearers formed up as the bands lifted their instruments to their mouths. The growl and roar of engines being started filled the air with noise.

Standing just behind the saluting base, the generals, in their field-grey uniforms and gleaming medals, the red and gold of their rank at their throats, awaited the arrival of the Führer, Adolf Hitler. There were dignitaries from many countries present, amongst them, Major Claud Brown and Sir Robert Albright of His Majesty's Secret Service.

Stretching down the wide Unter den Linden on both sides as far as the eye could see, were thousands of cheering Berliners, the crowds being held back by an army of SA and SS men, sometimes unsuccessfully. Enterprising young Hitler Youth sat astride the tops of streetlights to get a better view, their hair rippling in the breeze. The roar of the crowd got louder and louder, as the cavalcade drove slowly down the highway. Hitler stood in the front of a huge Mercedes Benz staff car, wearing a simple brown uniform with swastika armband and the Iron Cross first class pinned to his right, breast pocket. Sitting in the back were Reichsführer Heinrich Himmler and Reichsmarshal Hermann Göring. From time to time, Hitler raised his right arm in salute to the adoring crowd. 'Sieg Heil! Sieg Heil!' they shouted with delirious enthusiasm. Arriving at the saluting stand, the car drew to a halt. Hitler climbed down, walked over to the podium and returned the salutes of his officers. He stood on the stand and once more raised his right arm. Göring and Himmler stood on either side and below their master.

The head of the procession came into view: row upon row of goose-stepping men in field grey led by the massed infantry bands. Behind them, the colourful flags of the various regiments fluttered in the wind. The dark blue of the navy, the lighter blue of the air force and the black of the SS followed in seemingly endless formation. The crowd gave roar after roar of appreciation as the tanks, field guns and mechanised infantry went slowly past. Huge swastika banners lined the route with smaller ones being waved by the children as the Führer acknowledged his mighty war machine. Line after line marched past, seemingly never ending, and the sky above was darkened as the bombers and fighter planes of the Airforce flew overhead in salute to their leader and master. Standing among the generals, General Altmann muttered to himself, 'You fools! You damned fools! If only you could see.'

Later, in the afternoon, a sea of thousands of faces looked up at the balcony of the Reich Chancellery, swaying backwards and forwards, a never ending movement, like an ocean. Hitler, accompanied by Göring, stepped out as the crowd below gave a huge cry and shouted themselves hoarse. Turning to the fat Reich-Marshal as he acknowledged the crowds below, Hitler said, 'They are mine; I can do with them what I will. They'll follow me wherever I lead. I have the people in the palm of my hand.'

62

London, June 1939.

Expertly balancing the tea tray in the crook of her left arm, Angela Bradbury knocked and entered the inner sanctum of her beloved chief, Sir Robert Albright, head of the Secret Intelligence Service, also known as MI6.

'Ah, Angela, you're an angel. Its Earl Grey, I hope?'

'Of course, Sir Robert, just as you like it,' said the middle-aged spinster, who'd have gladly laid down her life for Sir R, as she called him. She'd climbed the ladder from the bottom. Starting life in the typing pool as a young girl, her fiancée lying dead in the Flanders mud, she'd risen through the ranks and had now reached the pinnacle of her career. Privy to many of Sir Robert's secrets, she could be trusted with her life, the soul of discretion.

'Thank you, Angela. Keep the wolves from the door, there's an angel; we don't want to be disturbed.'

'Of course, Sir Robert, don't worry. Unless the King or Mr Churchill calls,' she said on the way out.

'Do you know, Gentlemen, I'd be totally lost without that woman. You pour, please Claud.'

Watching the whole proceedings with a look of bewilderment on his face sat Stefan Wagner, who'd flown in from Basel that morning and had been met by Claud Brown.

'Milk and sugar, Stefan?' asked Claud.

'Sugar, no milk, thank you,' replied Stefan.

Sir Robert, Claud and Stefan were sitting in armchairs around a low coffee table. Turning to Stefan, Claud said, 'Now, to business. We need to talk about the Circle. Can you bring us up to date, Stefan?'

'Right,' replied Stefan. 'Firstly, Rudi and Bruno. It's nearly time to get them out of Germany permanently, by the end of August at the latest. I've received information from the General that on the twenty-third of last month Hitler told the General Staff that war with Poland was inevitable. I think that the writing's on the wall. It's now only a matter of time.'

Claud and Sir Robert nodded. Taking out his silver cigarette case, Claud lit up and inhaled, blowing the smoke towards the ceiling. 'As you probably know, at the end of March, we and the French signed an agreement guaranteeing that we'd help Poland if attacked. Since the so called 'Pact of Steel' between Germany and Italy was signed during May and Hitler's show of military strength in April — very impressive I must say———war's now inevitable.'

Sir Robert sighed. 'As Winston said recently, the storm clouds are gathering. Now, Rudi and Bruno, when they come out, I want them to fly to England and join us here. I have plans to set up, if possible, a group inside Germany when war starts.'

'Well, on that subject, I've some very interesting news,' said Stefan. 'Max is at the moment setting up the nucleus of a resistance group in Berlin. Max is a bit of a mystery, even to me. He acts the part of my servant from time to time, but don't let that fool you. Let me tell you, Gentlemen, he's a wealthy man in his own right. He owns a very large house on one of the Berlin lakes, a place that I've never seen incidentally. However, I believe that it's extremely well situated and equipped for what he has in mind. So, there already exists a safe and secure place to operate from.'

'That is good news,' said Sir Robert. 'You say that he's setting up a group, so where's he getting his people from?'

Stefan smiled, and replied, 'That's the beauty of it. He's recruiting young Jews to work for him. They, after all, have very good reason to detest the Nazis. His idea is to have a small group of about five young people. If we add Rudi and Bruno, we'll have a very substantial group in place, don't you think?'

'I'll say,' said Brown. 'You've got to hand it to our Max, he's bloody efficient. All that we have to decide is the best way of using the group to our advantage.'

'I've made my decision and I don't see any problem selling it to our masters in Whitehall, especially as Winston's so much in favour. We'd be irresponsible fools in the extreme not to take advantage of this situation. This, Claud, will be your baby. I think that we need to get a radio receiver-transmitter to Berlin and we'll need to train an operator.'

'Well,' replied Claud, 'we can get a radio in through the diplomatic bag. As for an operator, Rudi's the most obvious choice.'

Turning to Stefan, Albright said, 'There's something that puzzles us and perhaps you can help to throw some light on the matter?'

'Certainly, if I can,' replied Stefan.

'For the past couple of years we've being receiving, through the Altmann group, information of more of an intelligence rather than military nature, as if it's coming from a secondary source. It's damned accurate. However, the information's not something that the General could possibly know anything about. You mentioned earlier that Max was a bit of a mystery to you. Is it possible that he has another source of information that we know nothing about? Of course, we know of the young Abwehr Lieutenant, Weinburger, but this information is far too important to be coming from him. I'll give you an example. We now have a list of names of people operating out of the German Embassy here in London — spies. We've passed their names on to our special branch and they're now under surveillance. We also know about a number of people outside of the Embassy operating all over the country and working for the Germans. We'll roll them up when the time's right. Well, any ideas?'

Stefan smiled and nodded, 'That sounds like Max, to answer your question. It wouldn't surprise me in the least if he had another source of information. Max has his fingers in many pies, so it's entirely possible. Perhaps he doesn't want to reveal his sources to us.'

'Yes,' said Claud, 'that makes sense. I know Max well and it wouldn't surprise me at all; he's a man of many faces.'

Looking thoughtful, Sir Robert, obviously making a decision, continued, 'There's something else that scares the life out of me. This source, whoever they are, has suggested that we may have someone passing information on to another country. In other words, a mole in our midst, and that frightens me very much indeed. They couldn't, or wouldn't, be more positive, but the trouble is it's too vague to act on. We must, however, be on our guard.'

'That sounds very serious. I hope that whoever this source is, they're wrong,' said Stefan. 'Oh, by the way, Robert, Rudi is now the proud father of a baby boy. Talking of which, Otto his grandfather, Rachel's father, has turned out to be a great asset to the Circle. He makes the most incredible forgeries; they're superb and I defy anyone to tell them from the real thing. He's forging passports, ID cards and papers for Max's Jewish group. Max has managed to get his hands on the correct paper, with the right watermarks- don't ask me where from- but it's brilliant.'

Brown chuckled, 'This gets better and better, so we now have our own forger. Would he be prepared to come over and work with us here in London?'

'Most certainly. He's a Jew remember, and loathes the Nazis. He's only too glad to be able to be of use in the fight. Don't worry, all you need to do is ask.'

'What about Rudi's wife? I believe that there's also a brother,' said Sir Robert, 'Will they stay in Switzerland?'

'I doubt it,' said Stefan, 'Rachel won't agree to being separated from Rudi, of that I'm sure.'

'Very well, no problem. Well, Gentlemen, everything seems to be falling into place,' said Sir Robert, stretching. He continued, 'However, don't forget what they say about the best laid plans of mice and men. Now, Claud, why don't you take Stefan for some lunch and this afternoon go sightseeing. I'll meet you at my club this evening for dinner. Now, if you'll excuse me, I have to see the First Secretary in five minutes time.'

Standing, Albright extended his hand to Stefan, and said, 'We're grateful to you for everything that you've done for us. The country has reason to be thankful to you, the General and all of the members of the Circle. I promise you that we won't forget.'

'Sir Robert, I pray that we'll be allowed to work together until the scourge of Hitler and his crew are wiped off the face of the earth.'

Watching their retreating backs as they left the office, Sir Robert's face was thoughtful. *I wish to Christ I knew just who this secondary source is. I don't like being in the dark, and are they right about us having a traitor in our midst?* He mused.

63

It was 10pm on a hot evening in early August when Johann Klein, running up to the entrance of German Army Headquarters on the Bendlerstraße, showed his pass to the sentry and continued up the stairs and along the corridor towards his office. The General's door was closed, as was his. He turned the handle and walked into his office and immediately noticed that the connecting door to the General's office was open slightly. There was a diffused light coming into his room and he could hear voices emanating from the General's room next door. Immediately curious, he went quietly to the partially open door and listened.

Werner said to the General, 'Stefan was in London in June and had a meeting with Sir Robert Albright. They're very pleased with the information that we've managed to get out to them. They want to set up a group here in Berlin, if possible, before war comes.'

The General grunted. 'They've had some first class intelligence from us over the past few years. I just hope that the English put it to good use when that madman plunges us over the abyss and into a disastrous war. You do realise, don't you, Werner, that by the end of this month we'll be invading Poland? After that, I don't know if we'll still be able to pass on information to the British. If I can get hold of the battle plan, I'll microfilm it and pass it on, but after that … ,' his voice trailed off. 'God, Werner, I'm sick and tired of all of this. I'm tempted to resign my commission, but what good would that do? Anyway, I can't be the only person in a position of authority in this country who's prepared to bring Hitler down. There must be others. I just wish to God I knew who they were.'

'Sir, you're just tired. This country needs people like you to lead us after Hitler and his crew have gone. I'm having a meeting in The Black Cat later this week. It'll soon be time for Rudi and Bruno to leave Germany for good. If you do manage to get hold of anything, I'll pass it on and they can take it with them.'

'It won't be this week, but yes, if I do manage to get anything, and I'll have a damned good try, I'll pass it on to you. Although what the British and French can do to help the poor Poles, God only knows.' The General gave a sigh. 'You're right, Werner, I'm tired. Come on, take me home. I feel that I could sleep for a week.'

Johann heard movement from the office as the light went out, leaving him in complete darkness.

'Just a moment,' he heard Werner say from the corridor. 'I could have sworn that Klein's office door was closed when we came in.'

Johann quickly stepped into the recently vacated office, as his room was flooded with light. Holding his breath, he pressed himself against the wall, praying that Werner wouldn't check this office. He waited, scarcely daring to breathe. After a few moments, the light in his office was extinguished, leaving him in the dark once more. Moving carefully, his heart beat returning to something like normal, he edged his way slowly around the room and looked out of the window. Down below, he could see the General and Werner climbing into Werner's car. He waited for them to drive away and moved swiftly over to his desk, turning on the light. Snatching a pen and note pad, he wrote, 'Sir Robert Albright? The Black Cat? Microfilm. England,' feeling nauseous and totally uncomprehending.

'I can't believe it. The man's a traitor. I heard it with my own ears but it can't be true, can it?' he muttered to himself almost feverishly, a fine film of sweat covering his brow. Leaning forward slightly, he lifted the telephone and dialled. 'Come on Papa,' he said, glancing at his watch. It was 10.45pm. After what seemed like an age, the telephone was answered and he heard his father's voice. Frederick Klein was a diplomat and Johann hoped that he would be able to answer an important question.

'Father its Johann. Look, I know it's late, but it's important.'

'Yes, Johann, what is it?'

'Father, you served at our Embassy in London, didn't you?'

'Yes, my boy, you know that I did.'

'Does the name, Albright, Robert Albright mean anything to you?' There was silence at the end of the line for a moment, seeming like eternity to Johann.

'Is this something to do with your work, Johann?' his father said quietly.

'Yes, something like that.' He waited for the reply.

'Johann, it's Sir Robert Albright. I've met him a number of times, a charming man.'

'Please, Father, just answer the question,' he almost shouted down the phone.

'Sir Robert is the head of the British Intelligence Service. Does that answer your question?'

'Yes, Papa, it does indeed, thank you.' Gently replacing the receiver, he stared into space. 'What do I do now?' he asked himself. Quickly coming to a decision, he again lifted the telephone and dialled.

The phone was answered almost immediately.

'Heinz.'

'Heinrich! Thank God you're there, its Johann Klein.'

'Christ! Johann do you know what time it is?'

'Never mind the time. I've got to see you, now!'

'Now? Why now? It can't be that urgent, surely.'

'Listen, Heinrich,' he said, very quietly, as if frightened of being overheard, 'Believe me when I say that it's a matter of national security.'

At the mention of security, Heinrich's ears pricked up and he became instantly alert, making an instant decision. 'Alright. Do you know the "Blue Angel" on the Ku-Damm?'

'Yes,'

'Meet me there in half an hour.' The line went dead.

At 11.45pm Heinrich Heinz walked into the Blue Angel, stopped and looked around. The rugged, blond-haired young man at twenty-six was four years older than Johann and a member of the Gestapo. His badly disfigured nose, broken by Bruno the previous year, added to his good looks rather than detracted from them. Spotting Johann sitting in an alcove in the far corner of the room he walked over and sat down.

Facing the younger man, he said, 'Hello Johann. Now, what's this all about?'

Before he replied, Johann lifted his hand and signalled to the waiter, indicating that he wanted two beers.

He looked at Heinrich and said, 'Earlier this evening, I discovered that my chief is passing military secrets to the British. I know that it sounds mad, but I swear Heinrich that it's true.'

Seeing how serious his young friend was, Heinrich said, 'Explain.' Listening intently as Johann told him about the events of the evening, he nodded from time to time but said nothing, not wanting to interrupt.

'So, after they left, I called my father and he told me that this Sir Robert Albright's the Head of British Intelligence, and then I called you.

The trouble is, Heinrich, no one's going to take my word against one of the most senior and respected generals in the German Army.'

'I agree. Even we wouldn't arrest someone as high up as that without some substantial evidence. You say that this Major Werner mentioned a bar or club called The Black Cat?'

'Yes, it seems that they use it as some kind of meeting place.'

Heinrich grunted, took a swig of beer and looked at Johann. 'Right, my boy, the first thing that we need to do is get some evidence, something a little more concrete.'

'How are we going to do that?'

'The first thing that we need to do, is to find out just where this Black Cat is.' Heinrich looked around the room and caught the waiter's eye, calling him over.

The old man approached and said, 'Yes, sir,'

'Two things, my friend,' said Heinrich jovially, 'First and most important, a beer for my friend and I and a little something for yourself.'

The old man's face lit up. 'Why, thank you, Sir, and what was the second?'

'We hope that you may be able to help us with a little information. Tell me, do you know a club or bar called The Black Cat?'

The old man's face split into a wide grin. 'Well, Sir, I've been serving beers in this city for more than thirty years and I know of only one bar called The Black Cat. Actually, it's not too far from here, in Wormser Straße. You see, it had quite a reputation in the old days.' The old waiter nodded to himself.

'A reputation?' asked Johann.

'Why, yes, young Sir, it was a bar used by queers and transvestites. All gone now, of course. I'll get your beers and thanks again for buying me a drink, very thoughtful, I'm sure.'

'Not at all, thank you,' said Heinrich, looking across at Johann, 'Now, that's interesting, Wormser Straße. I'll check that at the office tomorrow, or should I say, today. Listen, Johann, we're going to do some checking of our own.'

'What do you have in mind?'

'Well, your man Werner said that there was going to be a meeting sometime this week, right?'

Johann nodded and said, 'Yes, that's right.'

'Very well, we'll find this bar and go and have a look for ourselves. If your man, Werner turns up, we'll have something more solid to take to our masters. That would be enough, as it would confirm our suspicions. We can then take it further. What do you say?'

Johann's face lit up, 'Heinrich, you're a genius. We're going to have to be careful, though; if I'm recognised … ,'

'Of course, we might have to go there for a few nights running or we may strike lucky the first time around. Listen, I'll phone you later today. I need to check that there's only one Black Cat, as the old man says. If there is, we'll meet early in the evening. If your man doesn't turn up though, we'll have to think again. Look on the bright side, Johann, if you're right, this little lot will do our promotion prospects no harm at all, eh? However, Johann,' he said, more seriously, 'be careful. If these people suspect that we're on to them, it could get very dangerous. I don't want to hear that you've been found floating face down in the Spree.'

'I'll tell you what I think,' said Johann, 'we'll give it two nights. If Werner doesn't turn up in that time, we'll go to the SD and they can do what they want. Agreed?' he held out his hand.

Leaning across the table, Heinrich took the proffered hand, shook it, and said, 'Agreed.'

64

A pall of cigarette smoke hung in the sultry air, the bar full with people enjoying a night out. The Black Cat was doing good business this evening. Sitting in the corner, with a good view of the entrance, but well-hidden themselves, were Johann and Heinrich.

Swirling his beer around in his glass, Johann glanced over at the entrance, as someone came down the stairs and entered. He was by now beginning to think that he'd dreamt the conversation that he'd heard in the General's office two nights previously.

He gave a sigh and looked at Heinrich. 'If nothing happens tonight, I'm going to see the SD tomorrow,' he said. 'We could be here for ever.'

'We'll just give it another half an hour.' Heinrich was about to say something more, when he visibly stiffened as he looked in the direction of the entrance. 'Well I'll be fucked!'

Following his glance, Johann looked over, 'It's him. Werner.'

'Is that the man with the two younger ones?' Heinrich said, urgently.

'Yes it looks like it, although I don't know them.'

'I do. That stocky bastard's the one that messed me up last year. His name's Bruno and the other one's called Rudi, I think. Well, well, why am I not surprised that those two are mixed up in this? Keep your head down, Johann,' he muttered 'We've got them.'

Werner, Rudi and Bruno pushed their way through the crowd, headed towards the door at the back of the bar and walked through.

'You know the younger ones?'

'Yes, they did their labour service at the same time as me, last year. I had that fight. The big one made a real mess of me. Now it's my turn. What a coincidence though.'

'What should we do now?'

'You stay there for a moment. Jesus, I wish I was armed. I'm going to try and see where they've gone. If I'm not back in five minutes, go and get help,' he said, standing and heading towards the door.

Pushing it open he walked through. The dimly lit corridor was quiet and empty as he listened, hoping for a sign of where they'd gone.

Glancing into the room on the left he could see that it was empty. He walked to the foot of the staircase on the right-hand side and looked up into the gloom. Walking slowly and carefully upward, he arrived on the first landing and saw the dark entrance to the disused bar. Carrying on upwards, he passed the entrance to Gustav's apartment, pausing only for a second before he carried on. Quietly and cautiously he made his way up onto the last landing. There was a light showing under the door and he could hear the murmur of voices. Satisfied, he slowly retreated down the way he'd come.

Johann looked anxiously towards the door and gave a sigh of relief as he saw Heinrich coming back out. He'd been gone for less than three minutes.

Walking over, he looked at Johann, smiled and nodded, 'Come on, let's get the fuck out of here.' The two men walked over to the entrance, climbed the stairs and walked out in to the warm, summer night.

65

The early morning sunlight poured in through the large double window in Langers' office, as Dieter knocked and entered. 'Morning, Dieter,' said Langers, barely glancing up from the papers spread across his desk.

'Morning, Chief,' replied Dieter, casually giving the Hitler salute, 'We've a Gestapo man and an army lieutenant outside asking to see you. They say it's urgent.'

Langers grunted. 'Do they say what it's about?' He looked up at Dieter, a frown crossing his face, interested despite his large workload.

'Not to me, Sir. However, I've a feeling that you should see them.'

'Very well, wheel them in.' Langers put down his pen and waited.

The two marched in, the lieutenant immaculately dressed in uniform and the Gestapo man in civilian clothes. They halted, the young army officer giving the correct military salute, while the Gestapo agent gave the Hitler salute.

'Good morning, Gentlemen. Now, what can I do for you?'

Johann Klein stepped forward, looking towards Heinz, and said, hesitantly, 'I regret, Sir, that I have to report my senior officer for treason.'

'What?' said Langers, very quietly, 'Who is your superior officer?' he asked.

'General Frederick Altmann, Sir.'

Langers was unable to conceal his shock, a look of horror crossing his face, 'Lieutenant, are you absolutely sure? Be careful, that is a very serious charge.'

'I can confirm that, Sir, at least in part,' said Heinrich.

'Alright, pull up some chairs and tell me about it, from the beginning.'

'So, the three of them turned up at this Black Cat last night?' asked Langers.

'Yes Sir. I recognised Werner, of course,' said Johann, 'and it confirmed what I'd overheard two nights before, so here we are.'

Turning to Heinrich, Langers said, 'And you recognised the other two?'

'Yes, Sir, we did our labour service at the same time. The big one, Bruno, and I had a fight.' Heinrich's face turned slightly pink as he continued, 'I was seriously injured and so I'm not likely to forget him.'

Dieter looked at Heinrich and asked, 'The other one, do you know his name?'

'Well, Sir, it's Rudi I think, although I'm not sure.'

Dieter looked closely at Heinrich and said quietly, 'Is it possible, I wonder? Sir, I'll get a complete list of names of the people in the camp at that time.'

Langers nodded, tapping his pen rhythmically on the desk. 'Good Lord,' he murmured, as he lifted the telephone and asked to speak to Heydrich's secretary. He spoke quietly for a few minutes and replaced the receiver. Looking over at the three young men facing him, he said, 'We have a meeting with General Heydrich in thirty minutes time. Gentlemen, I think that the shit's about to hit the fan.'

'Right, come in,' said Langers as they returned to his office an hour later. 'As you heard, I'm in charge of this case. You, Heinz, as of now, are working for me. You, Lieutenant, will go back to the Bendlerstraße. I don't have to tell you to act perfectly normally so make some excuse for your absence this morning. Your involvement is, for the time being at least, at an end. I've no doubt that when it comes to a trial, you'll be the star witness. For the moment, you keep out. Now, for the last time, are you absolutely sure that you're not suspected by them?'

'Positive, Sir.'

'Very well, off you go, and Klein?'

'Yes, Sir'

'Well done.'

Johann nodded, stood up, saluted and walked out of the office.

Watching his retreating back for a few seconds, Langers turned to Dieter and said, 'Get hold of Zauber, I want a meeting in this office at 1400 hours sharp.'

'Yes, Sir,' said Dieter, following Klein out of the door.

The atmosphere in the office was tense. Zauber, the Gestapo chief, walked quickly in and sat looking expectantly towards Langers.

'Right, Gentlemen,' murmured Langers quietly, 'we've a lot to do and a short time to do it in. I want everything in place by the end of the afternoon. You, Zauber, will arrange a twenty-four hour surveillance of The Black Cat, that's a Gestapo matter.' Turning towards Heinz, he said, abruptly, 'What's facing the bar?'

'An apartment building, sir.'

'Right, I want the second floor apartment taken over by us, I don't care if the occupants stay or leave, and I want a Gestapo presence there from this evening. What about the back?'

Dieter answered, 'I sent a man down there this morning, Sir. There's an alley leading from the back of the bar into Wittenbergplatz. If we place a car there it shouldn't be spotted easily as it's a busy road.'

'Good. I've a photograph of Major Werner Koenig and I'm having copies run off now. Have you got that list yet, Dieter?'

'It's on its way Sir, later this afternoon,'

'I want to positively identify these two- what were they called again?' he said looking at Heinz.

'Bruno and Rudi, Sir.'

Nodding, Langers continued, 'As soon as you have it, Dieter, and they're identified, I want photographs of them. They must be on record somewhere. Get copies made. Now, the beauty of this situation is this: these people have no idea that we're on to them. We, on the other hand, know exactly who they are and where to find them and so, if necessary, can pick them up at any time. I don't, however, want to do that. What I want is to see where this leads us. There could be more people involved. If there are, I want them.'

'Sir, what about the General?' asked Dieter.

'Since early this afternoon, he's been put under discreet surveillance so we don't need to worry about him. This case takes priority and that comes from the top. It's a joint SD-Gestapo affair, with the Gestapo, under you Zauber, providing the manpower. I want a squad of men on standby twenty-four hours a day. They're to be ready to go instantly, is that understood?' Everyone around the room nodded. 'Right, let's get on with this and see where it takes us. Don't let there be any mistakes. If there are, heads will roll, that I promise you. Get on with it.'

66

The car turned into Wormser Straße and glided to a halt outside the apartment block facing The Black Cat. Four men got out, walked through the entrance and climbed to the second floor. One of the men knocked quietly on the door of apartment twelve and waited. They heard approaching footsteps and the door was opened by a middle-aged man.

Lifting his badge, the senior of the men said, 'Gestapo,' pushed his way past and entered, followed by the others.

The man's face drained of all colour, his heart starting to race as the four men walked into the living room. The man's wife was reading a magazine. Ignoring her completely, one of the agents walked over to the side of the window and parted the curtain slightly. He looked through, turned to his companions and nodded.

The woman stood, dropping the magazine. Her mouth opened as if about to protest as her husband said quietly, 'It's the Gestapo, my dear.' Her mouth closed quickly, and she too turned pale.

The senior man turned to the couple, and said, 'This is business of the state. We need to use this apartment for a while and I don't know how long we'll be here. You have a choice. You can stay if you wish or, if you prefer, you can go and stay with friends or relatives.' He raised his eyebrow, looking from one to the other.

There was a silence as the two looked at each other. 'Well, sir,' said the man, 'we don't have any relatives here in Berlin. My wife and I are from Frankfurt originally and know very few people.'

'Very well, you can stay,' said the senior man, 'but you'll have to keep out of this room. Do you have a spare bedroom?'

'Yes,' answered the wife.

'Good, we can use that too. As from now we're here for as long as it takes.'

Two of the men were setting up a tripod and screwing a powerful camera to the top, pointing it towards the other side of the street at a downward angle.

'Would you like a cup of coffee?' asked the woman.

'You're an angel,' said the senior man, grinning. 'I think we're going to enjoy it here.' He lifted a finger and looked from one to the other. He said, suddenly very serious, 'You are not under any circumstances to talk to anybody of our presence here. If you do, the consequences will be very serious for you both. Now, try to go about your daily lives as normal, but no gossiping about us at the shops,' he said looking towards the woman.

'Don't worry, sir,' said the man, 'We know when to keep our mouths shut. We're both loyal Germans.'

'Good,' said the senior man, 'that's the end of the matter.'

67

Briskly walking into the office with a file tucked under his arm, Dieter, with a smile of triumph playing at the corner of his mouth, said to Langers, 'I've got those lists, Chief, and, surprise, surprise, Rudi Wagner was with Bruno Meyer at the labour service camp.'

'Was he now? It looks like young Wagner will go the way of his father.'

'That's not all. I've been doing some digging in the files,' Dieter sat facing Langers, the older man looking on with interest. 'In 1929, Bruno's father was shot to death in an alley in Wedding. He was a communist and the murderer was never caught. However, it was widely known at the time who the murderer was. It seems that the party used a Brownshirt called Neiper as a sort of unofficial hit man and everyone was sure that it was him that killed Bruno's father.'

'Go on,' murmured Langers.

'Guess whose body was found in a car near a Brownshirt beer hall a few weeks ago?' Without waiting for a reply, Dieter continued, 'Deputy-Gauleiter Neiper. After the murder, the police questioned people who were in the hall that night and three young Brownshirts remember a young man who talked to them. He was dressed as a Brownshirt and fits the description of Bruno Meyer.'

'This gets more interesting.'

'Much more, Chief,' he continued, 'After the murder, a senior customs officer from Tempelhof airport came forward and reported that he'd been approached by Neiper. He said that Neiper had asked him to make sure that a Jewish family who were emigrating were given a smooth passage through customs. Apparently, that was no problem as their documents were perfectly in order. I suspect that Neiper bribed this man.'

'Interesting. Now why would a Deputy-Gauleiter help a Jewish family?'

'Exactly. I think that he was being blackmailed for some reason. Anyway, I checked the passenger list for that flight and found — wait for it — that Robert Wagner's wife, Astrid, and Rudi were booked on the same flight.'

'Where was this flight going to?'

'Basel. Now, Robert Wagner's brother, Stefan, lives in Basel. He's a very rich man, a banker. This afternoon, I phoned our embassy and spoke to our man there and he tells me that Wagner's known to have connections with both Swiss and British intelligence. Apparently he's a close friend of an Englishman called Claud Brown, who's the resident spook at the British Embassy.'

'Christ,' muttered Langers, 'go on.'

'Now for the icing on the cake: not only did Stefan Wagner serve under Altmann in the 1914 war, but they've been close friends ever since.'

'So, there's our connection. Altmann's passing on information to the English through Stefan Wagner?'

'Yes, I'd say so, and one other thing. Our man made some discreet enquiries. He just called me back. Apparently, a few days after they'd arrived, Rudi married the Jewish daughter and they now have a baby son.'

Langers looked at Rudi and smiled, 'That, my boy is a good bit of work. I wonder how the half-Jew bastard will get on without a father? Now we've cast our net, all we have to do is wait and see who we catch in it.'

'Yes sir,' said Dieter with a smile, 'Do you know, I think that I might have underestimated my friend, Rudi. Maybe he does have some balls, after all.'

68

The warm evening sunshine poured down onto the leafy suburb of Treptow as Werner turned into the drive of the secluded house. Climbing out of the car, he walked towards the massive oak door and rang the bell. The General, dressed in civilian clothes, answered and stood aside to let Werner enter.

'Good evening, Werner. Let's go into the library and have a drink,' said the General, leading the way. Once inside, the General walked over to the large sideboard and poured two generous measures of whisky, offering one to Werner.

'Thank you, Sir,' said Werner taking the drink, 'I suppose that this will be the last time that we send anything to Switzerland, at least for a while.'

'Probably. Do you realise that in less than two weeks we'll be at war. The invasion of Poland is set for the 1st of September and I'm sure that Britain and France won't sit back and do nothing this time. I've a copy of the battle plans on microfilm here. When are Rudi and Bruno planning to leave?'

'Well, we're having a meeting in The Black Cat tomorrow night at midnight. After that I assume that they'll leave very soon, within two days.'

'Good. At least the English will know what's going to happen, although I suspect that they'll be in no position to help the Poles. God help them.'

Werner nodded. 'I'm sure that it's no consolation to you to know that everything that you've being predicting for the last few years is now happening?'

The General sighed. 'None whatsoever. Oh, by the way, within the next few days Germany and Russia are going to sign a non-aggression pact. Ironic, isn't it? Hitler's signed a pact with the communists, his avowed enemies — a matter of expediency while he takes care of the Poles. However, Werner, make no mistake, it won't be long before he turns his attentions further east and then Stalin had better look out. I expect to be called to take over my divisions within the next few days.

I've asked for you to join me. You have no objections I take it? I'm inclined to recommend you for promotion. God knows you deserve it.'

'Of course not, Sir. We've been together for a long time now and I want to carry on working with you. As for promotion, I've no great desire to command a regiment. If it comes in the future, then alright, but for the moment…' he shrugged his shoulders and smiled, 'Anyway, who's going to keep their eye on you?'

The General chuckled. 'You cheeky young pup.'

'Do you know, General, if we never do anything again, we'll have done an enormous amount over the past few years. Our part in this is almost at an end. We've done our best to damage this regime and I think that we've a lot to be proud of.'

'Yes, I agree, but you know Werner, it makes my heart bleed to see what's happened to our beloved country since 1933. I've great fear for the future. This will eventually end in disaster for Germany, mark my words.'

'Oh, I'm sure that you're right. The people seem to be prepared to follow him like sheep, but they'll live to regret it. Mind you, let's not forget our friend Max. He has his hideaway down on the lake and I'm sure that he has some plan of his own. Let him take over where we've left off.'

'You're quite right, Werner,' said Altmann, cheering a little, 'We've done all that we can, now let fate decide what it will.'

Werner put down his glass and looked at his superior and friend.

The General walked over to him and took his hand in both of his. 'Werner, I regard you as my second son. I have no regrets. You're right — we've done some good work over the years.' There was a tear in his eye as he embraced the younger man. 'God be with you and with us all,' he said.

A feeling of absolute dread overcame Werner as he embraced the old soldier. 'Goodbye Chief,' he muttered.

69

'Yes! Yes! At last, you bastard,' murmured the Gestapo agent as he looked down to the entrance of The Black Cat from the second floor vantage point. His colleague jumped up off the settee where he'd been dozing and moved quickly to join his companion at the window. Wormser Straße was dimly lit, pools of light illuminating the areas underneath the street lamps, the rest cast in shadow on this sweltering August night.

'What is it?' asked the Gestapo man, suddenly alert.

'The one they call Werner's just gone inside.'

'Shall I make the call?'

'No, wait — let's see if the others turn up first.' The two men stood silently side by side, excited, as, at last, something was happening. 'There, look, they've just turned the corner.'

'Three of them,' said the second man, 'I recognise Rudi and Bruno, not the other one though.'

'We'll give them a few more minutes. Look the light's just gone on in the apartment.' They watched as Werner walked to the window and closed the curtains, seemingly close enough to touch.

'It's time,' said the senior man as he walked over towards the telephone, 'When I've made the call, we'll go downstairs and wait.'

Rudi, Bruno and Joseph walked into the apartment.

'Christ, it's hot in here,' exclaimed Bruno, 'Can't we open a window?'

'No,' said Werner. 'Anyway, we won't be here for long.'

Lying on the coffee table, were two automatic pistols with spare clips of ammunition, and two leather shoulder holsters. 'They're for you two,' Werner said, looking at Rudi and Bruno, 'You may need them. When are you planning to leave Germany?'

'The day after tomorrow; we're taking the car,' said Rudi as he and Bruno removed their light summer jackets and put on the shoulder holsters.

'Joseph, do you want one of those?' asked Werner, indicating the pistols now being worn by Bruno and Rudi.

Joseph laughed. 'You must be joking. I'm more likely to shoot myself than the Gestapo.'

'Come on let's have a drink. Who knows how long it'll be before we see each other again,' said Werner, pouring four whiskies. Turning towards Rudi, Werner continued, 'Here's the last microfilm, Rudi. You should try and get it to the English as soon as possible. I should tell you that within two weeks we'll be at war.'

'As soon as that?' said Joseph.

'Yes, I'm afraid so,' replied Werner, 'The General and I are expecting our embarkation orders any day now. We expect to be sent to the Polish frontier. The invasion's planned for the 1st of September.'

'Well, I'm glad that something's happening at last. We can now get out of this God-forsaken country and start doing some real work against these bastards,' said Bruno. 'I can't wait to get to England and start making a real difference.'

Rudi smiled. 'We may be back here sooner than you expect, Bruno. At least I think that's the plan. New identities, the whole works. Something puzzles me though, just where are we going to operate from?'

Bruno shrugged, as Werner smiled and said to himself, '*If you knew, Rudi, you'd be very surprised.*'

70

'Fucking Gestapo!' shouted the young policeman aloud as he approached the desk in the main police station by the Berlin Zoo. 'The bastards think that they own my patch. They've been camped out there for the past fucking three days to my knowledge at least, maybe longer.'

'What's upsetting you, young man?' said the older and infinitely more experienced desk sergeant. It was approaching midnight and he'd just come on duty along with Inspector Weinburger. The two had been having a quiet discussion when the young man had entered, his shift finished.

'The Gestapo, Sergeant. They must have someone or something under surveillance. As I say, they've been sitting out there for days now,' he chuckled. 'It must be fucking boring. Serve the bastards right.'

'Eh, mind your language in front of the inspector, young man,' said the sergeant.

'Sorry, Sir,' said the policeman.

Looking keenly at the young man standing in front of him, Inspector Wolfgang Weinburger was immediately on the alert. His mental antenna quivering, he said, 'Where are they exactly?'

'In Wittenbergplatz, Chief.'

'*Christ! The Black Cat,*' thought Weinburger, 'And you say that they've been there for a few days now?'

'Yes, Sir.'

Affecting disinterest, Weinburger shrugged his shoulders and said, 'Well, it's nothing to do with us; the Gestapo are a law unto themselves. Sergeant, I'm just going out to buy some cigarettes. Hold the fort until I get back, will you?'

'Yes, Inspector,' said the older man, eyeing the Inspector's retreating back shrewdly and thinking to himself, *'That's interesting, he doesn't smoke.'*

Weinburger, ran down the police station steps into the humid night air. 'Where's the nearest public telephone?' he muttered to himself as he halted on the pavement, looking to the left and right. He quickly walked in the direction of the railway station and arrived at a public phone booth slightly out of breath. It was occupied by an old woman. Without hesitation he took out his warrant card and pulled open the door to the kiosk. The woman looked up, startled, 'Police, I need that phone, now!' he shouted. The woman looked as if she were about to protest, thought better of it, and said into the phone, 'Fernand I have to go, I'll call you back.' She quickly replaced the receiver and without a word pushed past the inspector. Fumbling in his trouser pocket for change, he inserted the coins, dialled the number and waited. It was answered almost immediately. Recognising Werner's voice, he said, quietly but urgently, 'Werner, it's Weinberger. They're on to you, get out now!' Without waiting for a reply, Wolfgang hung up. 'I hope to Christ I'm not too late,' he muttered to himself as he walked back in the direction of the police station.

71

Werner calmly replaced the receiver and looked from Rudi to Bruno and Joseph. Without any hint of panic in his voice, he said quietly, 'That was Weinberger. We're being watched. It's time to get out of here. Rudi, you've got the micro film?'

'Yes.'

'Good, now come on.' T

The four headed towards the door.

Four black saloon cars sped around the corner into Wormser Straße and screeched to a halt outside The Black Cat. The doors were flung open as nine Gestapo agents jumped out, some armed with sub-machine guns. Dieter, in the lead car, walked over to the two Gestapo men who'd had the bar under surveillance and said, 'Well?'

'There are four of them in there, Sir,' said the senior man.

'Very well. You two stay here, cover the entrance, the rest of you come with me.' Dieter ran down the stairs followed by his men as he drew his pistol. The bar was about half full as they entered.

Dieter shouted, 'Gestapo! Get out of the way.' He and his men pushed their way through as the customers, seeing the armed men, erupted into panic. There were screams and shouts as the bar was plunged into darkness. Gustav, guessing what was happening, pulled down the master switch behind the bar and prepared to get out as soon as possible. In almost total darkness, the Gestapo, using the butts of their machine pistols, mercilessly beat a way through the crowd and burst into the corridor with Dieter in the lead.

Werner, leading the way, was about half way down as the Gestapo came through the downstairs door. The lights suddenly came on again, as one of the Gestapo men found the master switch. Werner looked down as the first of the men started to run up the stairs and opened fire.

Rudi and Bruno aimed their weapons. In the split second before he fired Bruno looked into the eyes of Heinrich Heinz. He smiled and squeezed the trigger. '*I told you that I'd kill you if you ever crossed my path again, you bastard*,' he thought to himself. The bullet smashed into Heinrich's forehead, killing him instantly. Rudi's shot hit the other man in the throat, throwing him backwards. Werner's shot embedded itself in the wall just above Dieter's head. The three men continued firing, pouring shots down the stairs as the remaining Nazis crouched and returned the fire.

Realising the situation, Werner shouted, 'Get back! Now! Move!' As they turned, under a hail of fire, several bullets hit Joseph in the back, toppling him over backwards. His body slid slowly down the stairs towards the men below, leaving a trail of blood, his eyes staring sightlessly at the ceiling.

The three men ran into the room. Werner walked quickly over to the cupboard and opened the drawer, taking out two hand grenades. He walked back over to the door, pulled the pin on one of the grenades and tossed it down the stairs. It flew in a slow arc, hit the stair carpet and erupted in smoke and flame, shooting red hot shrapnel amongst the men below, killing two and seriously wounding three more.

'Pull back!' shouted Dieter. His ears buzzed with the incredibly loud detonations and flying shrapnel in the enclosed space. He was lucky to have escaped serious injury himself. 'Stay there,' he said to the remaining men as he walked quickly back to the door leading to the bar. It was totally empty now, chairs and tables scattered all over the floor. He ran quickly back up the stairs and into the street as reinforcements arrived. A truck full of uniformed SS men pulled up and jumped down, Brigadier Langers sitting in the front.

'What's happening?' said Langers as he climbed down from the truck's cab.

'We've got them trapped, Sir, but they're well-armed and fighting back. I've had a number of men killed and wounded but we've shot one of them.' Turning to the Gestapo men who'd had the bar under surveillance, he said, 'Take two of the SS soldiers, go up to the apartment opposite and spray the hide-out with machine gun fire.'

'Don't open fire until I give the order,' said the young SS lieutenant who'd arrived with the men. I don't want you shooting our own people. It was obvious who was now leading the operation. Nodding, he led the SS across the road and into the building. 'The rest of you men come with me,' said the young officer. Dieter was happy to hand over to the more experienced and trained soldier.

Werner turned to Rudi and Bruno. 'That should keep them quiet for a while, but not for long. Right, you two, it's time to go. Get up into the ceiling and across to the building next door and get out that way. I'll try to hold them off a bit longer.'

Bruno, said, 'But what about you? We can't just … .'

'Don't worry about me, just do as you're told and that's an order. Get to a phone and try to warn the General in case I can't, and then get on to Max. Now go! And good luck.'

Without looking at them he walked over to the door and opened it slowly. Looking cautiously out, he saw the top of a man's head and shoulders appearing very slowly around the top of the stairs. He opened fire, the man gave a cry, and was flung back. Werner pulled the pin on a second grenade and rolled it to the head of the stairs. As it exploded with a roar, a sheet of flame rose into the air, sending shrapnel flying in all directions. 'That should keep their fucking heads down for a while.' Although he knew now that it was only a matter of time.

Rudi and Bruno crawled as quickly as possible through the passage in the roof and jumped down into the dark building. Cautiously, they walked down the stairs, through the large offices, and down to the main entrance. They stood by the door and waited. Slowly opening the door, Rudi peered to his right and looked in the direction of The Black Cat. There was a crowd around the entrance, cars with their doors wide open and an army lorry. No one was looking in their direction as he and Bruno slipped quietly away and around the corner.

Standing in an alcove at the bottom of the stairs in The Black Cat, Dieter, Langers and the SS Lieutenant were talking quietly. 'I suggest that when your men open fire from the other side of the street, you storm the apartment door, unless you have a better idea?' said Langers.

'We'll storm it immediately the firing stops. This has gone on for long enough. I'm not going to allow these people to hold us up for much longer. However, I can't guarantee that anyone will survive.' Looking around at the dead, he continued, 'I'm not prepared to put my men's lives at risk unnecessarily.' The air around them was filled with the reek of cordite. One of the wooden panels along the side of the stairs was smouldering as if about to burst into flames. They'd managed to pull the wounded away. The occasional groan came from the bar where they'd been laid on the floor. In the distance the wail of ambulance sirens could be heard.

'Do you know, Sir,' said Dieter to Langers, 'I think that they were tipped off. They were ready for us.'

'No matter, we've got them trapped now. It's gone very quiet up there.' Looking towards the young Waffen SS Lieutenant, Langers said quietly, 'Lieutenant, if you could take at least one alive, I'd be grateful.'

'I'll do my best, Sir, but I can't make any promises.'

Leading the way into the room facing The Black Cat on the opposite side of the road, the Gestapo man pointed to the window. The two SS men walked over and looked out. The apartment window opposite was faintly lit, the diffused light coming through the curtains. Lifting a dining chair, the SS man swung it in an arc above his head and smashed the window. The two stood with their machine guns pointing across the road.

There was no sign of movement from downstairs as Werner waited. 'It must be soon now,' he muttered to himself. Keeping his eye on the door, he moved slowly backwards into the centre of the room. Eyeing the bottle of whisky on the table, he grinned and said, 'What the fuck,' as he lifted the bottle and took a swig. Looking down at the telephone on the coffee table, he made an instant decision as he lifted the receiver and tucked the handset under his chin. With the pistol aimed unwaveringly towards the door, he dialled the General's number. 'Come on General, I don't have much time.'

The phone was answered on the second ring.

'Altmann,'

'Sir, its Werner, don't say anything. The Gestapo are on to us. I only have a short time. Rudi and Bruno have managed to escape. I'm afraid my time's up. I can't hold them off much longer. I'm going to try to get out now. You must leave, save yourself, now! Go to Max's.'

'You said Rudi and Bruno, what about Joseph?' asked the General, quietly.

'I'm sorry, Sir.' Werner said no more, knowing that the General would understand.

'Goodbye, Werner,' murmured the General quietly, 'May God bless you.'

The line went dead.

'Right, time to get the fuck out before they storm the place,' muttered Werner. 'I might just have a chance. Go on, you can do it,' he urged himself, as he replaced the receiver.

The two SS men in the apartment opposite waited, aware of movement in the apartment on the other side of the road. 'Come on,' snarled one of the men, 'Give the fucking order before it's too late.

From downstairs, someone shouted, 'Fire now!'

They aimed their weapons and squeezed the triggers simultaneously. The window imploded with a huge explosion as Werner started to move towards the hall. The chatter of machine gun fire filled the air as the room was raked with bullets, gouging great chips of wood out of the furniture. Werner's back was stitched with machine gun bullets as they pierced his body and slammed into his upper torso like hammer blows. The force of the 9mm bullets pushed his body forward as he fell dead, face down on the floor.

As soon as the guns stopped firing, the SS soldiers stormed the room, kicking open the door. The first thing they saw was Werner's body as they moved cautiously from room to room, their weapons at the ready.

Langers and Dieter walked in and looked around at the destruction, 'Where are the others?' said Langers, 'his voice filled with fury, 'There should be two more. Where the fuck are they?'

Dieter walked over to Werner's body. With the tip of his boot he turned the Major over and looked down. 'Treacherous bastard,' he muttered to himself. Turning towards Langers, he said, 'Chief, the other one on the stairs is Altmann's son I think.'

He was puzzled as he slowly walked down the hallway and stopped. There was a draught coming from above his head. He looked up and saw the gaping black square hole. In fury, he turned and smashed his fist with full force into the wall. 'That's where they went. This one,' he said, indicating Werner, 'gave them the chance to escape. He's Altmann's aid. Do you know Sir, this group's very well organised. I'll hunt down Rudi and Bruno if it's the last thing I do, and when I have them I swear to Christ they'll be screaming for mercy before I'm finished with them.'

'Dieter, send some men and arrest that fucking traitor, Altmann. I want him alive,' said Langers, his tone icy.

72

General Altmann put down the telephone, tears stinging his eyes as he moved slowly over to his desk and sat down. The house was completely silent, the only light coming from the desk lamp. He pushed the tears away with his hand. 'Joseph, what have I done? My only son, dead. You were never meant to be a soldier, that was my job,' the General spoke to the room. He made no effort to leave, no haste to get out, his decision already made. He continued talking to himself, 'Where would I go? England.' He snorted. 'England and do what? Be a figurehead? No, it's better to go out now, do the correct military thing. I will not have the humiliation of the torture chamber and a show trial.' The room was briefly illuminated, as two pairs of car headlights pierced the drawn curtains.

'So, you've arrived already, have you? You black uniformed thugs. Well, you'll be too late. When you've been destroyed, as eventually you will be, I pray that my fellow countrymen will not see me as a traitor. Let history be my judge. I have not one regret, except that I won't be alive to see your end.'

He heard the car doors slammed shut and the sound of approaching footsteps crunching on the gravel as he opened the desk drawer and took out his service pistol. He looked down at the dull, well-oiled weapon for a second, placed the barrel into his mouth and pulled the trigger.

73

The crowds walking up and down the Kurfürstendamm were still large even at 1am, as if no one wanted to be home in bed on this warm balmy night. Rudi and Bruno mingled with the crowds, both feeling slightly vulnerable and aware of the need to get to a phone as quickly as possible. After escaping from The Black Cat, they'd driven the short distance to the Anhalter station and left the car in a side street.

Rudi glanced at his watch, unable to believe that it'd been less than an hour since they'd first entered the secret apartment and the surprise attack by the Gestapo. 'Let's get off the main street and find a quiet bar, Bruno. We must find a phone.'

'Yes, you're right. I feel as if everyone's watching us. Look, down there,' he said, pointing to an illuminated Schultheiß Brewery sign, 'Let's go in.'

They entered a small, dark bar. Standing in the entrance, Rudi looked around for a telephone sign. 'Over there, out the back by the toilets. Find a seat and order two beers. I'll be as quick as I can.' The room was filled with the chatter of people, the air a fog of cigarette smoke. Pushing his way through, Rudi walked out to the corridor and saw the telephone booth on the right, its concertina doors open. He entered, closed the doors and lifted the receiver. Dialling the General's number first, he waited, the hair on his forehead matted with sweat. He could hear the phone ringing at the other end, seeming to go on forever. 'Nothing. Well I tried,' he muttered to himself as he replaced the receiver, 'Maybe Werner's already spoken to him.' He dialled next the number that he had for Max. Again the phone rang. 'Come on Max, for Christ's sake, answer.' Again, nothing. Replacing the receiver he headed back towards the bar. 'We have to get under-cover and quickly,' he muttered to himself.

Max and Simon were sitting down in the secret room in the cellar of the house on the lake. Each had an ice-cold beer and from time to time took a swig. In front of them, they had a mound of ammunition and a pile of pistol magazines and were loading them. As they finished they stacked them to one side. Neither of them heard the urgent ringing of the telephone above their heads.

Rudi walked into the bar, looked around and spotted Bruno sitting in a corner booth. He walked over and sat down as Bruno looked up. 'Well?' he asked.

'Nothing! Nobody's answering. Listen, Bruno, we'll give it another half an hour. If we get no reply from Max we're going to have to find some shelter until tomorrow. Before long every Gestapo officer and policeman in Berlin will be out looking for us. What a fuck up, how did they get on to us?'

'Your guess is as good as mine, but one thing's for sure, we have to lie low. Any ideas?'

'Yes, as it happens, but I'm reluctant to put these people in danger. Mind you, it'll only be for a short time, I hope.'

'Who is it?' said Bruno, taking a swig of beer.

'The Hoffmanns.'

'What! Dieter's parents?'

'Yes, I had a conversation with his father a few months ago. There's a hiding place up in the attic that we can use. I've even got a front door key. Bruno, we don't have any choice. Glancing up, Rudi froze. 'Shit!' he murmured, 'Don't turn around, two policemen have just walked in.'

Instinctively, Bruno lifted his right hand and placed it on the butt of the pistol nestling under his jacket. 'What are they doing?'

'Talking to the owner.' Rudi saw the proprietor gesture to the other side of the room. The policemen looked and walked over. Craning his neck, Rudi could see the two policemen bending down and grasping a drunk under the armpits. They pulled him up, and, one on each side, escorted him out. 'It's alright, just a drunk.' Bruno visibly relaxed. 'That's it; one more call and then we get out of here.' Rudi stood.

'I wonder what's happened to Werner?' said Bruno quietly.

'I don't know, but for now we have to think of ourselves. I'm going to make that call.'

Putting the loaded magazines into an ammunition box, Max yawned and stretched. 'That's enough for one night,' he said looking at Simon,

'Tell me, are you happy here Simon?'

Simon put a cigarette in his mouth, struck a match and inhaled deeply before he replied, 'You bet. I enjoy chauffeuring you around and I've got a new identity. I've been asked for my papers twice and they must be good or I wouldn't be here talking to you!'

'Do you remember the night we first met?'

'Of course.'

'I asked you about your friends,' he smiled. 'I mean the ones that you can trust.'

'Yes, that's true. What about them?'

'Well, I think it's time that you paid them a visit. Look, Simon, we're on the brink of war, take it from me, I know. I think that we need another four or five; that should do it. Go into town and see if you can find them and sound them out without giving too much away. Once Germany's at war, things are going to get very bad for you Jews and so now is the time to get our little group in place.'

'Max, what do you have in mind for this group?'

Max gave a cold smile. 'What do I have in mind? I'll tell you — to cause as much trouble and chaos as possible to those bastards in the Wilhelmstraße.'

Simon smiled. 'Max,' he said, 'meeting you was the best thing that ever happened to me. Leave it with me. I'll set it up.'

'Good, now it's bedtime. Come on.' The two rose, turned out the lights and closed everything up. As they climbed the stairs, they heard the telephone ringing faintly in the lounge. Max ran up the last few stairs, just as the phone stopped ringing. 'Shit! I wonder who that was?' he said with a sense of foreboding.

Rudi replaced the receiver for the last time. His mind was made up as he headed back to the bar. 'No reply. Come on, we're going to the Hoffmanns. It's not far.'

They got up and walked out into the warm night. It was beginning to get quieter as people started to head home and think about work the next day.

74

As the two duty policemen were about to leave the police station that night, the desk sergeant had called them back. 'Look out for this vehicle: here's the registration. The Gestapo want to have a chat with the owner. Have you got copies of the photos of the two that we're looking for?'

'Yes, Sarge, we'll keep our eyes open. That was some shooting match at The Black Cat tonight, wasn't it?'

'Yes it was, now go on, clear out and stay alert, the pair of you.'

They now strolled slowly on their patrol by the Anhalter station. One of them had a cigarette cupped in his hand and surreptitiously took a drag, from time to time. They looked at the parked cars as they walked along.

They spotted the Mercedes Benz almost immediately. They stopped, and one turned on his torch, pointing it in the direction of the car's registration plate. 'We've got it, Fritz, look.'

Fritz bent forward slightly. 'Yeh, that's it. Go and call the station, I'll wait here.'

His colleague nodded and headed in the direction of the nearest police telephone.

Ten minutes later, a black car pulled in and parked a few metres away from the Mercedes. The driver turned off the ignition, looked at his companion and said, 'If they come back here, we'll have them.

Turning into the quiet side street, Bruno and Rudi, keeping to the shadows as much as possible, walked towards the Hoffmann's house. There was no one in sight at this hour. In the distance, they could hear the hum of the traffic as it travelled up and down the Kurfürstendamm. The streetlights made pools of light surrounded by shadow as the two young men walked quietly up the drive. Rudi put his hand in his pocket and took out a bunch of keys, sorting through them as he searched for the right one given to him by the professor all those months previously.

Both young men were sweating profusely as Rudi inserted the key and pushed open the front door. Quietly moving into the hall Rudi felt around for the light switch in the darkness. After fumbling for a few seconds, he found it and flooded the hall with light. Rudi walked to the foot of the stairs and called, 'Professor Hoffmann! Professor! It's Rudi Wagner. Don't be alarmed.'

There was movement from upstairs. 'Rudi, is that you? What time is it? What's happened?' The Professor appeared at the top of the stairs wearing pyjamas, his hair in disarray.

From behind him, Greta's voice could be heard. 'What is it Klaus? Who's there?'

'It's Rudi, Mother, don't fret.' Klaus walked down the stairs, rubbing the sleep from his eyes. 'Rudi, Bruno, what's happened? You look dreadful.' The professor was suddenly wide awake, as he looked from one to the other.

'We're in trouble, Professor. The Gestapo are after us and we need somewhere to shelter for a few hours.'

'Come into the lounge,' said the Professor as Greta appeared at the top of the stairs tying her dressing gown. Leading the way through the doorway, Klaus turned to the dishevelled young men and said, 'Now is not the time for questions. You can tell us all about it later. Is it likely that they'll think to come here?' he asked, grasping the seriousness of the situation.

'I don't know, but it's possible. Dieter's involved and he might think to come here. All we need to do is get to a phone. The danger is that yours might be tapped so we daren't use it.'

'That's no problem. I can go and use a public phone in the morning.'

Greta, seeing the state of Rudi and Bruno, poured two drinks and handed one to each of them. 'Klaus, do you want a drink?'

'Yes, my dear, a good idea,' he said, obviously thinking. 'Look, you should go into the attic. If anyone turns up here you can slip into the hidden room.'

'Yes, that's what I thought,' said Rudi. 'I'm sorry to put you in this position, but there was nowhere else to go. I'm sure that the police and Gestapo are scouring the city for us now.'

'Think nothing of it,' said the Professor, looking at Greta and taking a sip of his drink. 'Why do you think I told you about the room in the attic? I suspected that you were involved in something at the time.'

Rudi smiled. 'Ironically, I wasn't at the time, but I certainly am now.'

'Did you say that Dieter knows about this?' asked Greta.

'He certainly does,' answered Bruno. 'He was leading the raid. I'm sorry, you don't know. The Gestapo raided a bar in town earlier this evening. We'd been using it as a meeting place. How they found out about us, we don't know.'

Finishing their drinks, they put the empty glasses down on the sideboard as the Professor said, 'Let's go upstairs. As I say, you can wait in the attic. If anyone comes calling you'll have plenty of time to hide.'

Turning out the ground floor lights, they walked up the stairs. 'If you give me the number, I'll make that call tomorrow, early,' said the Professor, leading the way up to the attic. He turned the light on. 'You know how to get in there if you need to. I'll go back down now. We don't want to arouse anyone's suspicions if they turn up and see the house ablaze with lights at this time in the morning.' He turned and walked back down the stairs. Rudi and Bruno went and sat with their backs to the wall, saying nothing, going over in their minds the events of the past three hours. Bruno, covered in sweat, put his hand into his jacket pocket and pulled out a handkerchief. The card that he'd picked up in The Black Cat all those months ago, fluttered unseen to the floor as he wiped his brow.

Klaus Hoffmann walked into the bedroom and opened the bedside drawer. He took out the pistol that he'd shown Rudi, checked that there was a round in the chamber, and slipped it into his dressing gown pocket. 'I'll use this if I have to,' he muttered to himself.

75

The two black cars turned into Forckenbeckstraße in the district of Schmargendorf, and took the sixth turning on the right into Driburger Strasse. They pulled into the drive of Rudi's house with a squeal of tyres, coming to a halt outside the darkened building.

Jumping out, Dieter said to the five Gestapo men who accompanied him, 'Smash the door down and be quick.' He had little hope that anyone would be here. Rudi, he knew, wasn't that stupid. He'd heard the report of his car being found and of the death of General Altmann. As he waited, the door gave way with a crash and splintering of wood. 'Search the place from top to bottom! Don't miss anything!' he ordered.

Walking in through the shattered door, he went into the lounge on the left and over to the sideboard. Lifting the decanter he poured himself a large scotch, sat in an easy chair and put his jackbooted feet onto the coffee table. He looked around the room that he'd known since childhood, as he heard his men banging around the house. Full of fury, he lifted his left leg up and brought it crashing down on to the highly polished surface of the table, causing a deep scratch. He looked across the room at the large, glass-fronted display cabinet, full of his old friend's mother's collection of rare Meissen. He stood, picked up his sub-machine gun and walked over to the cabinet. Looking at his reflection in the mirror-like surface of the glass, out of sheer spite, he lifted the butt of the gun and smashed the glass, raking the butt along each shelf and breaking every piece of fragile porcelain.

'Where are you, you bastards? I want you!' he said to himself with a mixture of anger and frustration.

One of his men walked into the room and said, 'It looks like someone was planning a trip, Captain.'

'Oh, yes, what have you found?'

'Four packed suitcases on a bed upstairs.'

Nodding, Dieter said, 'Keep looking. Pull the fucking place apart. See if you can find anything incriminating.' Dieter paced up and down and said aloud, 'I wonder, would they dare? I'm sure that my dear father and mother would give them shelter if they asked.' Making a decision, he drained his glass, walked to the door and called, 'Dorff, come here.' Dorff came down the stairs and said, 'Yes, Sir?'

'Dorff, guess who lives within walking distance of this house?' The whiskey had gone to his head, a result of not eating for a long time.

'I don't know Sir,' said Dorff, puzzled.

'Well, I'll tell you: my parents. Do you know, I used to play in this house as a child. It's true, Rudi Wagner and I used to be the best of friends at one time. It's absolutely true.'

Dorff didn't know what to say. He just looked at the young SD captain.

'I'll tell you what we're going to do, Dorff. You and I are going to take a little walk and pay my parents a visit, have a little nose around. Tell the sergeant that you and I are going to walk up to Nenndorfer Strasse. It's number thirty-six. When they've finished here they can meet us there.'

'Alright, Sir. It'd be nice to have a stroll,' he said, as he walked out of the door. Picking up the sub-machine gun Dieter walked to the front door and waited.

Professor Hoffmann was sitting in a chair by the bedroom window, sleep now impossible. He jolted upright as, suddenly, there was hammering on the front door and a continuous ringing of the doorbell. 'They're here, Greta,' he said, his heart thumping in his chest. Getting up, he walked down the stairs as Greta put on her dressing gown for the second time that night.

Rudi and Bruno heard the noise downstairs. Opening the cupboard door, they pushed open the false back and crawled inside the small, airless room.

Klaus shouted, 'I'm coming! Be patient, I'm coming!' He opened the door to be confronted by his son and a man in civilian clothes.

Dieter's mood had worsened on the walk to his parent's house: the whiskey, anger and frustration, a dangerous combination. 'Good morning, Mother, Father. 'I'm sorry to call so early, but as this isn't a social call, I'm sure that you won't mind.' He pushed his way past his father and walked into the lounge.

'What can we do for you, Captain?' said Klaus.

'A very good question, Father. Tell me, have you seen anything of my old friend, Rudi Wagner tonight? Oh, you don't mind if I have a small glass of whiskey, do you?' he said walking over to the sideboard. He immediately spotted the three dirty glasses, but said nothing as he poured, thinking to himself, '*Maybe this visit was worth it after all.*' Turning he looked at his father and mother, raised an eyebrow and said, 'Well?'

'Greta answered, 'No, we haven't seen Rudi for a long time.'

'In that case, you won't mind if we take a look, will you? Dorff, start in the cellar, through there.' Dorff nodded and left the room. 'Be very thorough, Dorff,' called Dieter. 'Why don't you join me, Father?' he said, lifting his glass.

'No, thank you. A little early, I think,' he said, putting his hand inside his dressing gown pocket and feeling the pistol. '*God, each time I see you I loathe you more and more, you jumped up little pup,*' he thought to himself.

'Aren't you interested to know why I want to see him?' Dieter said. 'Well, I'll tell you anyway; our friend's been a very naughty boy. At this moment he's probably the most wanted man in this country. Him and his accomplice, Bruno Meyer, are both traitors and have been betraying this country for a long time. I intend to take them, preferably alive, and when I get my hands on them they'll wish they'd never been born. That I promise you.'

'I've no doubt, Captain, that you're very good at what you do. However, I repeat, we haven't seen Rudi for a long time,' said Greta, with ice in her voice.

At that moment, Dorff came through the door and shook his head.

'Right, let's look upstairs, shall we? You lead the way, Father. You come too Mother; let's all stay together, shall we? Oh, by the way, Father, I hope that you haven't forgotten what it's like to be inside a concentration camp?' Klaus said nothing as he led the way upstairs, finding the feel of the pistol in his pocket comforting. Dieter and Dorff thoroughly searched the bedrooms as Klaus and Greta looked on. 'Now,' said Dieter smiling, 'the attic. Do you know, I haven't been up there since I was a boy.'

They walked into the darkness. Dieter turned on the switch, flooding the attic with light. Very slowly he walked around, looking everywhere. Dorff went to the very back of the room rummaging through old furniture that had been stacked there over the years. The Hoffmann's stood side by side, their backs to the wall. Klaus's heart was hammering in his chest as he looked towards Greta. Dieter was beginning to feel a sense of disappointment as he walked over to the cupboard set in the wall and slowly opened the door. Nothing, empty. As he was about to turn away, his eye happened to see a white card lying on the floor. He bent and picked it up. Slowly turning it over in his hand, he read, 'The Black Cat, Wormser Straße. Telephone 66 11 55.'

He looked up and smiled coldly, a feeling of triumph overwhelming him as he lifted the machine gun and pointed it at his parents. 'Well, well,' he said quietly, 'It looks to me as if you'll both be inside a concentration camp for a very long time.' Klaus tensed, gripping the pistol even tighter. 'Rudi! Bruno! I know you're there. I have a machine-gun pointing at my parents. You have ten seconds to come out and then I start shooting.' He waited.

'Alright, we're coming out,' said a muffled voice from behind the cupboard door.

Dieter half turned towards the cupboard, lifting the machine gun, 'Come on, slowly.'

Inside the darkened room, Bruno drew his pistol, determined not to give up easily, as Rudi opened the false back of the cupboard.

Out of the corner of his eye, Dieter saw a movement as his father drew the gun. Instinctively he turned, lifted the machine gun and opened fire, just as his father squeezed the trigger. The bullet from his father's gun smashed into Dieter's left elbow, the force shattering the bone. He gave a squeal of agony. The machine gun was cradled in his right arm, his finger pulling hard on the trigger, pointing directly at his father. The bullets sprayed into his father's chest, slamming him back against the wall as Greta moved in front of her husband as if to protect him. The 9mm bullets hit her in the throat as Dieter fell to the floor and writhed in agony. Rudi and Bruno burst out of the cupboard as Dorff tried to pull out his weapon. Seeing him, Bruno lifted his gun and fired three times, hitting him in the head and chest. He fell, dead before he hit the floor.

Looking around at the carnage, Rudi walked slowly over to the bodies of Klaus and Greta. Greta sprawled on top of her husband like a broken doll, a raw gaping wound in her throat. Quivering with rage, Rudi drew his weapon, walked over to Dieter and looked down at his writhing body, his left elbow seeping blood and lying at an impossible angle. His face was ashen and his eyes were clouded with pain as he looked up at Rudi.

Rudi pointed the gun directly at Dieters forehead as he said, his voice dripping with venom, 'You filthy piece of shit. You murdered your own parents in cold blood. Now I am going to kill you.'

'Fuck off you traitorous bastard,' said Dieter hoarsely as Rudi pulled the trigger.

'Click! Click! Click!' In anger and frustration, Rudi cursed, realising that the weapon was empty, the bullets used up in The Black Cat. 'You filthy bastard, I swear to God that I'll kill you if I ever see you again.'

'Come on Rudi, let's get the fuck out of here. Now! Move!' The two young men ran down the stairs and out into the darkness. Dieter's men arrived five minutes later. They found him lying unconscious on the floor.

76

Lieutenant Axel Weinburger drove down the Havelchaussee. On his left, bathed in moonlight, was the large park area known as the Grunewald, and on the right the river Havel. Glancing at his watch he saw that it was 3am as he pulled into the drive that led to Max's secluded house. The young army intelligence officer parked in the wide driveway, got out of the car and knocked persistently on the door. A light appeared and Max opened the door. He looked at Axel and motioned for him to enter, not at all put out by the lateness of the hour.

'I take it that this is not a social call at this hour, Axel. What's happened?' said Max.

'Sorry, but it's bad news I'm afraid. I had a call from Father. I've just come from his office.'

'The Circle?'

'Yes, the Gestapo raided The Black Cat at midnight. Father managed to phone and warn Werner, but it was too late. I'm afraid that Werner and Joseph Altmann were killed but your two boys escaped and are rolling about Berlin somewhere. The police and Gestapo are out in force looking for them now. I'm afraid that it gets worse: the General shot himself in the head just as the Gestapo arrived. He's dead.'

'Shit!' murmured Max as he crossed the room and telephoned the Krant's family at the small house which they occupied in the grounds. He waited, tapping his fingers on the table. 'Hello, Fritz. Sorry to wake you. Will you go and tell Simon to get dressed and come over here? It's urgent. Thank you.' He replaced the receiver and turned towards Axel. 'I wonder how they got on to us? I knew that it was a good idea to keep the two operations separate. No one knows about this place, thank God. The phone rang not long ago and I was too late to answer it. I bet it was Rudi and Bruno.'

'Well, Max, I hope that you get to them before the Gestapo do.'

'They've both got their heads screwed on, Axel. I expect they'll contact me as soon as they can. We'll just have to be ready when they do.

The front door opened and Simon walked in. 'What's the matter?' he enquired.

'We might have to go out. Make us all some coffee and then run downstairs. Get me the SS-Colonels uniform and a Privates uniform for yourself.' Simon nodded and headed for the kitchen. Max glanced at the clock. 'It happened about three hours ago, you say?'

'Yes, poor old Werner and Joseph, not to mention the General.'

Max sighed. 'That's the game we play and the risk that we take, I'm afraid, Axel. I'd like to know who betrayed them, though. You don't have any idea I suppose?'

'No, not at the moment, but we'll find out eventually. Sooner or later a report will land on our desks at headquarters.'

Simon came walking in, balancing a tray on his left arm. 'Ah, coffee, let's all have a drink. Then we have no choice but to wait. I hope that they phone quickly though. It'll soon be dawn and I'd like to get them undercover before it gets light.'

77

A s Rudi and Bruno ran out of the Hoffmanns drive, Rudi said, breathlessly, 'The Schmargendorf S-Bahn station's about two minutes from here. We need to get out of the centre of town and find a phone. I hope to God that Max is around now.'

They quickly walked into the station hall. The clock on the wall said 4am as they approached the ticket counter. 'Where's the next train going to?' asked Rudi.

The bleary-eyed ticket collector mumbled, 'Spandau, but you'd better hurry, it's about to leave.'

They ran up the stairs and jumped on to the train as the doors closed behind them and it pulled out of the station.

'Jesus, Rudi, that was close. I thought that our time was up. We've been very lucky in the past few hours. It can't stay this way for much longer.'

'I know. Seeing the Hoffmann's bodies lying there — I can't get the sight of them out of my mind.' He gave a shudder. 'I blame myself. If we hadn't have gone there … '

'Listen, Rudi,' hissed Bruno, 'it's not your fault. We had no choice but to go there. It wasn't you who pulled that trigger, it was Dieter. Now, stop blaming yourself. If you want to blame anybody, blame the fucking regime that spawned the likes of Dieter.'

'It's easy for you to say,' said Rudi as the train swayed from side to side.

'Listen! Stop feeling sorry for yourself. A lot of good people have died tonight, not just the Hoffmanns, and we may be next. Rudi, the sooner you realise that we're fighting a fucking war here, the better.' Bruno softened his tone, 'Listen, old friend, stop blaming yourself. It wasn't your fault. What we have to think of now is getting out of this mess.'

'I'm sorry, Bruno, you're right. However, I'll never forget what happened tonight. If I ever lay eyes on Dieter again, I'll kill him, I swear it.'

'Yes, it's a pity that your fucking gun was empty. Go and put a fresh magazine into it now. The night's not over yet and you might need it, and don't worry, you'll get your chance with Dieter, just as I did with Heinrich tonight. Do you remember, I said at the labour camp that if I ever set eyes on him again, I'd kill him and now I have.'

Rudi stood and nodded, 'I'll go into the toilet and do it immediately,' he said.

The train headed in the direction of Spandau, stopping from time to time as early morning workers got on and off. No one paid them any attention.

They pulled into Pichelsberg station. 'Spandau next stop,' said Rudi. As the train slowly left the station, the two young men stood and headed for the doors. As they arrived in Berlin-Spandau, they jumped off the train, trotted down the stairs and into the street. It was starting to get lighter as they looked around, both of them unfamiliar with this part of Berlin.

'Just down there, look,' said Bruno as he spotted a night bar further along the road. 'Come on.' They walked into the dingy bar. Sitting around the tables were a number of working men. Some had a beer and schnapps in front of them and others were sipping at cups of coffee. Bruno walked over to the bar and ordered two coffees as Rudi walked into the back, looking for the telephone. He spotted it just next to the toilets, lifted the receiver and put in some coins. '*,Max, please be there'* he prayed to himself as a wave of fatigue overcame him. He dialled and waited.

The telephone was answered on the second ring,

'Max, thank Christ.'

'Where are you?' snapped Max.

'Spandau, in a bar on the high street.'

'What's it called?'

'Oh, shit!' said Rudi. 'Think, think.' He hesitated. The name came to him, 'The Golden Lion.'

'Alright, stay there. We'll be with you within half an hour. Don't move.' The line went dead.

Rudi gave a sigh of relief as he walked back into the almost deserted bar and sat down. He'd never felt so relieved or so tired in his life. 'Our luck's changed at last. I spoke to Max and he said half an hour.'

'Thank God. Do you know I'm exhausted. I could sleep for a week,' said Bruno as he took a sip of coffee.

'Yes, me too.'

The owner of the bar looked over at the two young men sitting in the corner. The radio was playing quietly in the background. He'd had it on all night and had heard the broadcast. The police were searching for two fugitives and those two over there fitted the description. 'Would you like two more coffees boys? On the house,' he called over.

'Thanks, we wouldn't say no,' said Bruno.

'I'll bring them over.'

Bruno looked at Rudi, and said, 'Free coffee in a place like this? I don't believe it.' He was immediately suspicious and now wide-awake. 'Keep your eye on him, Rudi. Can you see a telephone behind the bar?'

Rudi looked over. 'Yes.'

'If he goes anywhere near it, he's a dead man.'

The owner came over carrying the coffee and eyed Bruno and Rudi closely. *'It's them,'* he thought to himself, *'and there's a very big reward.'* The man smiled and put down the coffee. 'Here you are gents. You're around a bit early this morning aren't you?'

'Yeh, we've been hitting the night clubs in town,' said Bruno with a smile.

'Ah, you youngsters. Mind you, I did the same thing when I was your age.' Bruno noticed the beads of sweat on the man's forehead. He was nervously rubbing his hands together. 'Right then, I'll leave you to it,' he said as he turned and headed back towards the bar.

'He suspects us,' muttered Bruno, watching the man closely, 'Come on Max, hurry up.'

The owner made his decision and called over, 'I'm just going into the back for a minute; if anyone comes in tell them I won't be long.'

'Alright,' said Bruno. As soon as the man had disappeared, Bruno jumped up and followed him. Quietly pushing open the door a fraction, Bruno saw the man starting to dial a number. Without any hesitation, he pulled out his pistol and opened the door. The man turned and opened his mouth to speak as Bruno smashed the butt of the weapon onto the back of his skull. The man fell into a heap on the floor, unconscious. Grabbing him by the legs, Bruno dragged him into the men's toilets. His head bounced from side to side, leaving a trail of blood on the dirty linoleum floor.

He quickly walked back into the bar just as a man dressed in the uniform of an SS officer walked through the door.

Bruno started to pull his pistol out, as Rudi exclaimed, 'Max, thank God!'

Max gave a cold smile, and said, 'Let's get the fuck out of here you two.'

78

Pushing the bar door open, Max walked briskly into the street followed closely by Rudi and Bruno. The sky was beginning to lighten as dawn approached. Max motioned for them to follow him as he led them around the corner and into a side street. Standing next to the large, black Mercedes was a young man dressed in the uniform of a private in the SS. Neither Bruno nor Rudi recognised him.

'Simon, open the boot,' said Max as they approached the car. 'Get in you two, quickly.' Rudi and Bruno did as they were ordered and were engulfed in total darkness. Simon pulled away from the curb at speed, turning into the main street and heading towards the River Havel.

Two police cars went speeding past in the opposite direction. 'It looks as if we were just in time, Simon,' murmured Max.

'We may still have problems. I think that there's some kind of a roadblock up ahead.'

'Alright, keep calm and leave the talking to me.' Just up ahead, he could see a police car parked by the side of the road. Standing in the centre of the road was a policeman, who flagged them down as they approached. Max undid the holster on his belt and wound down the window, as Simon slowed and finally stopped. A policeman bent forward and looked into the interior of the car, shining his flashlight.

He immediately noticed Max's uniform and rank, and said, 'Good evening, Sir. I'm sorry to have stopped you, but we're searching for two fugitives ...'

'I know. I've just come from Gestapo headquarters. Is there any news?'

'Well, Sir, we've just had a call from the owner of a bar just back there in Spandau. He says that the two that we're looking for were in there a few minutes ago. He was attacked by one of them and knocked out. They're in this area, there's no doubt.'

'Right, keep your eyes open. Can I go now? I've an important meeting to go to in connection with this business, in fact.'

'Yes, Sir of course. Heil Hitler.'

Max nodded and said, 'Drive on,' breathing a huge sigh of relief as they pulled away.

The owner of the Golden Angel sat with his head in his hands, the hair on the back of his head matted with blood. 'I knew it was them as soon as I saw them,' he whispered. 'It's been on the news all night and then the bastard attacked me and nearly smashed my skull.'

Looking at the two men who'd been in the bar at the same time as Rudi and Bruno, a policeman asked, 'What about you two, did you see anything?'

'I didn't take much notice,' replied one. 'I haven't heard the news this morning yet.'

'I can tell you something, though,' said the second man.

'What's that?' asked the policeman.

'Well, an SS officer walked in and they left with him.'

'Oh, shit!'

The police car came screeching to a halt alongside the police roadblock on the outskirts of Spandau. The driver wound down the window and said, urgently, 'Has an SS officer gone past here?'

'Yes, about ten minutes ago, in a black Mercedes.'

'Fuck! Which direction did he go?'

'Straight ahead.'

Without saying anything, the driver roared off.

Simon pulled slowly into the drive and came to a halt inside the large garage. Jumping out, he rushed over and closed the doors. Max climbed out and walked around to the back, opening the boot, 'You're home, my boys. Come on.'

Rudi and Bruno climbed stiffly out and looked around, 'That was the worst night of my life,' said Bruno, 'Where the fuck are we?'

'The Grunewald,' said Max.

Outside, the police car cruised slowly past. 'No sign of them,' the driver said to his companion.'

'No, they could be anywhere by now. I wonder who this mysterious SS officer is?'

The two policemen inside never knew how close they were to their quarry.

79

Rudi shot up in the narrow bed wondering for a second where he was, as he felt someone's hand shaking his shoulder. He looked around the underground room and saw Bruno in the next bed, yawning and stretching, his hair in disarray. The events of the previous night came flooding back. Simon stood looking at him, holding a steaming mug of coffee in each hand.

'Thanks, Simon,' said Rudi, 'What time is it?'

'5pm' answered Simon. 'Max suggests that you both take a shower and join him upstairs. He's planning a meal tonight, to introduce you to everyone.'

'Thank God for that. I'm starving; fighting these Nazis makes you hungry,' said Bruno yawning.

Simon laughed. 'I'll see you both upstairs,' he said, leaving the room.

Bruno looked around and said, 'This place is incredible. Look at it, Rudi. You could hide down here for months.'

'Yes, Max never ceases to amaze me. I wonder what other surprises he has in store for us.'

'Well, my boy, the sooner we're showered, the sooner we'll find out,' said Bruno, jumping out of bed.

Standing by the large picture window, Max was admiring the view across the river as Rudi and Bruno entered. He'd spent the afternoon preparing the motor launch. Everything was now ready for their departure.

Turning, he smiled and said, 'So, the two adventurers are with us again. You gave us a fright last night. It was a close run thing. Sit down. We need to talk. Let's have a drink. Scotch?'

'Great idea,' said Bruno. 'I'll fix them.'

'And what do you both think of our little hideout?'

'Little! You could hide an army here,' said Rudi.

Max smiled and said, 'That's the idea. Now, to business. Early tomorrow morning we're leaving Berlin. You two are the most wanted men in Germany at the moment and we have to get you out. It's the twenty-fifth of August today, which gives us about five days. Germany intends to invade Poland on the 1st of September and we want you safely inside Switzerland before then. It's very sad that the Altmann Circle's been damaged, but it's not smashed, so we must put all this behind us now and look to the future. I'm sorry about all the deaths, but the General and the others understood the risks.'

Bruno handed round the drinks, and said, 'It's the Hoffmanns that I feel most sorry for, as they were totally innocent. Rudi blames himself, but we had no choice but to go there.'

'Yes, I'm sorry too. They were, I'm afraid, casualties of war, and you shouldn't blame yourself, Rudi. You see we had a problem. We wanted as few people as possible to know about this place and, if I'm honest, I realise now that that was a mistake. We should have told you,' he said shrugging. 'I'm sorry, but it's too late now.'

'So am I,' said Rudi. 'But you're right, we can do nothing. Can you tell us what the plan is now?'

'Right. Firstly, I want you both to choose a German army uniform from downstairs. Until we're clear of Berlin you'll have to keep out of sight. As you already know we're going by river. We'll go down the Rhine to a small village called Rheinweiler, about eighteen kilometres from the Swiss frontier. We'll be met by Major Weiss, you both know him, from Swiss customs?' they nodded. 'You'll swap boats and go with him into Switzerland, to Basel. Now, you won't be able to stay in Switzerland. If the Nazis find out where you are, they'll put huge pressure on the Swiss to hand you over and believe me, they will. The Swiss intend to stay neutral in this war and will do nothing to upset the Nazis.'

'But Max, we've already said that we won't stay there,' said Rudi as Bruno nodded his agreement.

'I know. The plan is this: Stefan's arranged a plane to fly you all to London.' He smiled at Rudi and continued, 'Rachel's made it clear that where you go, she and the baby go, too. Sam and Otto also want to leave and help in England. It's all arranged. The plan is that eventually you'll come back here. Don't ask me how, that's up to the British to decide.' He looked from one to the other and continued, 'You see, the Nazis think that the Circle's destroyed. That couldn't be further from the truth.'

'Where did Simon come from?' asked Bruno.

'Simon's a Jew and so are the Krant family and, with Simon's help, I'm going to recruit some more young Jews to join our group.'

Rudi gave a whistle. 'That's a brilliant idea.'

'They've all got false identities, thanks to Otto. I intend to cause as many problems as I can for our Nazi friends. Well, what do you say?'

Bruno and Rudi looked at each other, smiled and both lifted their glasses. 'To the continuation of the Altmann Circle,' said Rudi.

The other two raised their glasses. 'The Altmann Circle,' they said.

80

Propped up in bed, still feeling groggy from the anaesthetic, the stump of his arm throbbing with pain, Dieter watched the second hand of the clock on the wall moving around like the pulse of a heartbeat as it counted off each minute. He felt a huge wave of bitterness engulf him as he glanced down at what remained of his left arm, the stump left by the surgeon's knife swathed in gauze and bandages, the arm from just above the elbow amputated.

He looked over towards the door as it swung open and Langers entered.

'Dieter, my boy, how are you feeling?' he asked, full of bonhomie as if he had nothing more than the 'flu.

'Like shit. Although I suppose it could be worse — I could be dead.'

'Exactly. From what I hear, if your friend Rudi had had his way, you would be.'

'Do you have any news of those two?'

'No, they've disappeared into thin air. They were last seen in Spandau, but after that, nothing. We're watching all of the usual exits ... ' His voice trailed off for a second and then he continued. 'What worries me is this SS officer that met them. These people are too well organised for me. I suspect that there are more of them somewhere. Those two had help. What I want to know is who?'

'It's like I said to you at The Black Cat. They knew that we were on our way. If we'd been a few minutes later ... someone must have tipped them off.'

'Well, at least the traitor Altmann's dead. Mind you, I'd have preferred him alive. There are too many unanswered questions for my liking, Dieter. Should I say that I'm sorry about your parents?'

'Sorry, why sorry? They were harbouring traitors and I have my father to thank for this,' he said bitterly, looking down at what remained of his left arm. 'What's going to happen to me now, Sir? I suppose that my career's over.'

'Good God, no! Why should it be? Look, you're never going to be a combatant, but that was never your role anyway. You're far too valuable to us as an SD officer, one arm missing or not. No, when you're fit you'll return to us.' He hesitated and looked at Dieter lying in the bed, his face pale and drawn. He continued, 'Do you remember when you joined us in Berlin last year, and I said to you that it wasn't our job to get our hands dirty?'

'Yes, I do.'

'Well, the rules have just changed. I think from now on, we're going to get our hands very dirty indeed. When the army moves into Poland, the SD won't be far behind and our job won't be very pleasant — necessary — but not pleasant. Do you understand?'

'Perfectly. I'll do whatever I have to. Like I always have. I'll do my duty.'

'Good. I'm glad that we understand each other. Now, we want you to come and stay with us to recuperate when they let you out of here.'

'Thank you. I will. Do you have a cigarette?'

'Yes, of course.'

'Could I have one?'

'Have the packet — but you don't smoke,' he said, handing over the cigarettes and a box of matches.

'I just started.'

The Brigadier stood and left and Dieter watched his retreating back. With difficulty he lit the cigarette and inhaled, the smoke making him cough at first. He lay back, his left arm causing him pain, as he looked up at the ceiling. Tears welled up in his eyes and started to roll down his cheeks. 'Oh, Christ, what have I done?' he said aloud. He couldn't get the sight of his mother's and father's bullet-riddled bodies out his mind. He tried. They were, after all, traitors, weren't they? 'Why couldn't you have been different and taken our side? Why did you have to make me do this? You hated me and yet I was only doing my duty. In the end you forced me to kill you.' He sobbed uncontrollably. His pyjama jacket was wet with tears. 'I swear to God,' he murmured, 'that from now on, anyone that I regard as an enemy, I'll destroy. You, my parents, hated me for what I am. Well, now I promise to give you every reason to hate me from the grave. People will have good reason to fear the name of Dieter Hoffmann.' He wiped away the tears with his good arm and said, 'From now on, no matter what I'm called upon to do, I'll never shed another tear.'

81

The Captain of the German battleship Schleswig-Holstein stood on the bridge, his eyes fixed on the second hand of the gleaming brassbound clock. His ship was anchored in the harbour of the city of Danzig. Everyone's eyes watched tensely as the hand made its journey around the clock's face. As it reached 4.45am this senior officer of the German navy looked over at his gunnery officer and nodded. He, in turn, spoke one word into the microphone at his throat, 'Fire'. A huge barrage erupted from the ship's guns, aimed at the old fortress of Westerplatte four miles to the north of the city. It was Friday the 1st of September 1939. This was the opening salvo of the Second World War.

82

The long motor-launch started to slow as it approached the small village of Rheinweiler. Max looked ahead, searching for the flash of light that would indicate the position of the Swiss customs patrol boat.

'There! Just to our right,' muttered Rudi as he spotted the intermittent gleam of the small searchlight as it pulsed on and off three times.

Max nodded and said, 'Got it,' as he moved the wheel to the right and turned towards the other boat.

They pulled up alongside as Major Weiss said, 'Get across quickly. I don't want to hang around.'

Rudi and Bruno embraced Max, whispered, 'Good luck,' and jumped aboard the Swiss boat. Weiss quickly accelerated away, as Max's boat was almost immediately swallowed up by the darkness. He turned the wheel, the arc of the wake gleaming in the moonlight, and headed back in the opposite direction.

Colonel Max Adler of the German Military Intelligence service smiled, and said to himself, 'God be with you boys. See you both soon. I hope.'

The dawn sunlight turned the river crimson. The water glittered and gleamed as the rays seemed to hit and then bounce off. Looking over to his right, Rudi could see the twin spires of Basel Cathedral in the distance. His heart soared as he thought of the wife and son waiting for him.

Bruno, his face thoughtful, turned towards Rudi and said, with unusual seriousness, 'I wonder what the future holds for us, Rudi?'

'I don't know, but I'll tell you this. No matter what happens to us, we're doing the right thing. I've no doubt of that. Look at all the suffering that this regime has caused already, and the future will be infinitely worse.'

Bruno grunted, the seriousness of the moment passing, as he said, 'Well, London next stop, Rudi?'

'Yes,'

'Do you think that if I ask nicely, they'll let me see the Crown Jewels?'

A huge grin lit up Rudi's face, as he put his arm around Bruno, kissed him on the cheek, and said — 'Idiot!'

END

www.ingramcontent.com/pod-product-compliance
Lightning Source LLC
Chambersburg PA
CBHW031201020726
47499CB00002B/443